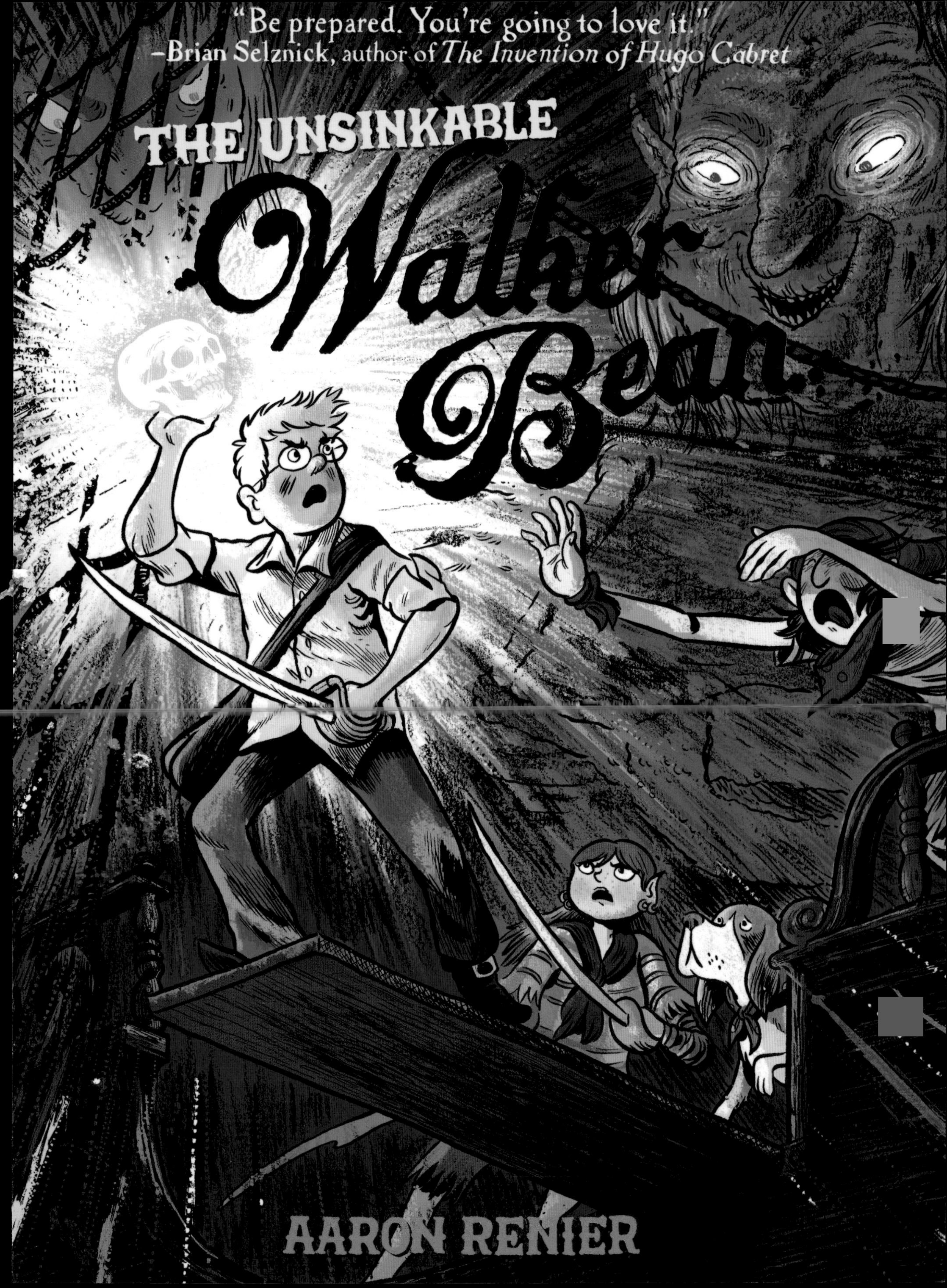
"Be prepared. You're going to love it."
–Brian Selznick, author of *The Invention of Hugo Cabret*
THE UNSINKABLE
Walker Bean
AARON RENIER

THE UNSINKABLE Walker Bean

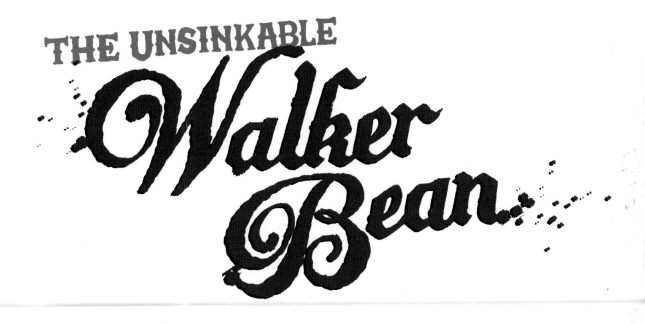

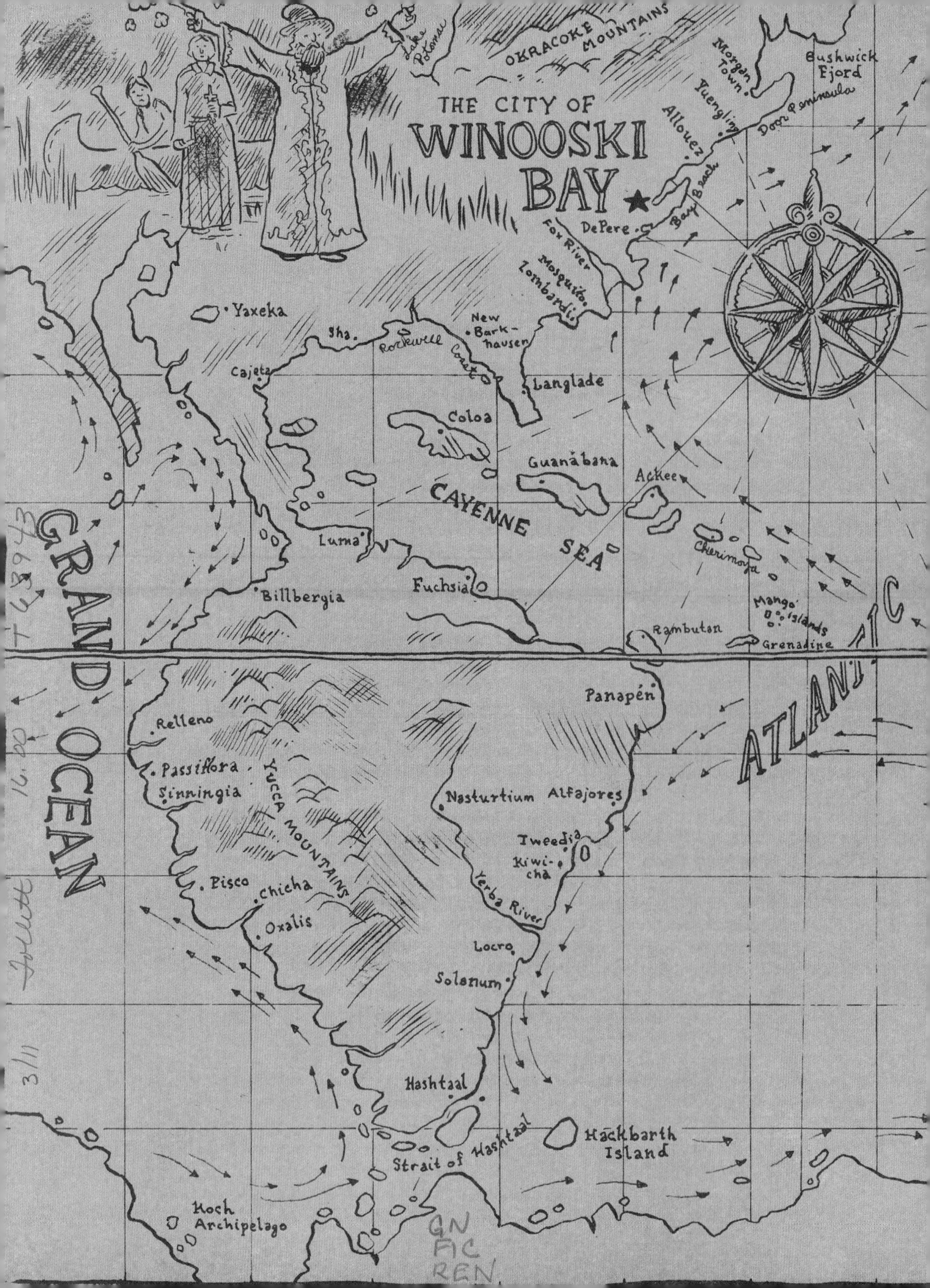

THE CITY OF
WINOOSKI
BAY
Lake Potomac
OKRACOKE MOUNTAINS
Morgan Town
Bushwick Fjord
Yuengling
Door Peninsula
Allouez
Bay Beach
DePere
Fox River
Mosquito
Lombardi
Yaxeka
Sha
Rockwell Coast
New Bark-hausen
Cajeta
Langlade
Coloa
Guanábana
Ackee
CAYENNE SEA
Luma
Cherimoya
Fuchsia
Billbergia
Mango Islands
Rambutan
Grenadine
GRAND OCEAN
ATLANTIC
Panapén
Relleno
Passiflora
Sinningia
YUCCA MOUNTAINS
Nasturtium
Alfajores
Tweedia
Kiwi-chá
Pisco
Chicha
Oxalis
Yerba River
Locro
Solanum
Hashtaal
Strait of Hashtaal
Hackbarth Island
Koch Archipelago

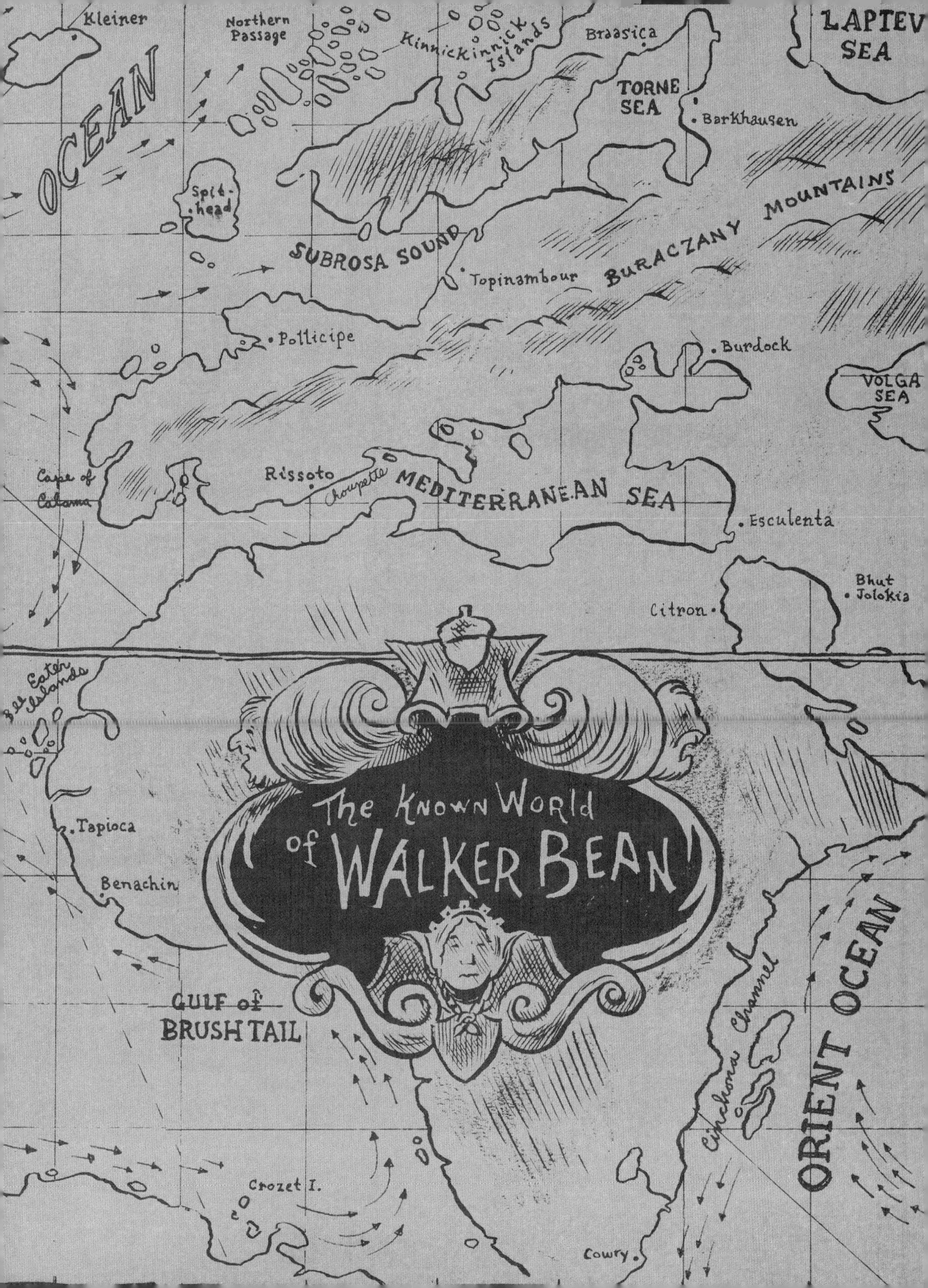
The Known World of WALKER BEAN
OCEAN
Kleiner
Northern Passage
Kinnickinnick Islands
Braasica
LAPTEV SEA
TORNE SEA
Barkhausen
Spit-head
BURACZANY MOUNTAINS
SUBROSA SOUND
Topinambour
Pollicipe
Burdock
VOLGA SEA
Cape of Calama
Rissoto
Choupette
MEDITERRANEAN SEA
Esculenta
Bhut Jolokia
Citron
Bee Eater Islands
Tapioca
Benachin
GULF of BRUSHTAIL
Cinchona Channel
ORIENT OCEAN
Crozet I.
Cowry

:01

First Second
New York & London

Copyright © 2010 by Aaron Renier

Published by First Second
First Second is an imprint of Roaring Brook Press,
a division of Holtzbrinck Publishing Holdings Limited Partnership,
175 Fifth Avenue, New York, NY 10010

Distributed in Canada by H. B. Fenn and Company Ltd.
Distributed in the United Kingdom by Macmillan Children's Books,
a division of Pan Macmillan.

Interior design by Aaron Renier and Colleen A F Venable

Colored by Alec Longstreth

Cataloging-in-Publication Data is on file at the Library of Congress.

ISBN: 978-1-59643-453-0

First Second books are available for special promotions and premiums
For details, contact: Director of Special Markets, Holtzbrinck Publishers.

First Edition September 2010
Printed in October 2010 in China
by South China Printing Co. Ltd.,
Dongguan City, Guangdong Province
3 4 5 6 7 8 9 10

THE UNSINKABLE Walker Bean

Written and illustrated by Aaron Renier

Colored by Alec Longstreth

:01

First Second

New York & London

With love to my mom.

For not only putting up with my nonsense,
but for taking it seriously.

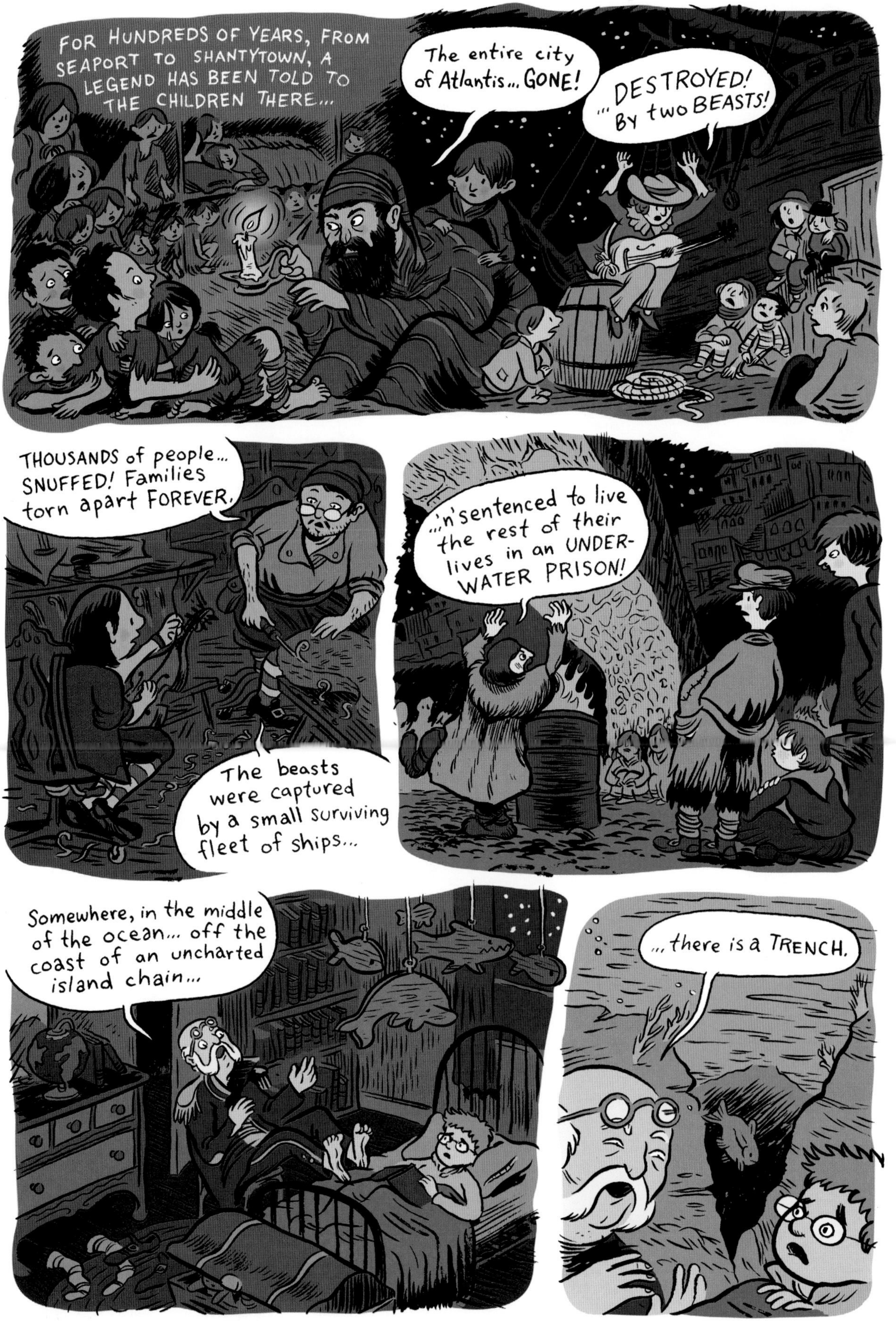
FOR HUNDREDS OF YEARS, FROM SEAPORT TO SHANTYTOWN, A LEGEND HAS BEEN TOLD TO THE CHILDREN THERE...
The entire city of Atlantis... GONE!
...DESTROYED! By two BEASTS!
THOUSANDS of people... SNUFFED! Families torn apart FOREVER.
The beasts were captured by a small surviving fleet of ships...
...'n' sentenced to live the rest of their lives in an UNDER-WATER PRISON!
Somewhere, in the middle of the ocean... off the coast of an uncharted island chain...
...there is a TRENCH.

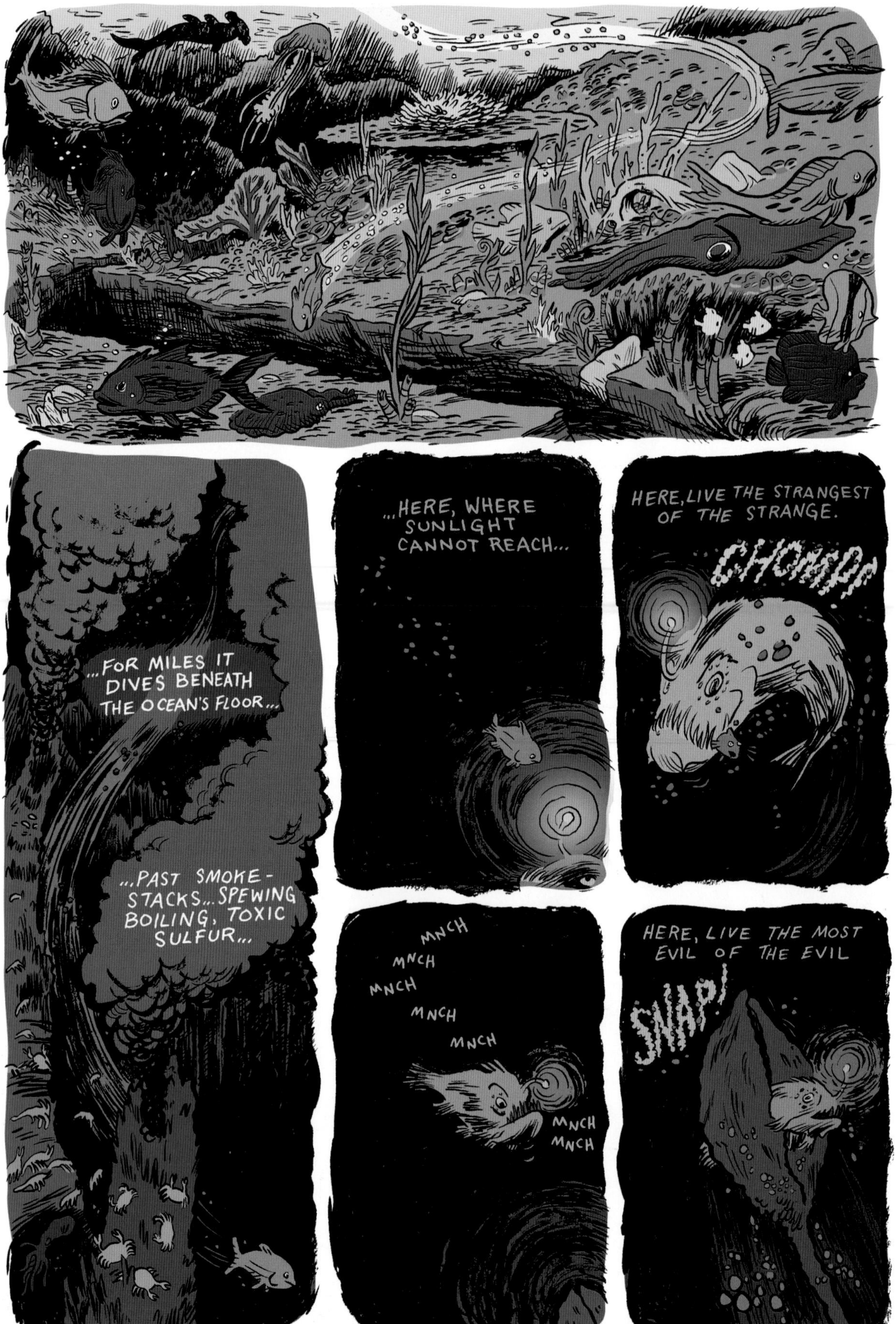
...FOR MILES IT DIVES BENEATH THE OCEAN'S FLOOR...
...PAST SMOKE-STACKS... SPEWING BOILING, TOXIC SULFUR...
...HERE, WHERE SUNLIGHT CANNOT REACH...
HERE, LIVE THE STRANGEST OF THE STRANGE.
CHOMP!
MNCH
MNCH
MNCH
MNCH
MNCH
MNCH
MNCH
HERE, LIVE THE MOST EVIL OF THE EVIL
SNAP!

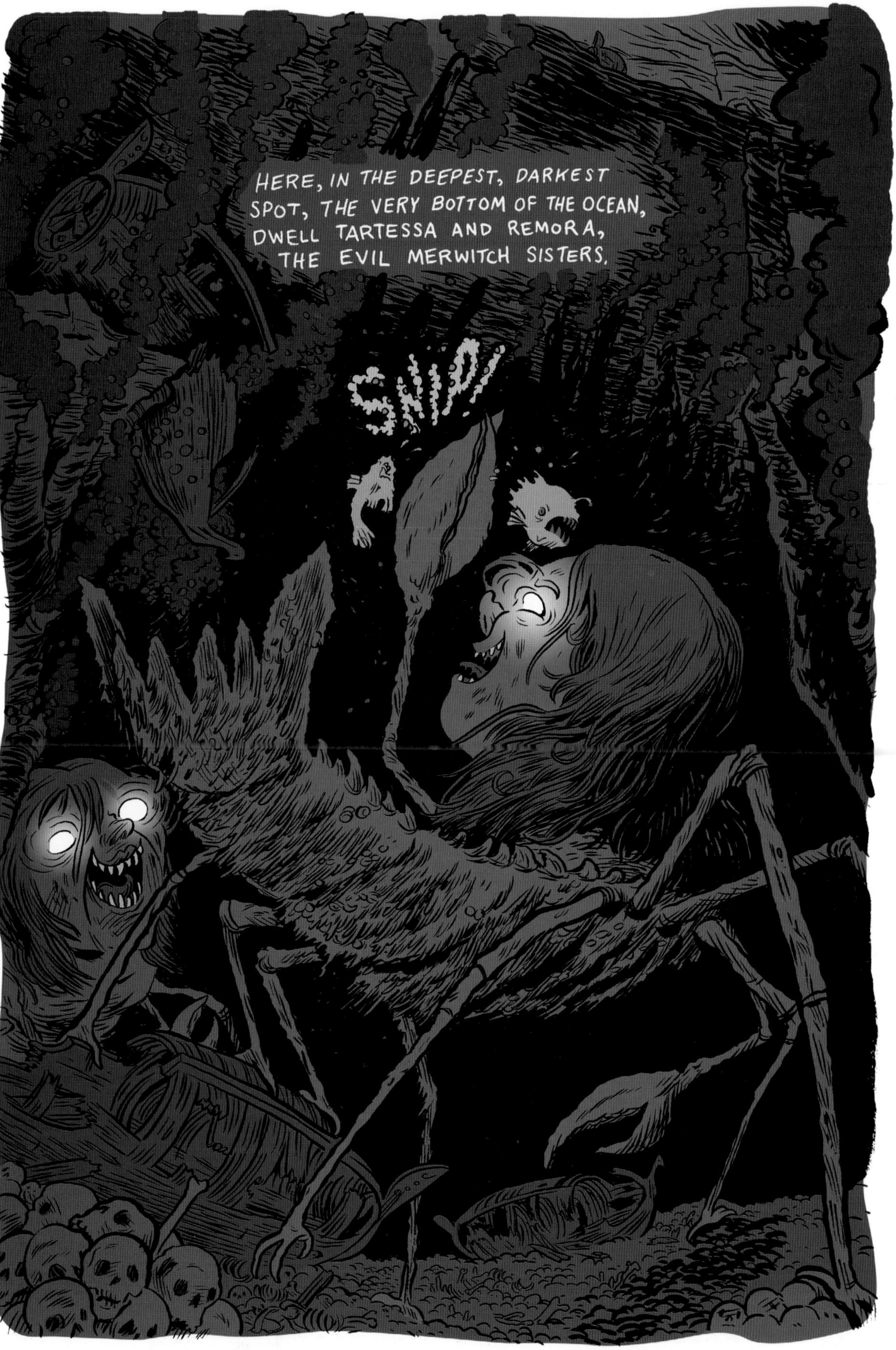
HERE, IN THE DEEPEST, DARKEST SPOT, THE VERY BOTTOM OF THE OCEAN, DWELL TARTESSA AND REMORA, THE EVIL MERWITCH SISTERS.
SNIP!

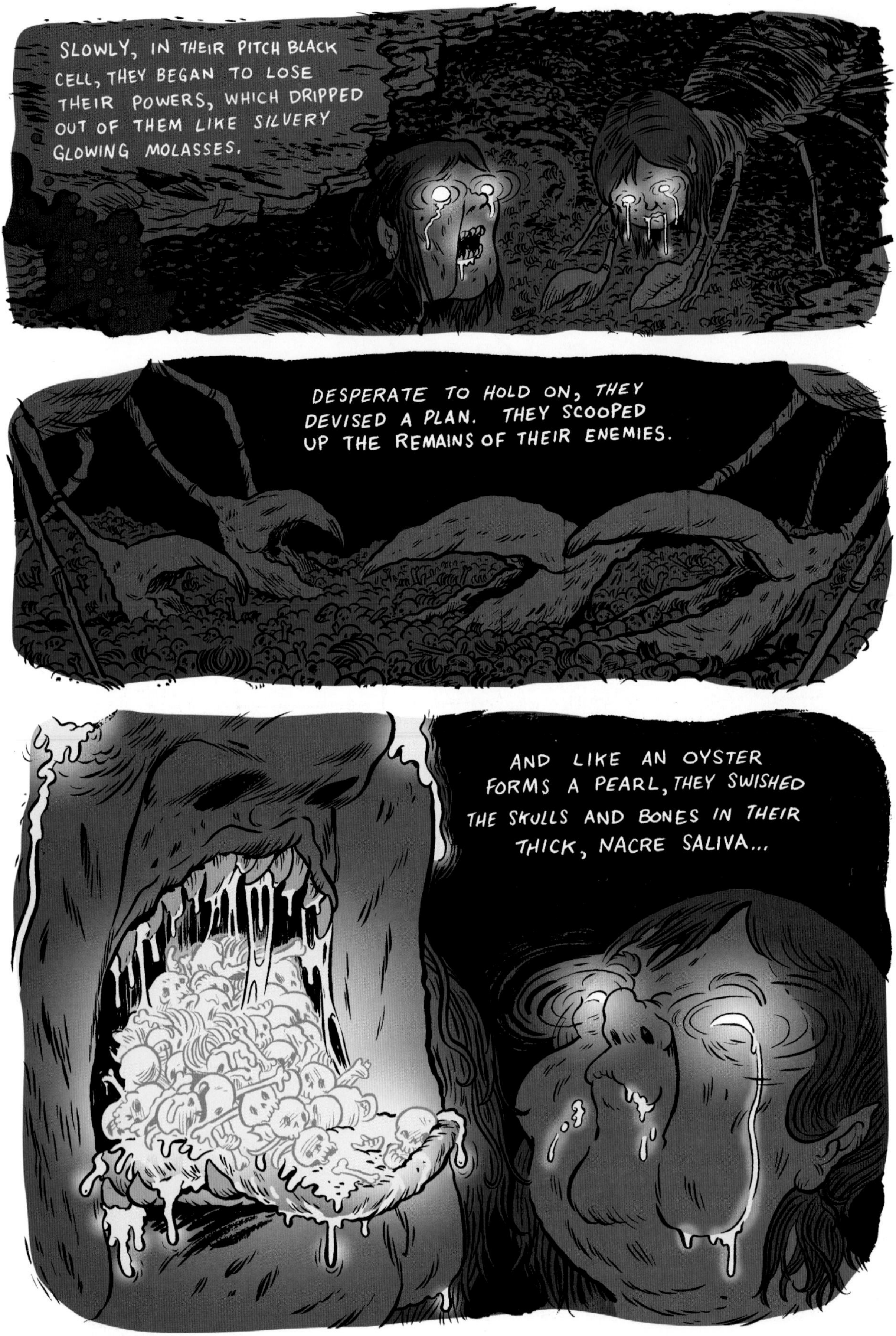
SLOWLY, IN THEIR PITCH BLACK CELL, THEY BEGAN TO LOSE THEIR POWERS, WHICH DRIPPED OUT OF THEM LIKE SILVERY GLOWING MOLASSES.
DESPERATE TO HOLD ON, THEY DEVISED A PLAN. THEY SCOOPED UP THE REMAINS OF THEIR ENEMIES.
AND LIKE AN OYSTER FORMS A PEARL, THEY SWISHED THE SKULLS AND BONES IN THEIR THICK, NACRE SALIVA...

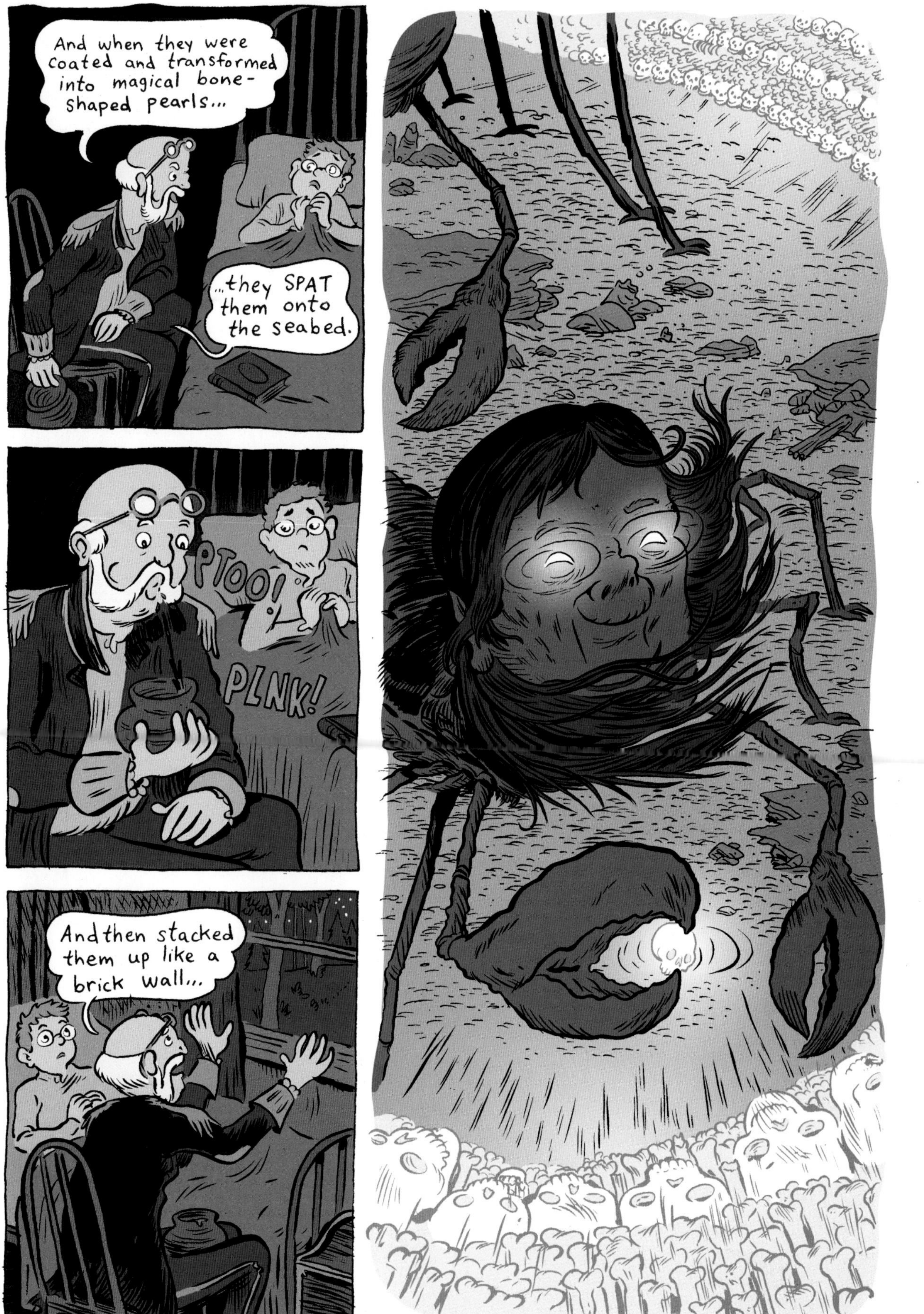
And when they were coated and transformed into magical bone-shaped pearls...
...they SPAT them onto the seabed.
PTOO!
PLNK!
And then stacked them up like a brick wall...

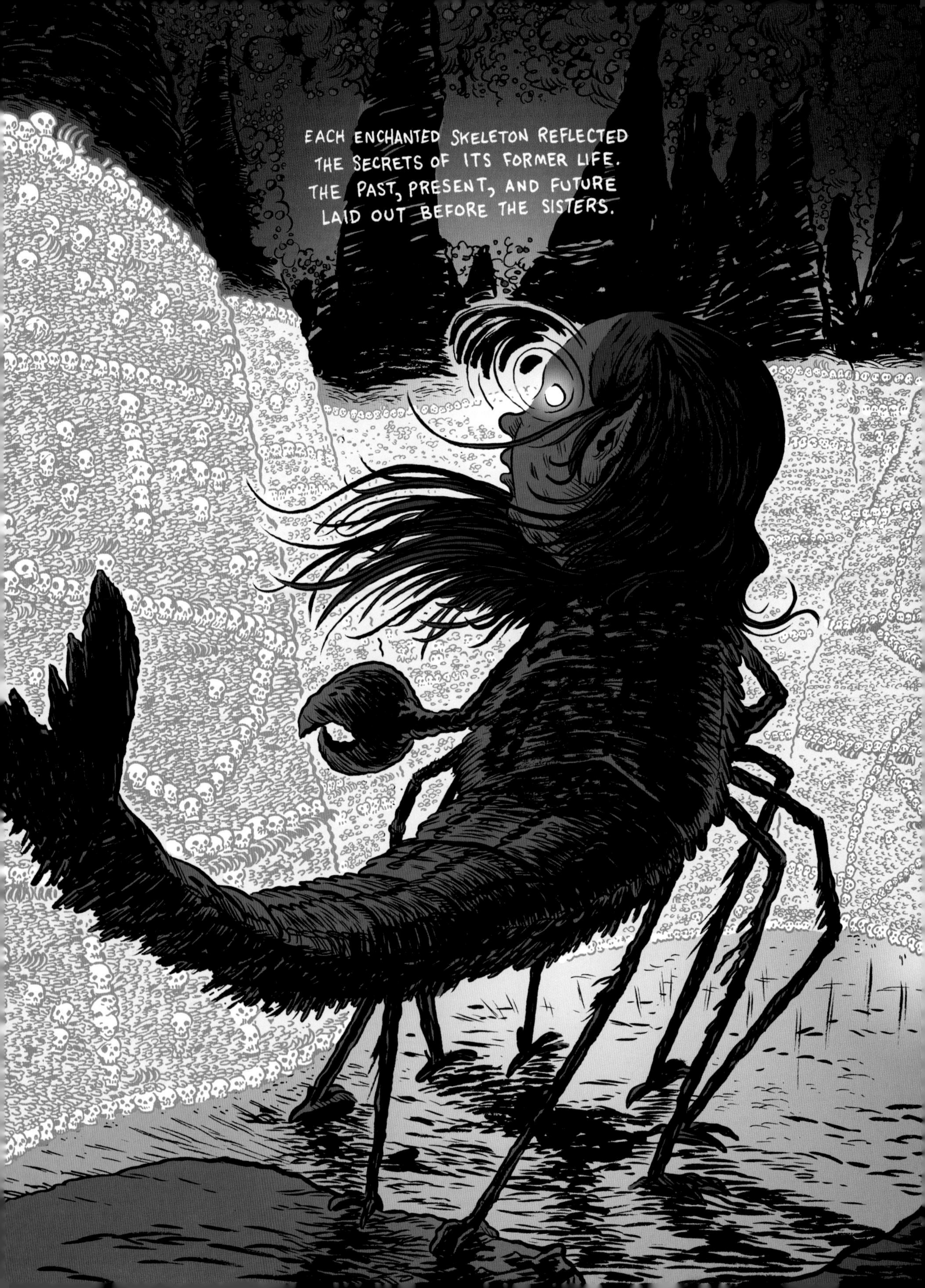
EACH ENCHANTED SKELETON REFLECTED
THE SECRETS OF ITS FORMER LIFE.
THE PAST, PRESENT, AND FUTURE
LAID OUT BEFORE THE SISTERS.

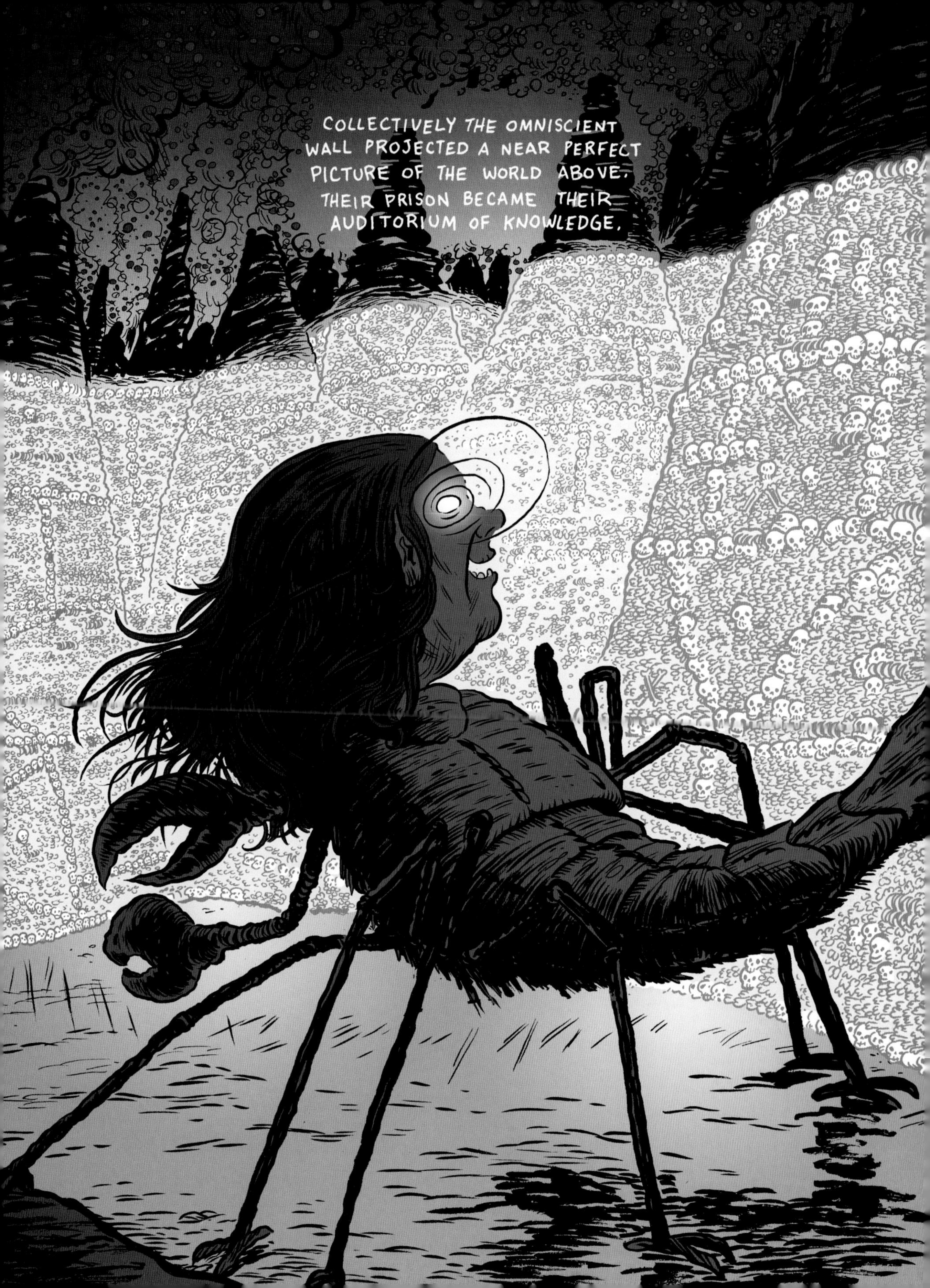
COLLECTIVELY THE OMNISCIENT WALL PROJECTED A NEAR PERFECT PICTURE OF THE WORLD ABOVE. THEIR PRISON BECAME THEIR AUDITORIUM OF KNOWLEDGE.

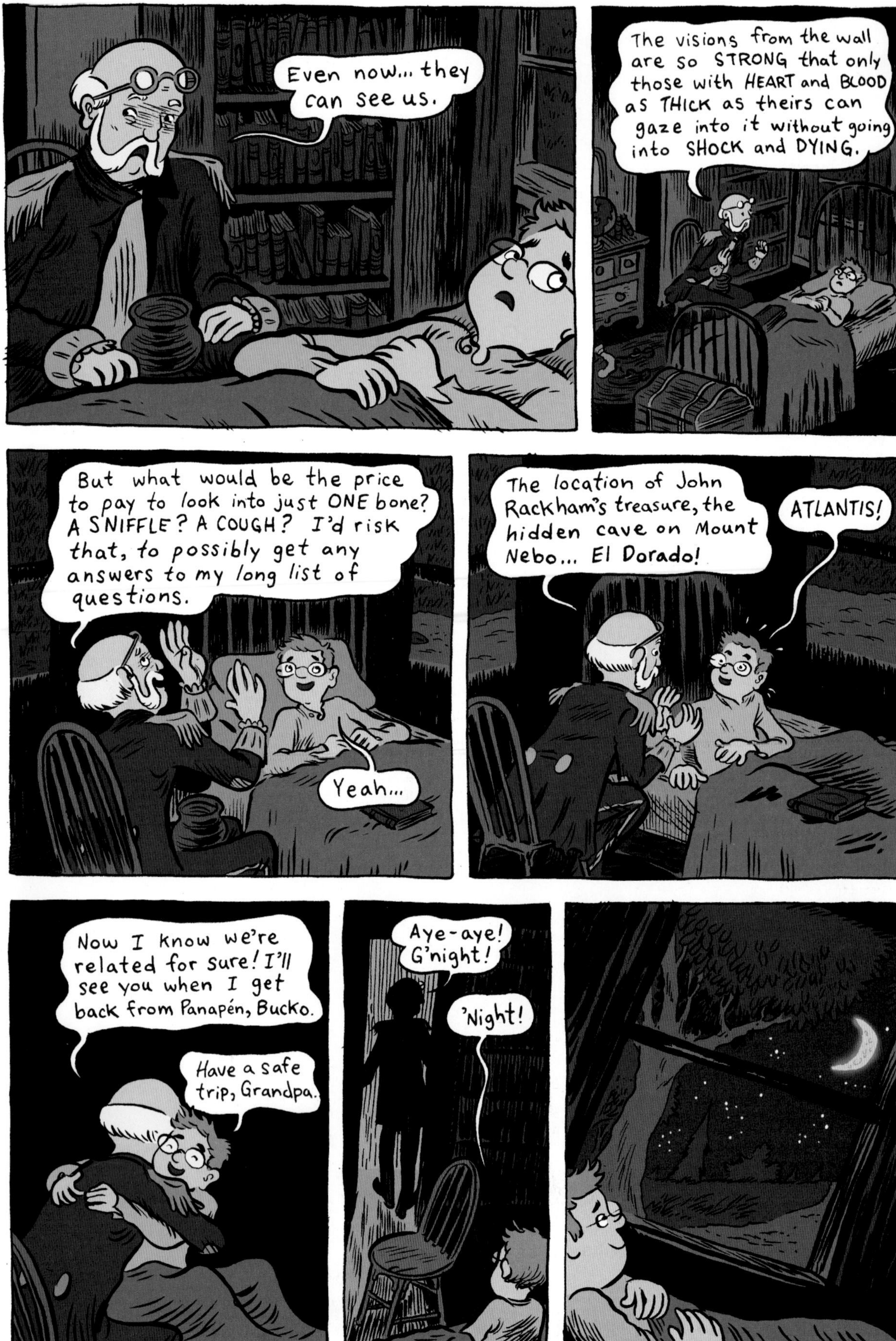
Even now... they can see us.
The visions from the wall are so STRONG that only those with HEART and BLOOD as THICK as theirs can gaze into it without going into SHOCK and DYING.
But what would be the price to pay to look into just ONE bone? A SNIFFLE? A COUGH? I'd risk that, to possibly get any answers to my long list of questions.
Yeah...
The location of John Rackham's treasure, the hidden cave on Mount Nebo... El Dorado!
ATLANTIS!
Now I know we're related for sure! I'll see you when I get back from Panapén, Bucko.
Have a safe trip, Grandpa.
Aye-aye! G'night!
'Night!

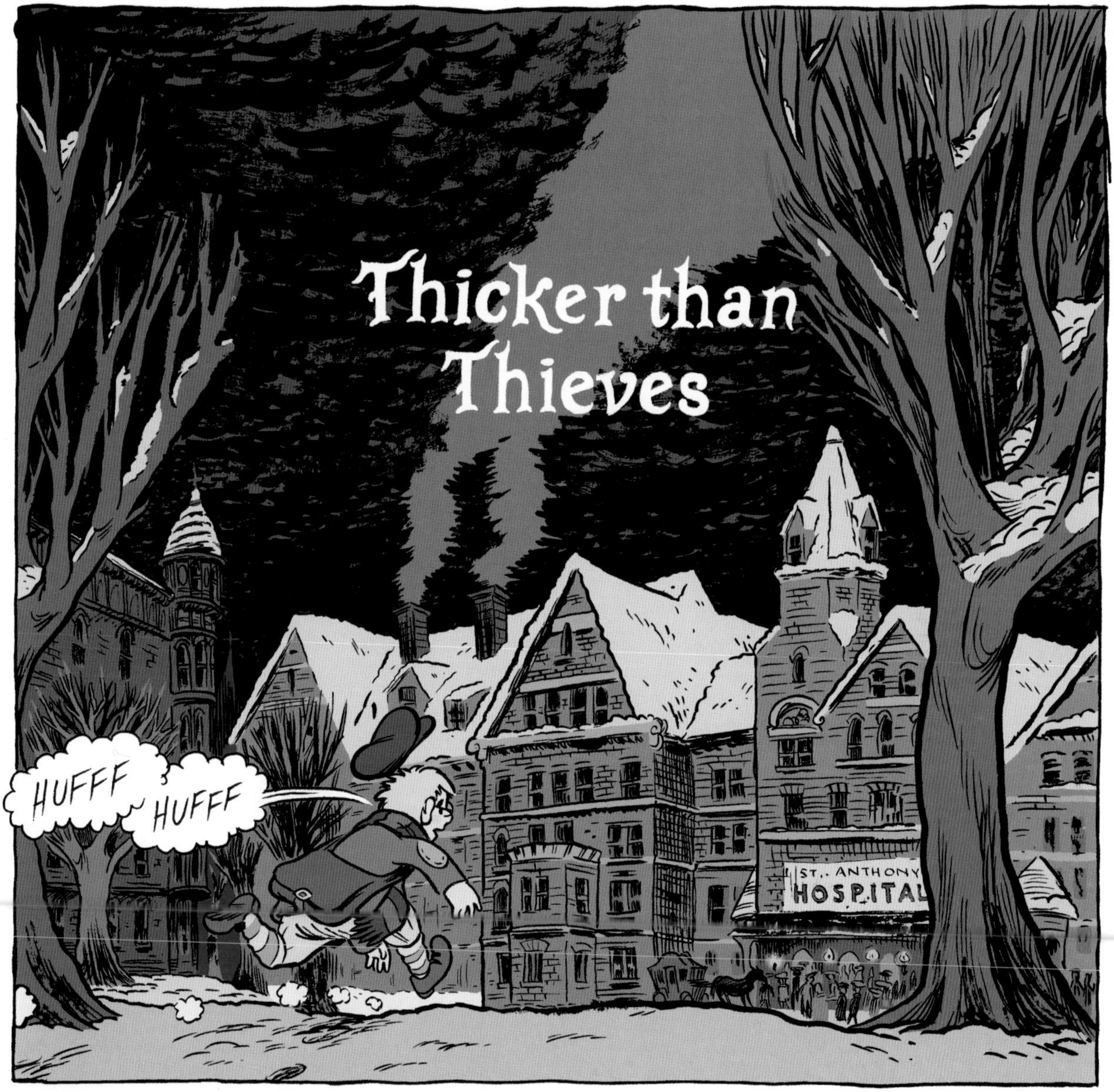
Thicker than Thieves
HUFFF
HUFFF
ST. ANTHONY'S
HOSPITAL

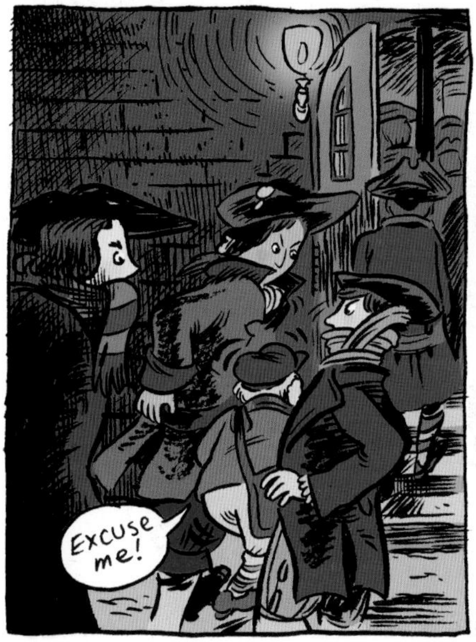
Excuse me!

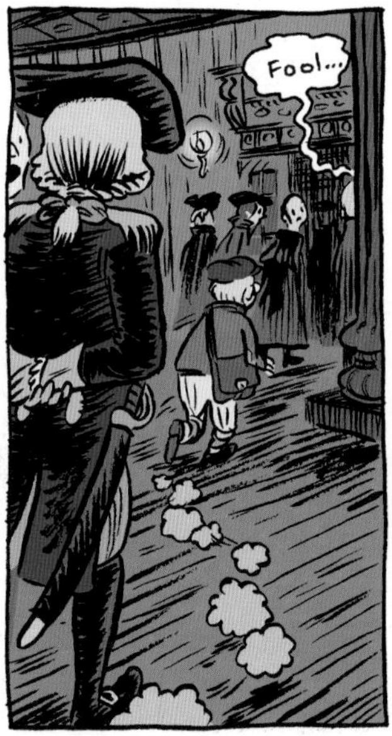
Fool...

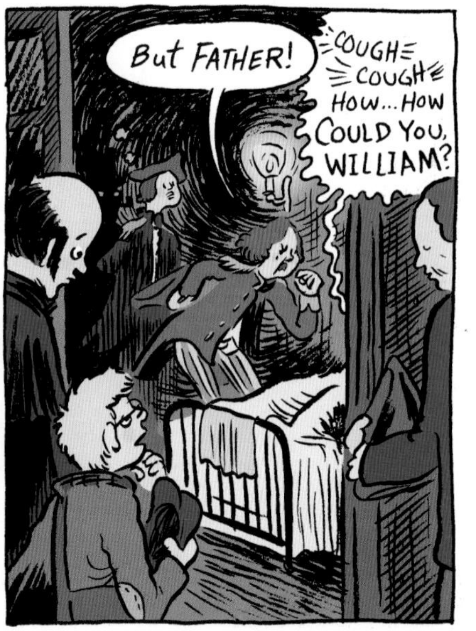
But FATHER!
COUGH
COUGH
HOW... HOW COULD YOU, WILLIAM?

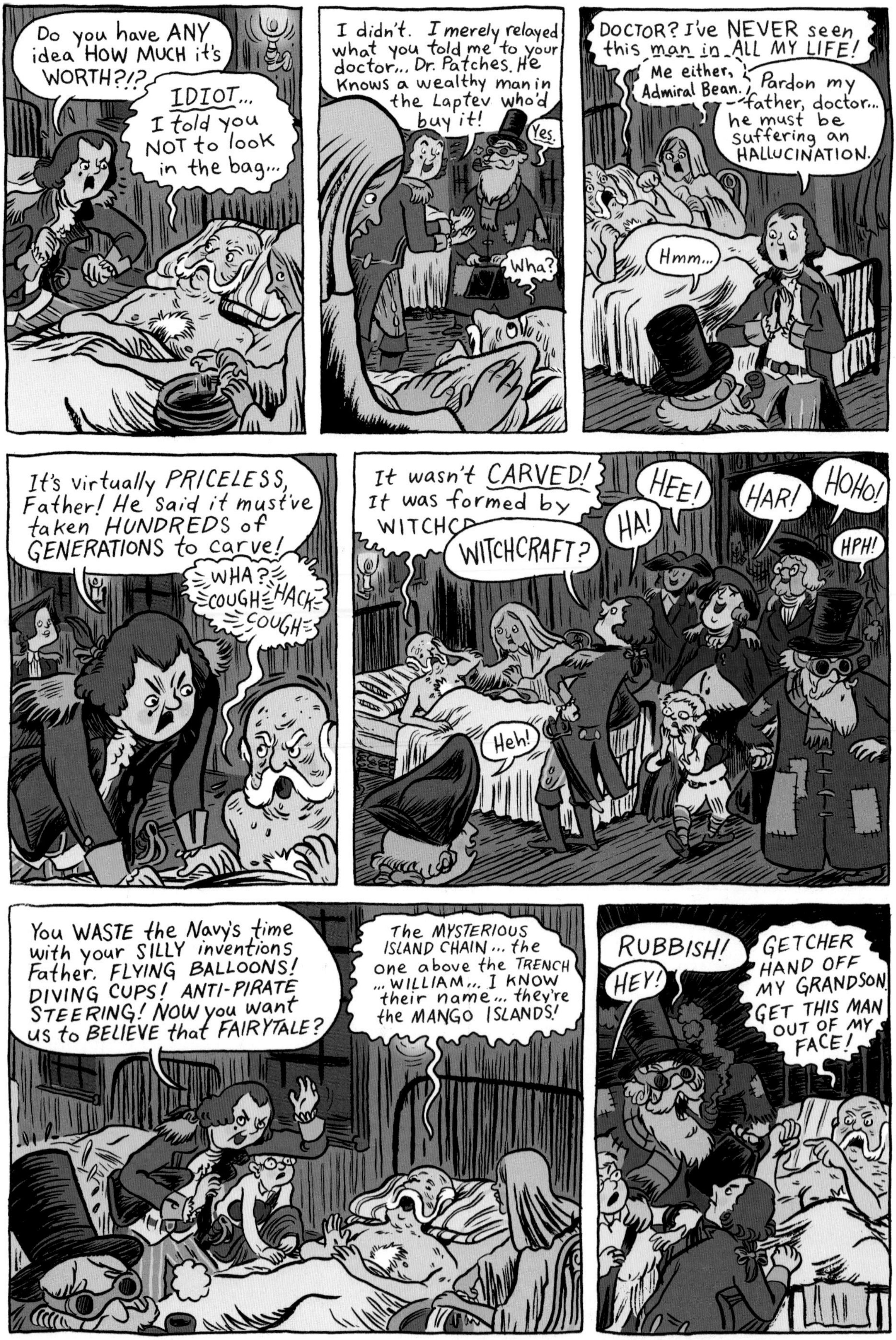

Do you have ANY idea HOW MUCH it's WORTH?!?
IDIOT... I told you NOT to look in the bag...
I didn't. I merely relayed what you told me to your doctor... Dr. Patches. He knows a wealthy man in the Laptev who'd buy it!
Yes.
Wha?
DOCTOR? I've NEVER seen this man in ALL MY LIFE!
Me either, Admiral Bean.
Pardon my father, doctor... he must be suffering an HALLUCINATION.
Hmm...
It's virtually PRICELESS, Father! He said it must've taken HUNDREDS of GENERATIONS to carve!
WHA? COUGH HACK COUGH
It wasn't CARVED! It was formed by WITCHC
WITCHCRAFT?
HA!
HEE!
HAR!
HOHO!
HPH!
Heh!
You WASTE the Navy's time with your SILLY inventions Father. FLYING BALLOONS! DIVING CUPS! ANTI-PIRATE STEERING! NOW you want us to BELIEVE that FAIRYTALE?
The MYSTERIOUS ISLAND CHAIN... the one above the TRENCH ...WILLIAM... I KNOW their name... they're the MANGO ISLANDS!
RUBBISH!
HEY!
GETCHER HAND OFF MY GRANDSON. GET THIS MAN OUT OF MY FACE!

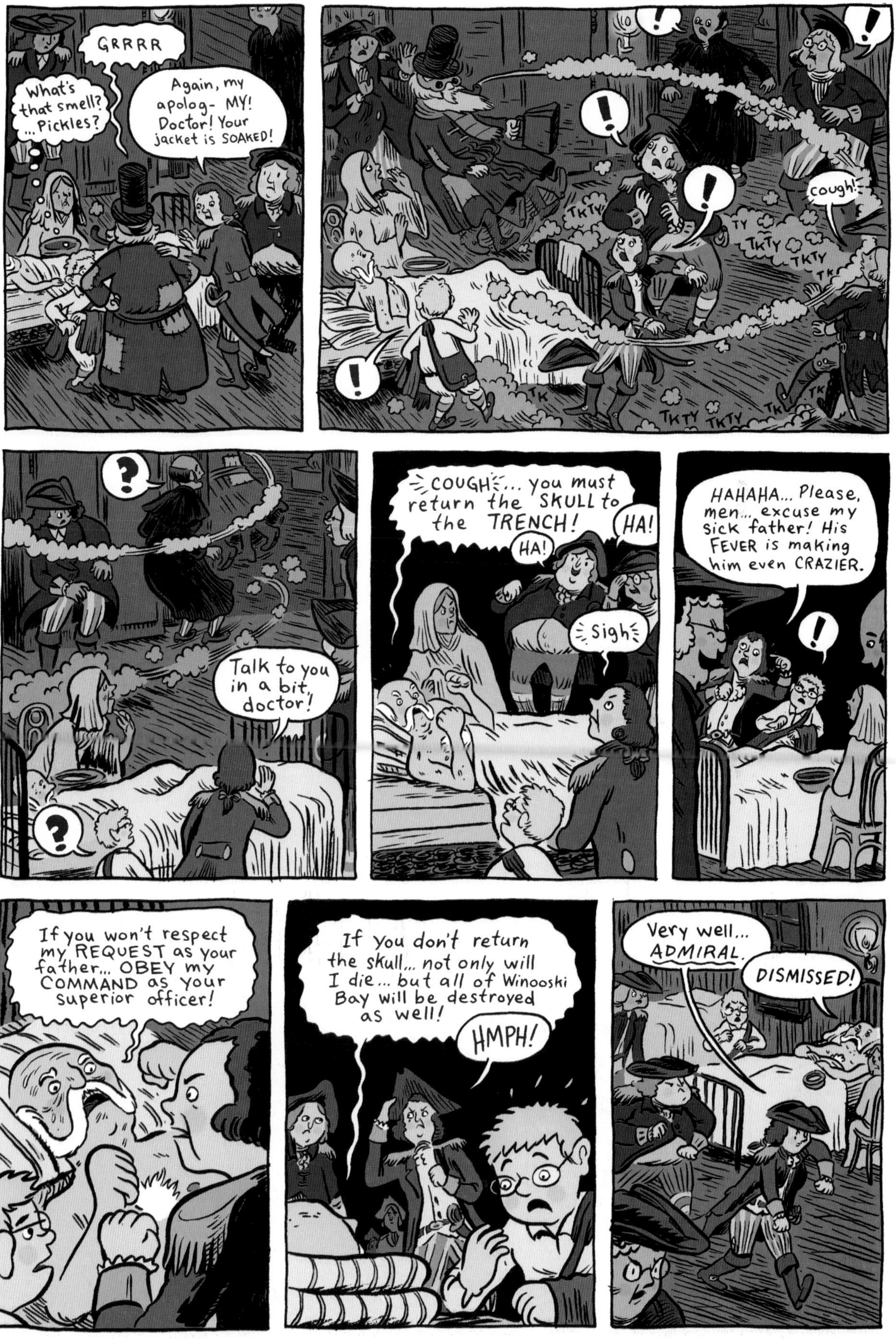

GRRRR
What's that smell? ...Pickles?
Again, my apolog- MY! Doctor! Your jacket is SOAKED!
!
!
!
!
!
TKTY
TY
TKTY
TKTY
TK
cough!
TK
TKTY
TKTY
TK
TK
?
?
Talk to you in a bit, doctor!
COUGH ... you must return the SKULL to the TRENCH!
HA!
HA!
Sigh
HAHAHA... Please, men... excuse my sick father! His FEVER is making him even CRAZIER.
!
If you won't respect my REQUEST as your father... OBEY my COMMAND as your superior officer!
If you don't return the skull... not only will I die... but all of Winooski Bay will be destroyed as well!
HMPH!
Very well... ADMIRAL.
DISMISSED!

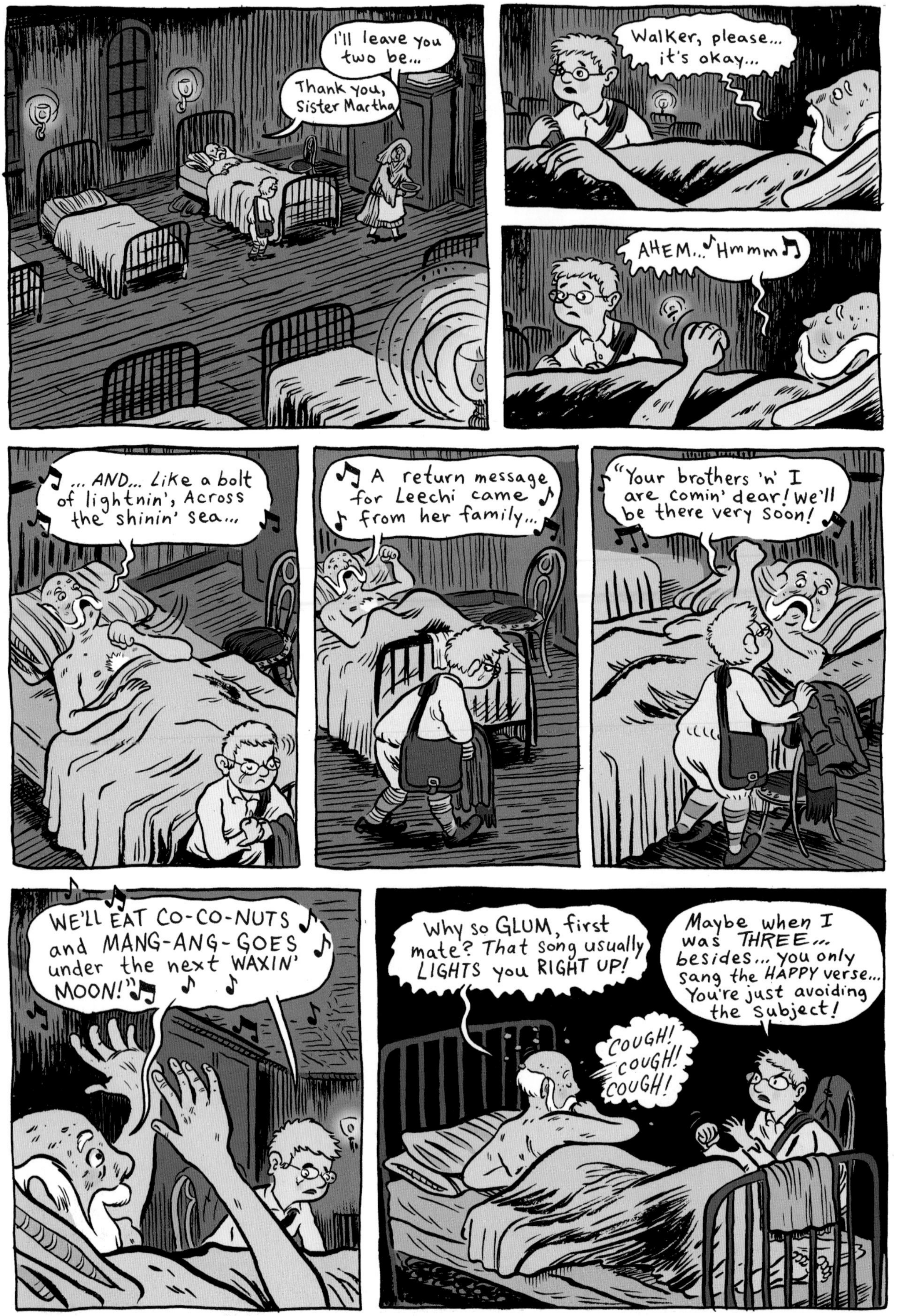
I'll leave you two be...
Thank you, Sister Martha
Walker, please... it's okay...
AHEM... ♪Hmmm♫
♫... AND... Like a bolt of lightnin', Across the shinin' sea...♫
♫ A return message for Leechi came ♪ from her family...♫
"Your brothers 'n' I are comin' dear! We'll be there very soon!♫
WE'LL EAT CO-CO-NUTS and MANG-ANG-GOES under the next WAXIN' MOON!"♫
Why so GLUM, first mate? That song usually LIGHTS you RIGHT UP!
Maybe when I was THREE... besides... you only sang the HAPPY verse... You're just avoiding the subject!
COUGH! COUGH! COUGH!

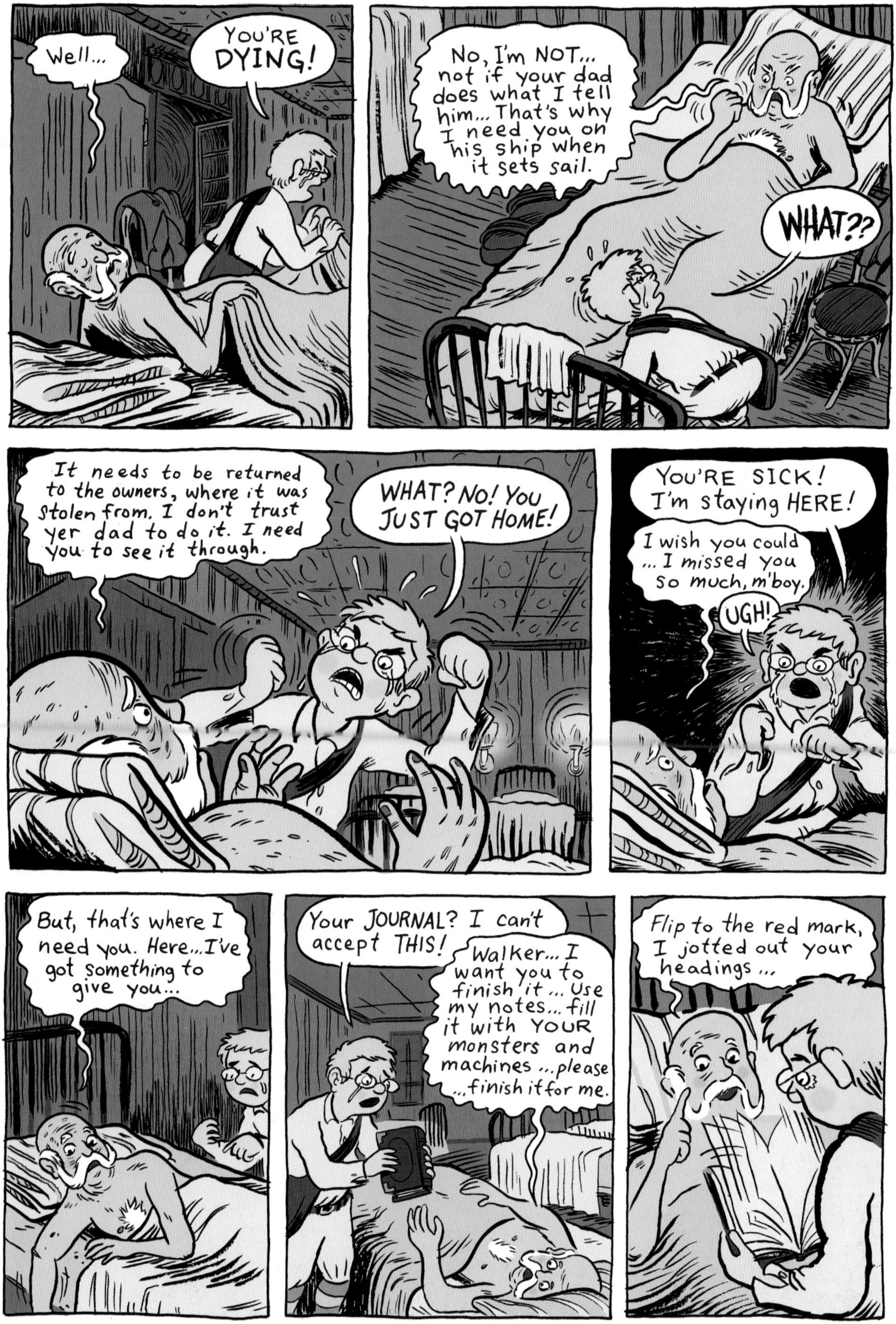
Well...
YOU'RE DYING!
No, I'm NOT... not if your dad does what I tell him... That's why I need you on his ship when it sets sail.
WHAT??
It needs to be returned to the owners, where it was stolen from. I don't trust yer dad to do it. I need you to see it through.
WHAT? NO! YOU JUST GOT HOME!
YOU'RE SICK! I'm staying HERE!
I wish you could ... I missed you so much, m'boy.
UGH!
But, that's where I need you. Here...I've got something to give you...
Your JOURNAL? I can't accept THIS!
Walker... I want you to finish it ... Use my notes... fill it with YOUR monsters and machines ...please ...finish it for me.
Flip to the red mark, I jotted out your headings ...

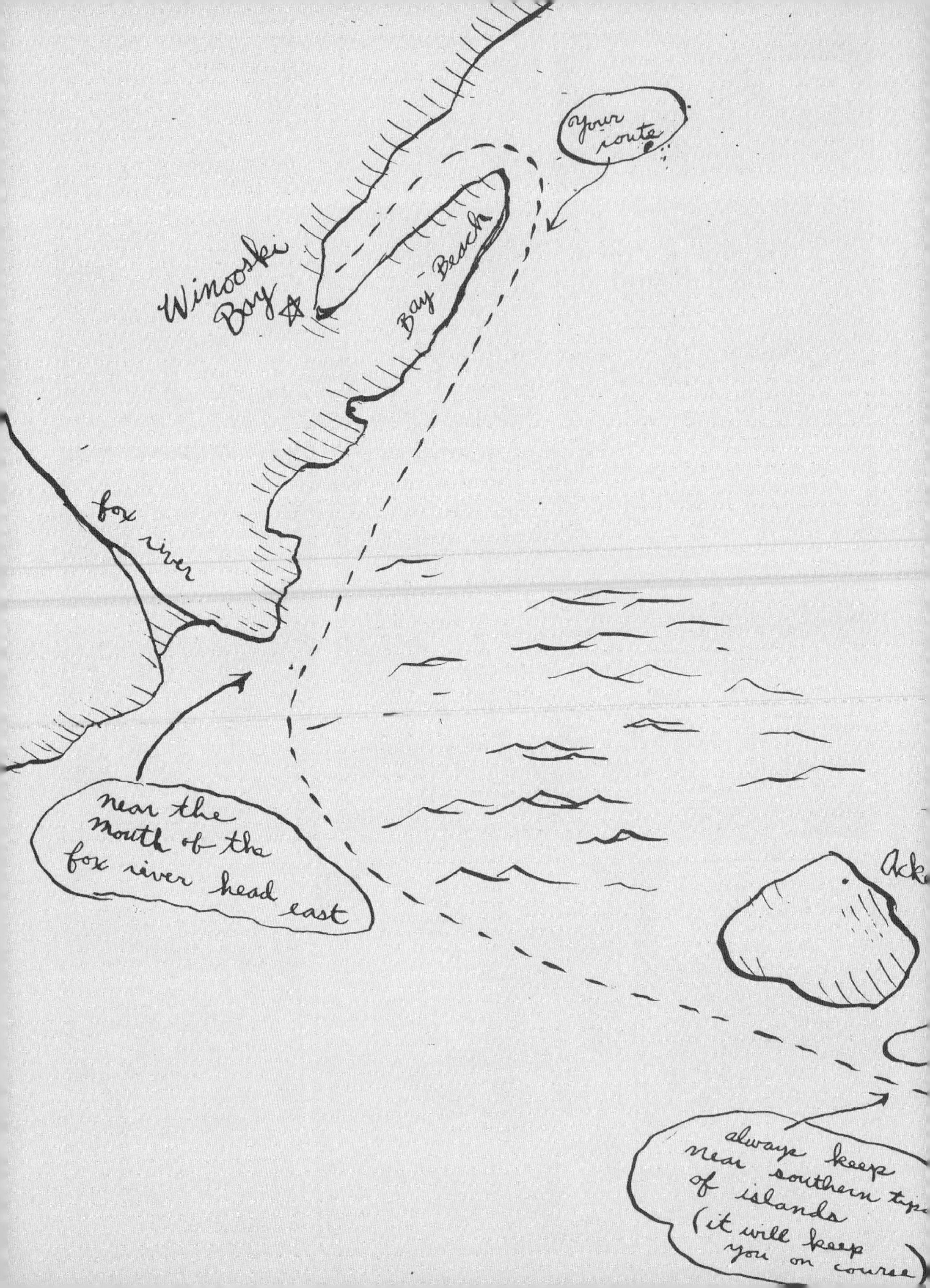

Your route
Winooski Bay
Bay Beach
fox river
near the mouth of the fox river head east
Ack
always keep near southern tip of islands (it will keep you on course)

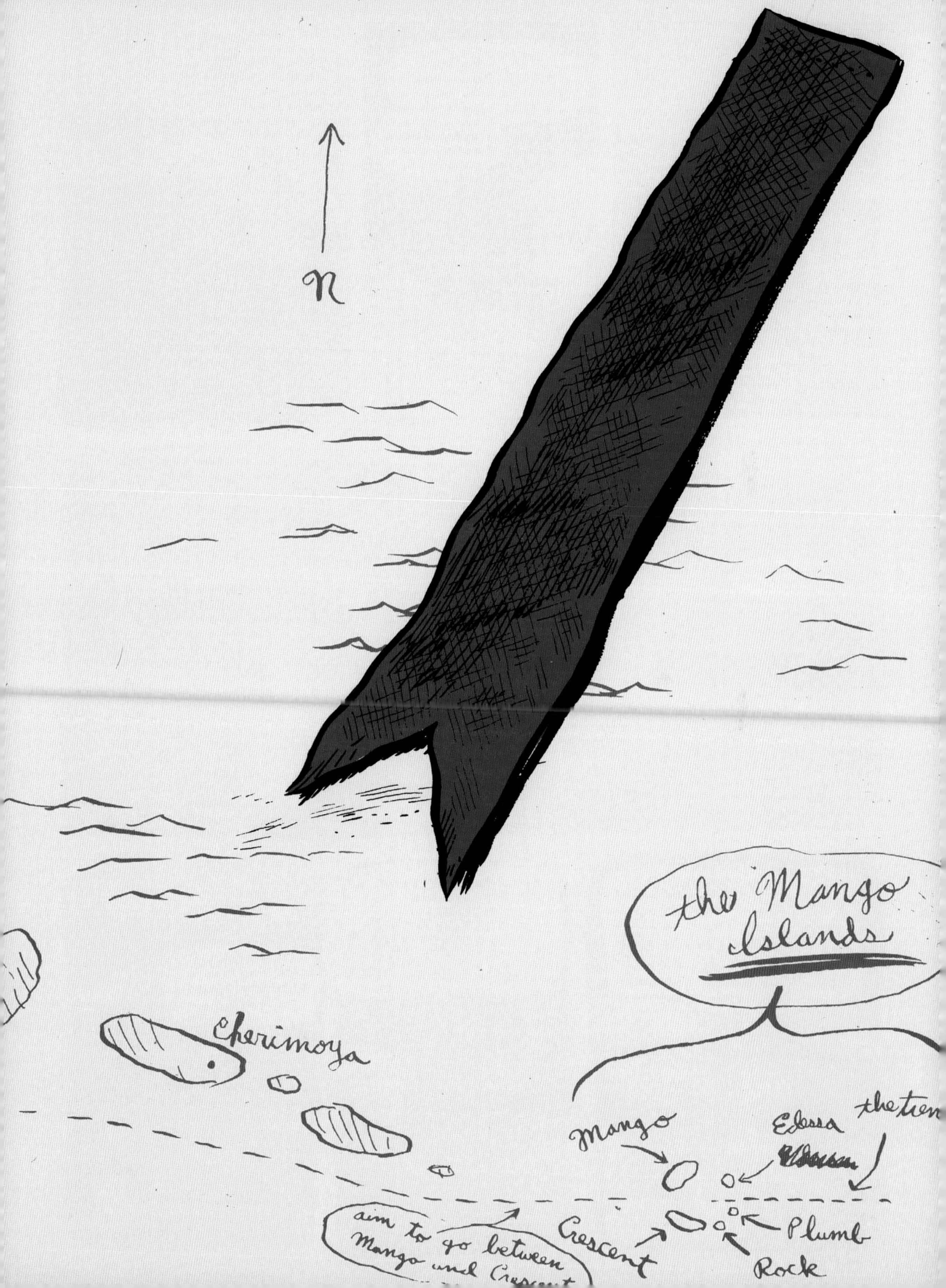

n
the Mango Islands
Cherimoya
Mango
Edessa
Crescent
Plumb
Rock
aim to go between
Mango and

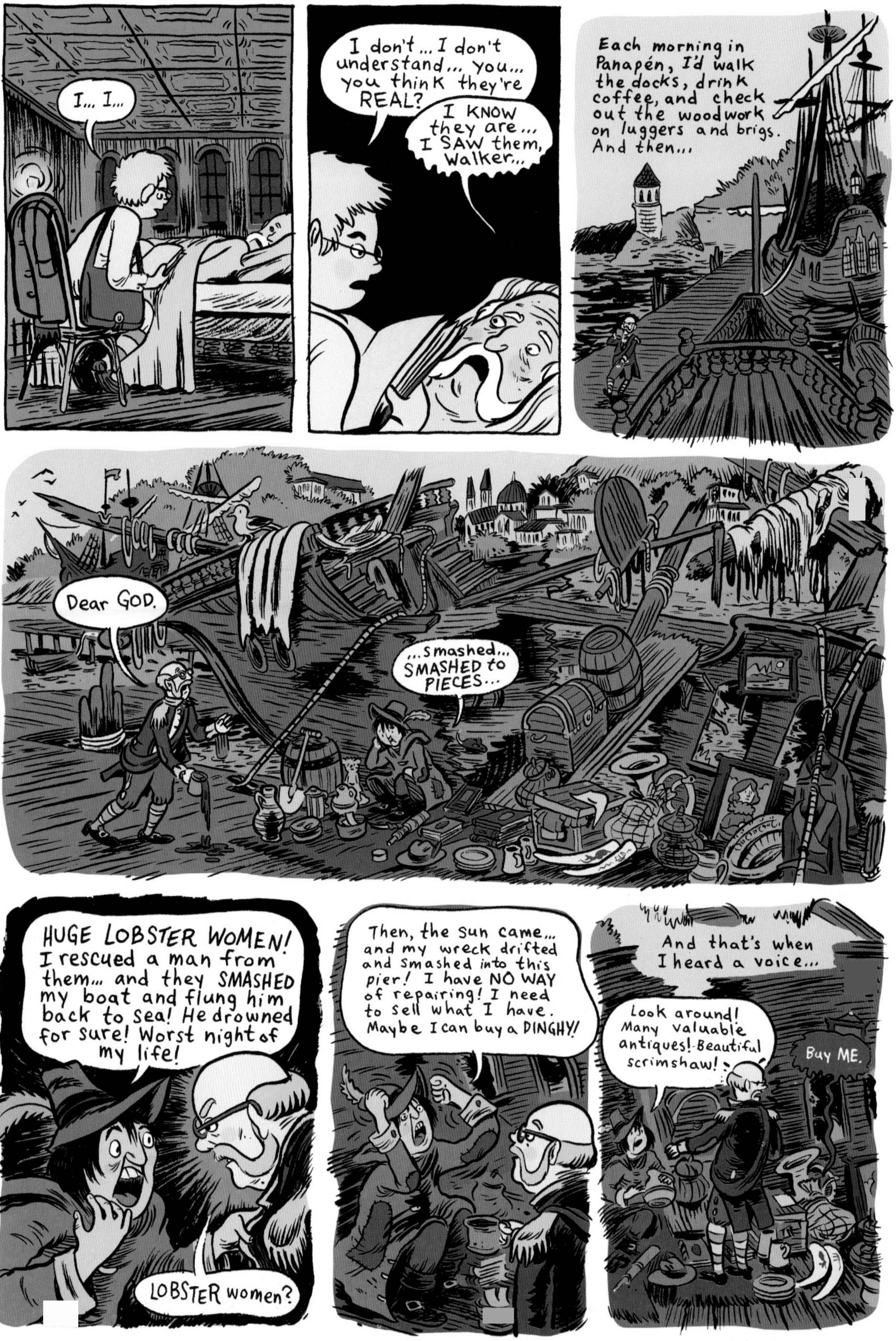

I... I...
I don't... I don't understand... you... you think they're REAL?
I KNOW they are... I SAW them, Walker...
Each morning in Panapén, I'd walk the docks, drink coffee, and check out the woodwork on luggers and brigs. And then...
Dear GOD.
...smashed... SMASHED to PIECES...
HUGE LOBSTER WOMEN! I rescued a man from them... and they SMASHED my boat and flung him back to sea! He drowned for sure! Worst night of my life!
LOBSTER women?
Then, the sun came... and my wreck drifted and smashed into this pier! I have NO WAY of repairing! I need to sell what I have. Maybe I can buy a DINGHY!
And that's when I heard a voice...
Look around! Many valuable antiques! Beautiful scrimshaw!
Buy ME.

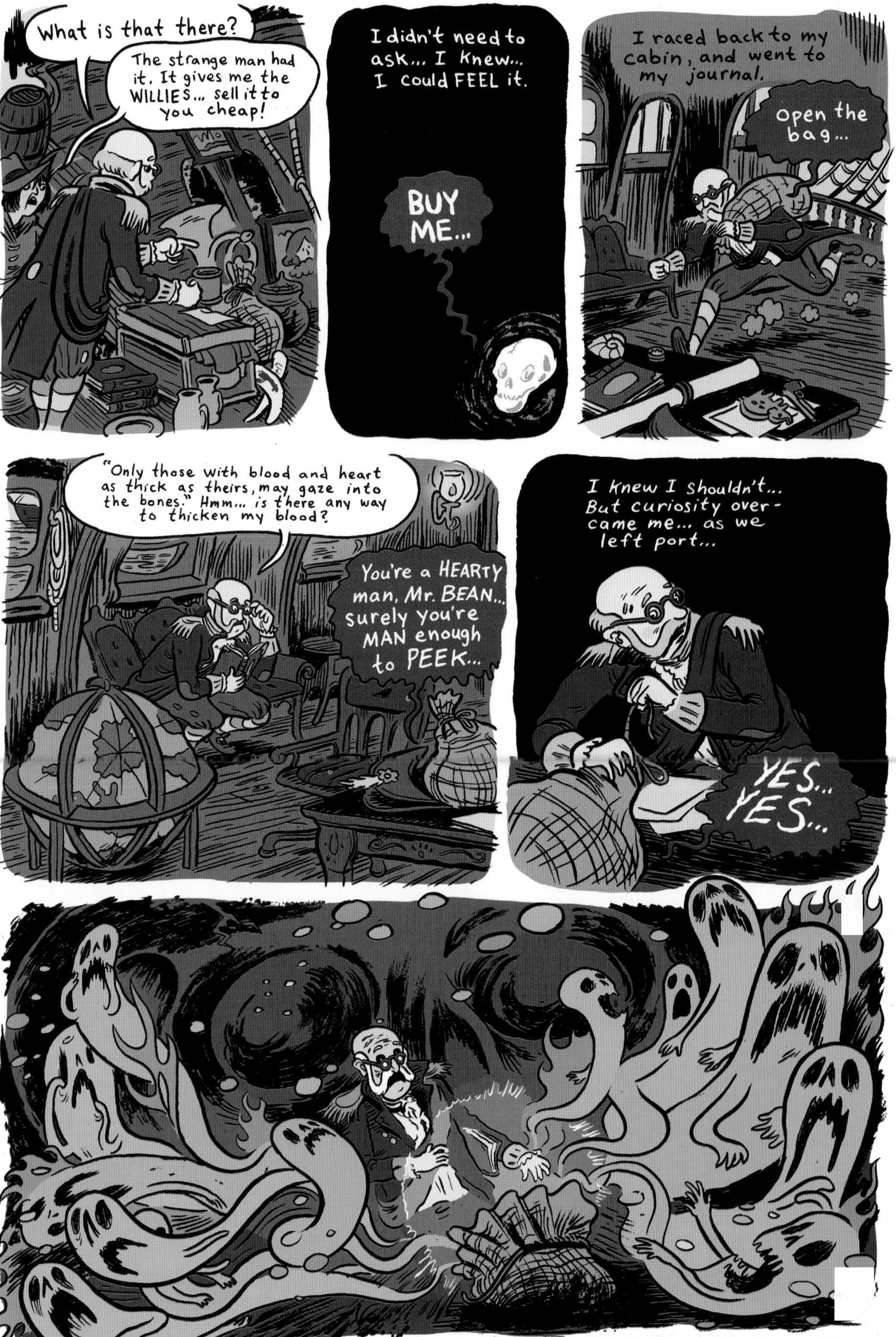
What is that there?
The strange man had it. It gives me the WILLIES... sell it to you cheap!
I didn't need to ask... I knew... I could FEEL it.
BUY ME...
I raced back to my cabin, and went to my journal.
Open the bag...
"Only those with blood and heart as thick as theirs, may gaze into the bones." Hmm... is there any way to thicken my blood?
You're a HEARTY man, Mr. BEAN... surely you're MAN enough to PEEK...
I knew I shouldn't... But curiosity overcame me... as we left port...
YES... YES...

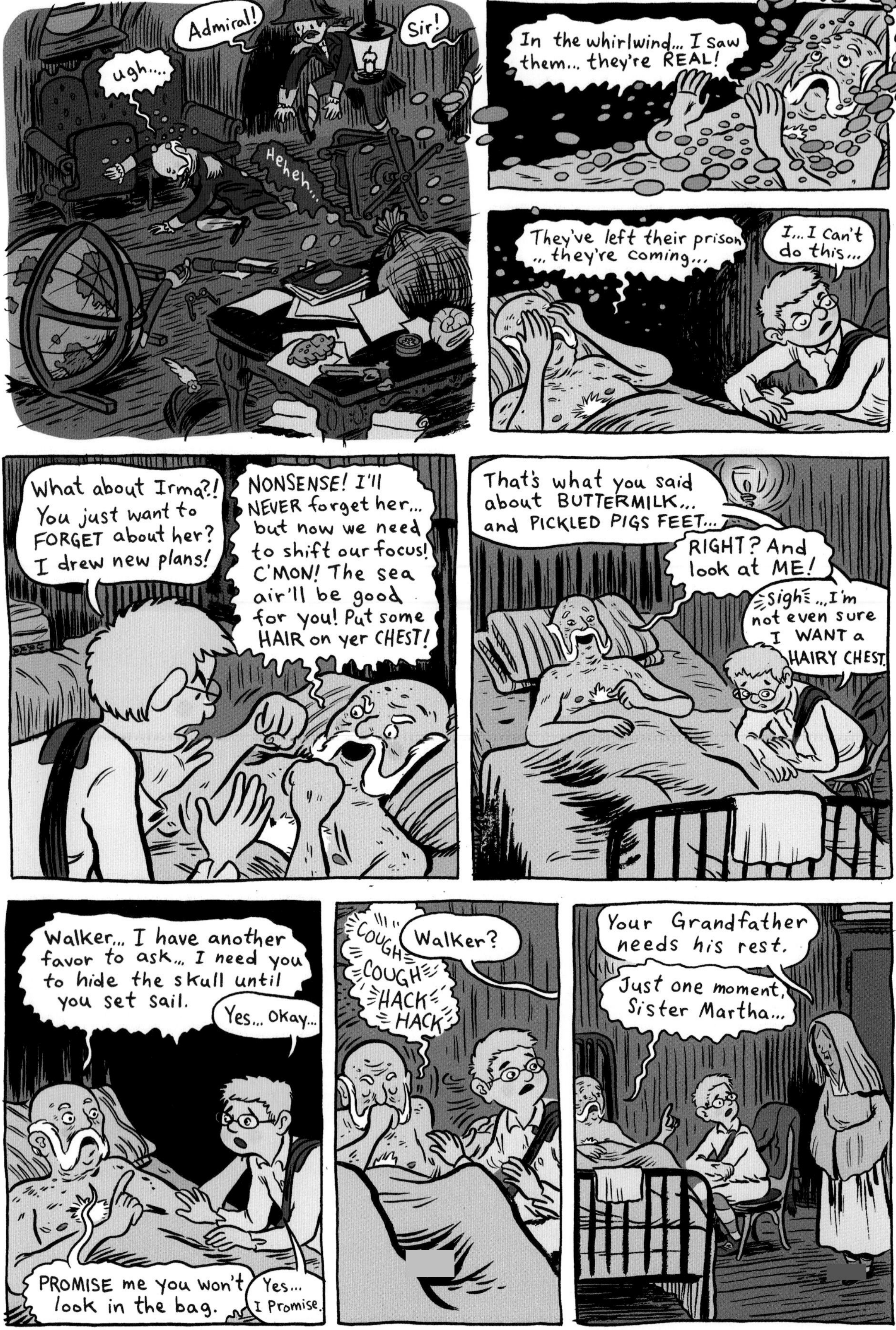
Admiral!
Sir!
ugh....
Heheh...
In the whirlwind... I saw them... they're REAL!
They've left their prison ... they're coming...
I... I can't do this...
What about Irma?! You just want to FORGET about her? I drew new plans!
NONSENSE! I'll NEVER forget her... but now we need to shift our focus! C'MON! The sea air'll be good for you! Put some HAIR on yer CHEST!
That's what you said about BUTTERMILK... and PICKLED PIGS FEET...
RIGHT? And look at ME!
Sigh ...I'm not even sure I WANT a HAIRY CHEST.
Walker... I have another favor to ask... I need you to hide the skull until you set sail.
Yes... Okay...
PROMISE me you won't look in the bag.
Yes... I Promise.
COUGH COUGH HACK HACK
Walker?
Your Grandfather needs his rest.
Just one moment, Sister Martha...

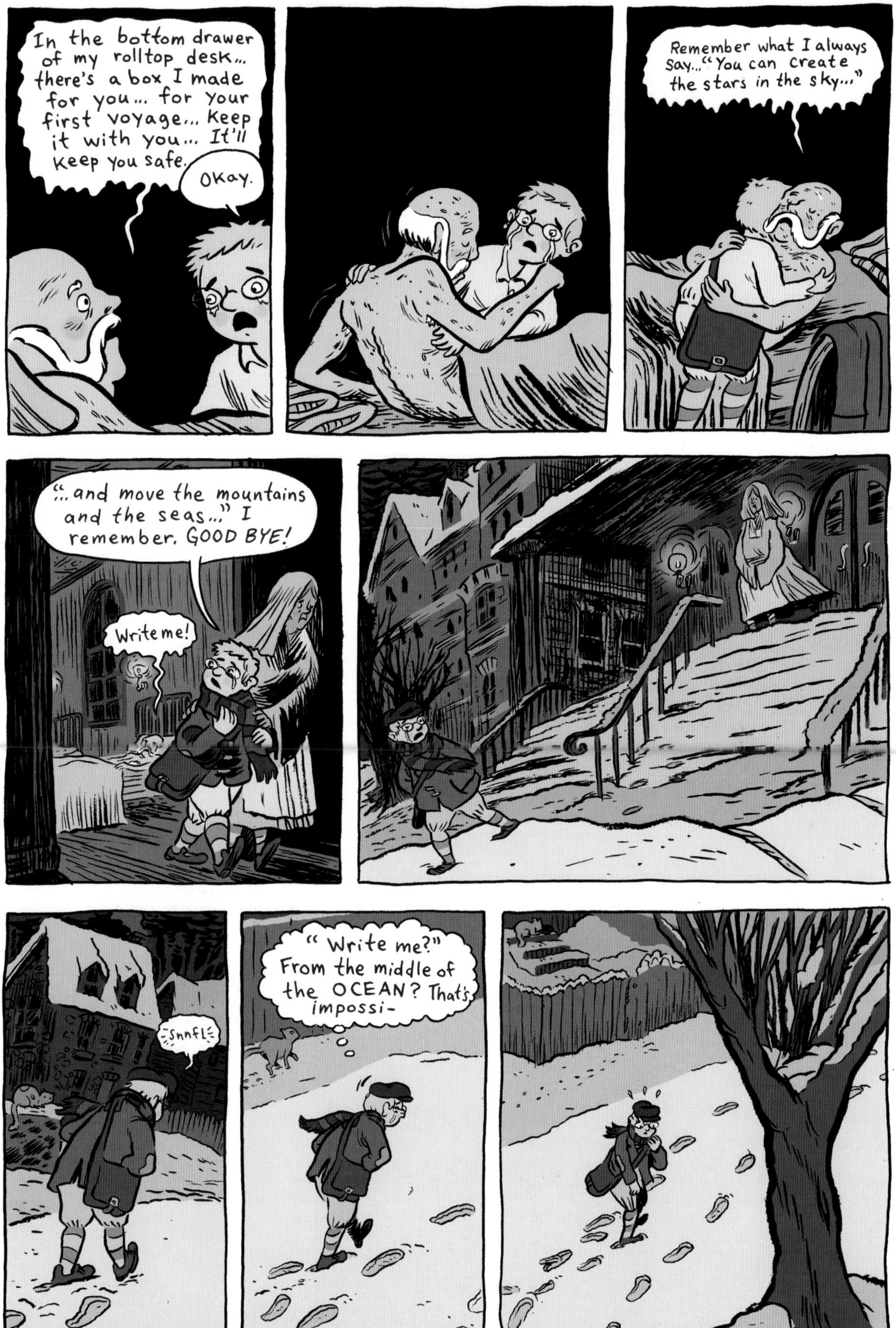
In the bottom drawer of my rolltop desk... there's a box I made for you... for your first voyage... Keep it with you... It'll keep you safe.
Okay.
Remember what I always say... "You can create the stars in the sky..."
"...and move the mountains and the seas..." I remember. GOOD BYE!
Write me!
Snnfl!
"Write me?" From the middle of the OCEAN? That's impossi-

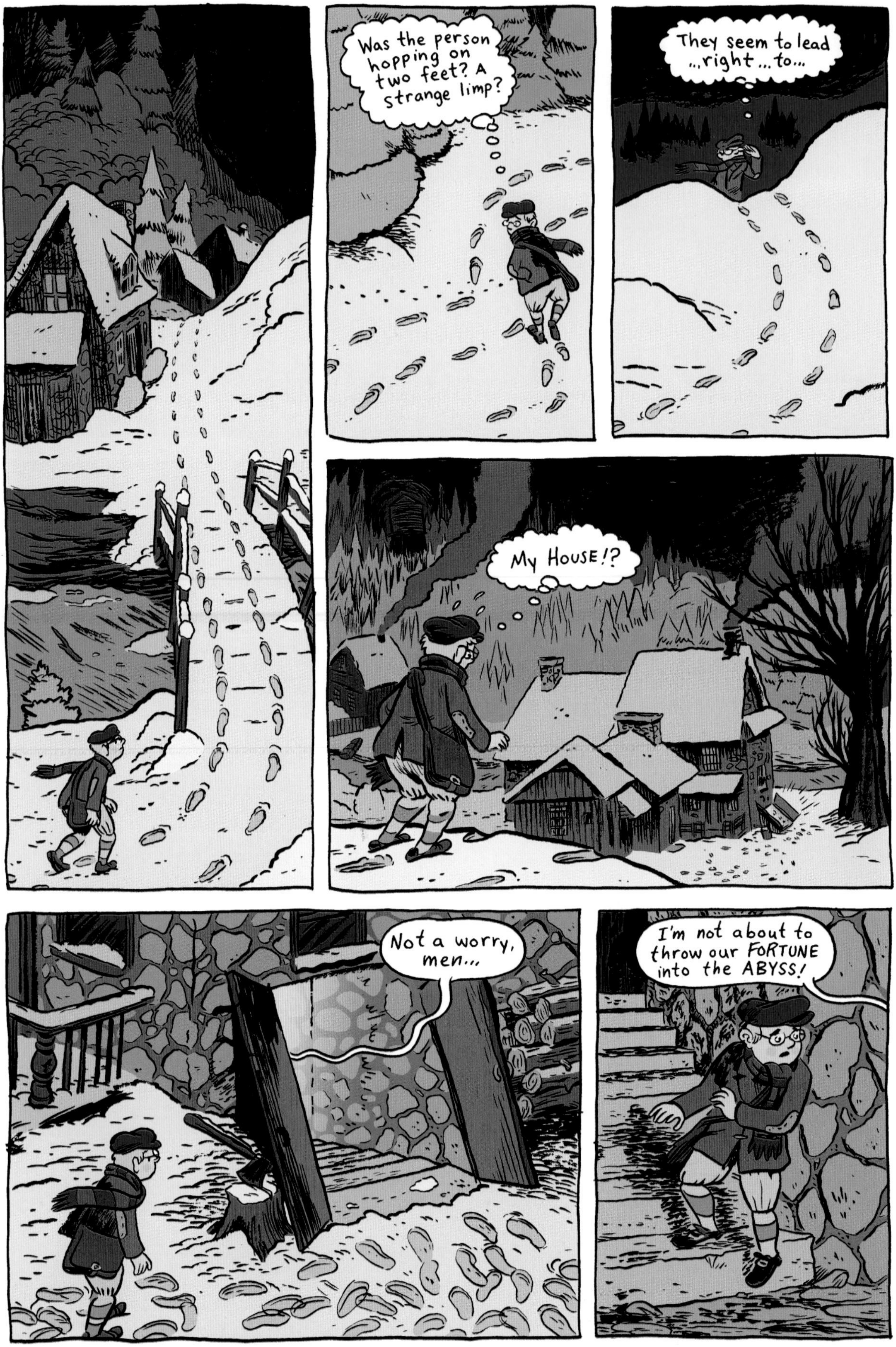

Was the person hopping on two feet? A strange limp?
They seem to lead ...right ... to...
My HOUSE!?
Not a worry, men...
I'm not about to throw our FORTUNE into the ABYSS!

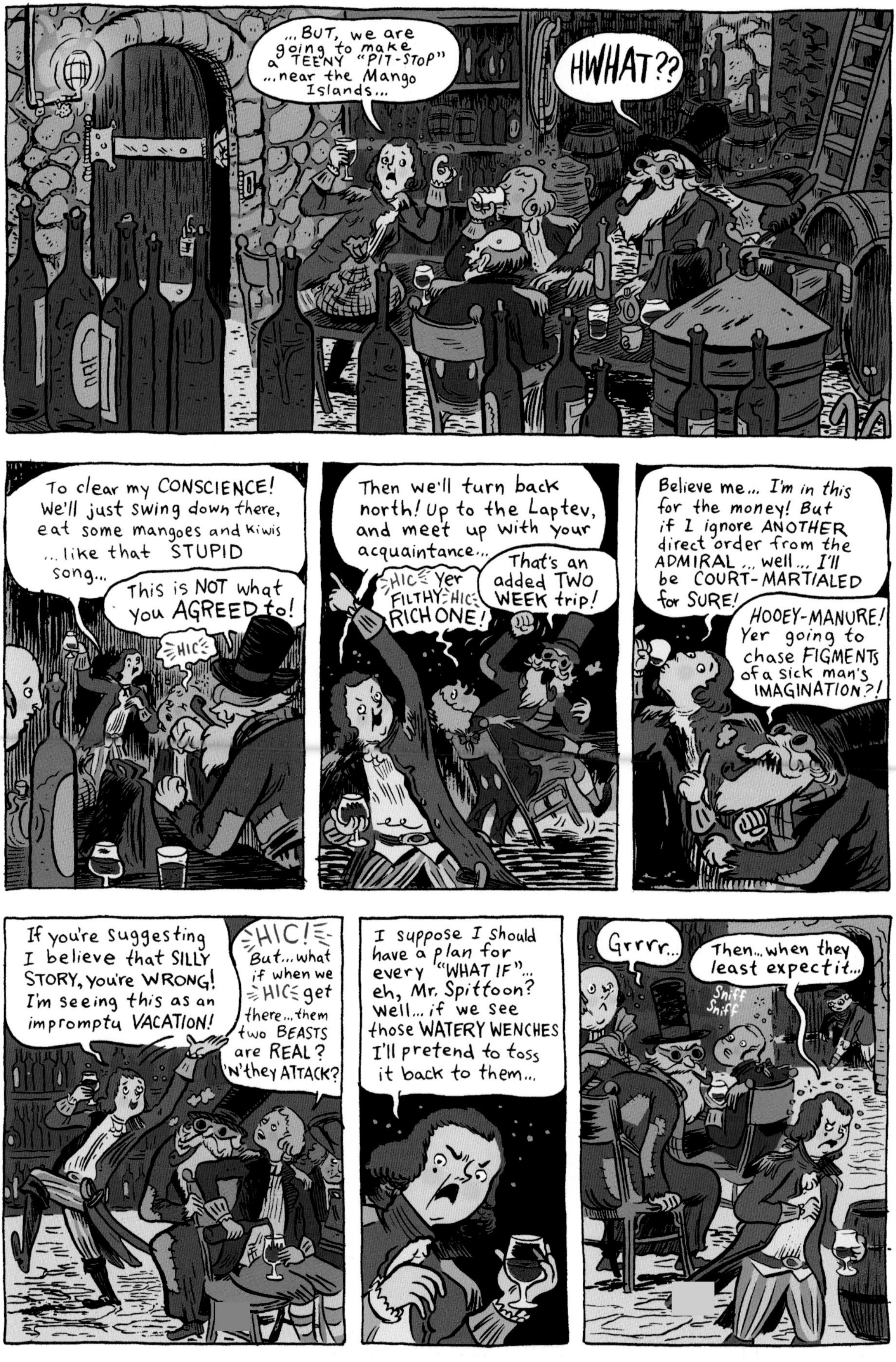

...BUT, we are going to make a TEENY "PIT-STOP" ...near the Mango Islands...
HWHAT??
To clear my CONSCIENCE! We'll just swing down there, eat some mangoes and kiwis ...like that STUPID song...
This is NOT what you AGREED to!
HIC
Then we'll turn back north! Up to the Laptev, and meet up with your acquaintance...
HIC Yer FILTHY HIC RICH ONE!
That's an added TWO WEEK trip!
Believe me... I'm in this for the money! But if I ignore ANOTHER direct order from the ADMIRAL... well... I'll be COURT-MARTIALED for SURE!
HOOEY-MANURE! Yer going to chase FIGMENTS of a sick man's IMAGINATION?!
If you're suggesting I believe that SILLY STORY, you're WRONG! I'm seeing this as an impromptu VACATION!
HIC! But... what if when we HIC get there... them two BEASTS are REAL? 'N'they ATTACK?
I suppose I should have a plan for every "WHAT IF"... eh, Mr. Spittoon? Well... if we see those WATERY WENCHES I'll pretend to toss it back to them...
Grrrr...
Then... when they least expect it...
Sniff Sniff

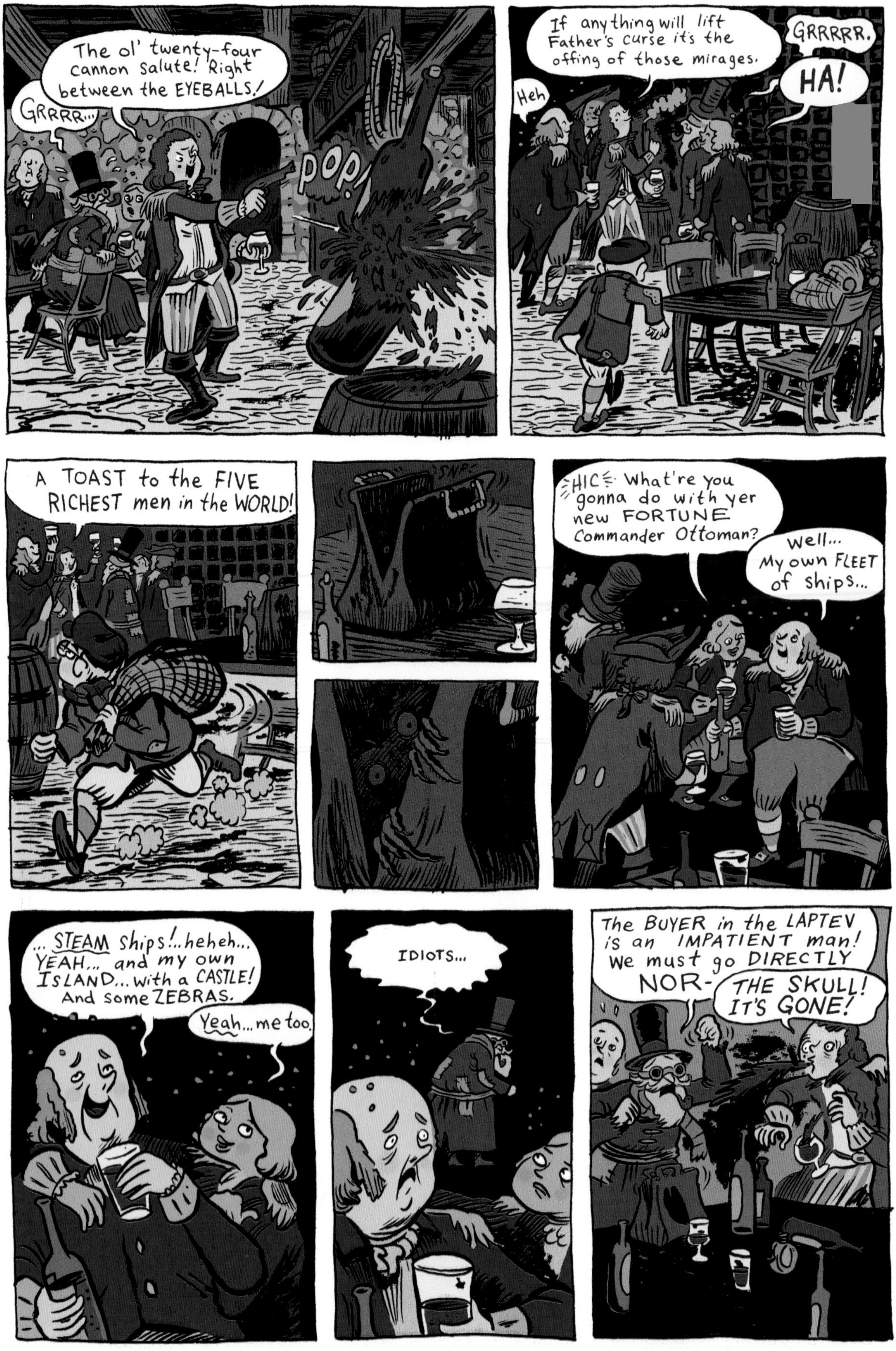

The ol' twenty-four cannon salute! Right between the EYEBALLS!
GRRRR...
POP!
If anything will lift Father's curse it's the offing of those mirages.
GRRRRR.
HA!
Heh
A TOAST to the FIVE RICHEST men in the WORLD!
HIC What're you gonna do with yer new FORTUNE Commander Ottoman?
Well... My own FLEET of ships...
...STEAM ships!...heheh... YEAH... and my own ISLAND... with a CASTLE! And some ZEBRAS.
Yeah... me too.
IDIOTS...
The BUYER in the LAPTEV is an IMPATIENT man! We must go DIRECTLY NOR-
THE SKULL! IT'S GONE!

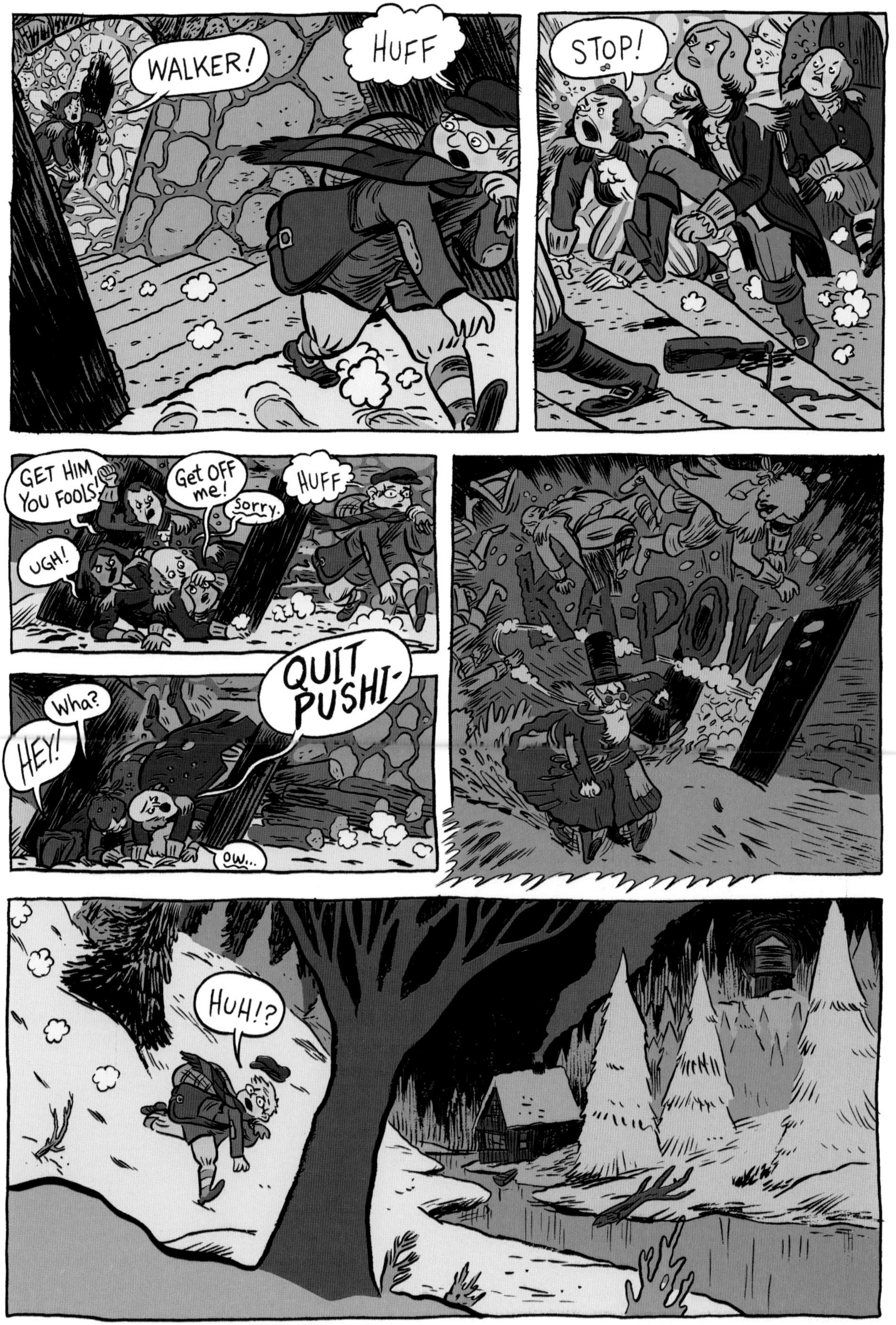
WALKER!
HUFF
STOP!
GET HIM YOU FOOLS!
Get OFF me!
Sorry.
HUFF
UGH!
HEY!
Wha?
QUIT PUSHI-
OW...
KA-POW
HUH!?

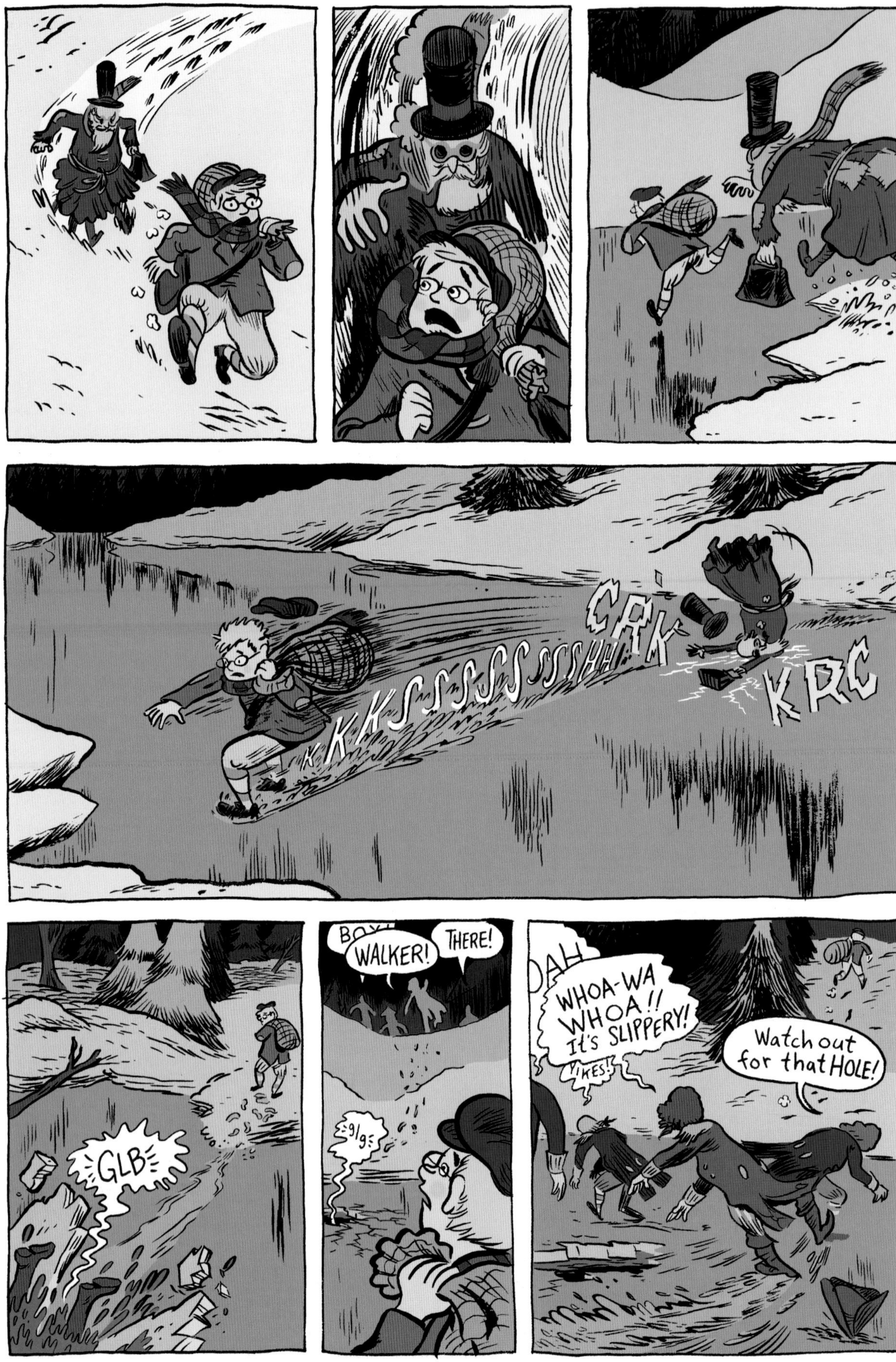
KKKSSSSSSSSSSSHH
CRK
KRC
GLB
WALKER!
THERE!
glg
OAH
WHOA-WA WHOA!! It's SLIPPERY!
YIKES!
Watch out for that HOLE!

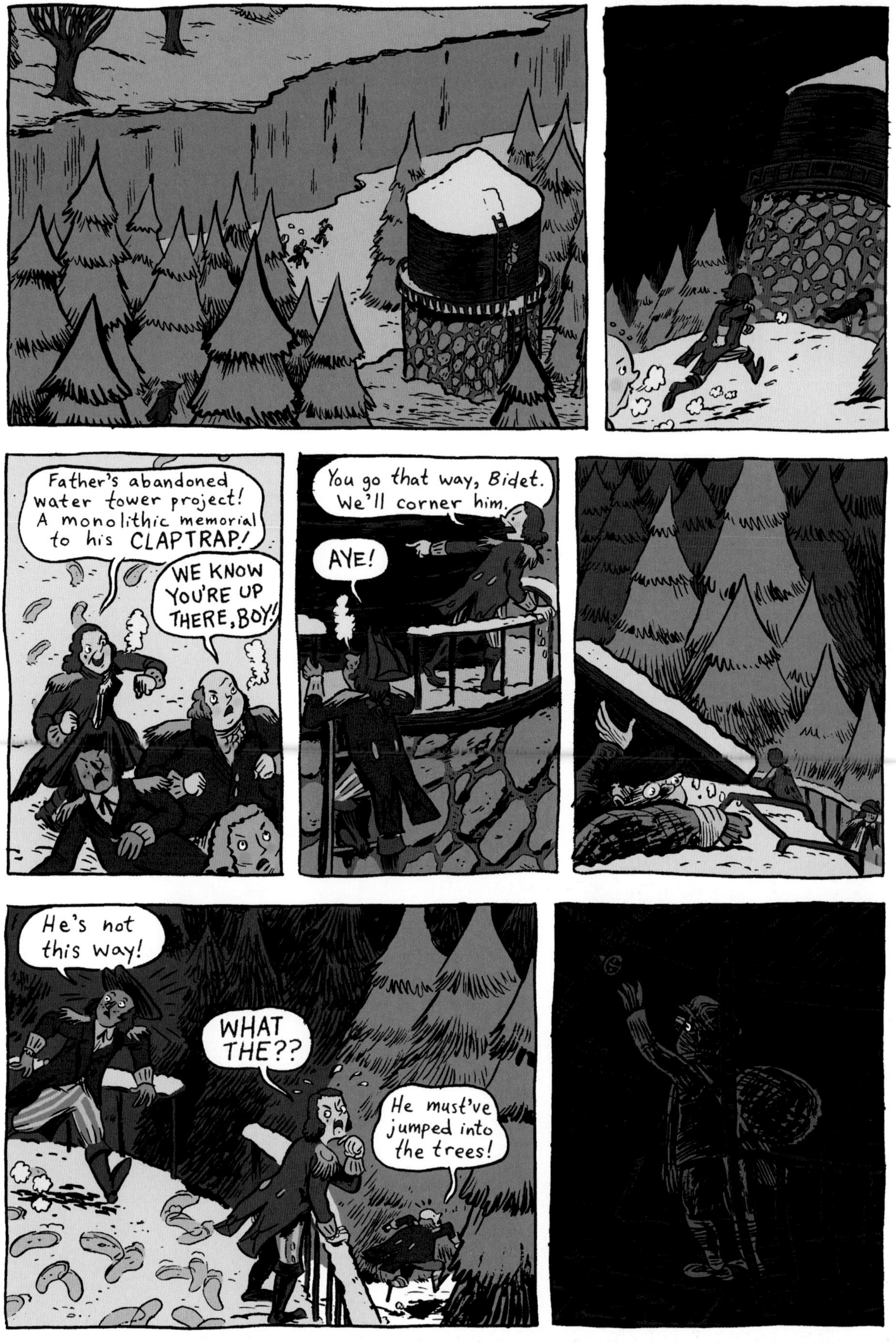
Father's abandoned water tower project! A monolithic memorial to his CLAPTRAP!
WE KNOW YOU'RE UP THERE, BOY!
You go that way, Bidet. We'll corner him.
AYE!
He's not this way!
WHAT THE??
He must've jumped into the trees!

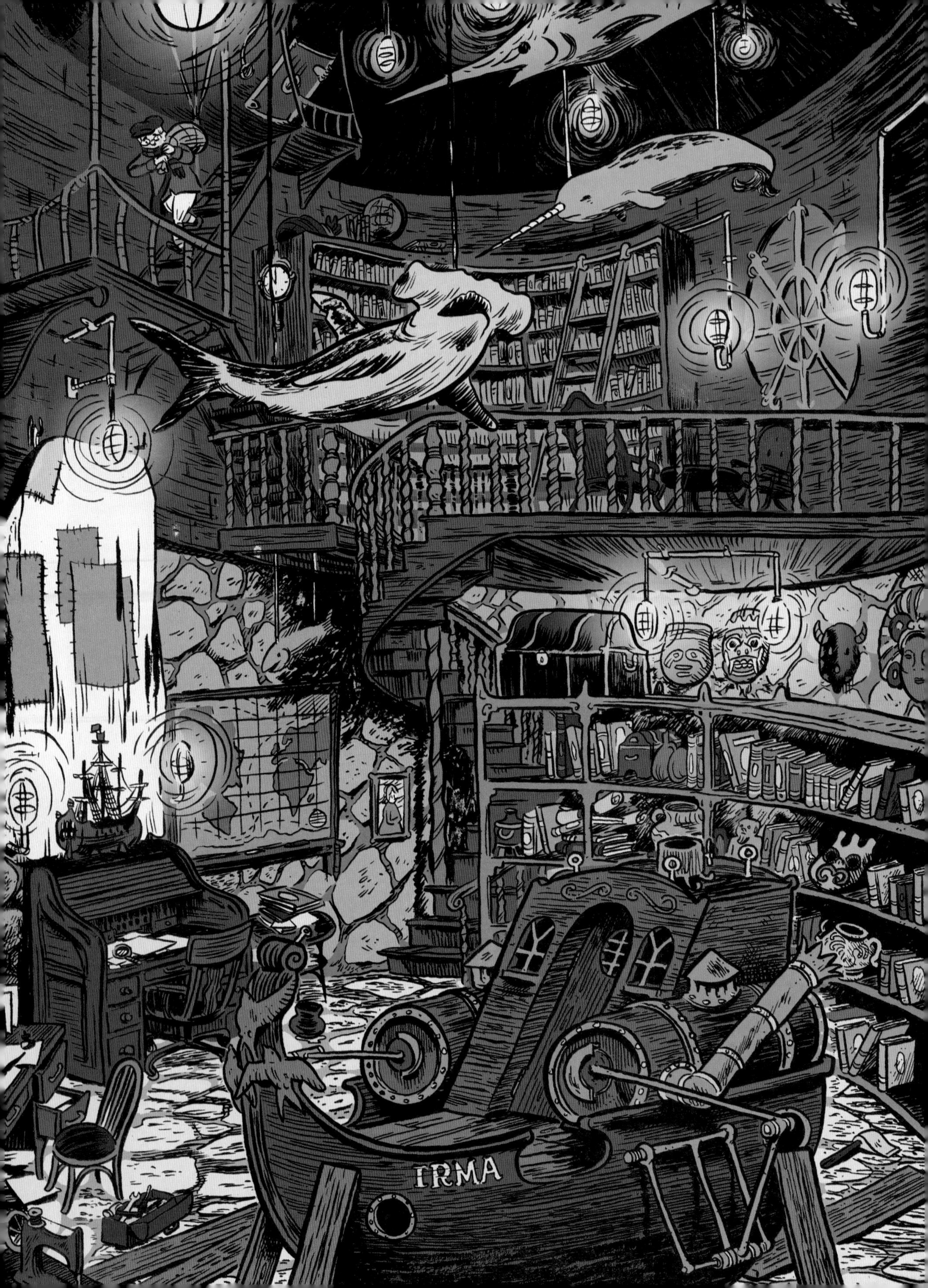
IRMA

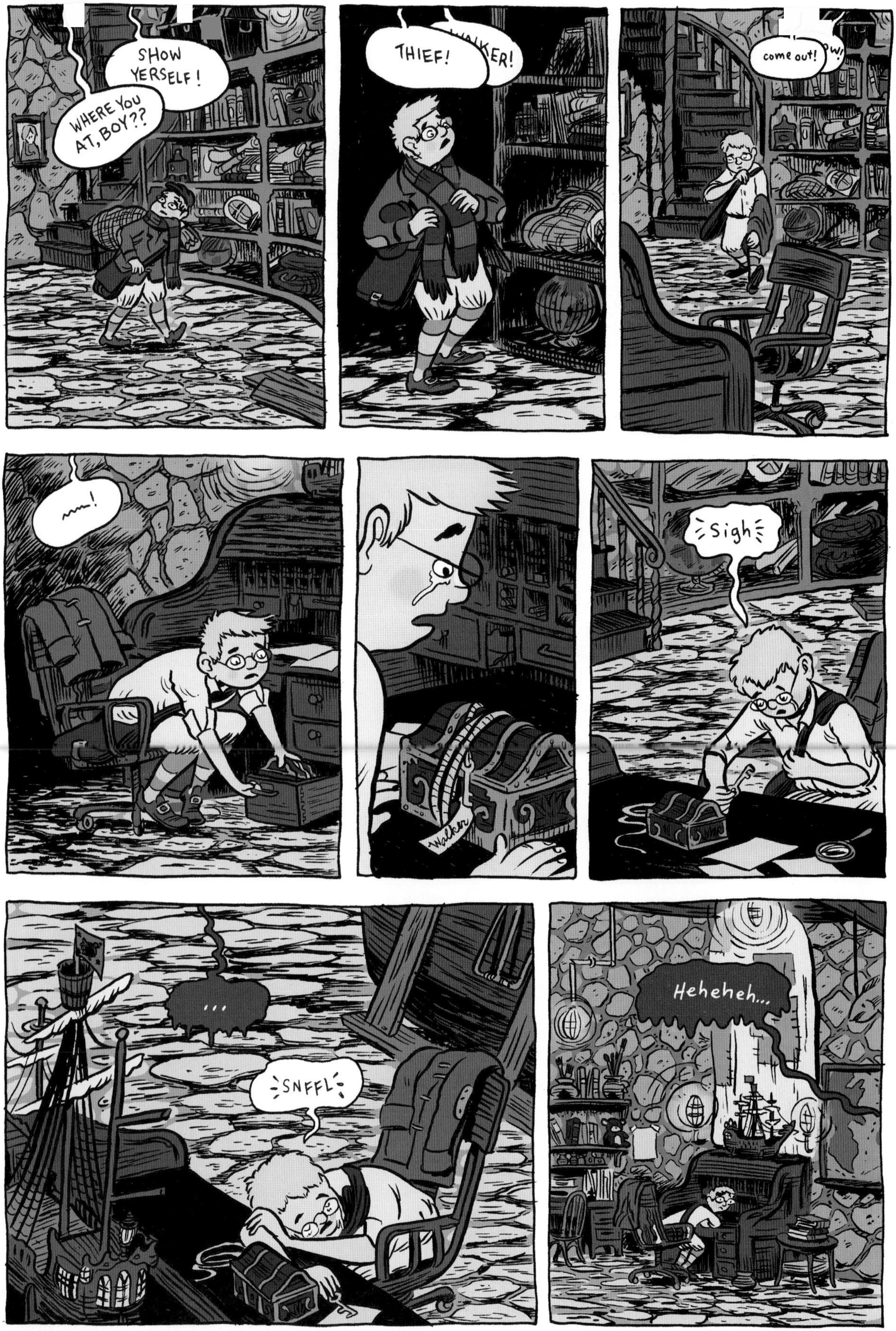
SHOW YERSELF!
WHERE YOU AT, BOY??
THIEF!
ER!
come out!
~~!
Sigh
...
SNFFL
Heheheh...

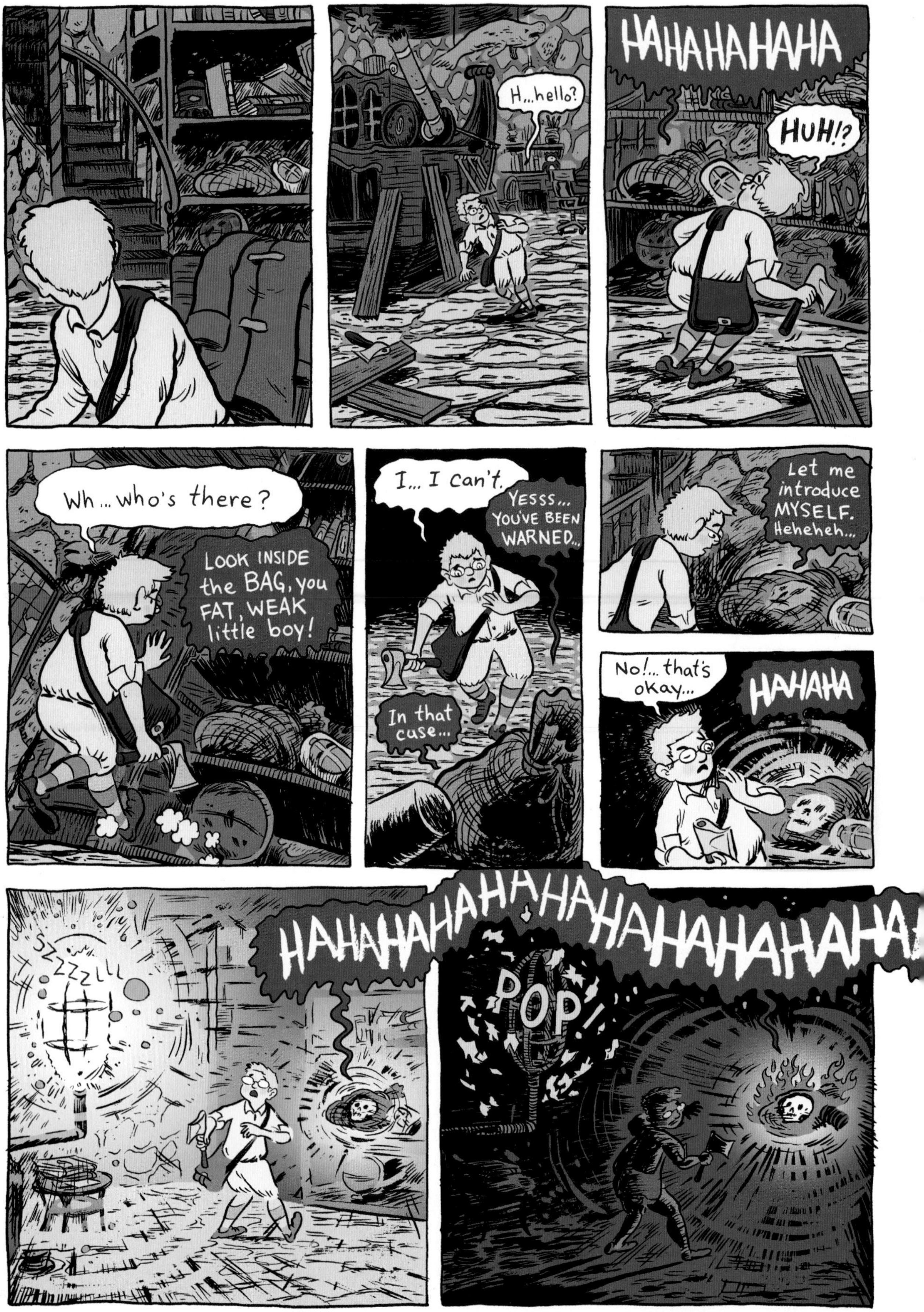
H... hello?
HAHAHAHAHAHA
HUH!?
Wh... who's there?
LOOK INSIDE the BAG, you FAT, WEAK little boy!
I... I can't.
YESSS... YOU'VE BEEN WARNED...
In that case...
Let me introduce MYSELF. Heheheh...
No!... that's okay...
HAHAHA
SZZZZLLL
HAHAHAHAHAHAHAHAHAHAHAHAHA!
POP!

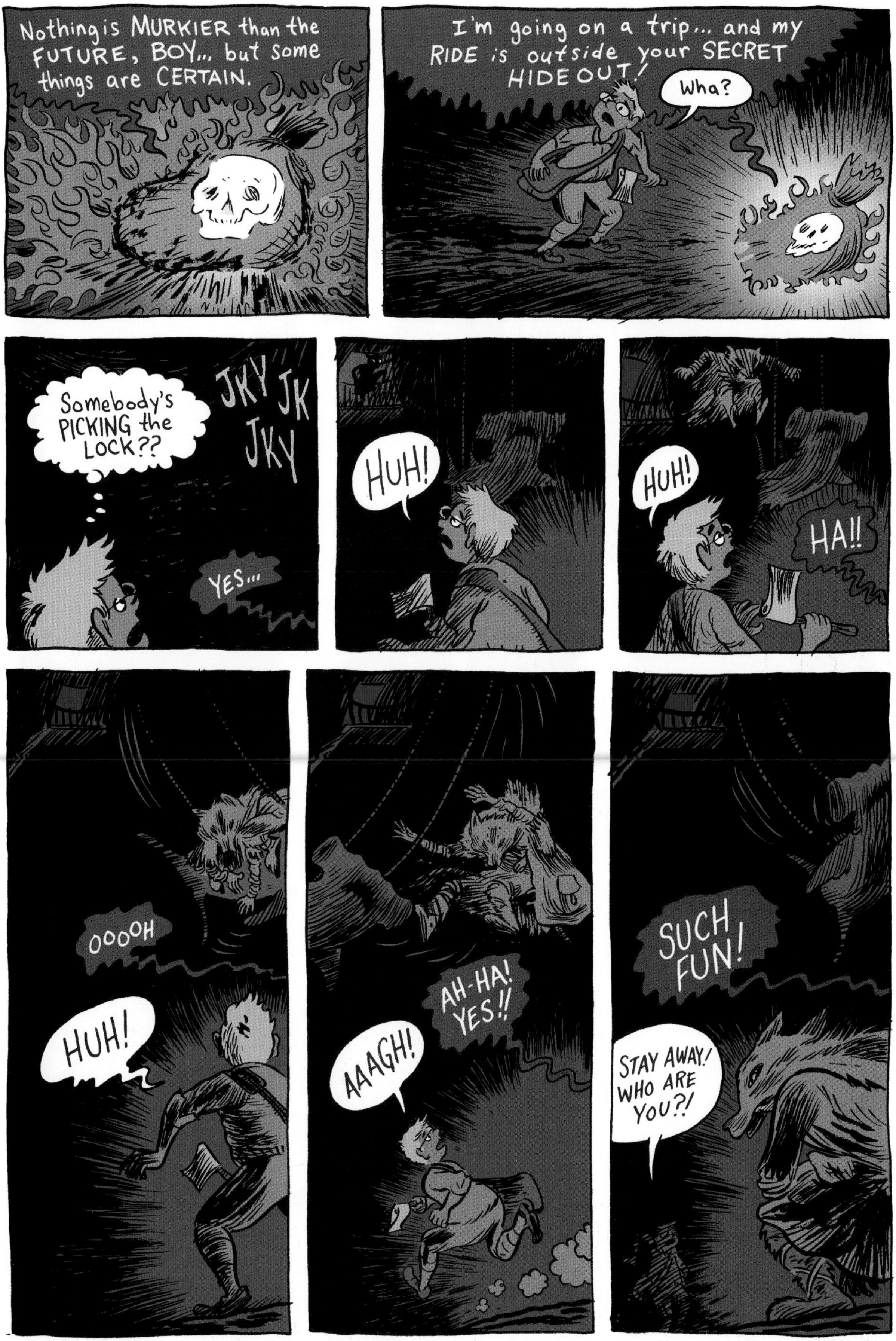
Nothing is MURKIER than the FUTURE, BOY... but some things are CERTAIN.
I'm going on a trip... and my RIDE is outside your SECRET HIDEOUT!
Wha?
Somebody's PICKING the LOCK??
JKY JK JKY
YES...
HUH!
HUH!
HA!!
OOOOH
HUH!
AH-HA! YES!!
AAAGH!
SUCH FUN!
STAY AWAY! WHO ARE YOU?!

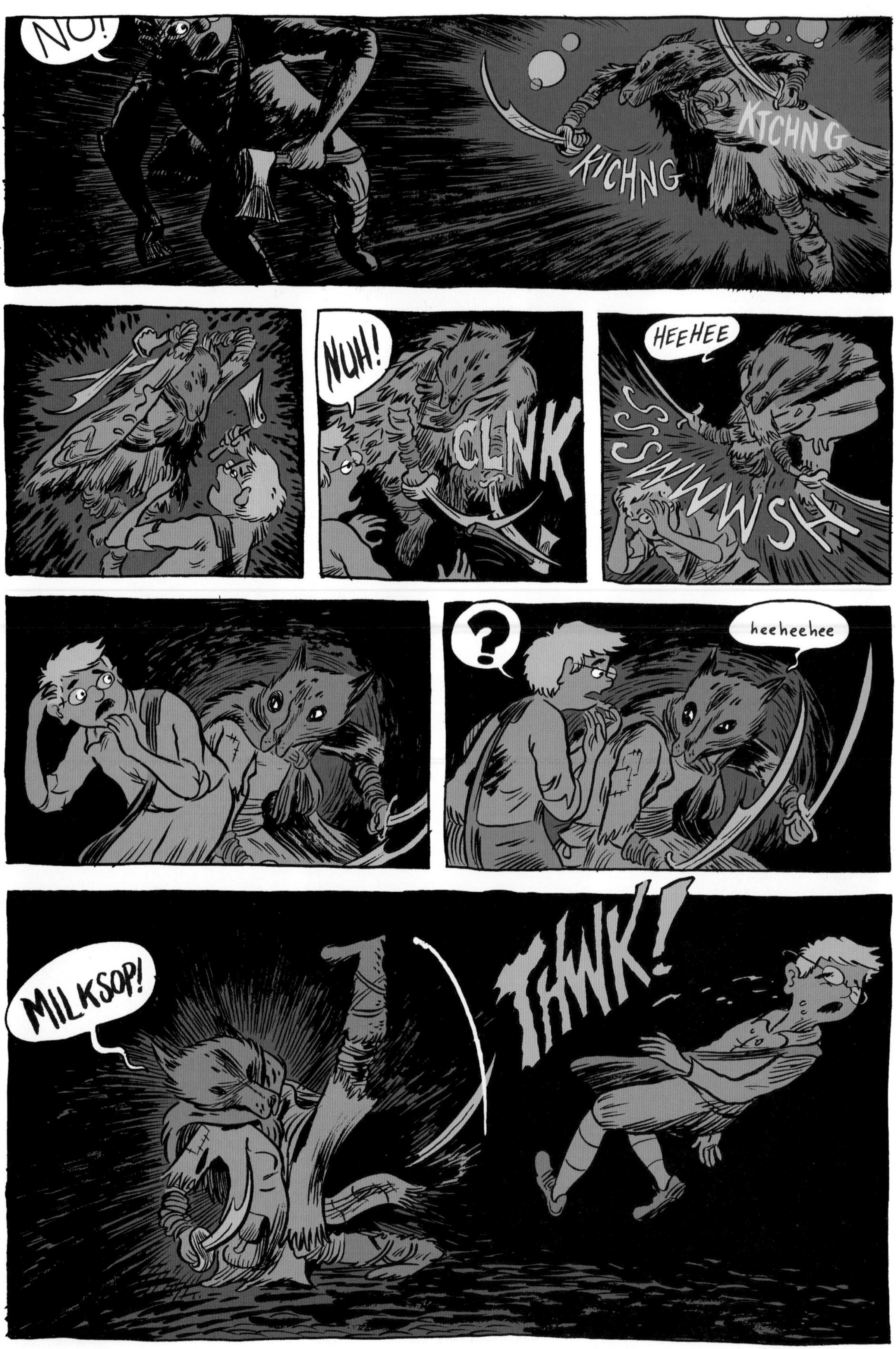
NO!
KICHNG
KICHNG
NUH!
CLNK
HEEHEE
SSWWWSH
?
heeheehee
MILKSOP!
THWK!

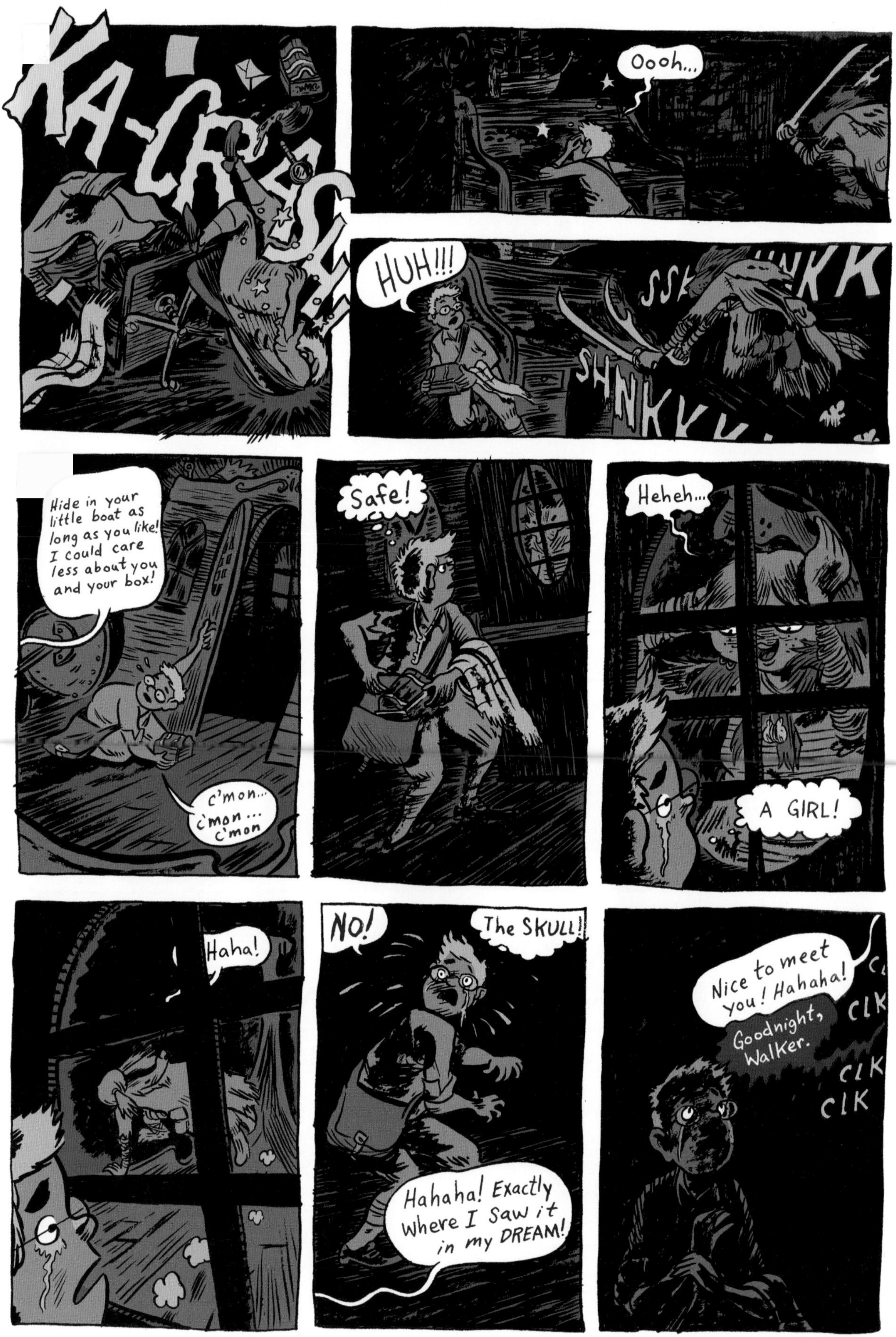
KA-CRASH
Oooh...
HUH!!!
SSHNKK
SHNKKKK
Hide in your little boat as long as you like! I could care less about you and your box!
c'mon... c'mon... c'mon
Safe!
Heheh...
A GIRL!
Haha!
NO!
The SKULL!
Hahaha! Exactly where I saw it in my DREAM!
Nice to meet you! Hahaha!
Goodnight, Walker.
CLK
CLK
CLK

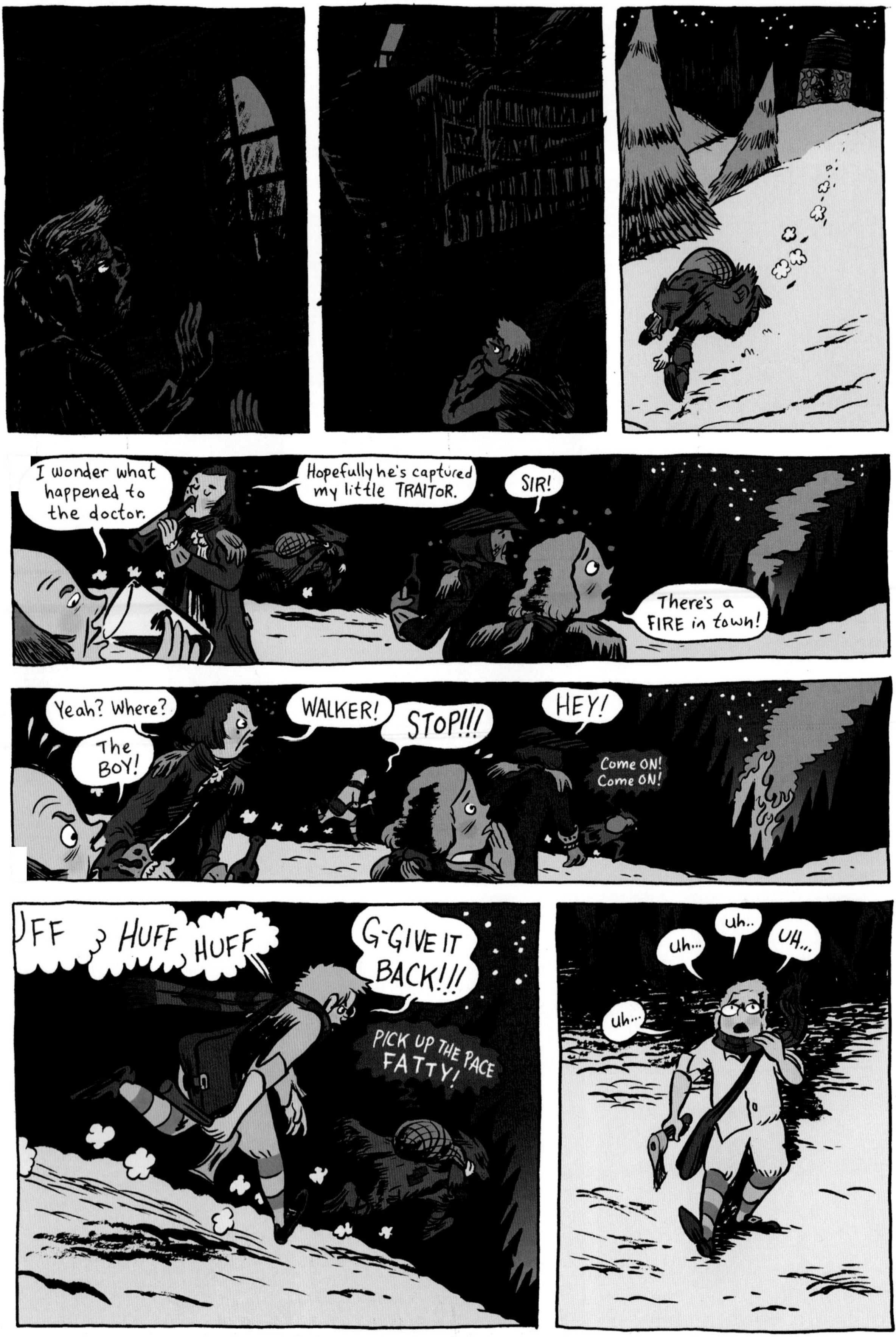
I wonder what happened to the doctor.
Hopefully he's captured my little TRAITOR.
SIR!
There's a FIRE in town!
Yeah? Where?
The BOY!
WALKER!
STOP!!!
HEY!
Come ON! Come ON!
UFF HUFF, HUFF
G-GIVE IT BACK!!!
PICK UP THE PACE FATTY!
uh...
uh..
UH...
uh...

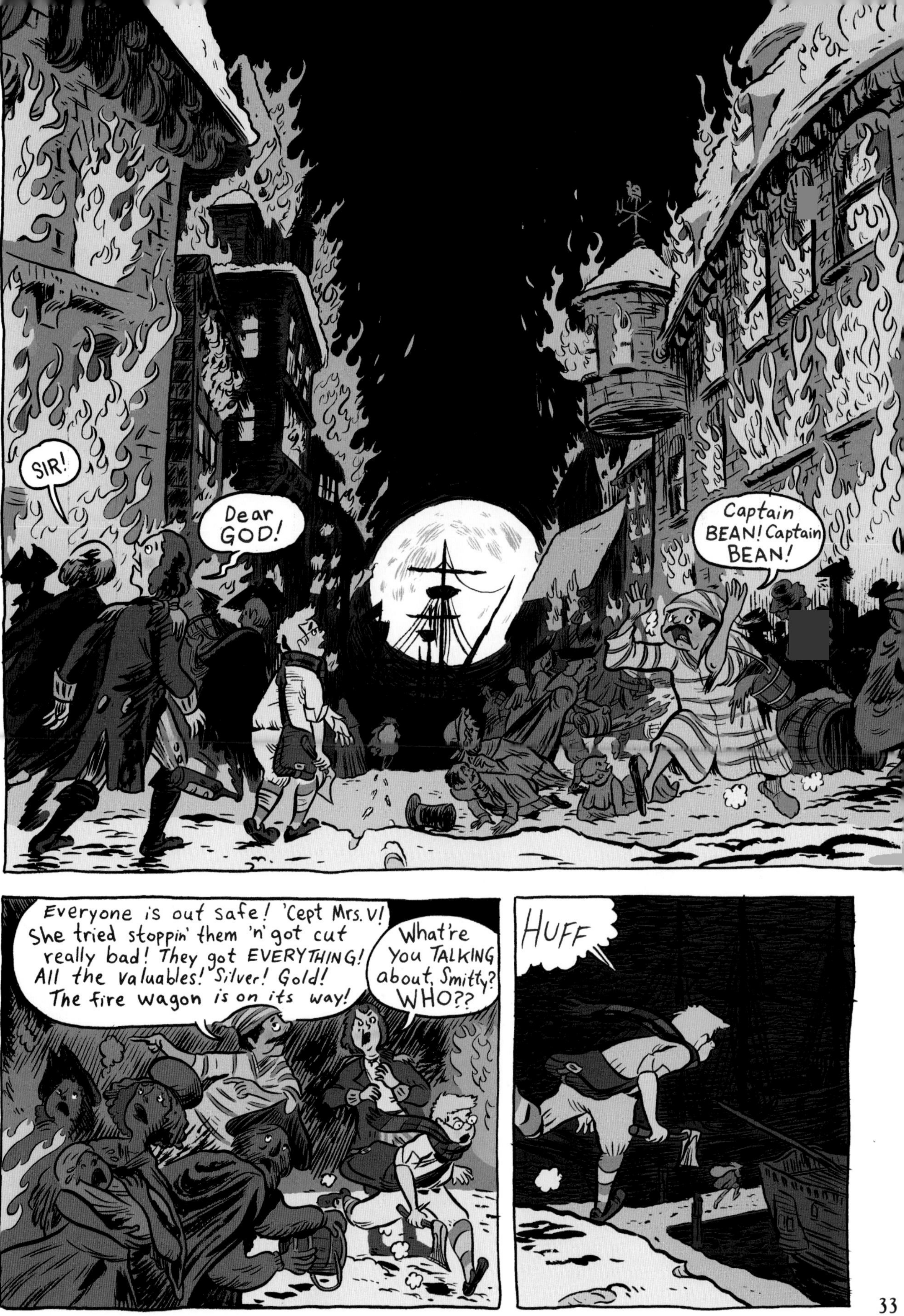
SIR!
Dear GOD!
Captain BEAN! Captain BEAN!
Everyone is out safe! 'Cept Mrs. V! She tried stoppin' them 'n' got cut really bad! They got EVERYTHING! All the valuables! Silver! Gold! The fire wagon is on its way!
What're You TALKING about, Smitty? WHO??
HUFF

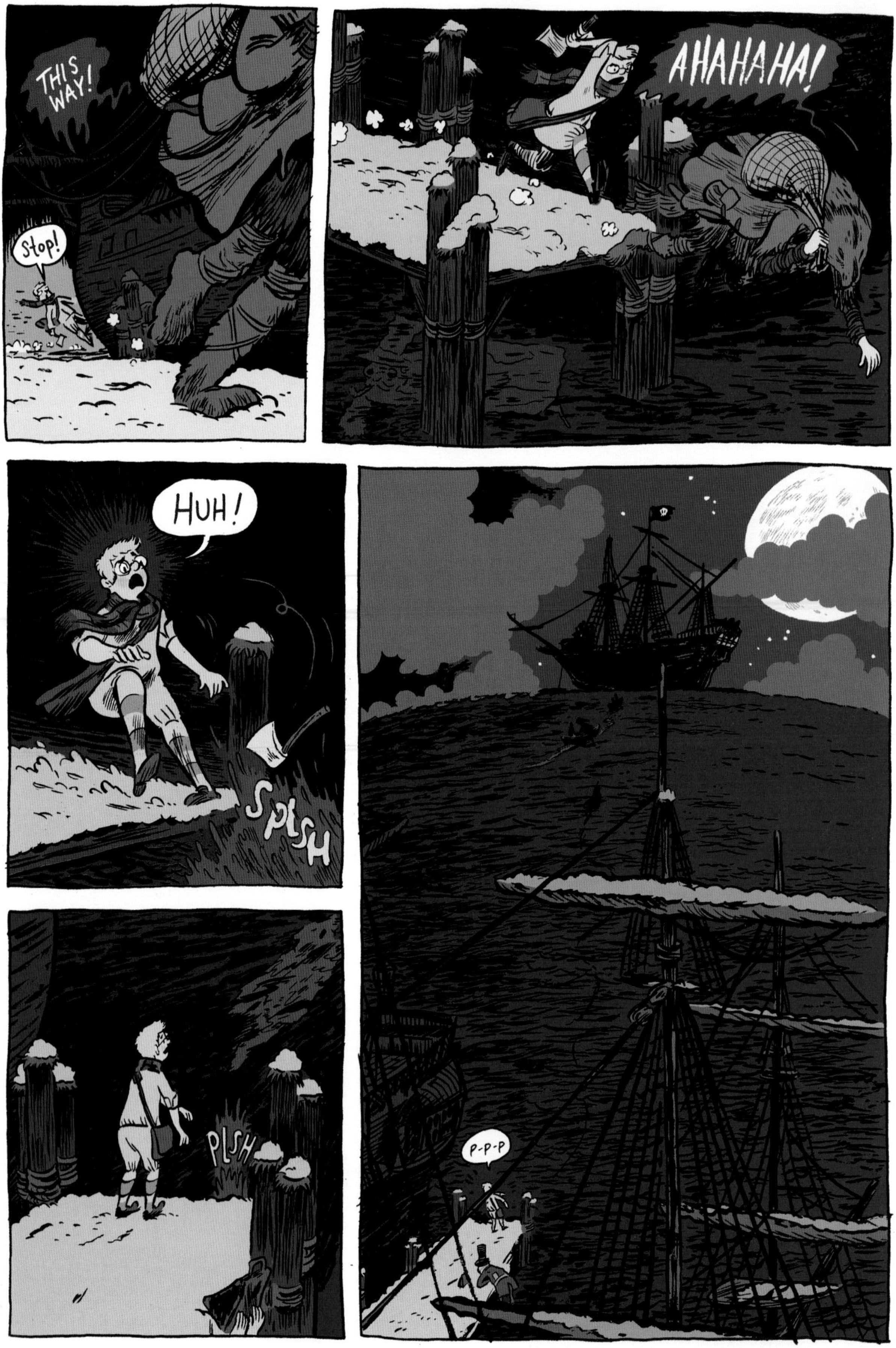
THIS WAY!
Stop!
AHAHAHA!
HUH!
SPLSH
PLSH
P-P-P

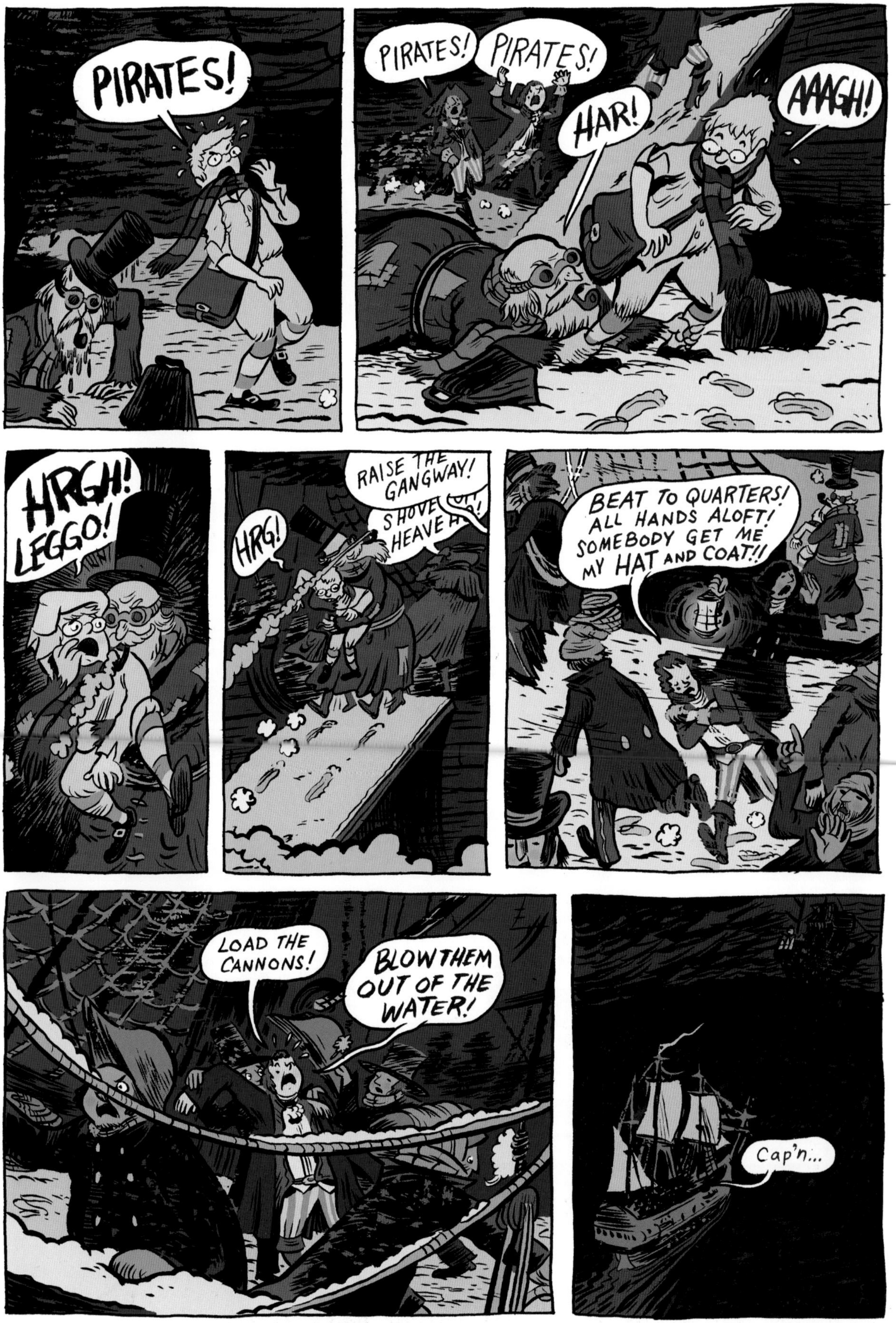
PIRATES!
PIRATES!
PIRATES!
HAR!
AAAGH!
HRGH! LEGGO!
HRG!
RAISE THE GANGWAY!
SHOVE
HEAVE
BEAT TO QUARTERS! ALL HANDS ALOFT! SOMEBODY GET ME MY HAT AND COAT!!
LOAD THE CANNONS!
BLOW THEM OUT OF THE WATER!
Cap'n...

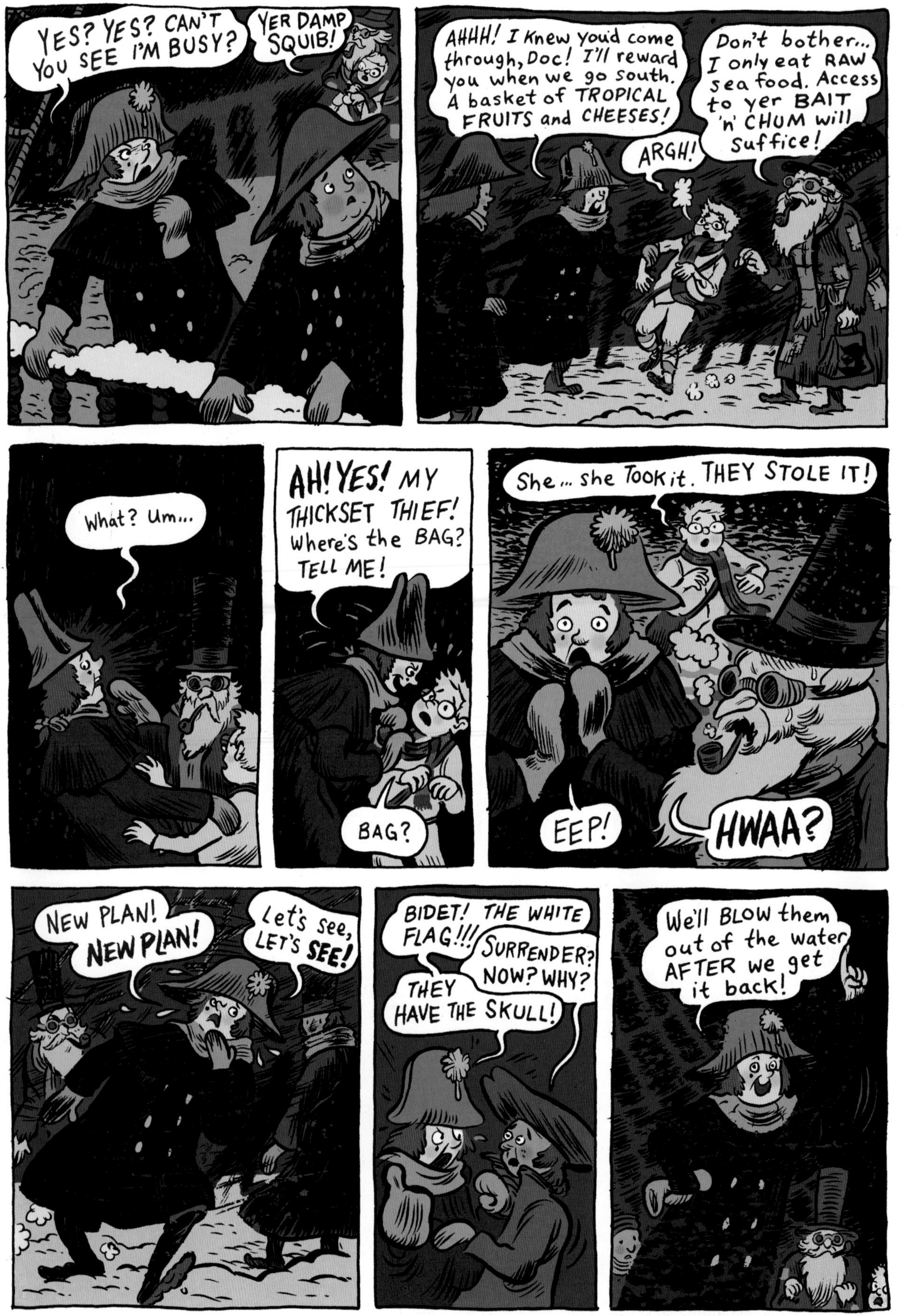
YES? YES? CAN'T YOU SEE I'M BUSY?
YER DAMP SQUIB!
AHHH! I knew you'd come through, Doc! I'll reward you when we go south. A basket of TROPICAL FRUITS and CHEESES!
Don't bother... I only eat RAW sea food. Access to yer BAIT 'n' CHUM will suffice!
ARGH!
What? Um...
AH! YES! MY THICKSET THIEF! Where's the BAG? TELL ME!
BAG?
She... she TOOK it. THEY STOLE IT!
EEP!
HWAA?
NEW PLAN! NEW PLAN!
Let's see, LET'S SEE!
BIDET! THE WHITE FLAG!!!
SURRENDER? NOW? WHY?
THEY HAVE THE SKULL!
We'll BLOW them out of the water AFTER we get it back!

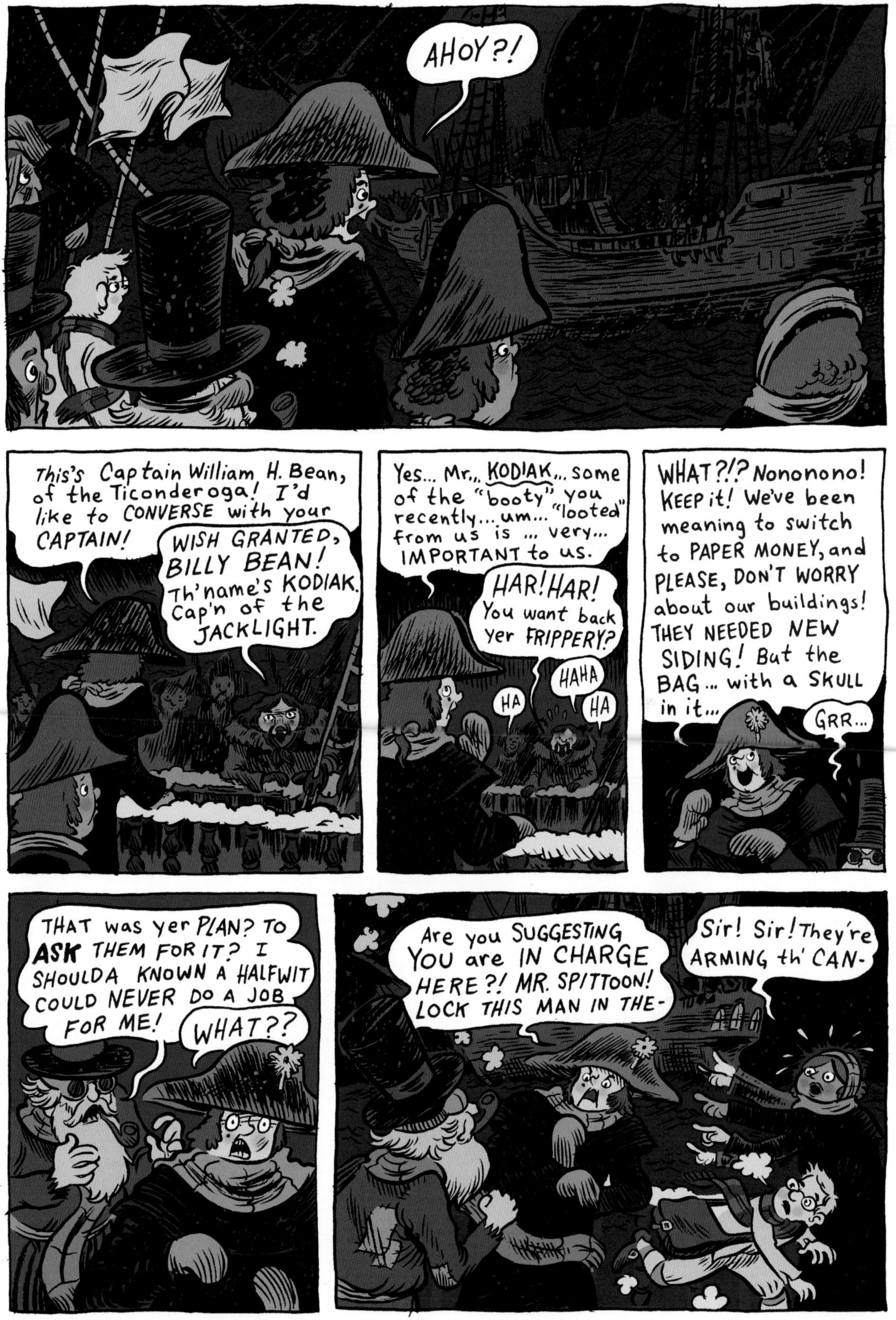

AHOY?!
This's Captain William H. Bean, of the Ticonderoga! I'd like to CONVERSE with your CAPTAIN!
WISH GRANTED, BILLY BEAN! Th'name's KODIAK. Cap'n of the JACKLIGHT.
Yes... Mr... KODIAK... some of the "booty" you recently... um... "looted" from us is ... very... IMPORTANT to us.
HAR! HAR! You want back yer FRIPPERY?
HA
HAHA
HA
WHAT?!? Nononono! KEEP it! We've been meaning to switch to PAPER MONEY, and PLEASE, DON'T WORRY about our buildings! THEY NEEDED NEW SIDING! But the BAG... with a SKULL in it...
GRR...
THAT was yer PLAN? TO ASK THEM FOR IT? I SHOULDA KNOWN A HALFWIT COULD NEVER DO A JOB FOR ME!
WHAT??
Are you SUGGESTING YOU are IN CHARGE HERE?! MR. SPITTOON! LOCK THIS MAN IN THE-
Sir! Sir! They're ARMING th' CAN-

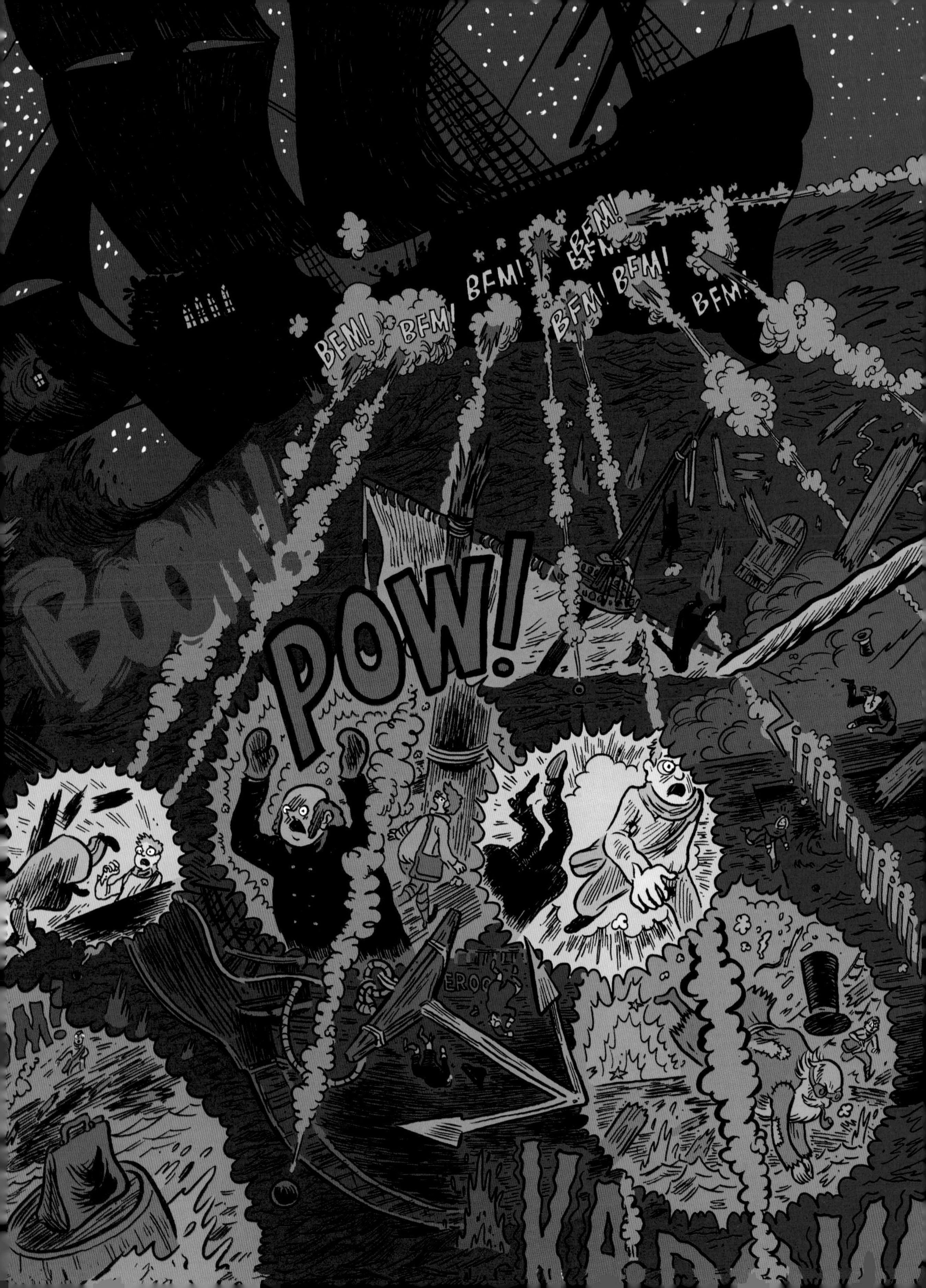
BFM!
BFM!
BFM!
BFM!
BFM!
BFM!
BFM!
BFM!
BOOM!
POW!

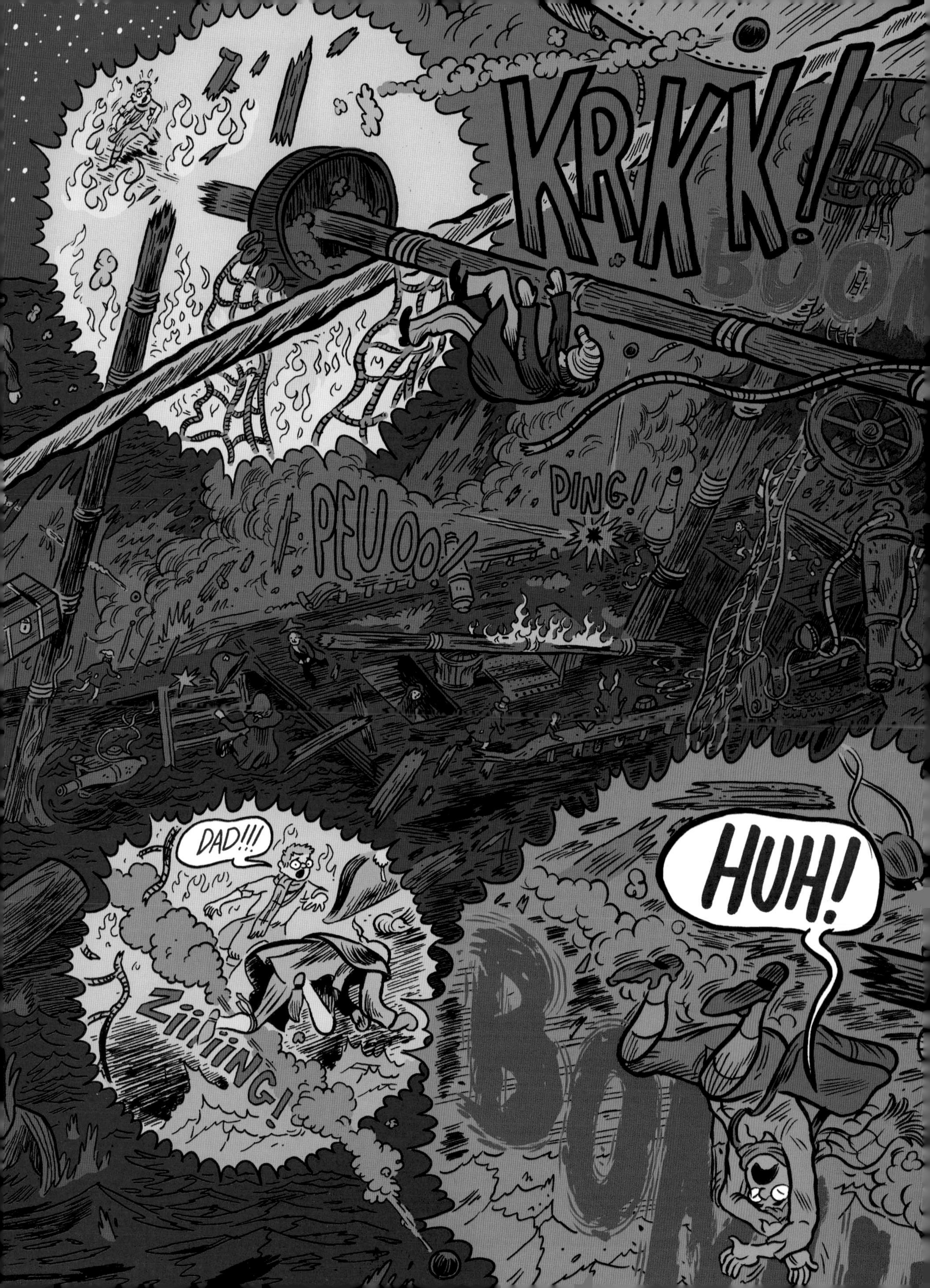
KRKK!
BOOM
PING!
PEUOOF!
DAD!!!
HUH!
ZiiiiiNG!
BOOM

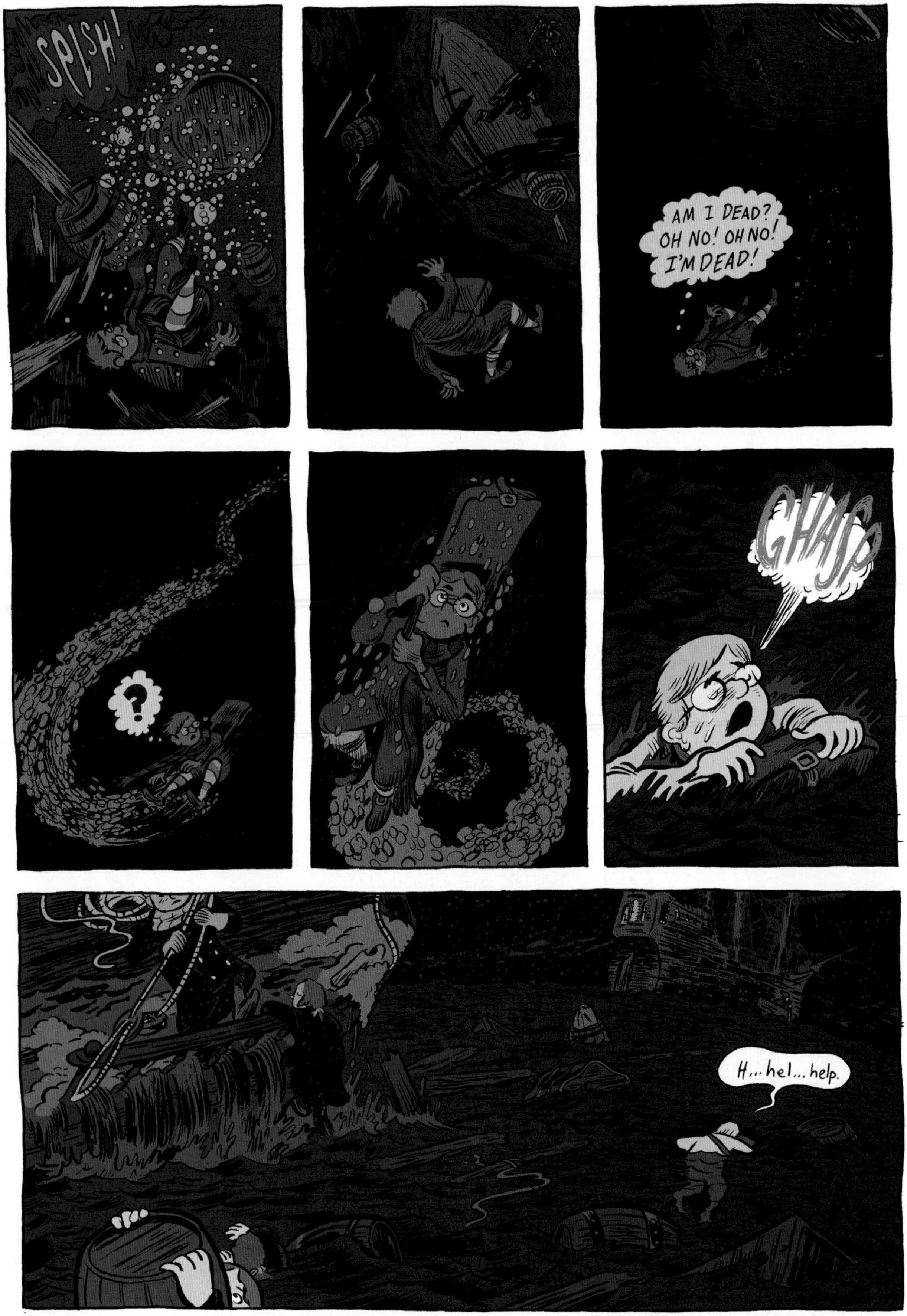
SPLSH!
AM I DEAD? OH NO! OH NO! I'M DEAD!
?
GHASP
H... hel... help.

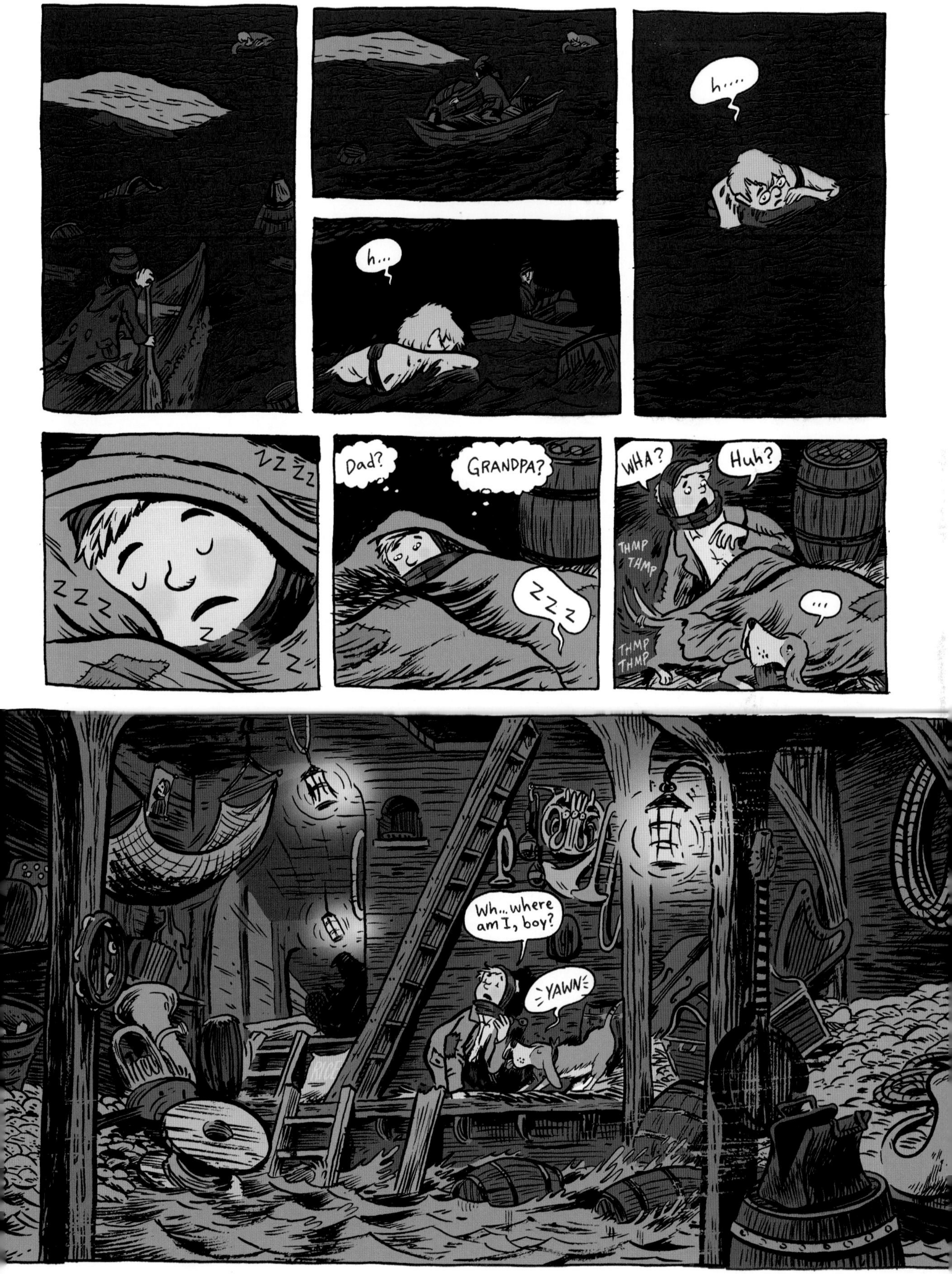
h...
h....
ZZZZ
ZZZ
ZZZZ
Dad?
GRANDPA?
ZZZ
WHA?
Huh?
THMP THMP
THMP THMP
...
Wh... where am I, boy?
YAWN

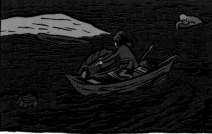

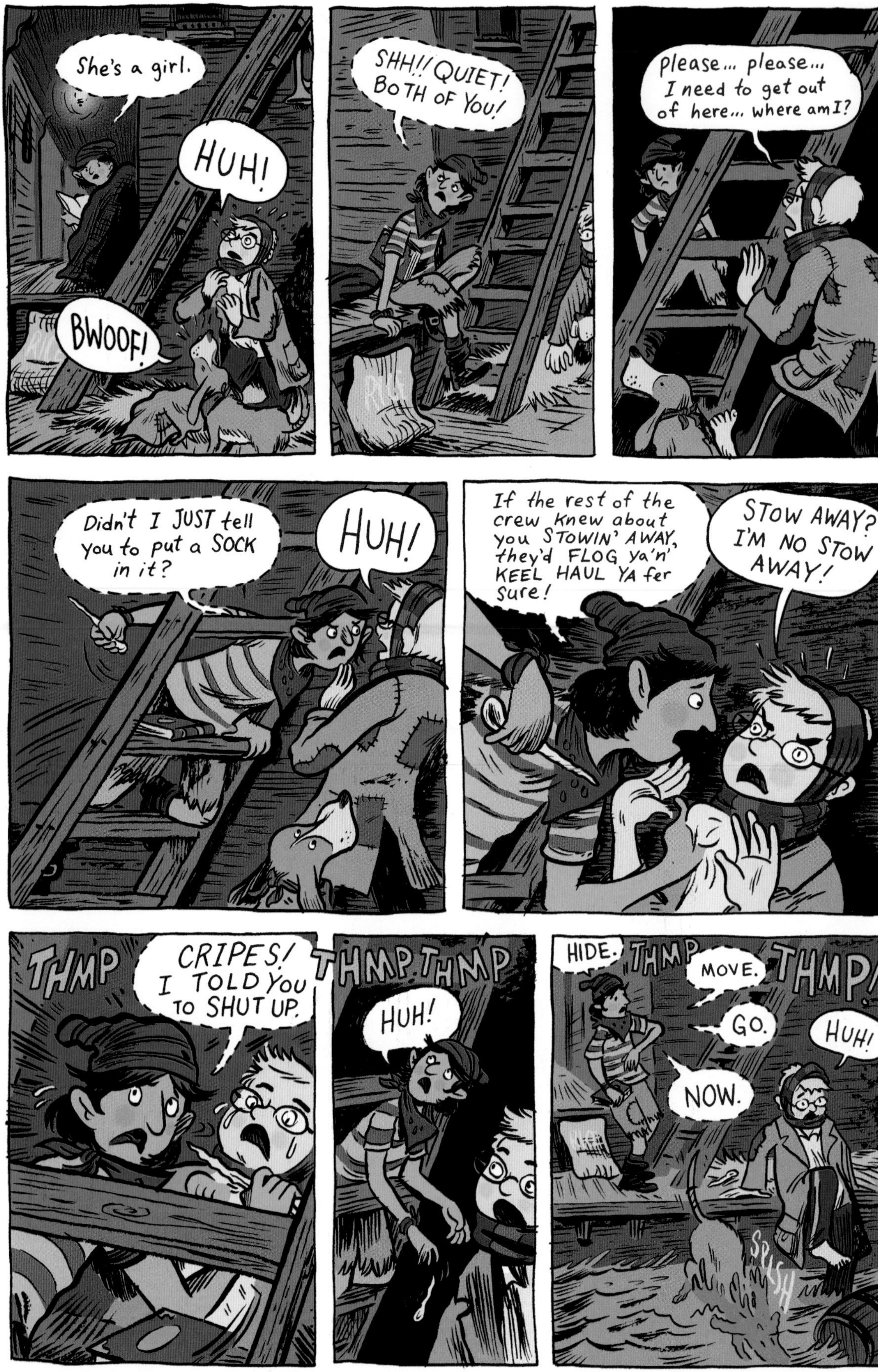
She's a girl.
HUH!
BWOOF!
SHH!! QUIET! BOTH OF YOU!
Please... please... I need to get out of here... where am I?
Didn't I JUST tell you to put a SOCK in it?
HUH!
If the rest of the crew knew about you STOWIN' AWAY, they'd FLOG ya'n' KEEL HAUL YA fer sure!
STOW AWAY? I'M NO STOW AWAY!
THMP
CRIPES! I TOLD YOU TO SHUT UP.
THMP THMP
HUH!
HIDE.
THMP
MOVE.
THMP!
GO.
HUH!
NOW.
SPLISH

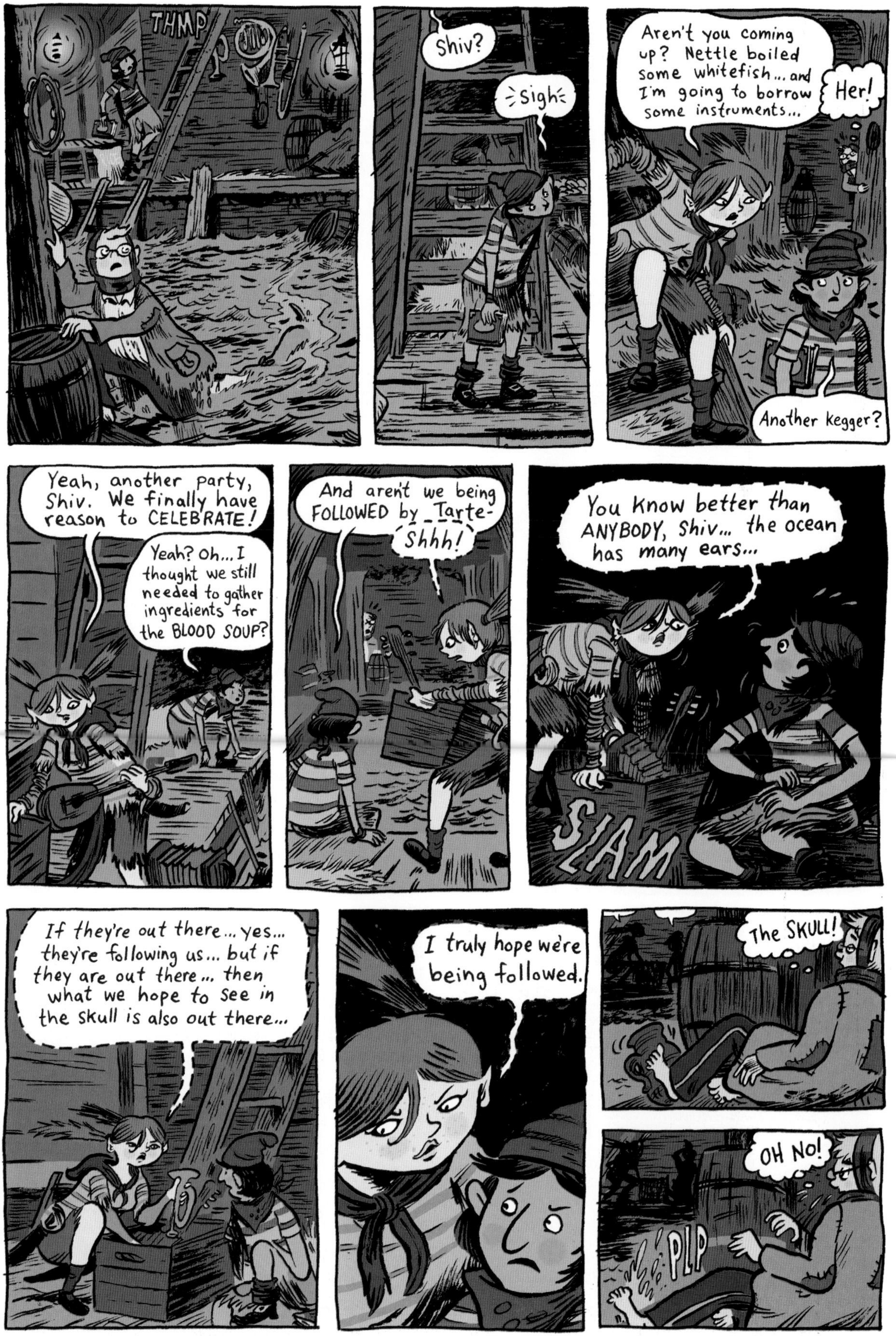
THMP
Shiv?
Sigh
Aren't you coming up? Nettle boiled some whitefish... and I'm going to borrow some instruments...
Her!
Another kegger?
Yeah, another party, Shiv. We finally have reason to CELEBRATE!
Yeah? Oh... I thought we still needed to gather ingredients for the BLOOD SOUP?
And aren't we being FOLLOWED by Tarte-
Shhh!
You know better than ANYBODY, Shiv... the ocean has many ears...
SLAM
If they're out there... yes... they're following us... but if they are out there... then what we hope to see in the skull is also out there...
I truly hope we're being followed.
The SKULL!
OH NO!
PLP

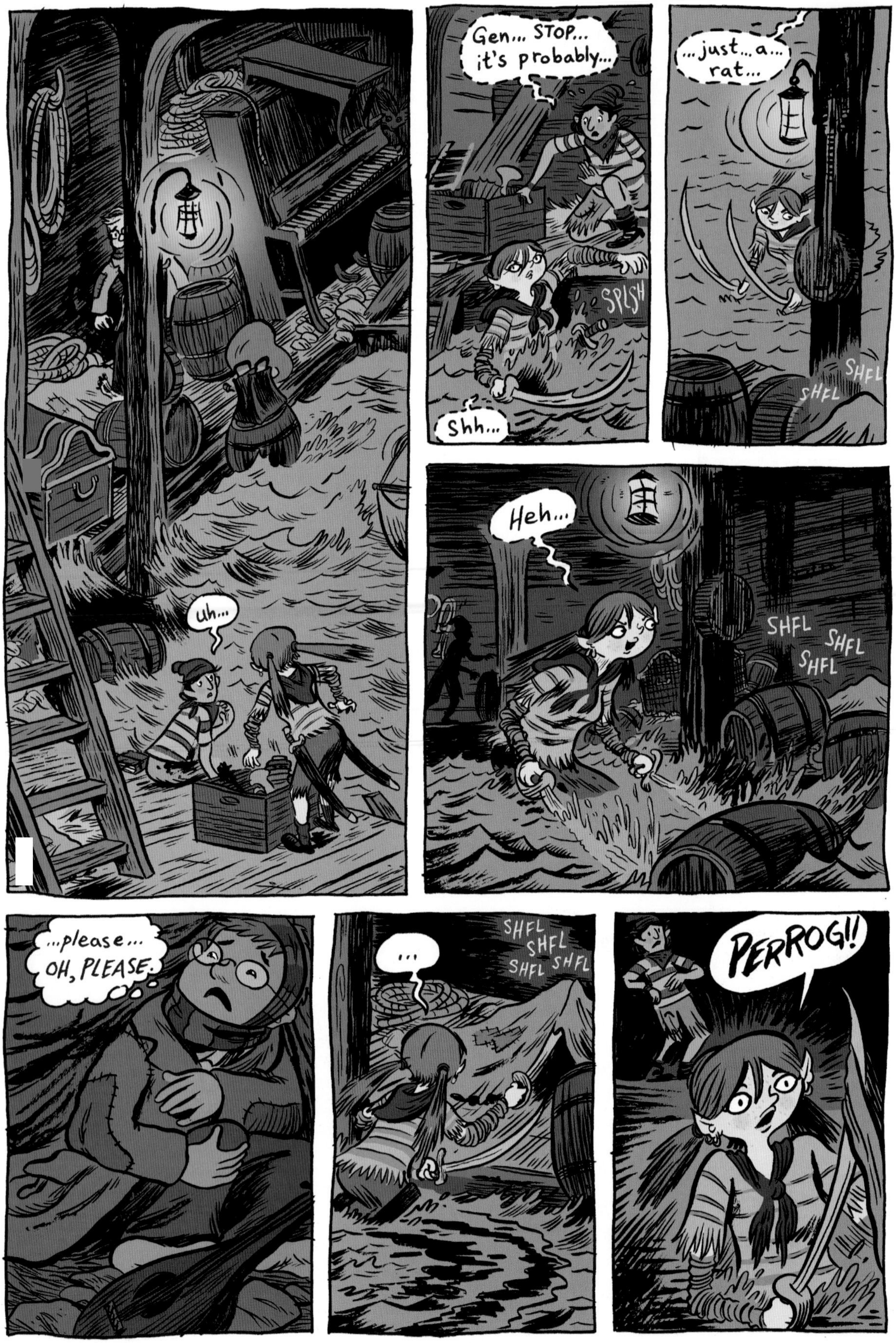
uh...
Gen... STOP... it's probably...
Shh...
SPLSH
...just... a... rat...
SHFL
SHFL
Heh...
SHFL
SHFL
SHFL
...please... OH, PLEASE.
...
SHFL
SHFL
SHFL SHFL
PERROG!!

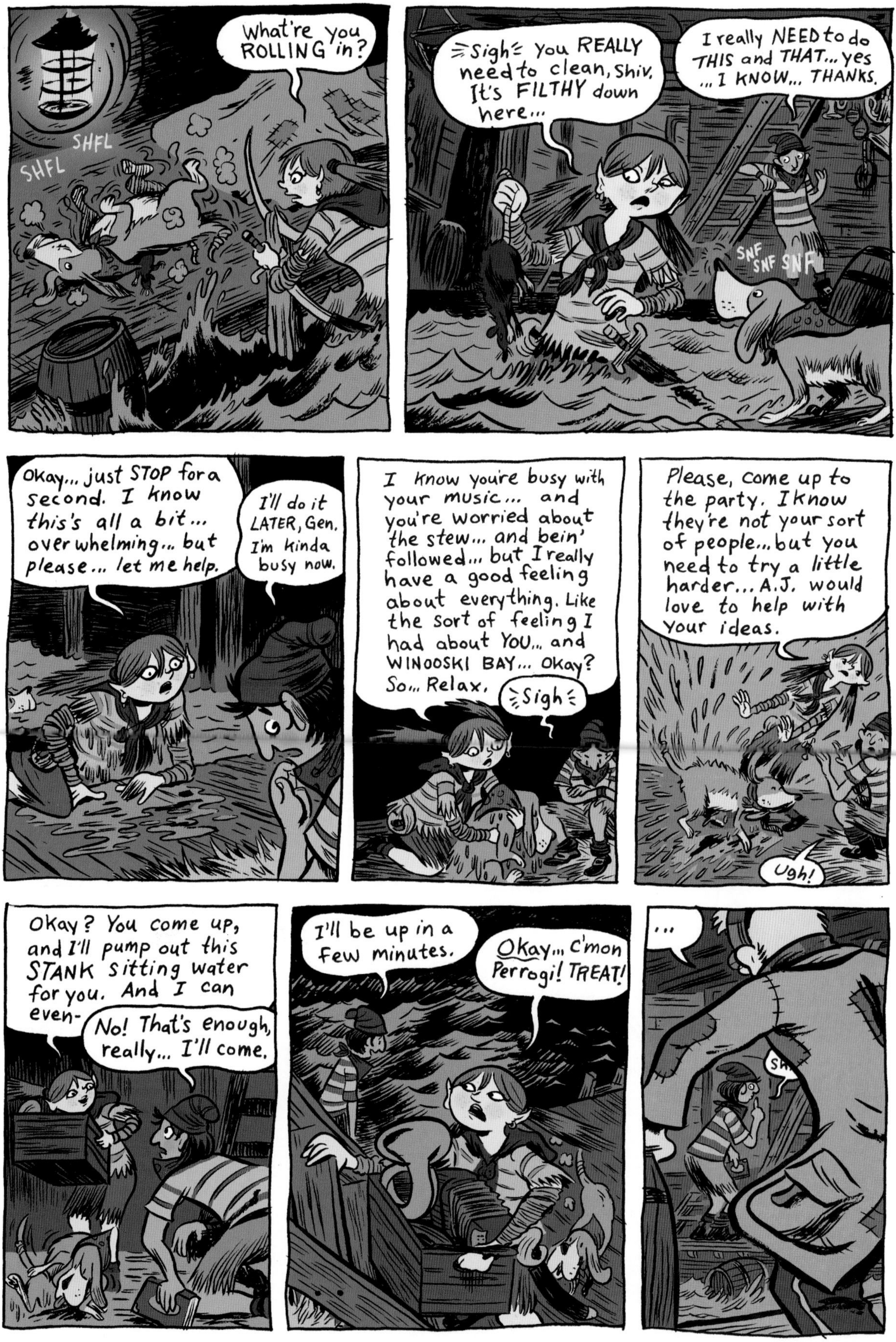

What're you ROLLING in?
SHFL
SHFL
≈Sigh≈ You REALLY need to clean, Shiv. It's FILTHY down here...
I really NEED to do THIS and THAT... yes ... I KNOW... THANKS.
SNF SNF SNF
Okay... just STOP for a second. I know this's all a bit... overwhelming... but please... let me help.
I'll do it LATER, Gen. I'm kinda busy now.
I know you're busy with your music... and you're worried about the stew... and bein' followed... but I really have a good feeling about everything. Like the sort of feeling I had about YOU... and WINOOSKI BAY... Okay? So... Relax.
≈Sigh≈
Please, come up to the party. I know they're not your sort of people... but you need to try a little harder... A.J. would love to help with your ideas.
Ugh!
Okay? You come up, and I'll pump out this STANK sitting water for you. And I can even-
No! That's enough, really... I'll come.
I'll be up in a few minutes.
Okay... C'mon Perrogi! TREAT!
...

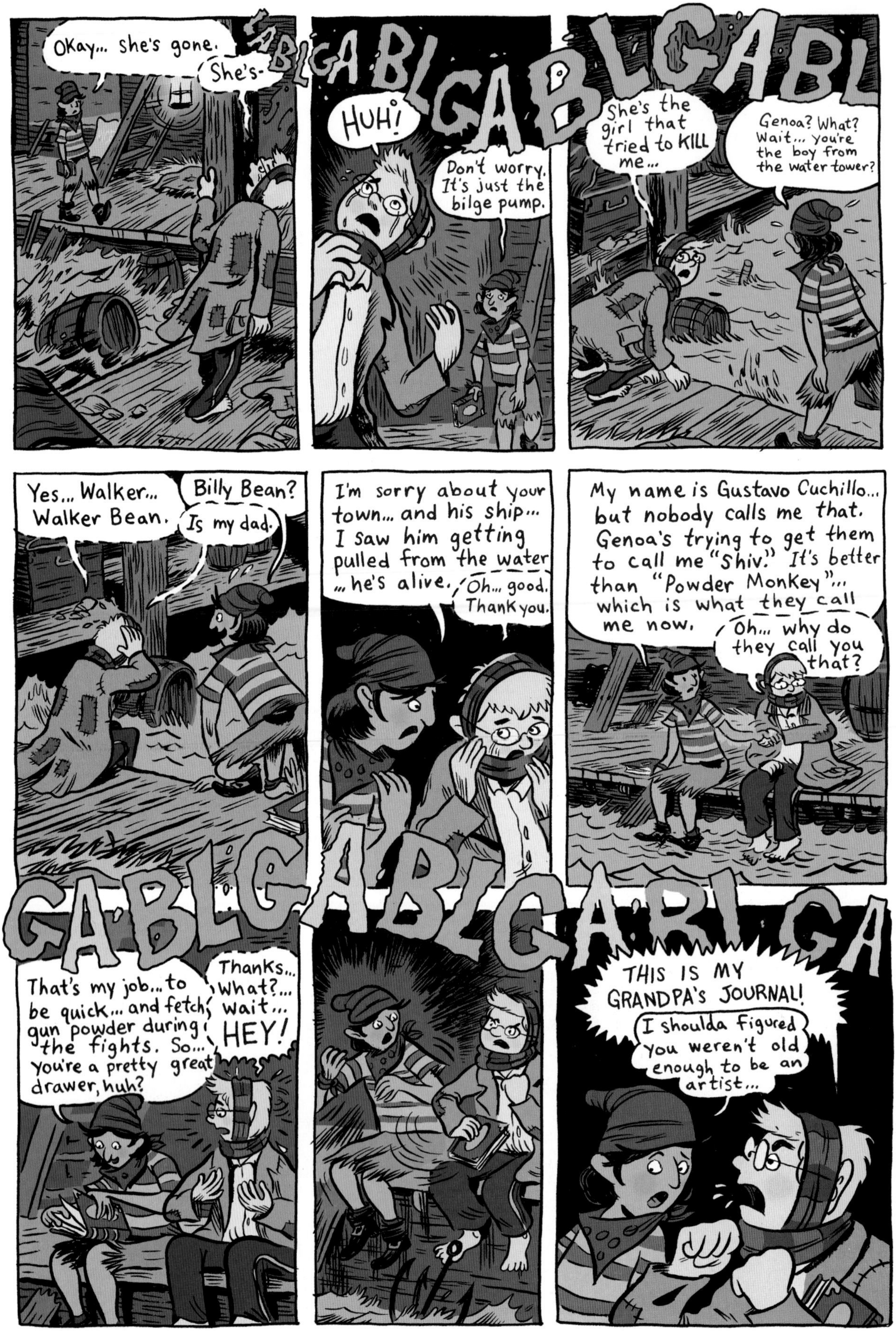

Okay... she's gone.
She's-
GABLGABLGABLGABL
HUH!
Don't worry. It's just the bilge pump.
She's the girl that tried to KILL me...
Genoa? What? Wait... you're the boy from the water tower?
Yes... Walker... Walker Bean.
Billy Bean?
Is my dad.
I'm sorry about your town... and his ship... I saw him getting pulled from the water ...he's alive.
Oh... good. Thank you.
My name is Gustavo Cuchillo... but nobody calls me that. Genoa's trying to get them to call me "Shiv." It's better than "Powder Monkey"... which is what they call me now.
Oh... why do they call you that?
GABLGABLGABLGA
That's my job... to be quick... and fetch gun powder during the fights. So... you're a pretty great drawer, huh?
Thanks... what?... wait... HEY!
THIS IS MY GRANDPA's JOURNAL!
I shoulda figured you weren't old enough to be an artist...

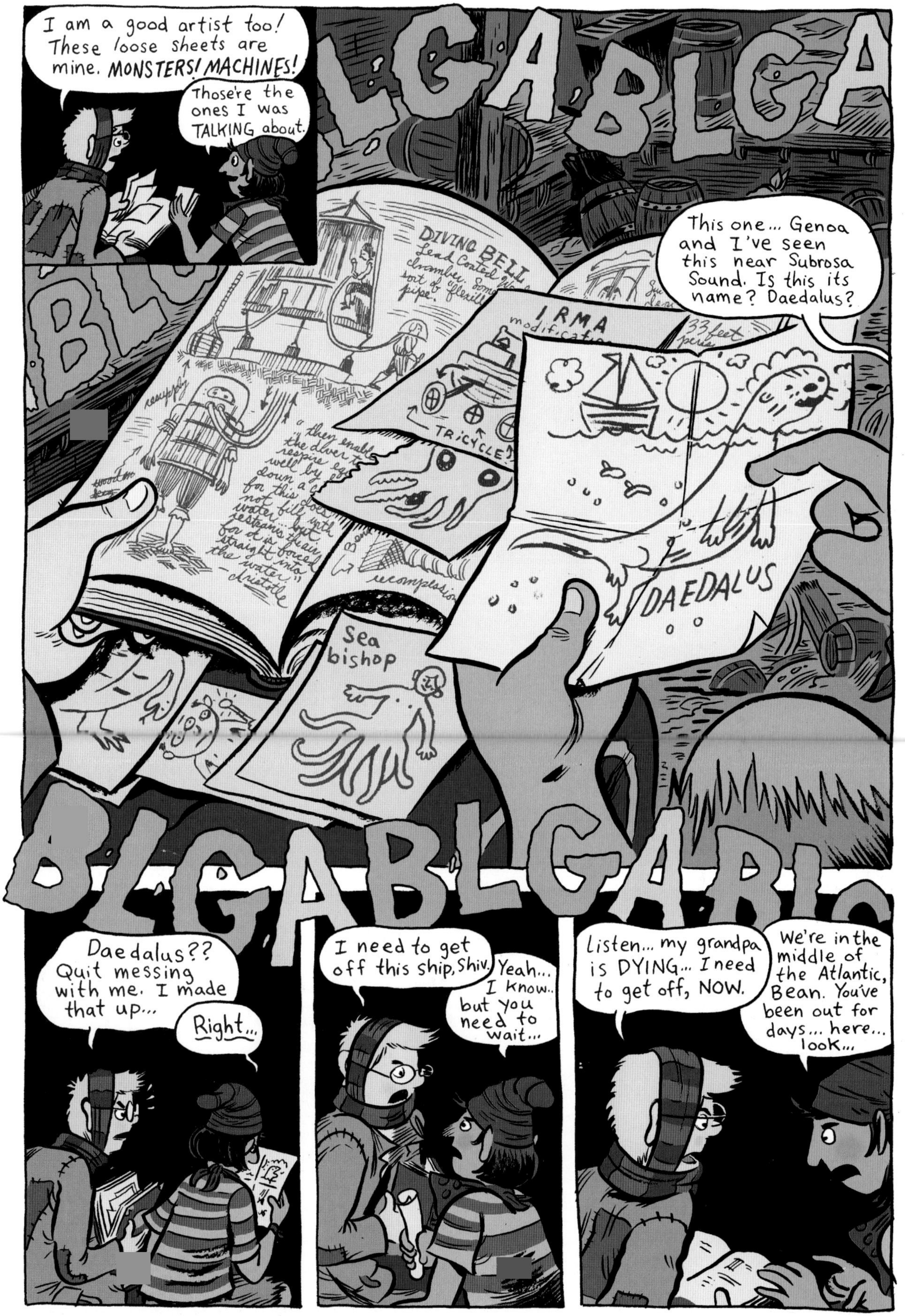
I am a good artist too! These loose sheets are mine. MONSTERS! MACHINES!
Those're the ones I was TALKING about.
BLGABLGA
DIVING BELL
IRMA
TRICYCLE
This one... Genoa and I've seen this near Subrosa Sound. Is this its name? Daedalus?
DAEDALUS
Sea bishop
BLGABLGABLG
Daedalus?? Quit messing with me. I made that up...
Right...
I need to get off this ship, Shiv.
Yeah... I know... but you need to wait...
Listen... my grandpa is DYING... I need to get off, NOW.
We're in the middle of the Atlantic, Bean. You've been out for days... here... look...

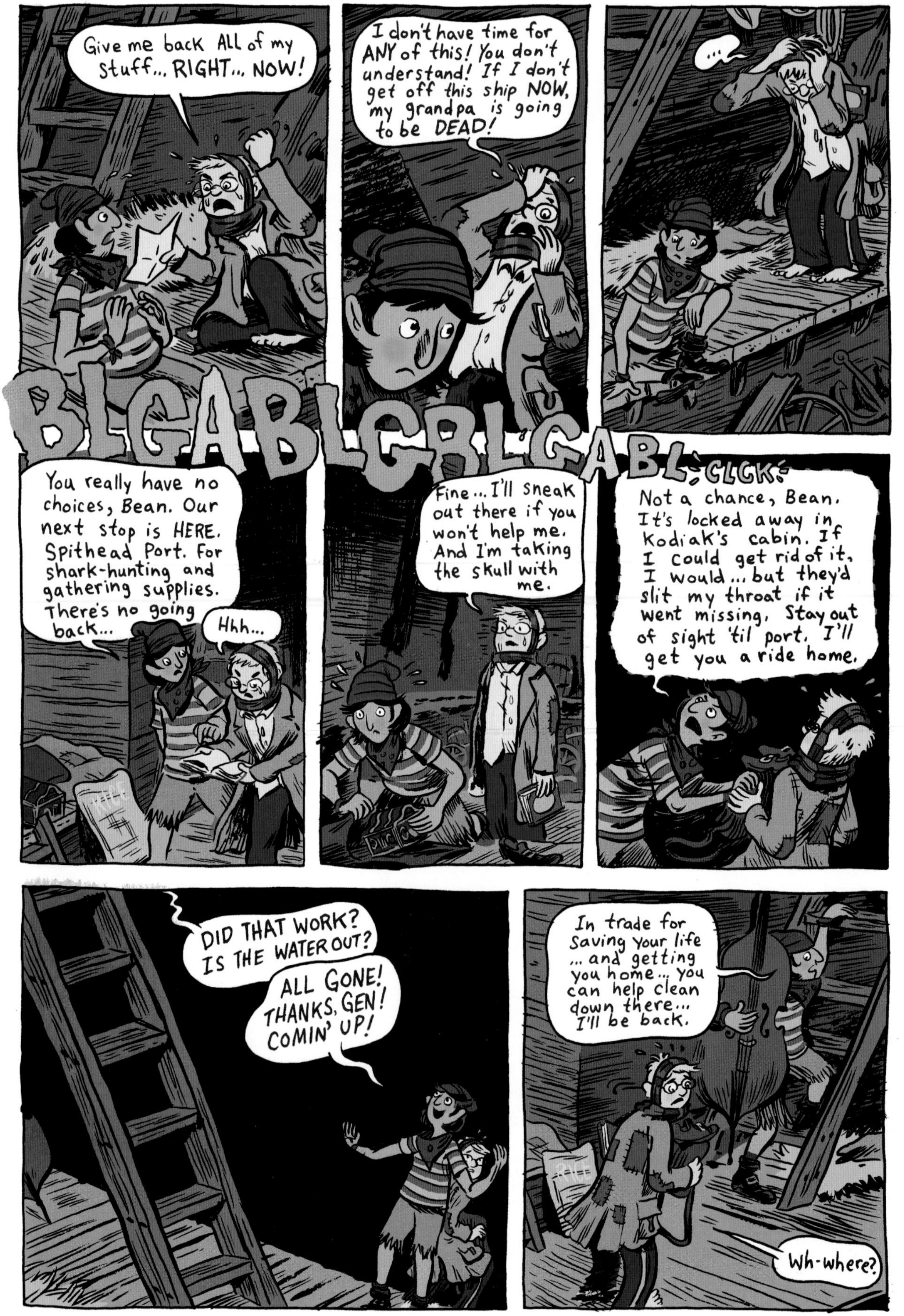
Give me back ALL of my stuff... RIGHT... NOW!
I don't have time for ANY of this! You don't understand! If I don't get off this ship NOW, my grandpa is going to be DEAD!
...
BLGABLGBLGABL
CLCK
You really have no choices, Bean. Our next stop is HERE. Spithead Port. For shark-hunting and gathering supplies. There's no going back...
Hhh...
Fine... I'll sneak out there if you won't help me. And I'm taking the skull with me.
Not a chance, Bean. It's locked away in Kodiak's cabin. If I could get rid of it, I would... but they'd slit my throat if it went missing. Stay out of sight 'til port. I'll get you a ride home.
DID THAT WORK? IS THE WATER OUT?
ALL GONE! THANKS, GEN! COMIN' UP!
In trade for saving your life ... and getting you home... you can help clean down there... I'll be back.
Wh-where?

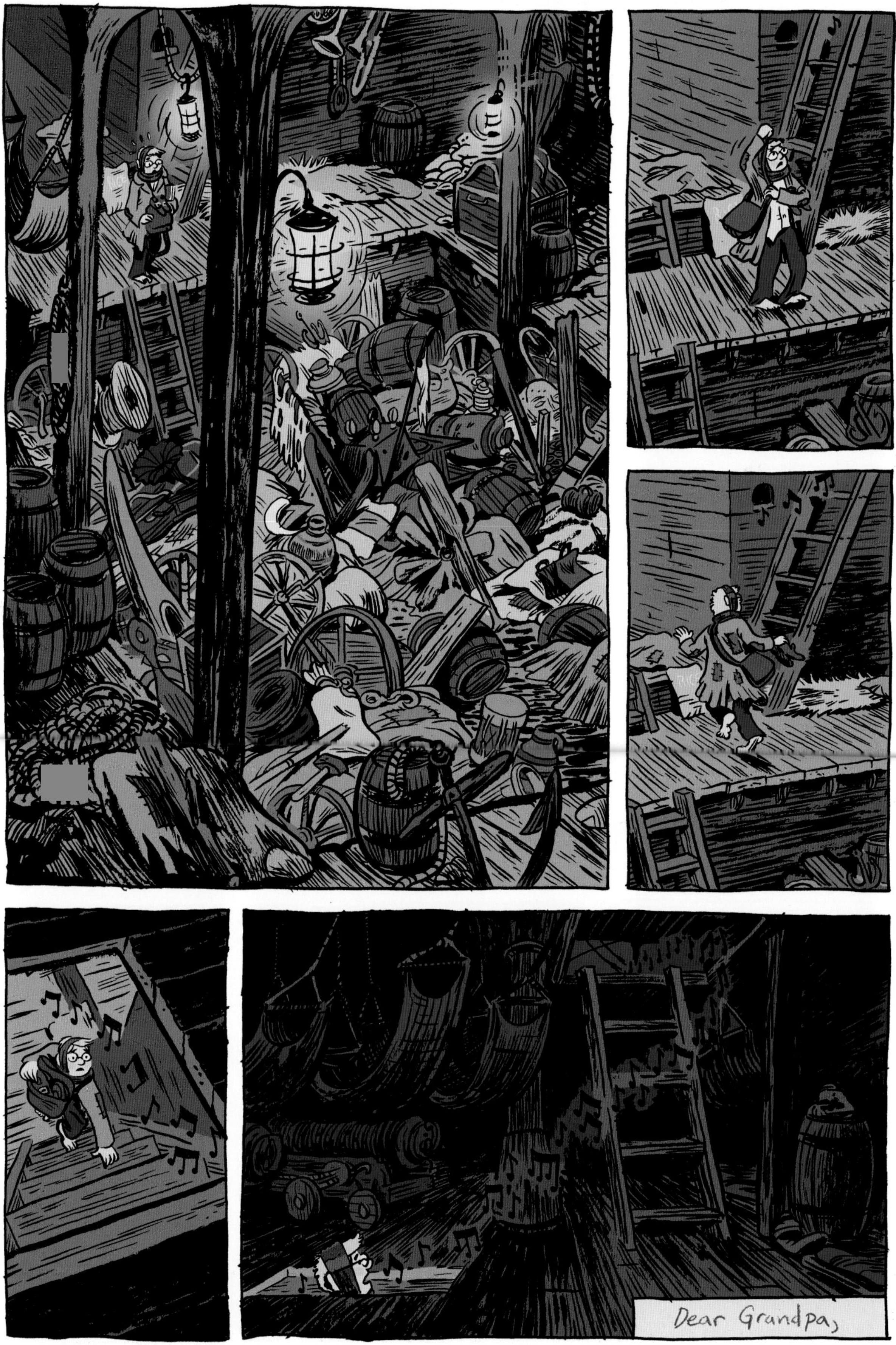
Dear Grandpa,

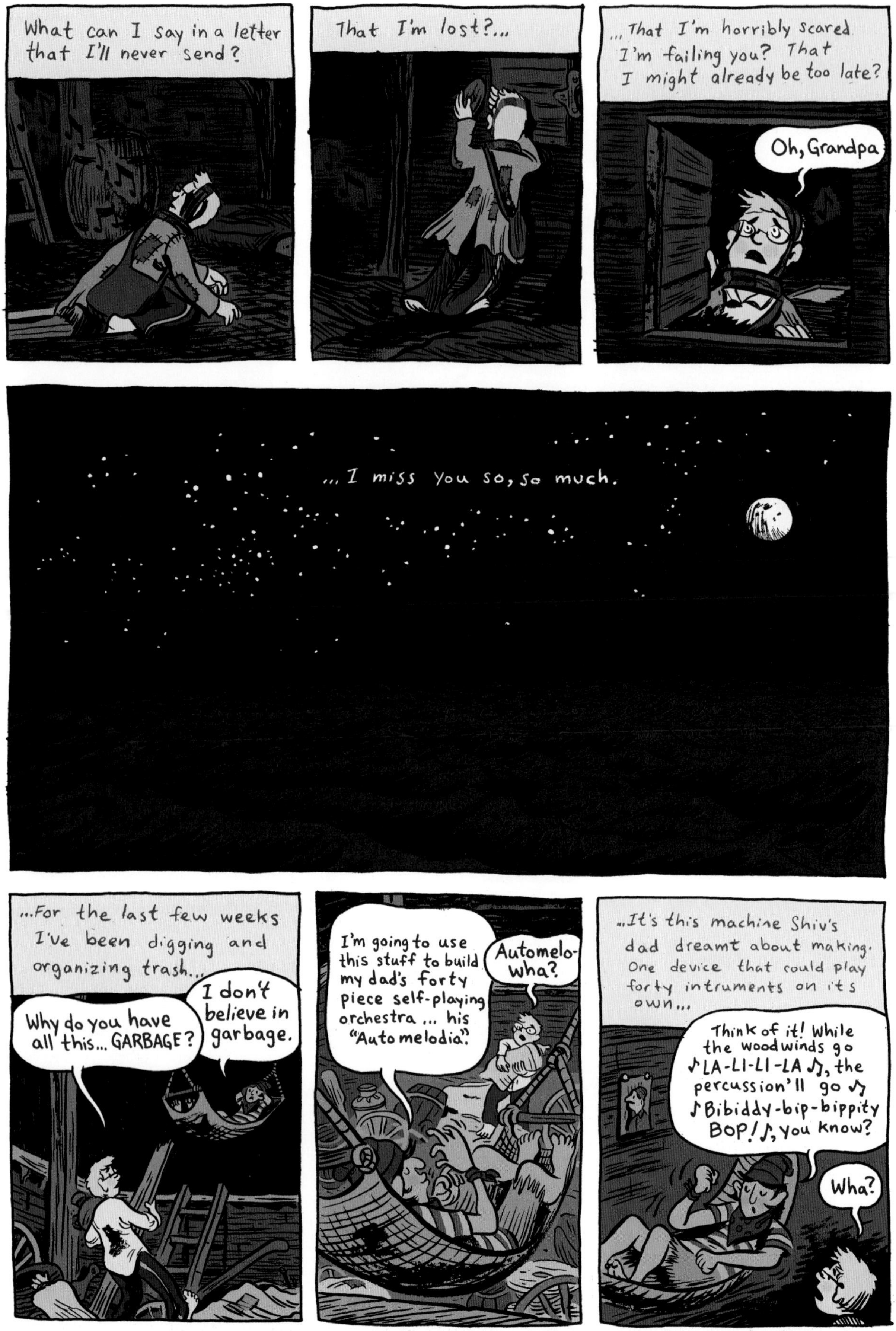
What can I say in a letter that I'll never send?
That I'm lost?...
...That I'm horribly scared I'm failing you? That I might already be too late?
Oh, Grandpa
...I miss you so, so much.
...For the last few weeks I've been digging and organizing trash...
Why do you have all this... GARBAGE?
I don't believe in garbage.
I'm going to use this stuff to build my dad's forty piece self-playing orchestra ... his "Automelodia."
Automelo-Wha?
...It's this machine Shiv's dad dreamt about making. One device that could play forty intruments on it's own...
Think of it! While the woodwinds go ♪LA-LI-LI-LA♫, the percussion'll go ♪♪Bibiddy-bip-bippity BOP!♫, you know?
Wha?

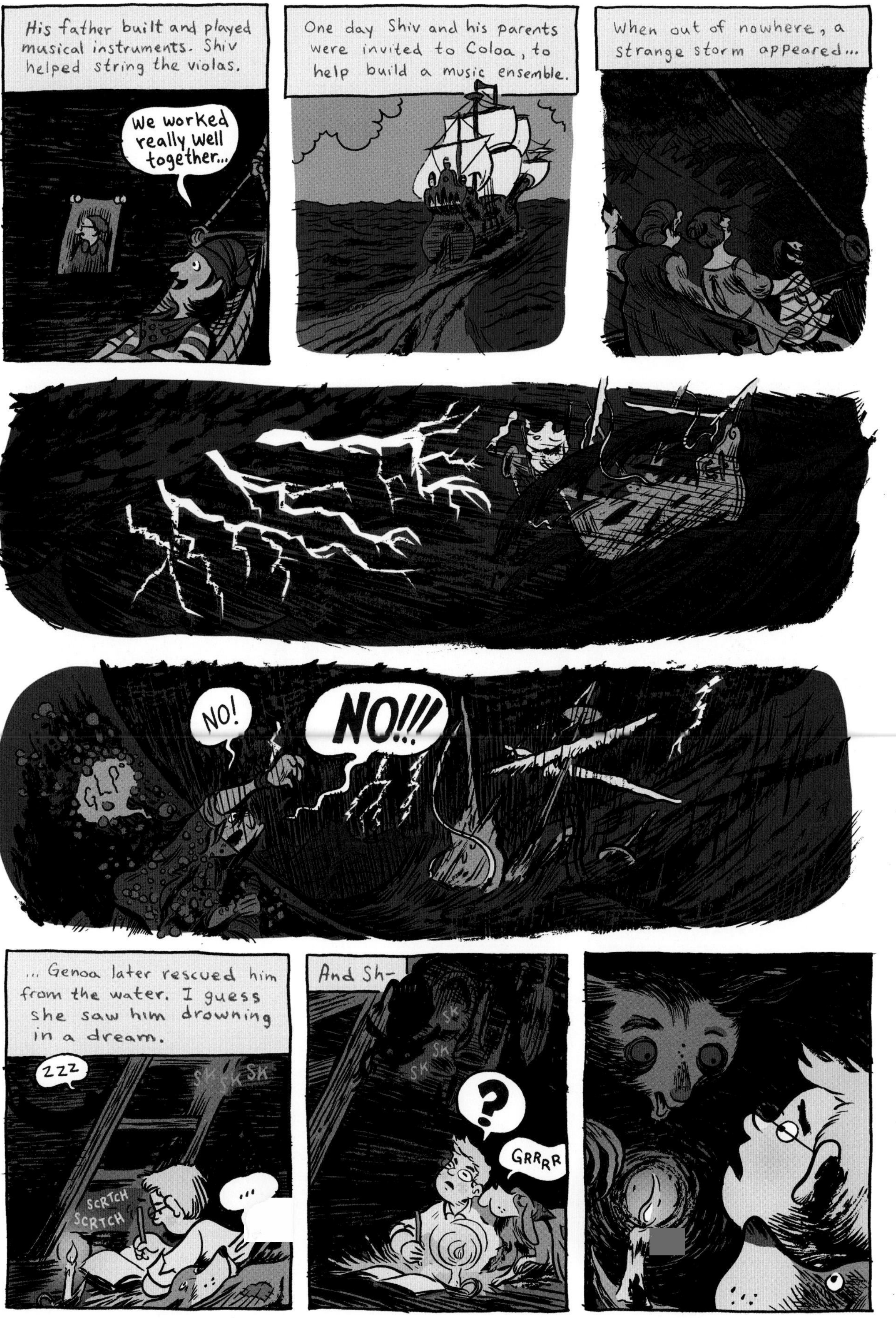
His father built and played musical instruments. Shiv helped string the violas.
We worked really well together...
One day Shiv and his parents were invited to Coloa, to help build a music ensemble.
When out of nowhere, a strange storm appeared...
NO!
NO!!!
... Genoa later rescued him from the water. I guess she saw him drowning in a dream.
ZZZ
SK SK SK
SCRTCH SCRTCH
...
And Sh-
SK SK SK
?
GRRRR

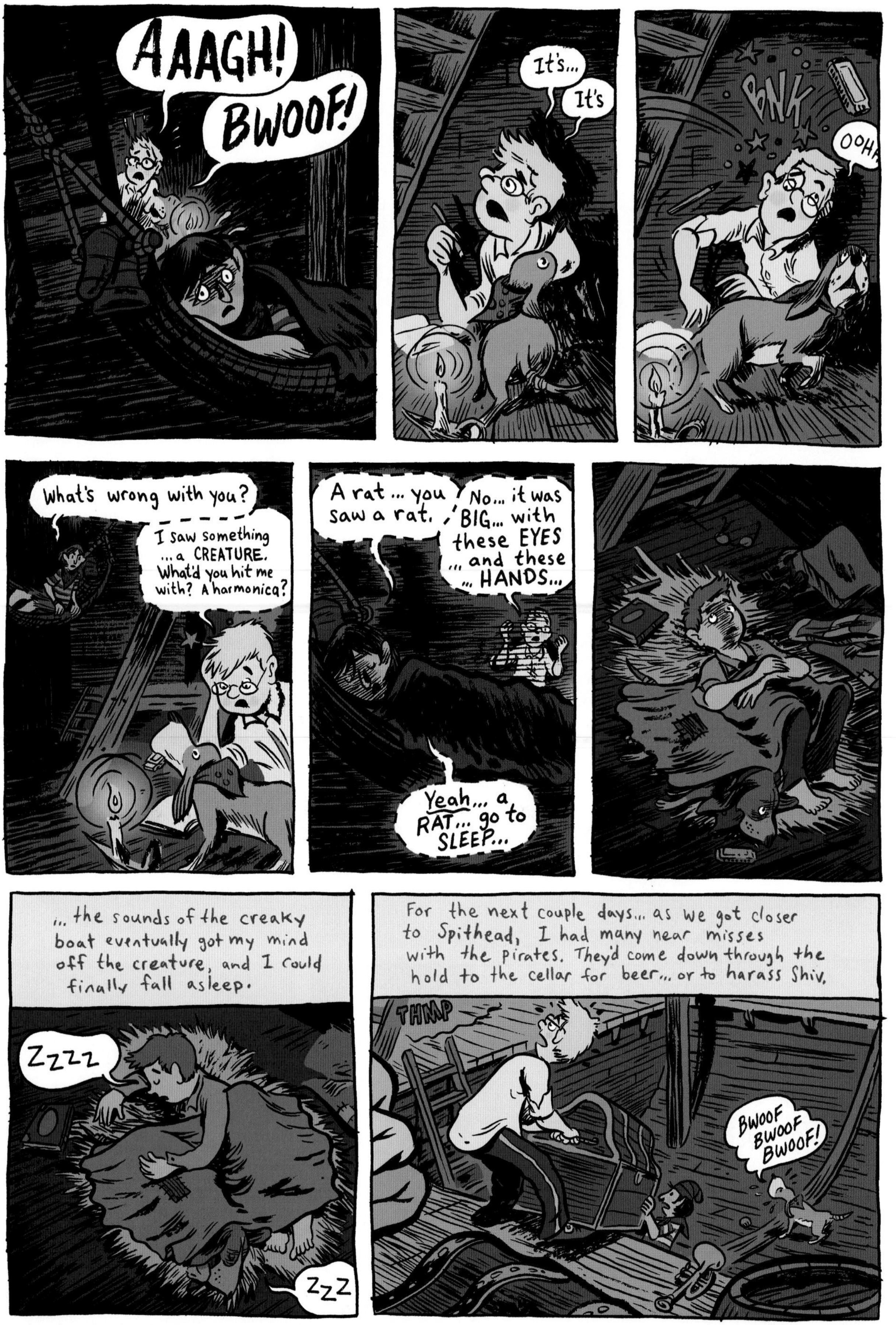
AAAGH!
BWOOF!
It's...
It's
BNK
OOHH
What's wrong with you?
I saw something ...a CREATURE. What'd you hit me with? A harmonica?
A rat... you saw a rat.
No... it was BIG... with these EYES ... and these ... HANDS...
Yeah... a RAT... go to SLEEP...
... the sounds of the creaky boat eventually got my mind off the creature, and I could finally fall asleep.
Zzzz
ZzZ
For the next couple days... as we got closer to Spithead, I had many near misses with the pirates. They'd come down through the hold to the cellar for beer... or to harass Shiv.
THMP
BWOOF BWOOF BWOOF!

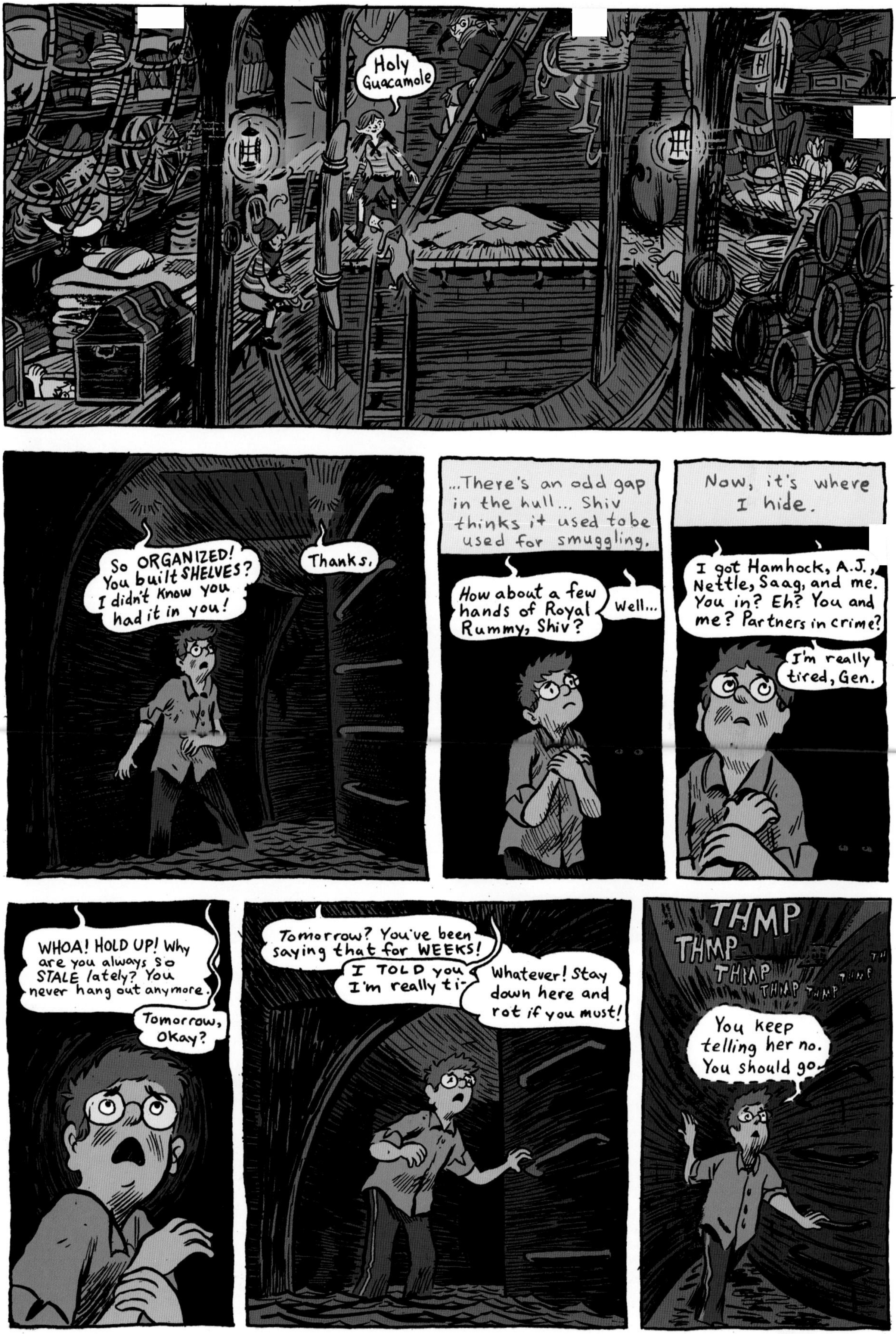
Holy Guacamole
So ORGANIZED! You built SHELVES? I didn't know you had it in you!
Thanks.
...There's an odd gap in the hull... Shiv thinks it used to be used for smuggling.
How about a few hands of Royal Rummy, Shiv?
Well...
Now, it's where I hide.
I got Hamhock, A.J., Nettle, Saag, and me. You in? Eh? You and me? Partners in crime?
I'm really tired, Gen.
WHOA! HOLD UP! Why are you always so STALE lately? You never hang out anymore.
Tomorrow, okay?
Tomorrow? You've been saying that for WEEKS!
I TOLD you I'm really ti-
Whatever! Stay down here and rot if you must!
THMP
THMP
THMP
THMP
You keep telling her no. You should go-

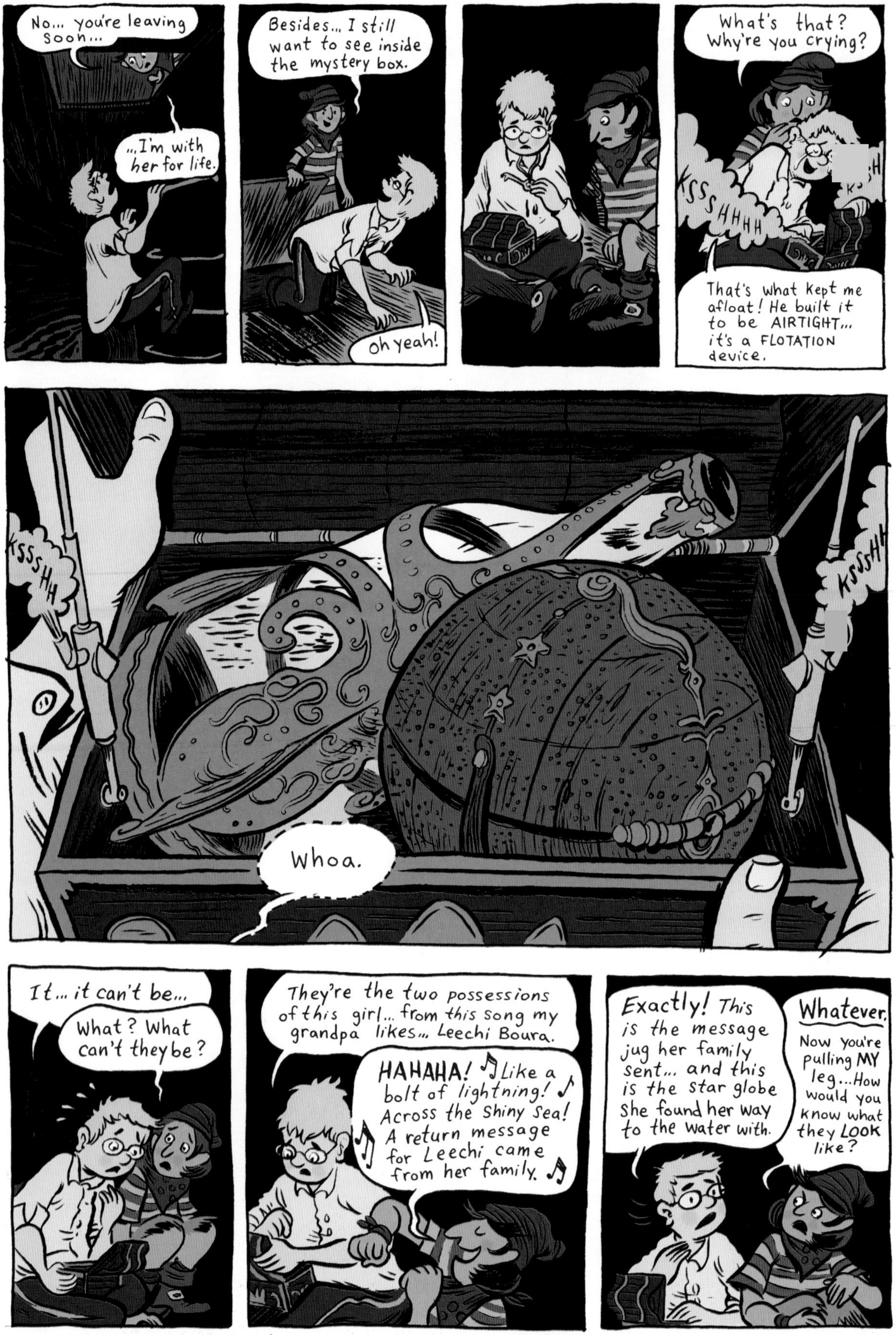

No... you're leaving soon...
...I'm with her for life.
Besides... I still want to see inside the mystery box.
Oh yeah!
What's that? Why're you crying?
KSSSHHHH
That's what kept me afloat! He built it to be AIRTIGHT... it's a FLOTATION device.
KSSSHH
KSSSHH
Whoa.
It... it can't be...
What? What can't they be?
They're the two possessions of this girl... from this song my grandpa likes... Leechi Boura.
HAHAHA! ♫ Like a bolt of lightning! ♪ Across the Shiny Sea! A return message for Leechi came from her family. ♪
Exactly! This is the message jug her family sent... and this is the star globe she found her way to the water with.
Whatever. Now you're pulling MY leg... How would you know what they LOOK like?

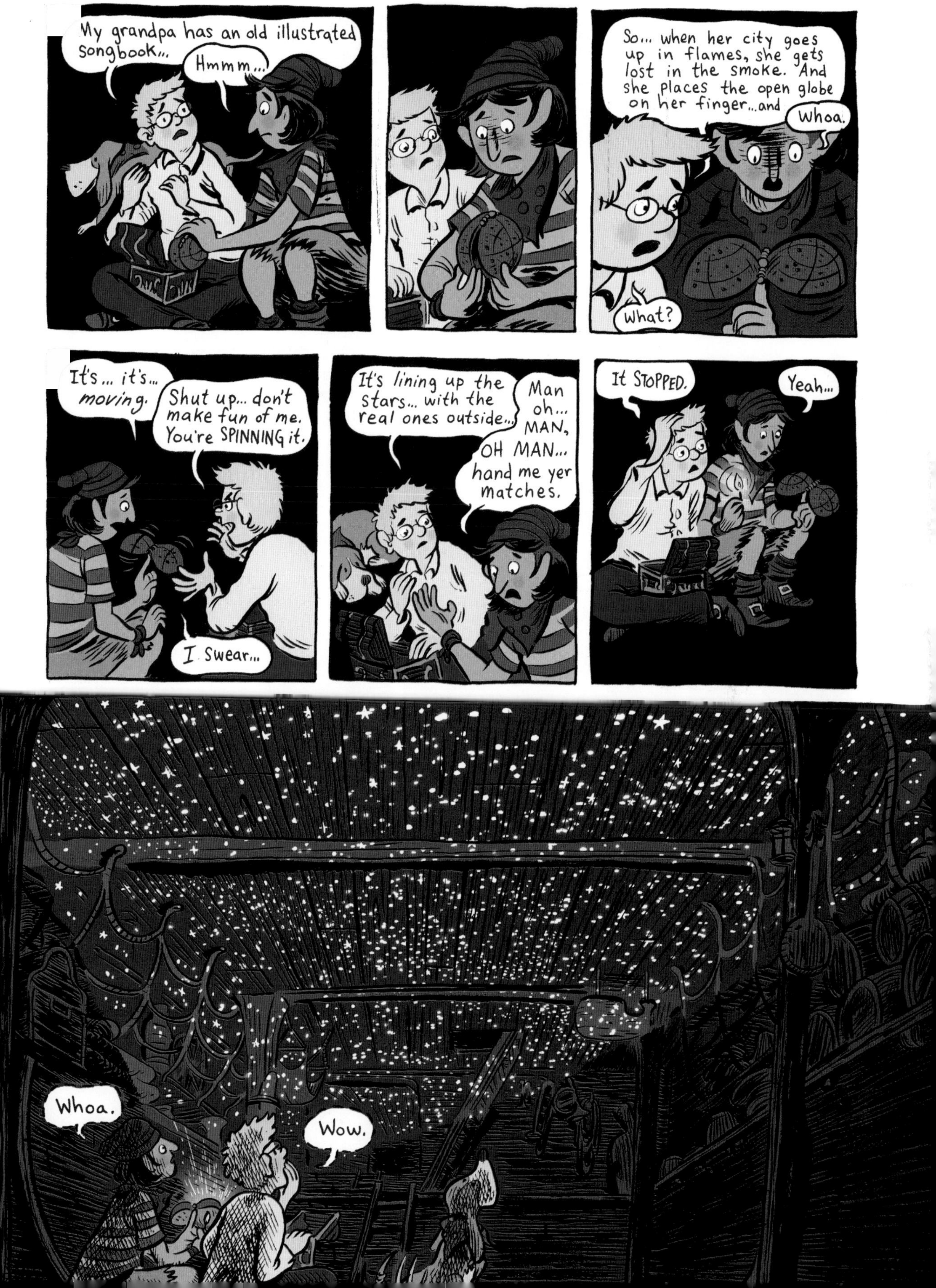
My grandpa has an old illustrated songbook...
Hmmm...
So... when her city goes up in flames, she gets lost in the smoke. And she places the open globe on her finger...and
Whoa.
What?
It's... it's... *moving*.
Shut up... don't make fun of me. You're SPINNING it.
I swear...
It's lining up the stars... with the real ones outside...
Man oh... MAN, OH MAN... hand me yer matches.
It STOPPED.
Yeah...
Whoa.
Wow.

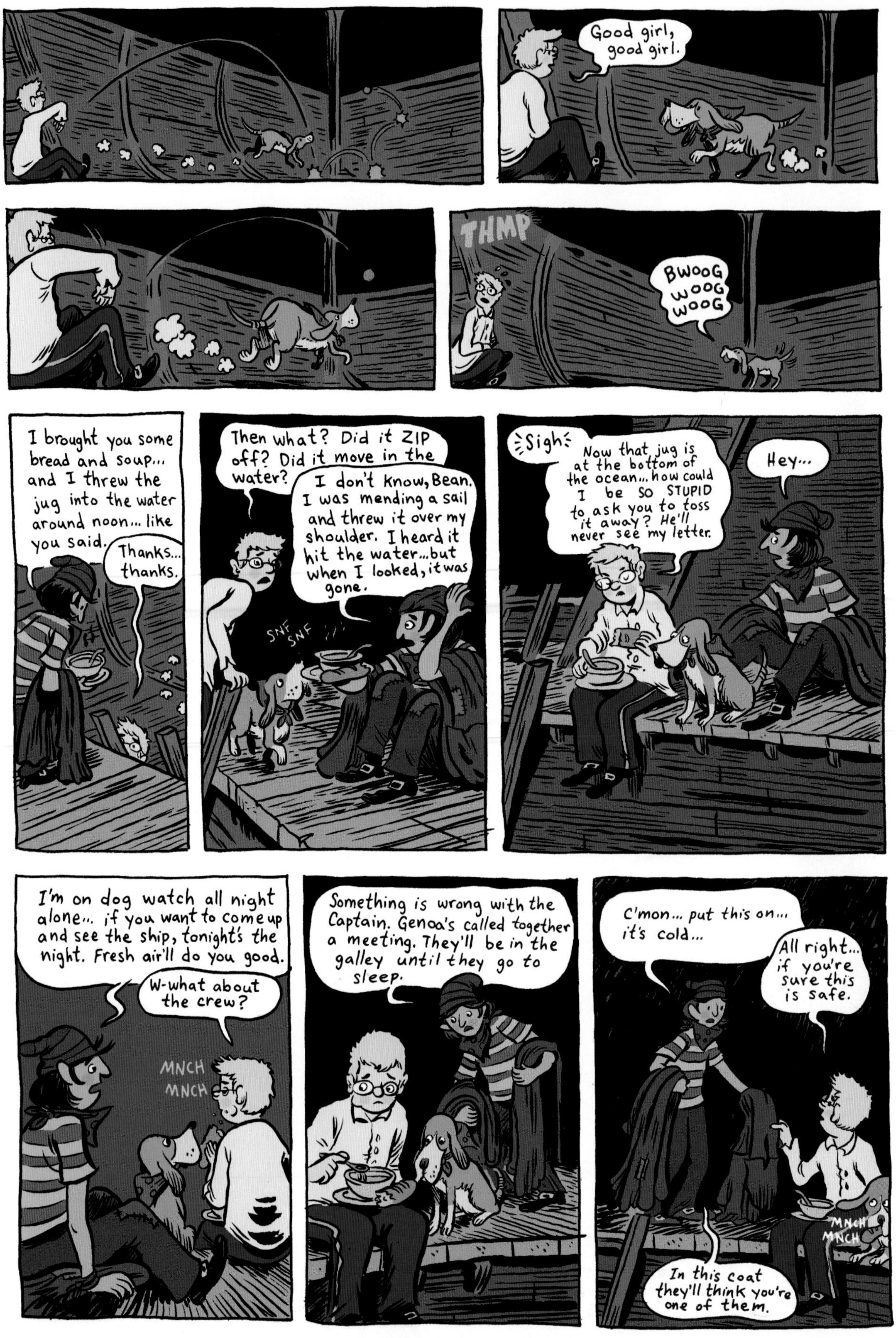

Good girl, good girl.
THMP
BWOOG WOOG WOOG
I brought you some bread and soup... and I threw the jug into the water around noon... like you said.
Thanks... thanks.
Then what? Did it ZIP off? Did it move in the water?
I don't know, Bean. I was mending a sail and threw it over my shoulder. I heard it hit the water...but when I looked, it was gone.
SNF SNF
Sigh
Now that jug is at the bottom of the ocean... how could I be SO STUPID to ask you to toss it away? He'll never see my letter.
Hey...
I'm on dog watch all night alone... if you want to come up and see the ship, tonight's the night. Fresh air'll do you good.
W-what about the crew?
MNCH MNCH
Something is wrong with the Captain. Genoa's called together a meeting. They'll be in the galley until they go to sleep.
C'mon... put this on... it's cold...
All right... if you're sure this is safe.
MNCH MNCH
In this coat they'll think you're one of them.

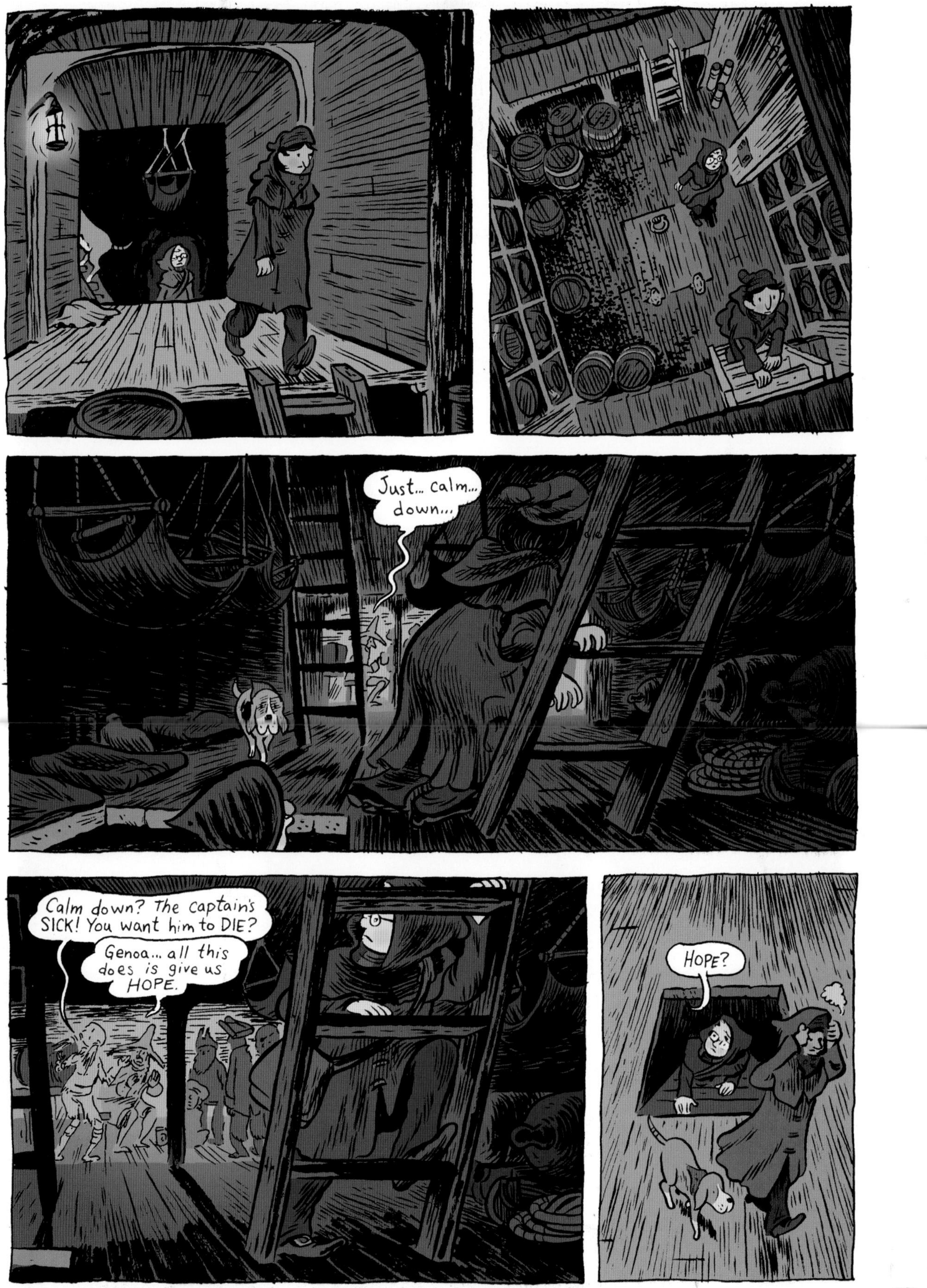

Just... calm... down...
Calm down? The captain's SICK! You want him to DIE?
Genoa... all this does is give us HOPE.
HOPE?

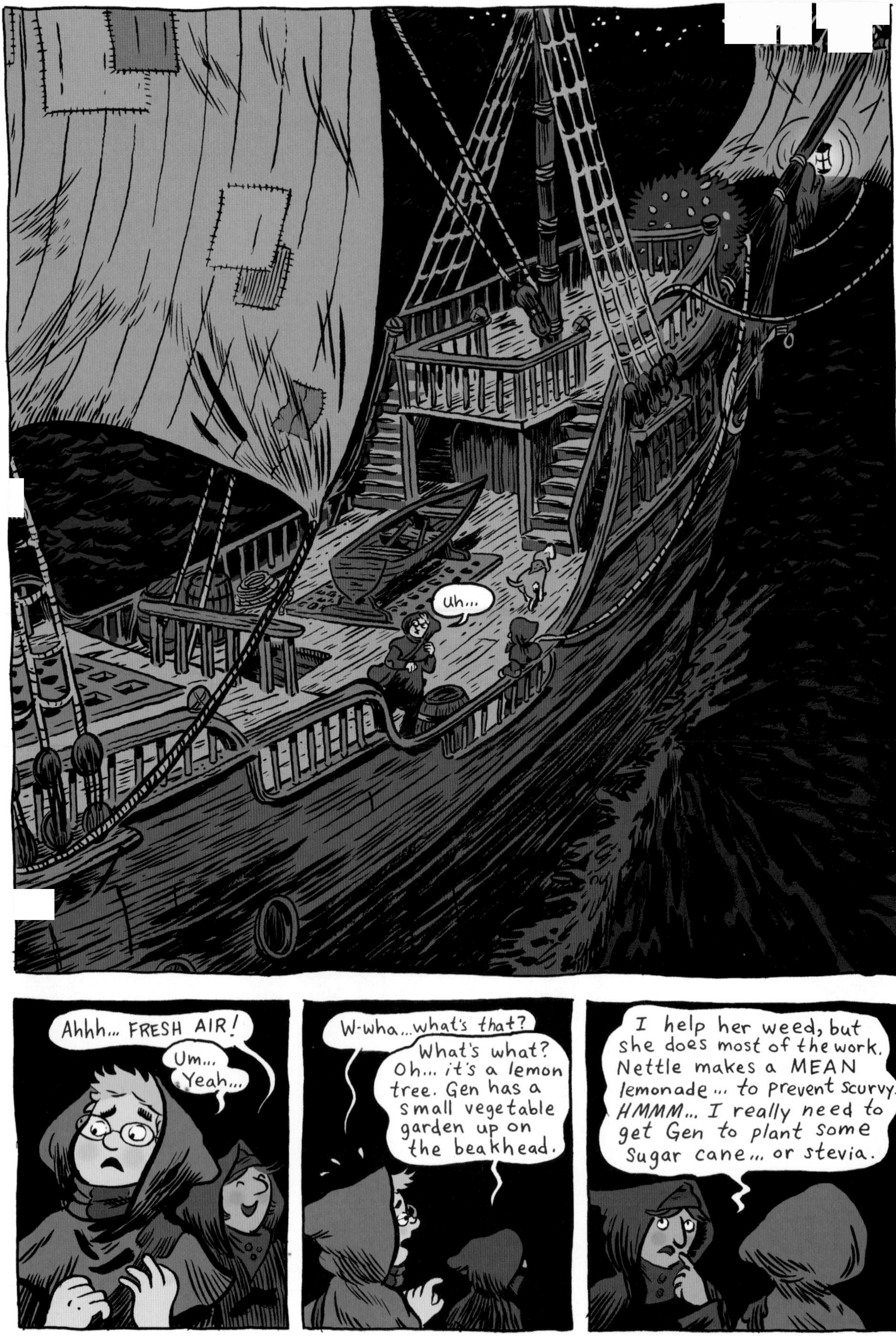

Uh...
Ahhh... FRESH AIR!
Um... Yeah...
W-wha...what's that?
What's what? Oh... it's a lemon tree. Gen has a small vegetable garden up on the beakhead.
I help her weed, but she does most of the work. Nettle makes a MEAN lemonade... to prevent scurvy. HMMM... I really need to get Gen to plant some sugar cane... or stevia.

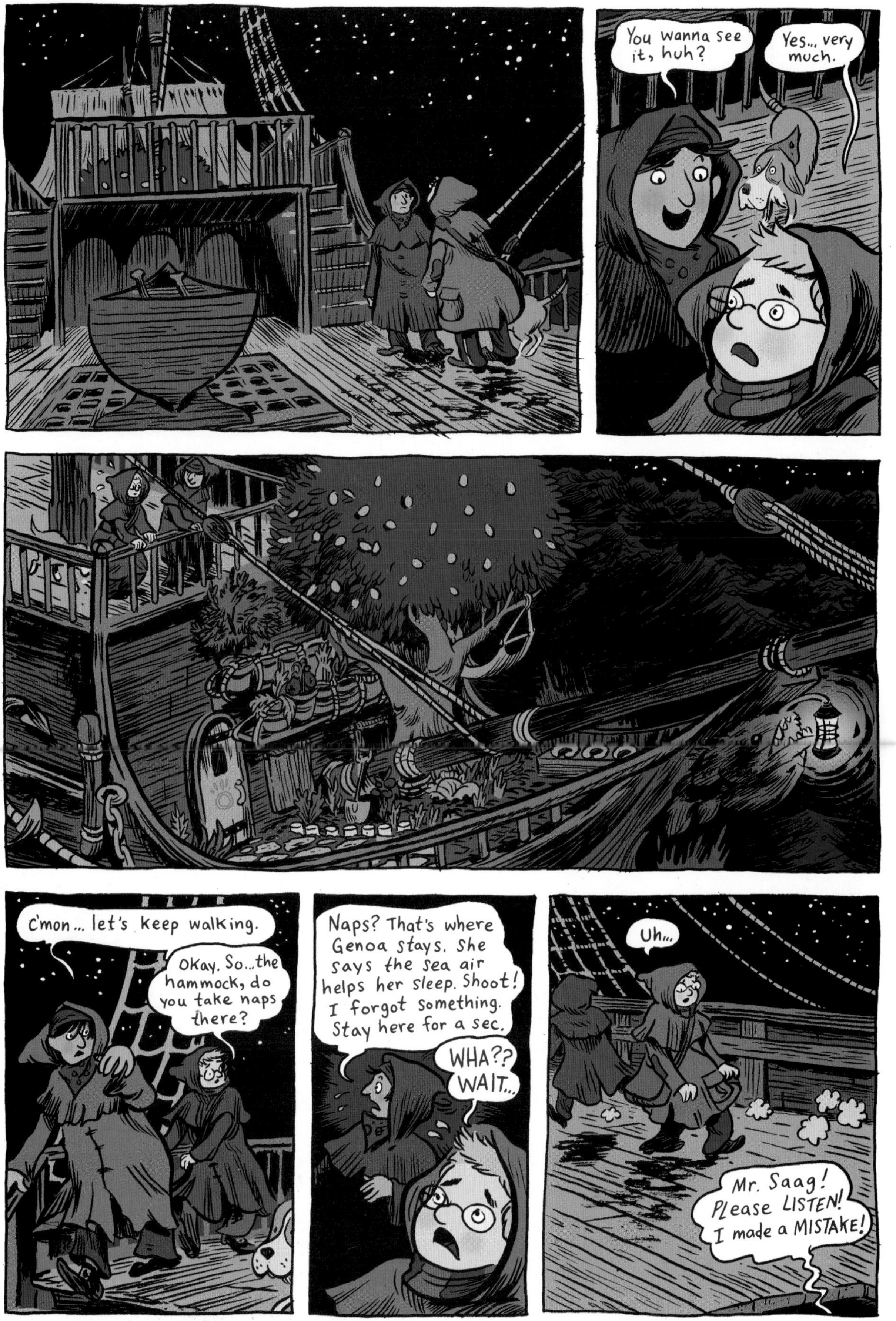
You wanna see it, huh?
Yes... very much.
C'mon... let's keep walking.
Okay. So... the hammock, do you take naps there?
Naps? That's where Genoa stays. She says the sea air helps her sleep. Shoot! I forgot something. Stay here for a sec.
WHA?? WAIT...
Uh...
Mr. Saag! Please LISTEN! I made a MISTAKE!

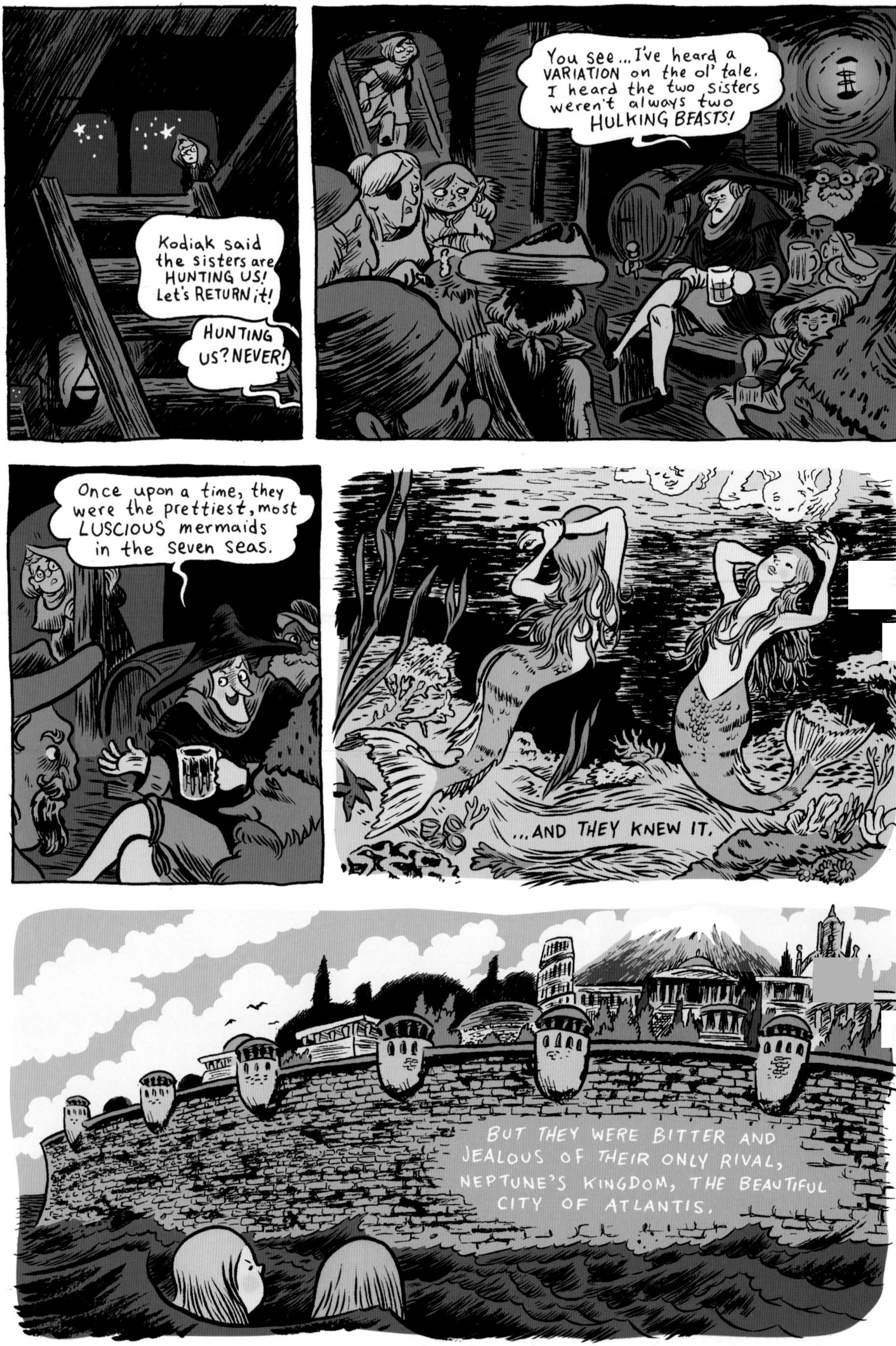
Kodiak said the sisters are HUNTING US! Let's RETURN it!
HUNTING US? NEVER!
You see... I've heard a VARIATION on the ol' tale. I heard the two sisters weren't always two HULKING BEASTS!
Once upon a time, they were the prettiest, most LUSCIOUS mermaids in the seven seas.
...AND THEY KNEW IT.
BUT THEY WERE BITTER AND JEALOUS OF THEIR ONLY RIVAL, NEPTUNE'S KINGDOM, THE BEAUTIFUL CITY OF ATLANTIS.

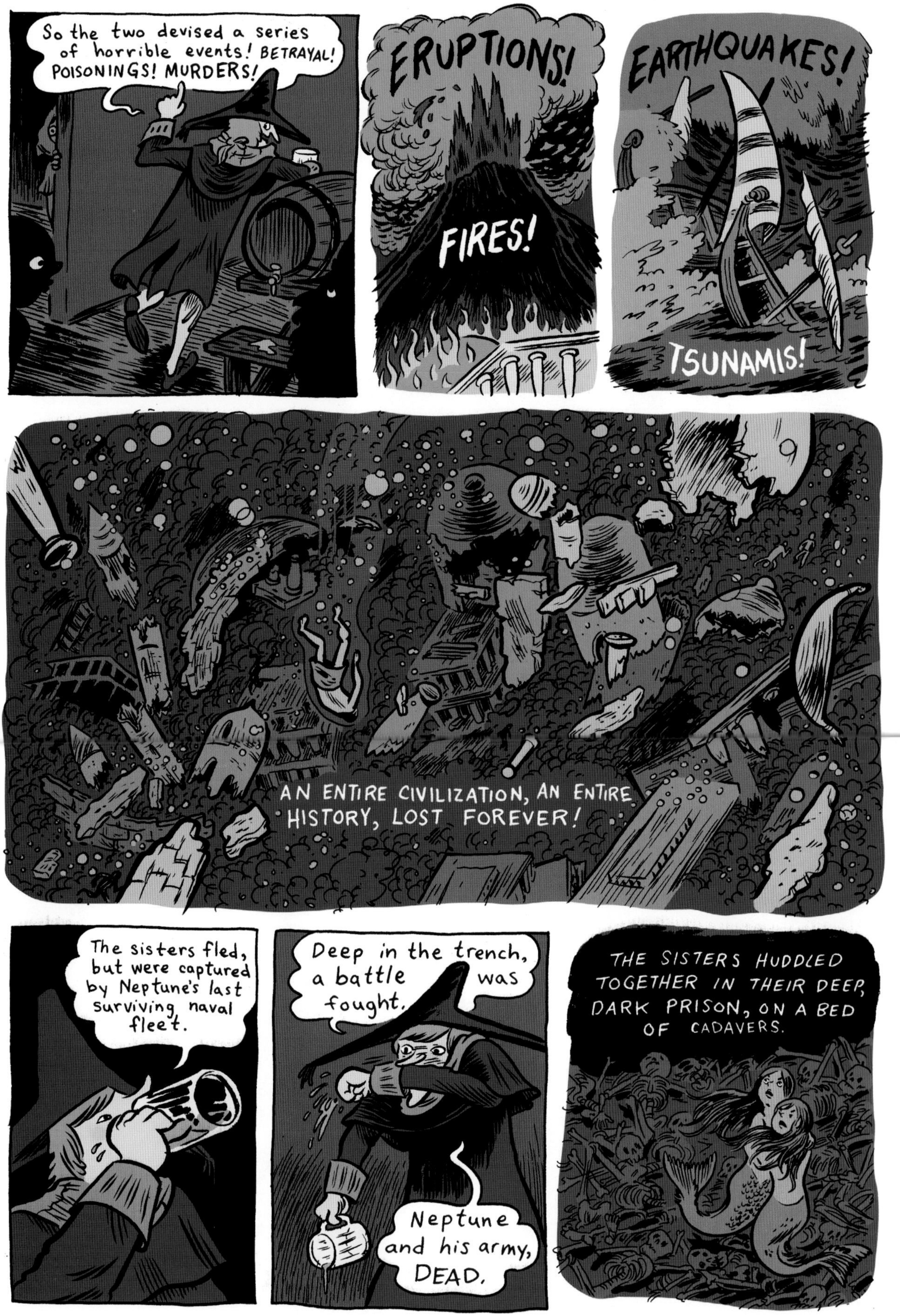
So the two devised a series of horrible events! BETRAYAL! POISONINGS! MURDERS!
ERUPTIONS!
FIRES!
EARTHQUAKES!
TSUNAMIS!
AN ENTIRE CIVILIZATION, AN ENTIRE HISTORY, LOST FOREVER!
The sisters fled, but were captured by Neptune's last surviving naval fleet.
Deep in the trench, a battle was fought.
Neptune and his army, DEAD.
THE SISTERS HUDDLED TOGETHER IN THEIR DEEP, DARK PRISON, ON A BED OF CADAVERS.

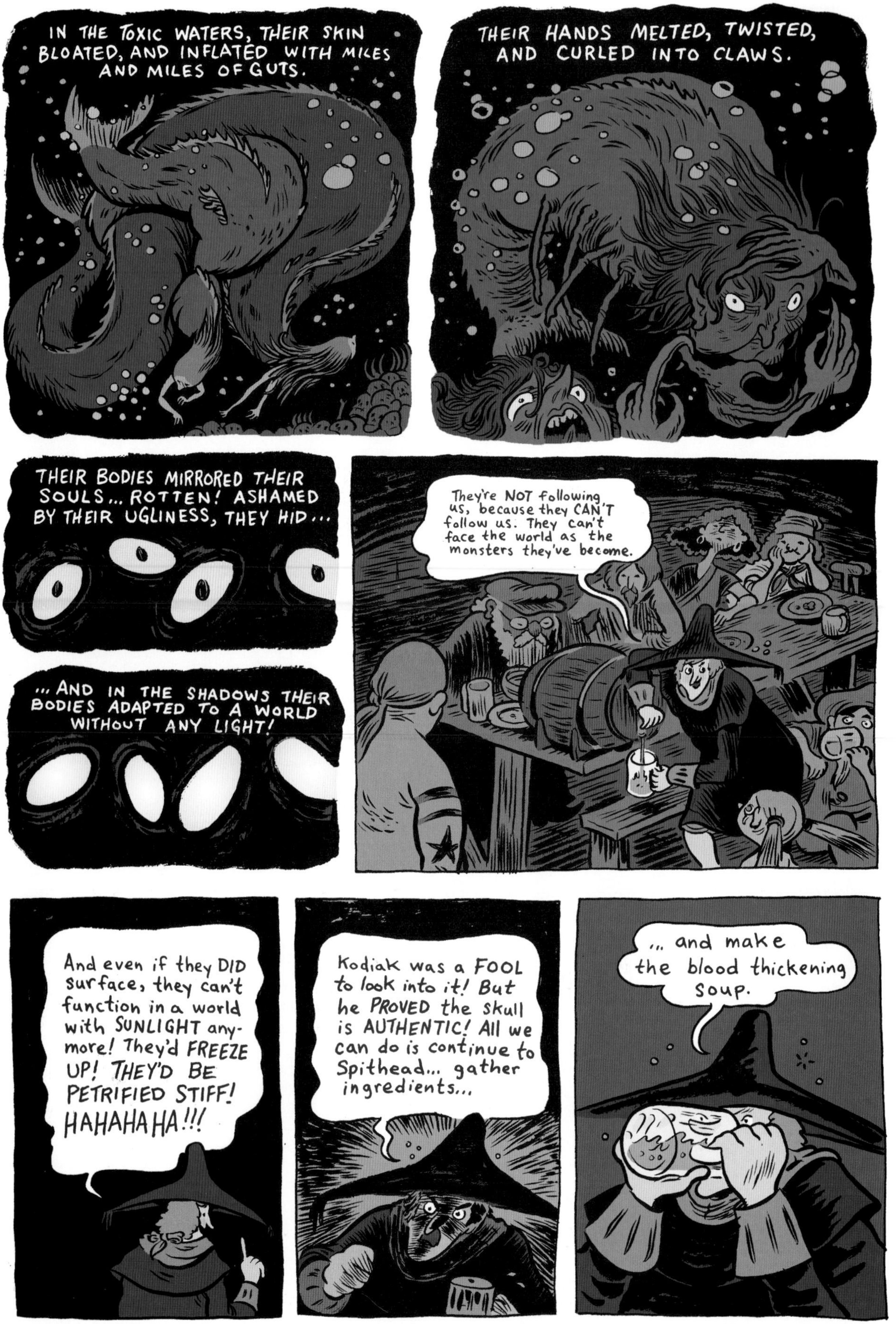
IN THE TOXIC WATERS, THEIR SKIN BLOATED, AND INFLATED WITH MILES AND MILES OF GUTS.
THEIR HANDS MELTED, TWISTED, AND CURLED INTO CLAWS.
THEIR BODIES MIRRORED THEIR SOULS... ROTTEN! ASHAMED BY THEIR UGLINESS, THEY HID...
...AND IN THE SHADOWS THEIR BODIES ADAPTED TO A WORLD WITHOUT ANY LIGHT!
They're NOT following us, because they CAN'T follow us. They can't face the world as the monsters they've become.
And even if they DID surface, they can't function in a world with SUNLIGHT anymore! They'd FREEZE UP! THEY'D BE PETRIFIED STIFF! HAHAHAHA!!!
Kodiak was a FOOL to look into it! But he PROVED the skull is AUTHENTIC! All we can do is continue to Spithead... gather ingredients...
... and make the blood thickening soup.

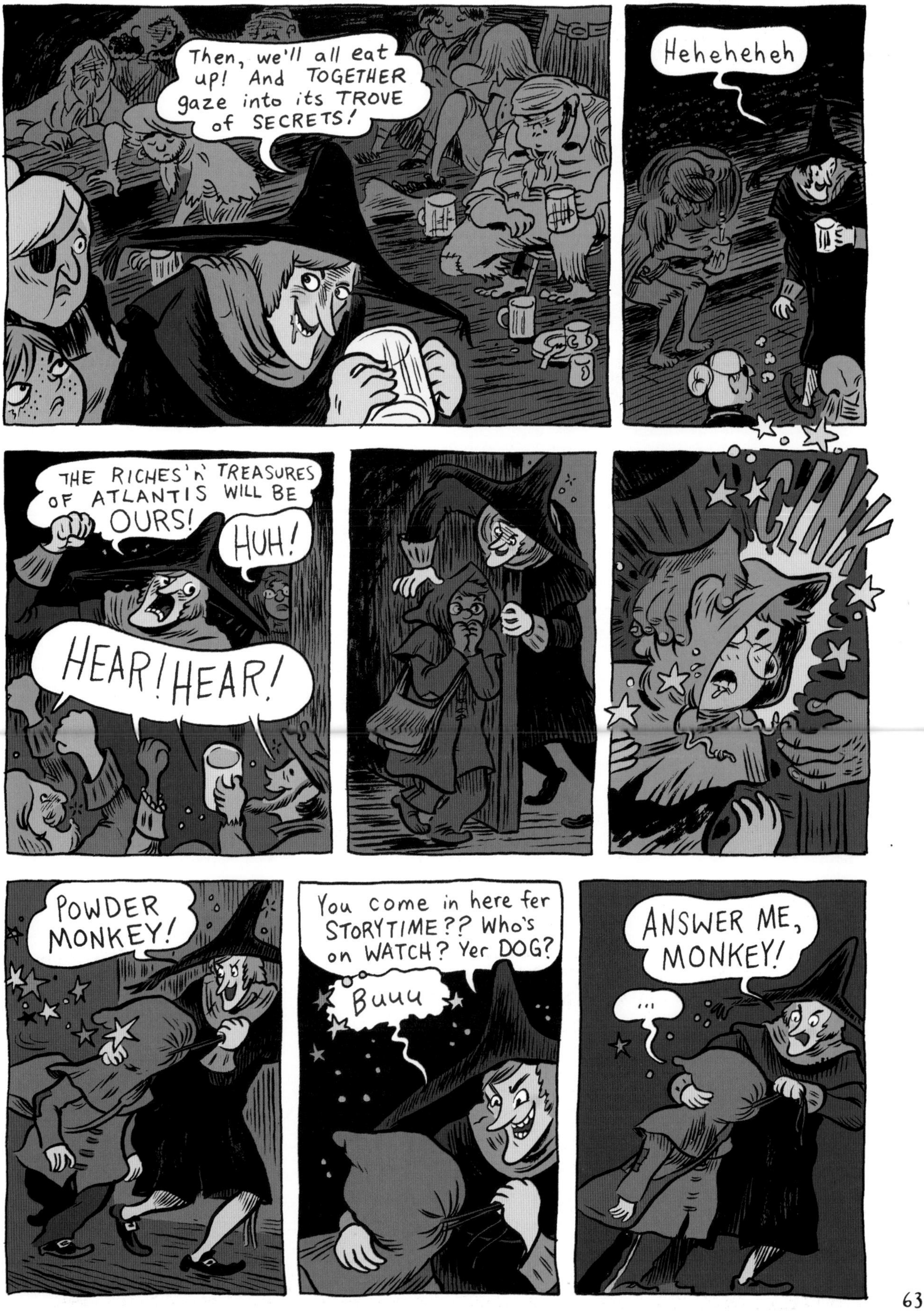

Then, we'll all eat up! And TOGETHER gaze into its TROVE of SECRETS!
Heheheheh
THE RICHES 'n' TREASURES OF ATLANTIS WILL BE OURS!
HUH!
HEAR! HEAR!
CLINK
POWDER MONKEY!
You come in here fer STORYTIME?? Who's on WATCH? Yer DOG?
Buuu
ANSWER ME, MONKEY!
...

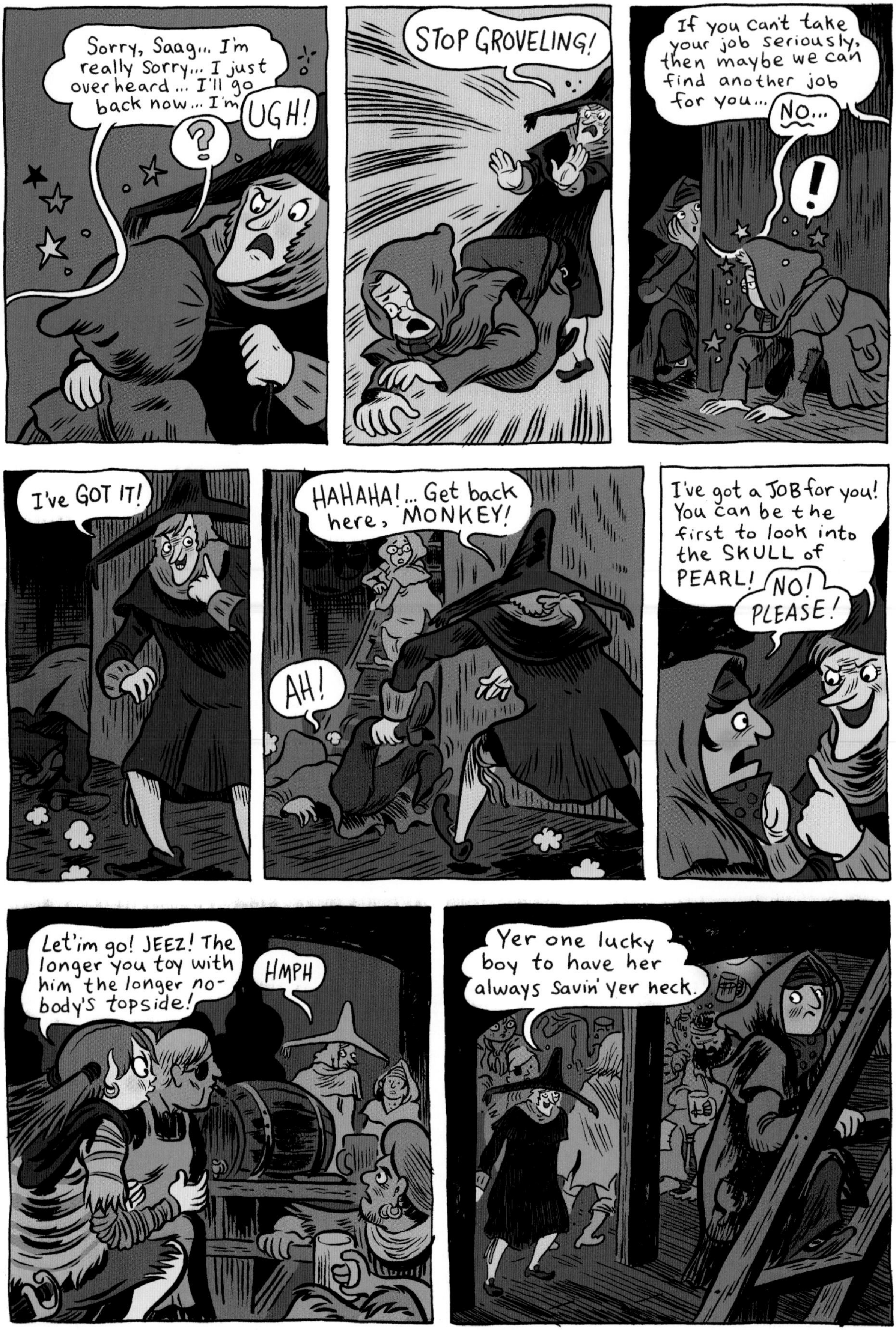
Sorry, Saag... I'm really sorry... I just overheard... I'll go back now... I'm
UGH!
?
STOP GROVELING!
If you can't take your job seriously, then maybe we can find another job for you...
NO...
!
I've GOT IT!
HAHAHA!... Get back here, MONKEY!
AH!
I've got a JOB for you! You can be the first to look into the SKULL of PEARL!
NO! PLEASE!
Let'im go! JEEZ! The longer you toy with him the longer nobody's topside!
HMPH
Yer one lucky boy to have her always savin' yer neck.

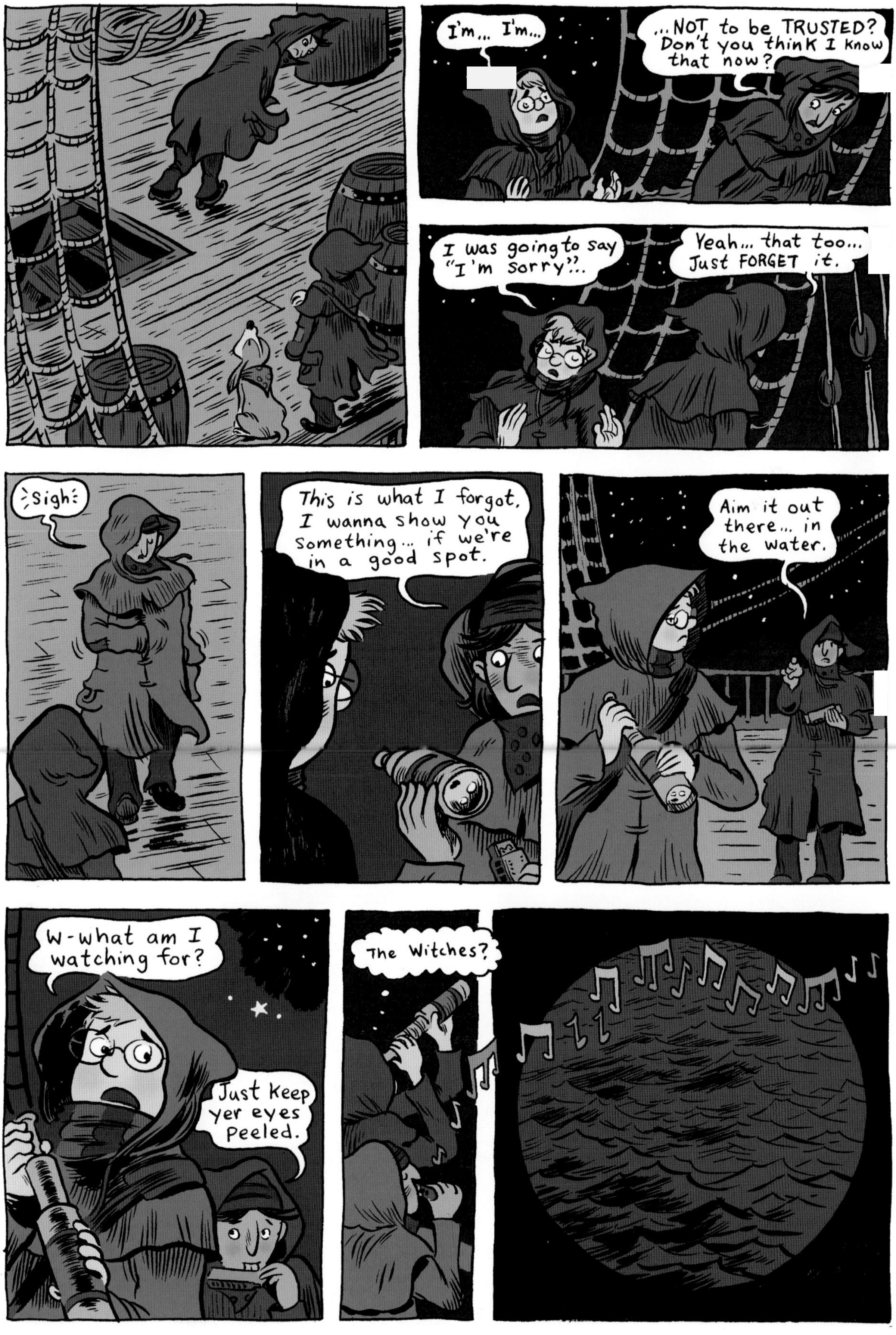

I'm... I'm...
...NOT to be TRUSTED? Don't you think I know that now?
I was going to say "I'm sorry"...
Yeah... that too... Just FORGET it.
Sigh
This is what I forgot, I wanna show you something... if we're in a good spot.
Aim it out there... in the water.
W-what am I watching for?
Just keep yer eyes peeled.
The Witches?

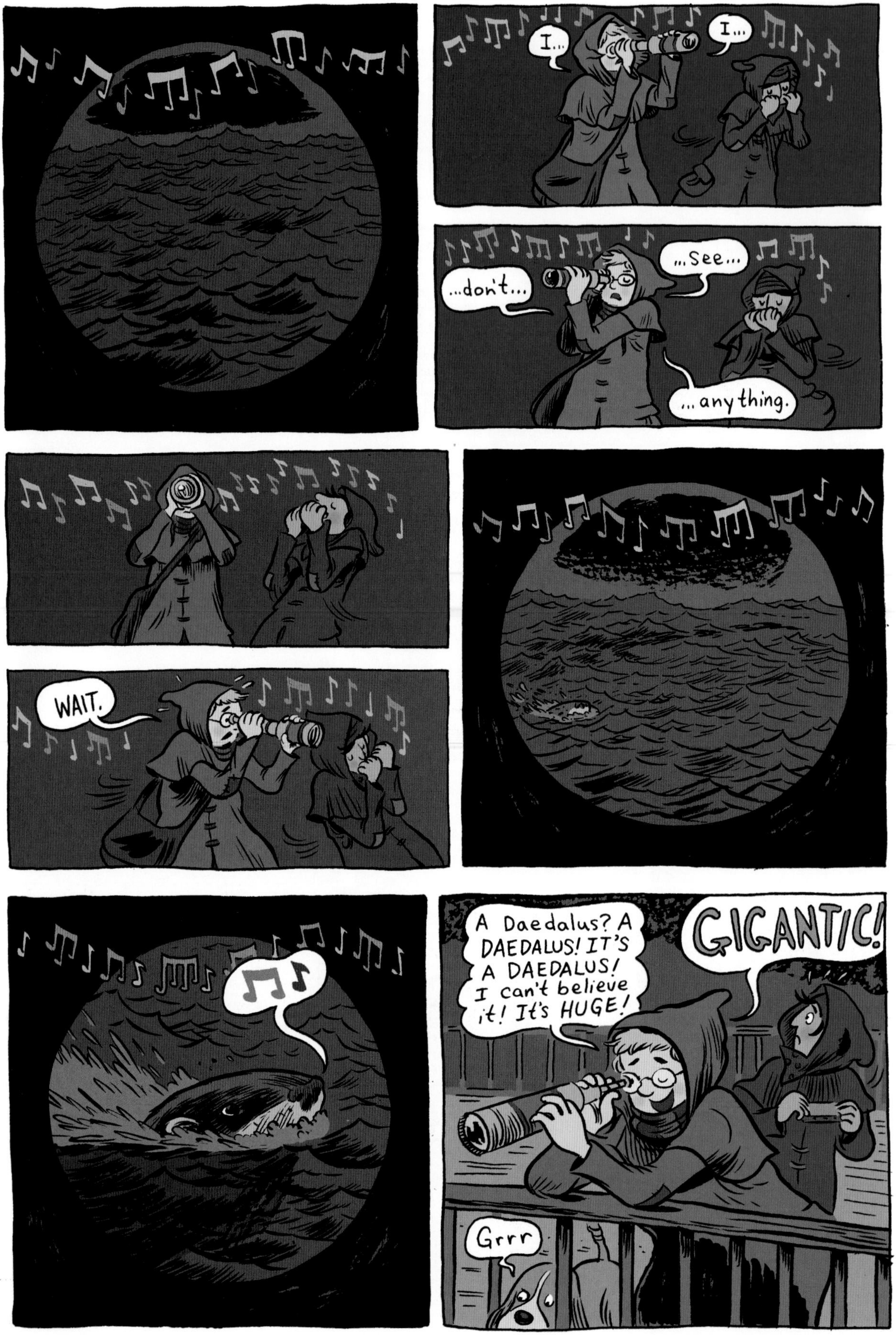
I...
I...
...don't...
...see...
...anything.
WAIT.
A Daedalus? A DAEDALUS! IT'S A DAEDALUS! I can't believe it! It's HUGE!
GIGANTIC!
Grrr

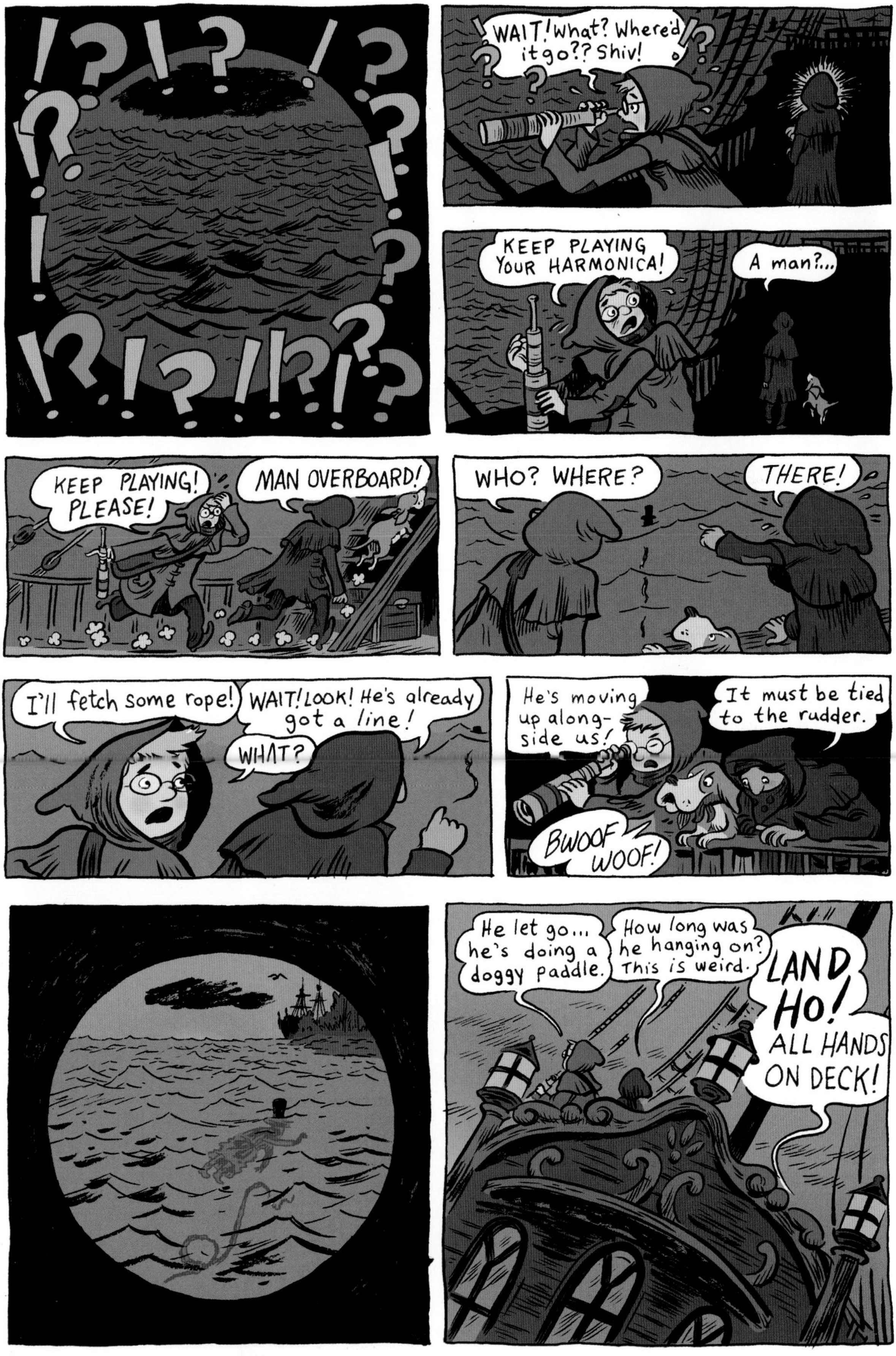
!?!?!?!?!?!?!?!?!?!?!?
WAIT! What? Where'd it go?? Shiv!
KEEP PLAYING YOUR HARMONICA!
A man?...
KEEP PLAYING! PLEASE!
MAN OVERBOARD!
WHO? WHERE?
THERE!
I'll fetch some rope!
WAIT! LOOK! He's already got a line!
WHAT?
He's moving up along-side us!
It must be tied to the rudder.
BWOOF WOOF!
He let go... he's doing a doggy paddle.
How long was he hanging on? This is weird.
LAND HO! ALL HANDS ON DECK!

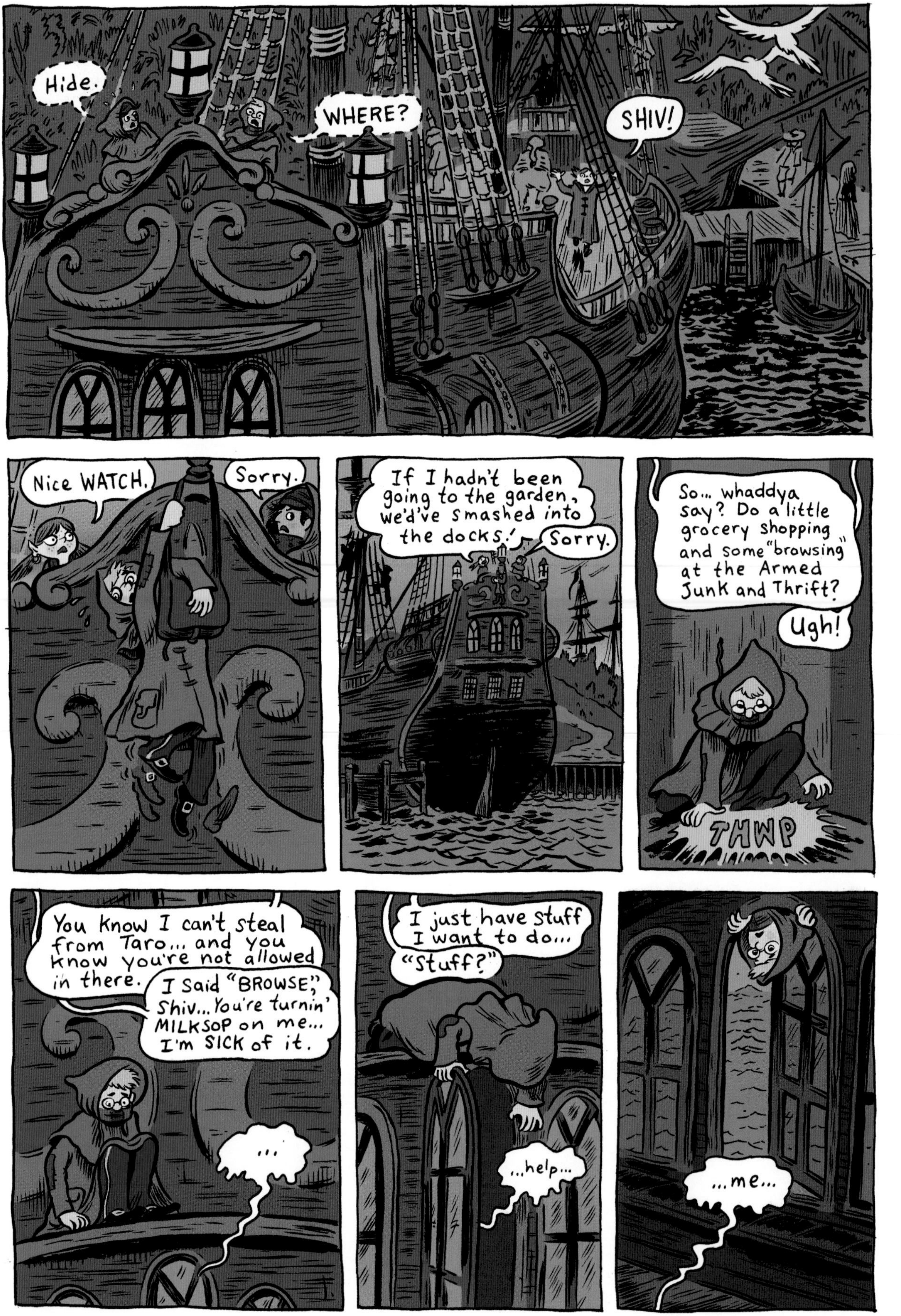
Hide.
WHERE?
SHIV!
Nice WATCH.
Sorry.
If I hadn't been going to the garden, we'd've smashed into the docks.
Sorry.
So... whaddya say? Do a little grocery shopping and some "browsing" at the Armed Junk and Thrift?
Ugh!
THWP
You know I can't steal from Taro... and you know you're not allowed in there.
I said "BROWSE," Shiv... You're turnin' MILKSOP on me... I'm SICK of it.
...
I just have stuff I want to do...
"Stuff?"
...help...
...me...

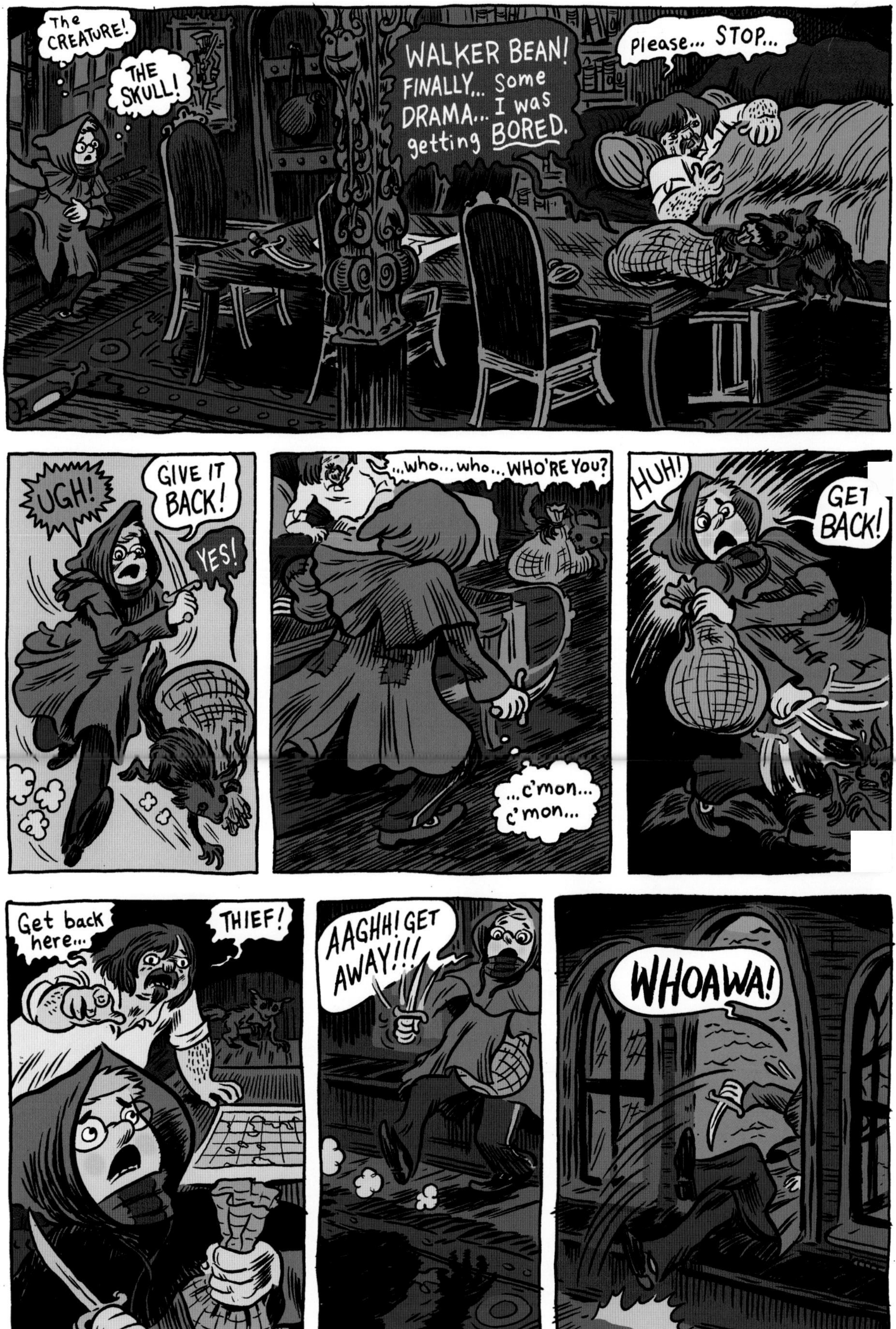

The CREATURE!
THE SKULL!
WALKER BEAN! FINALLY... Some DRAMA... I was getting BORED.
Please... STOP...
UGH!
GIVE IT BACK!
YES!
...who... who... WHO'RE YOU?
...c'mon... c'mon...
HUH!
GET BACK!
Get back here...
THIEF!
AAGHH! GET AWAY!!!
WHOAWA!

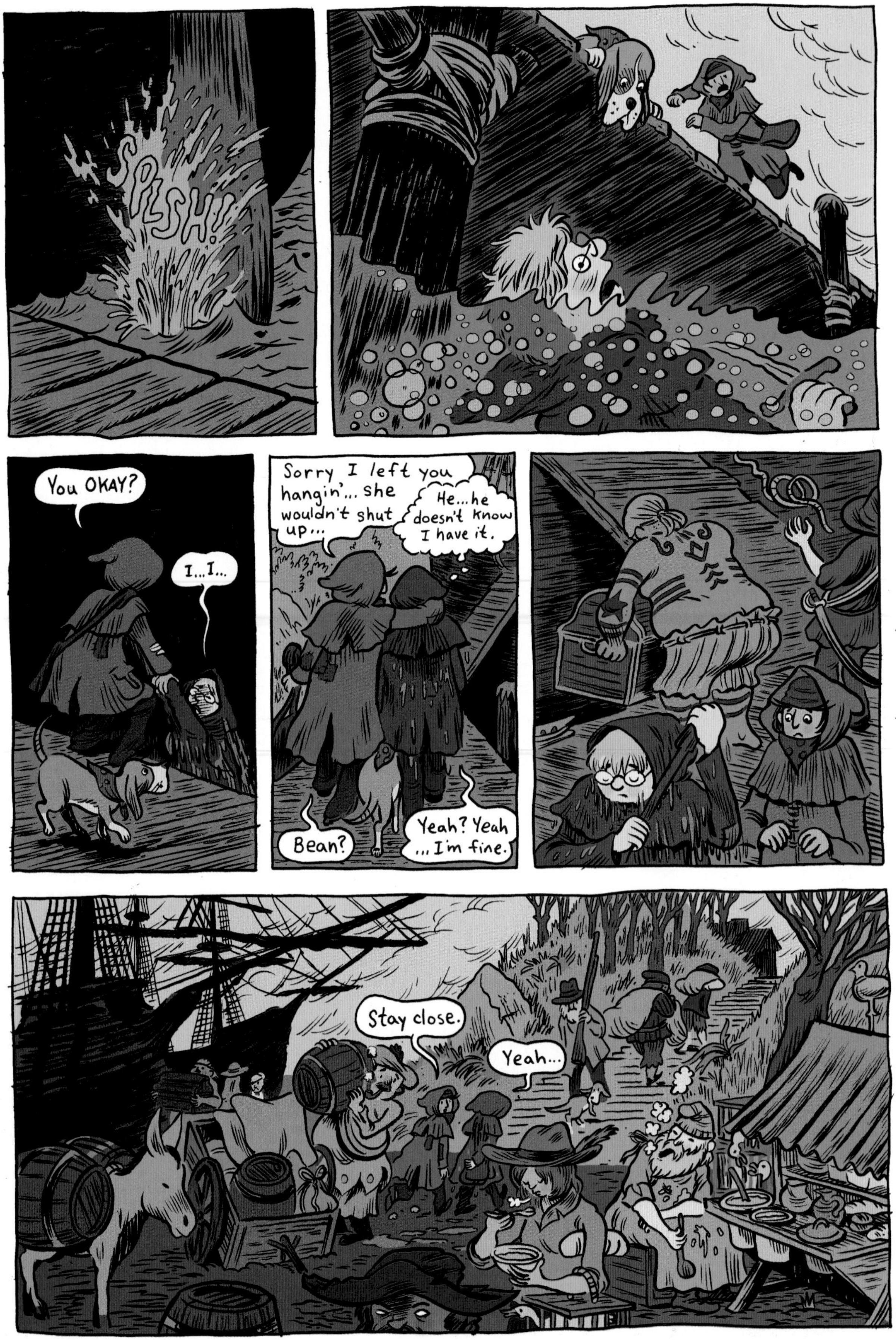
SPLSH!
You OKAY?
I...I...
Sorry I left you hangin'... she wouldn't shut up...
He...he doesn't know I have it.
Bean?
Yeah? Yeah ...I'm fine.
Stay close.
Yeah...

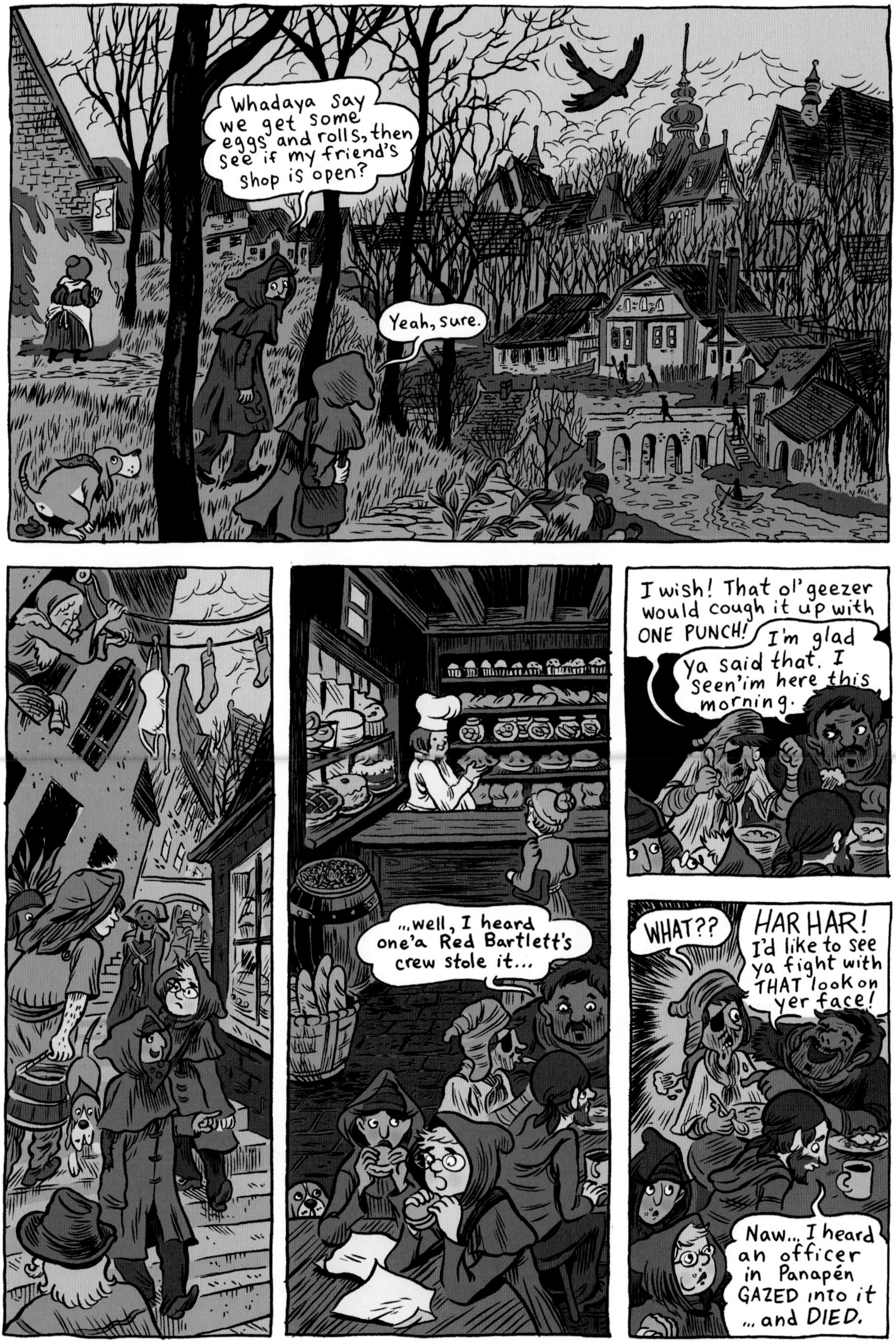

Whadaya say we get some eggs and rolls, then see if my friend's shop is open?
Yeah, sure.
...well, I heard one'a Red Bartlett's crew stole it...
I wish! That ol' geezer would cough it up with ONE PUNCH!
I'm glad ya said that. I seen'im here this morning.
WHAT??
HAR HAR! I'd like to see ya fight with THAT look on yer face!
Naw... I heard an officer in Panapén GAZED into it ... and DIED.

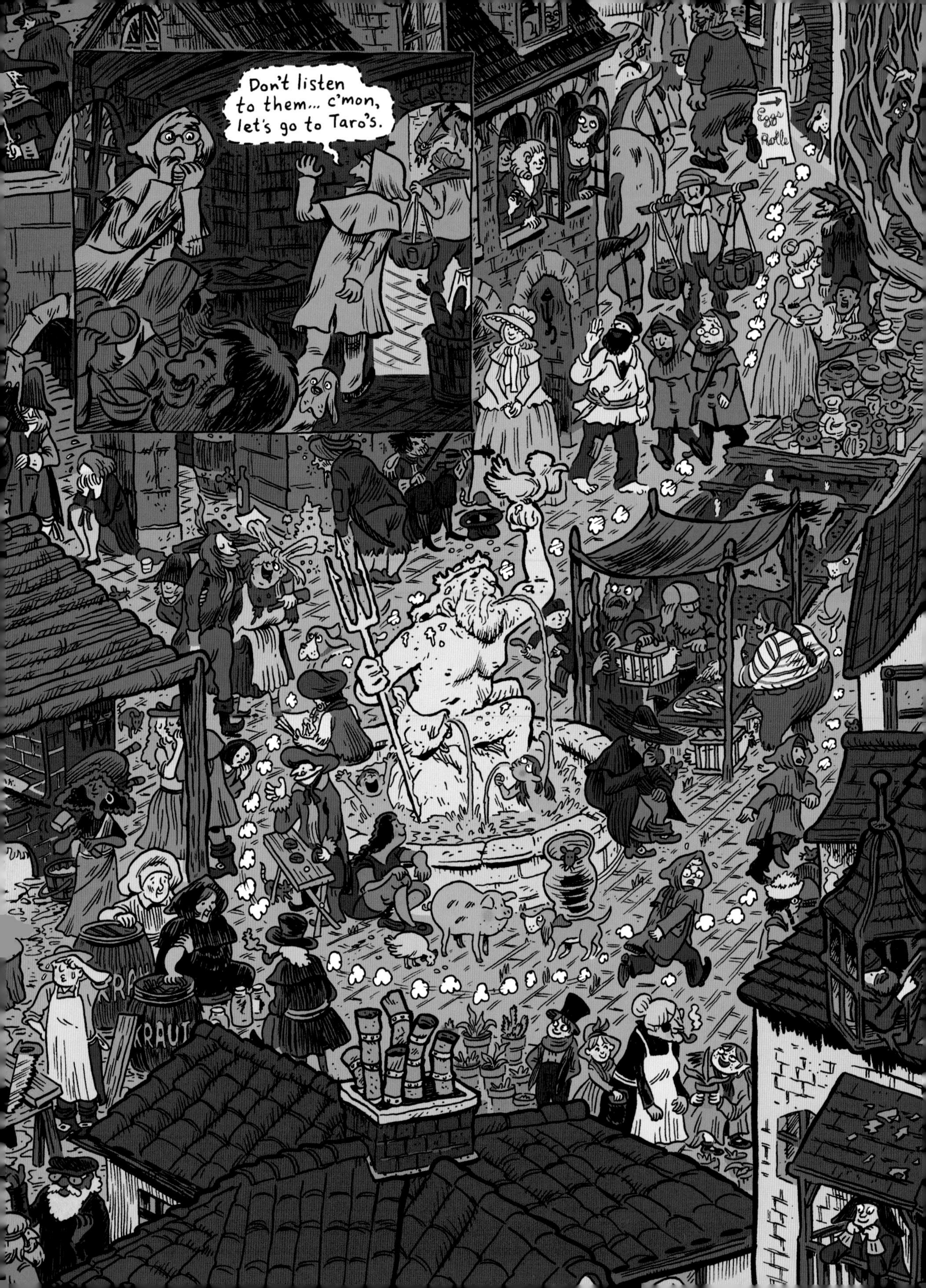
Don't listen to them... c'mon, let's go to Taro's.
Eggs Rolls
KRAUT

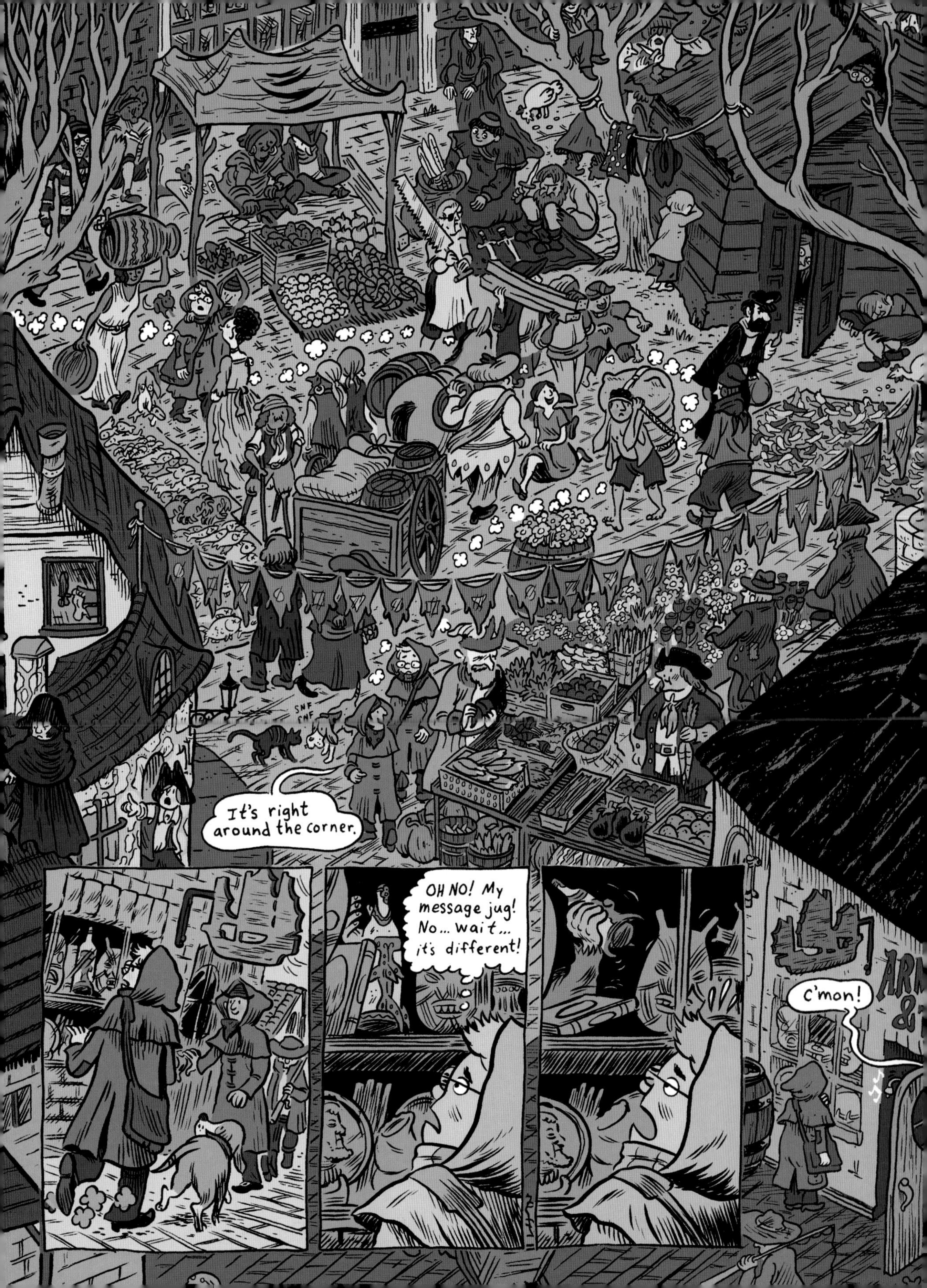
SNF SNF
It's right around the corner.
OH NO! My message jug! No... wait... it's different!
C'mon!

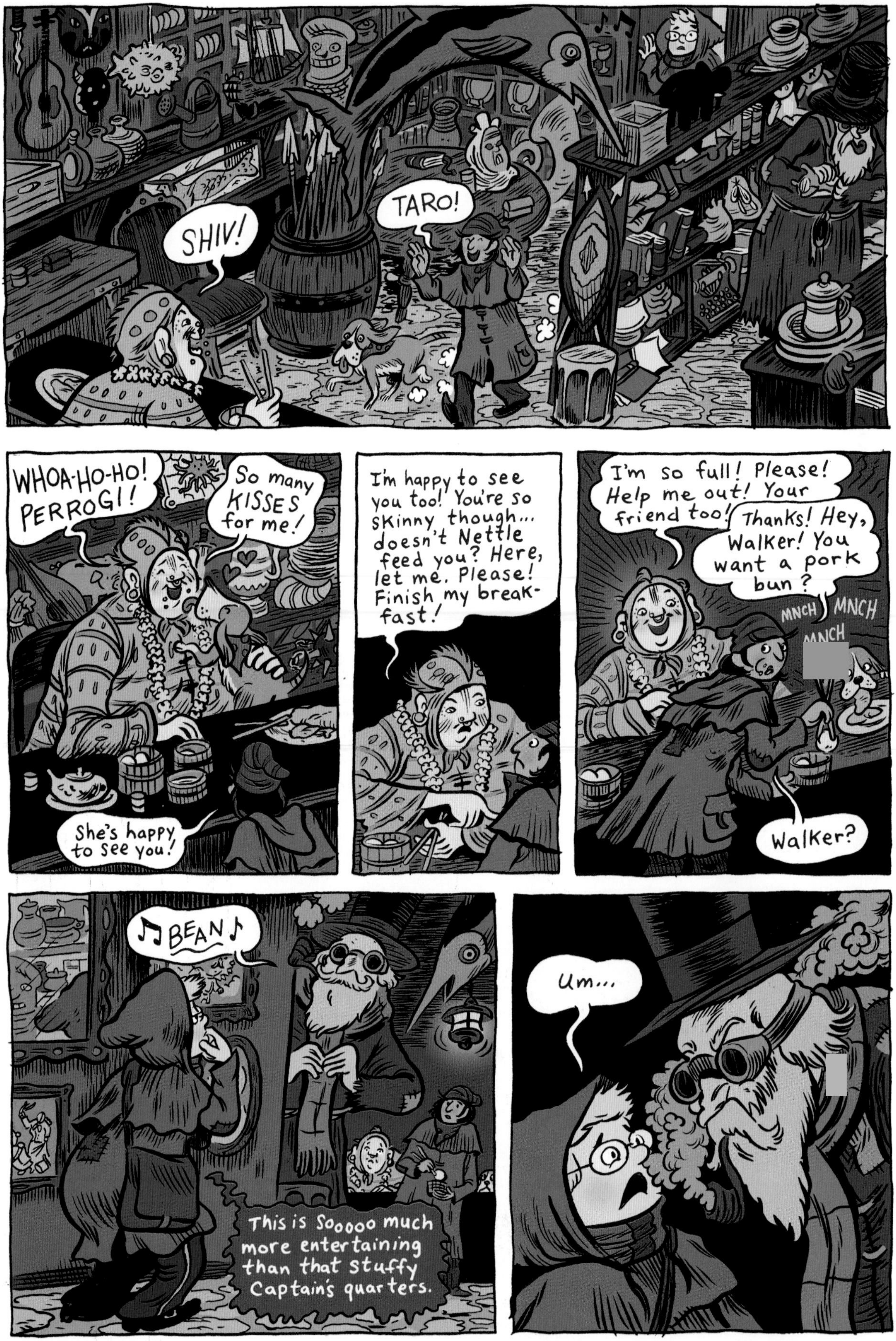

SHIV!
TARO!
WHOA-HO-HO! PERROGI!
So many KISSES for me!
She's happy to see you!
I'm happy to see you too! You're so skinny though... doesn't Nettle feed you? Here, let me. Please! Finish my break-fast!
I'm so full! Please! Help me out! Your friend too!
Thanks! Hey, Walker! You want a pork bun?
MNCH MNCH
Walker?
♫ BEAN ♪
This is Sooooo much more entertaining than that stuffy Captain's quarters.
Um...

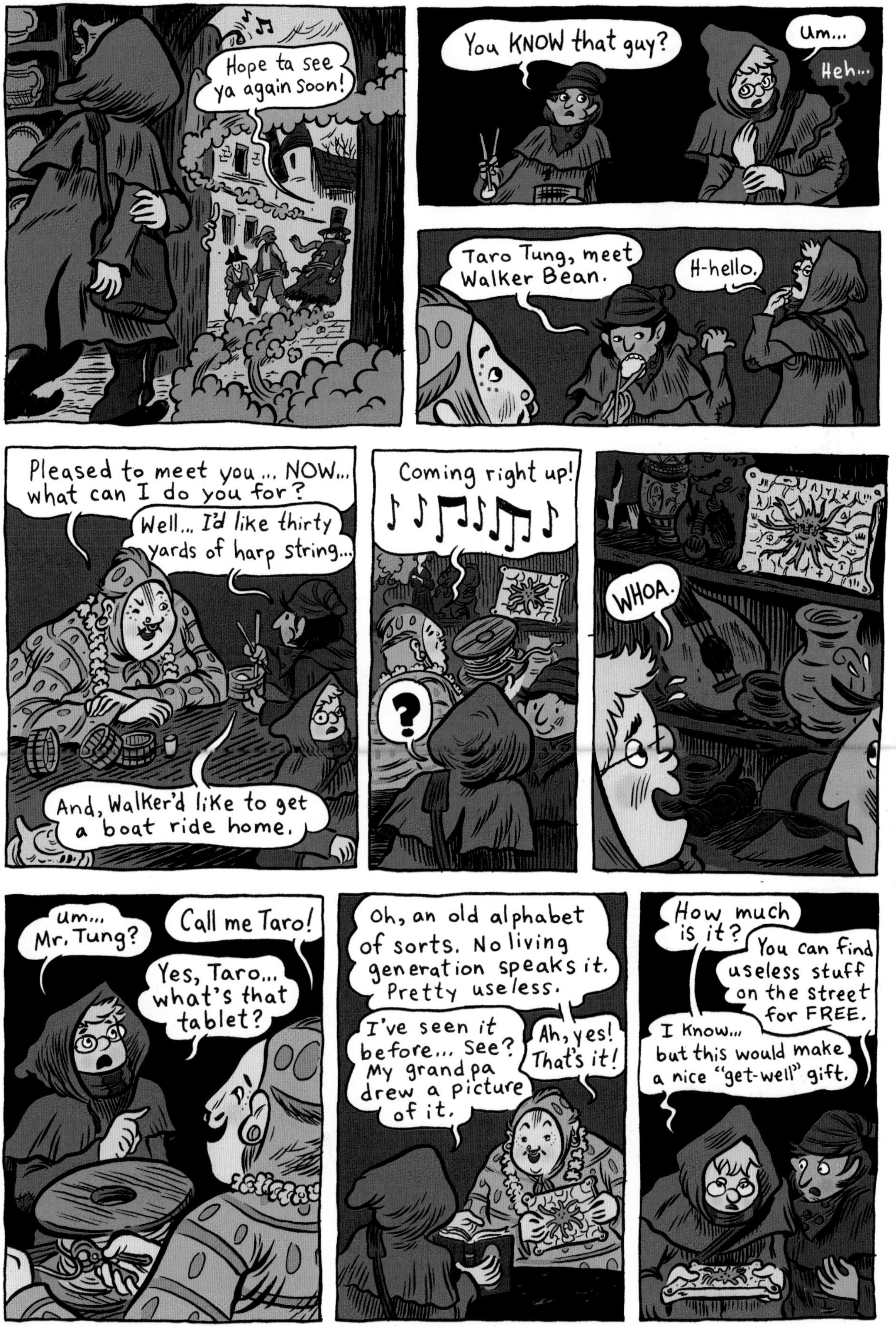
Hope ta see ya again soon!
You KNOW that guy?
Um...
Heh...
Taro Tung, meet Walker Bean.
H-hello.
Pleased to meet you... NOW... what can I do you for?
Well... I'd like thirty yards of harp string...
And, Walker'd like to get a boat ride home.
Coming right up!
WHOA.
um... Mr. Tung?
Call me Taro!
Yes, Taro... what's that tablet?
Oh, an old alphabet of sorts. No living generation speaks it. Pretty useless.
I've seen it before... See? My grandpa drew a picture of it.
Ah, yes! That's it!
How much is it?
You can find useless stuff on the street for FREE.
I know... but this would make a nice "get-well" gift.

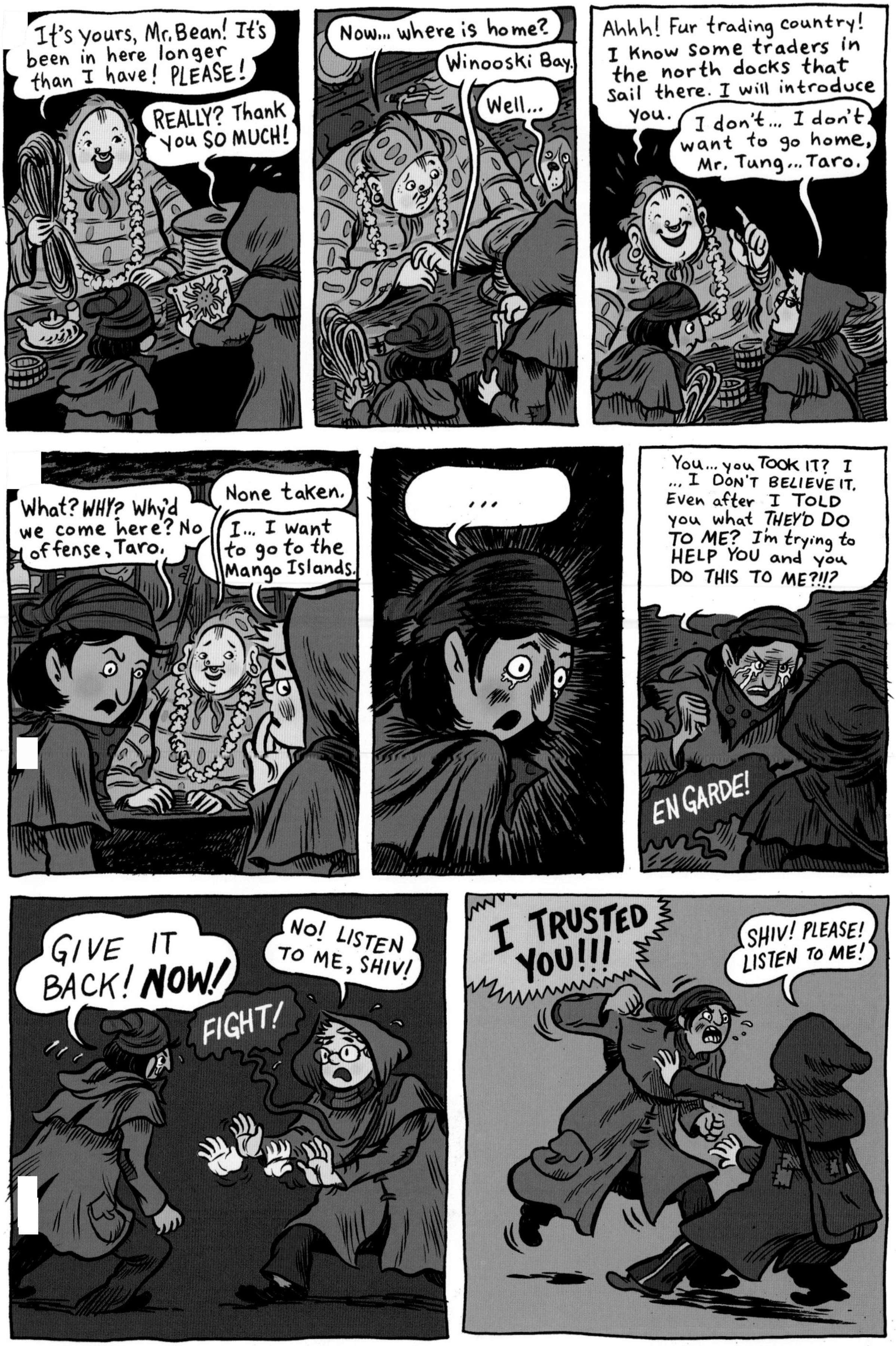

It's yours, Mr. Bean! It's been in here longer than I have! PLEASE!
REALLY? Thank you SO MUCH!
Now... where is home?
Winooski Bay.
Well...
Ahhh! Fur trading country! I know some traders in the north docks that sail there. I will introduce you.
I don't... I don't want to go home, Mr. Tung... Taro.
What? WHY? Why'd we come here? No offense, Taro.
None taken.
I... I want to go to the Mango Islands.
...
You... you TOOK IT? I ... I DON'T BELIEVE IT. Even after I TOLD you what THEY'D DO TO ME? I'm trying to HELP YOU and you DO THIS TO ME?!!?
EN GARDE!
GIVE IT BACK! NOW!
NO! LISTEN TO ME, SHIV!
FIGHT!
I TRUSTED YOU!!!
SHIV! PLEASE! LISTEN TO ME!

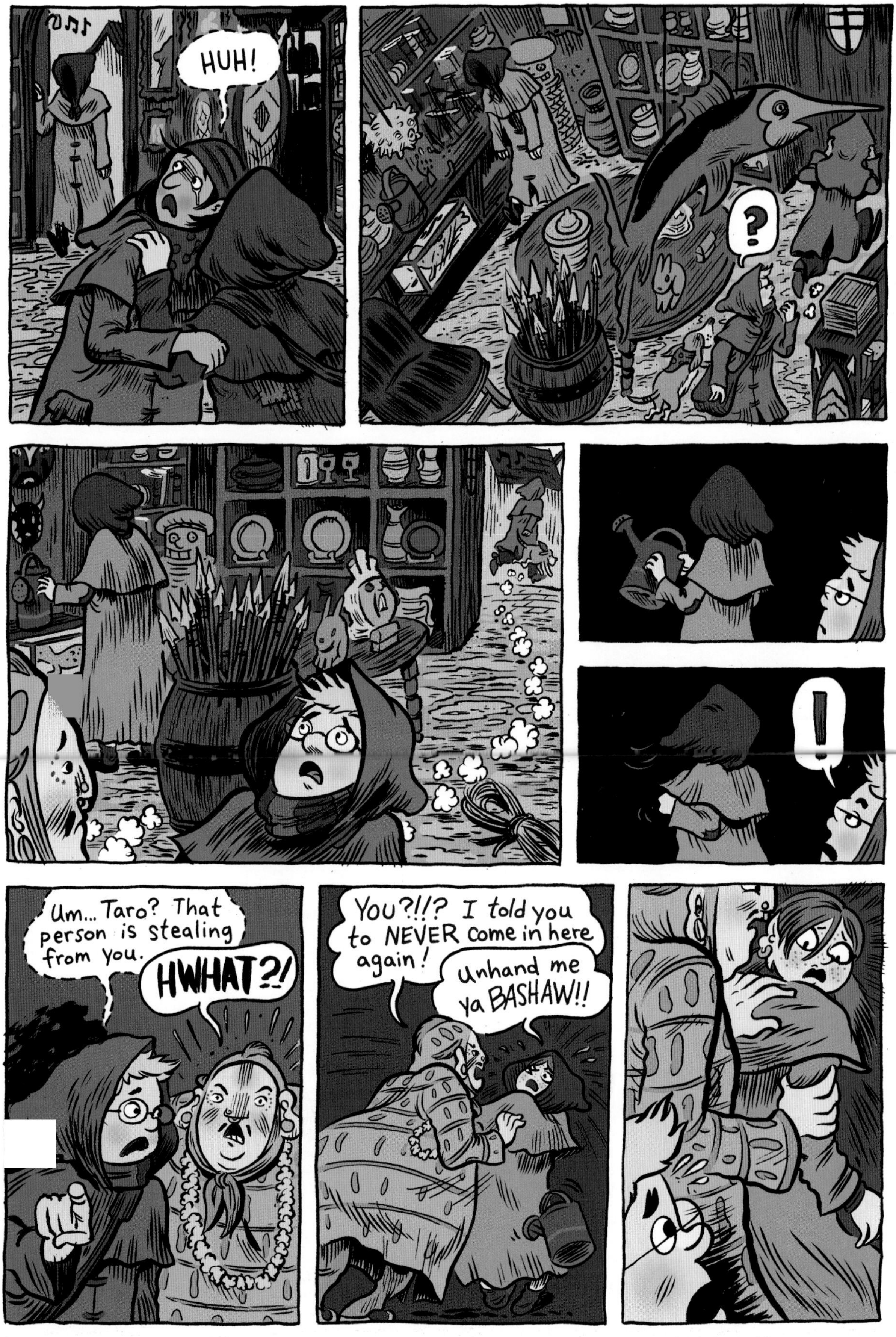
HUH!
?
!
Um... Taro? That person is stealing from you.
HWHAT?!
YOU?!!? I told you to NEVER come in here again!
Unhand me ya BASHAW!!

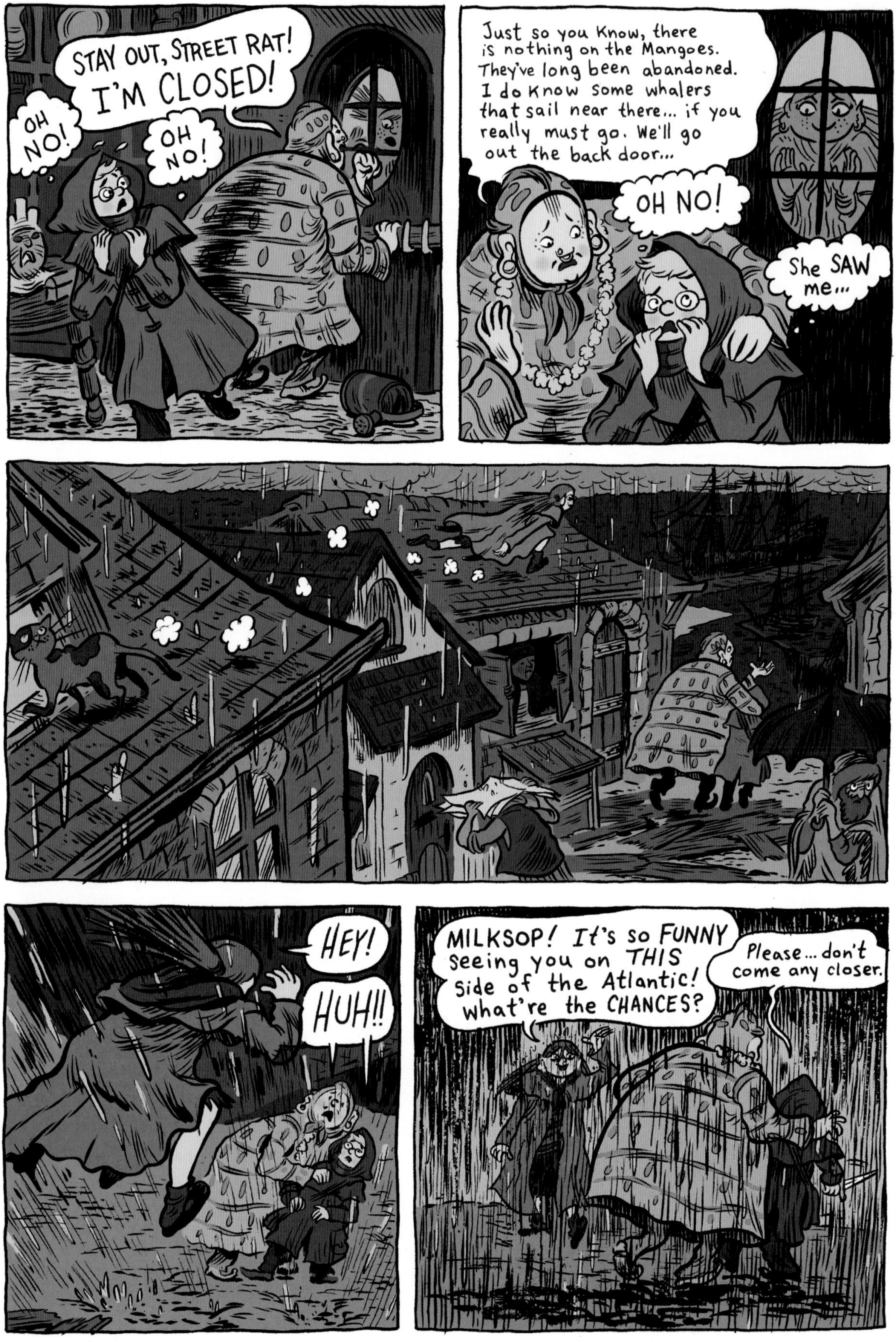
STAY OUT, STREET RAT! I'M CLOSED!
OH NO!
OH NO!
Just so you Know, there is nothing on the Mangoes. They've long been abandoned. I do Know some whalers that sail near there... if you really must go. We'll go out the back door...
OH NO!
She SAW me...
HEY!
HUH!!
MILKSOP! It's so FUNNY seeing you on THIS side of the Atlantic! what're the CHANCES?
Please... don't come any closer.

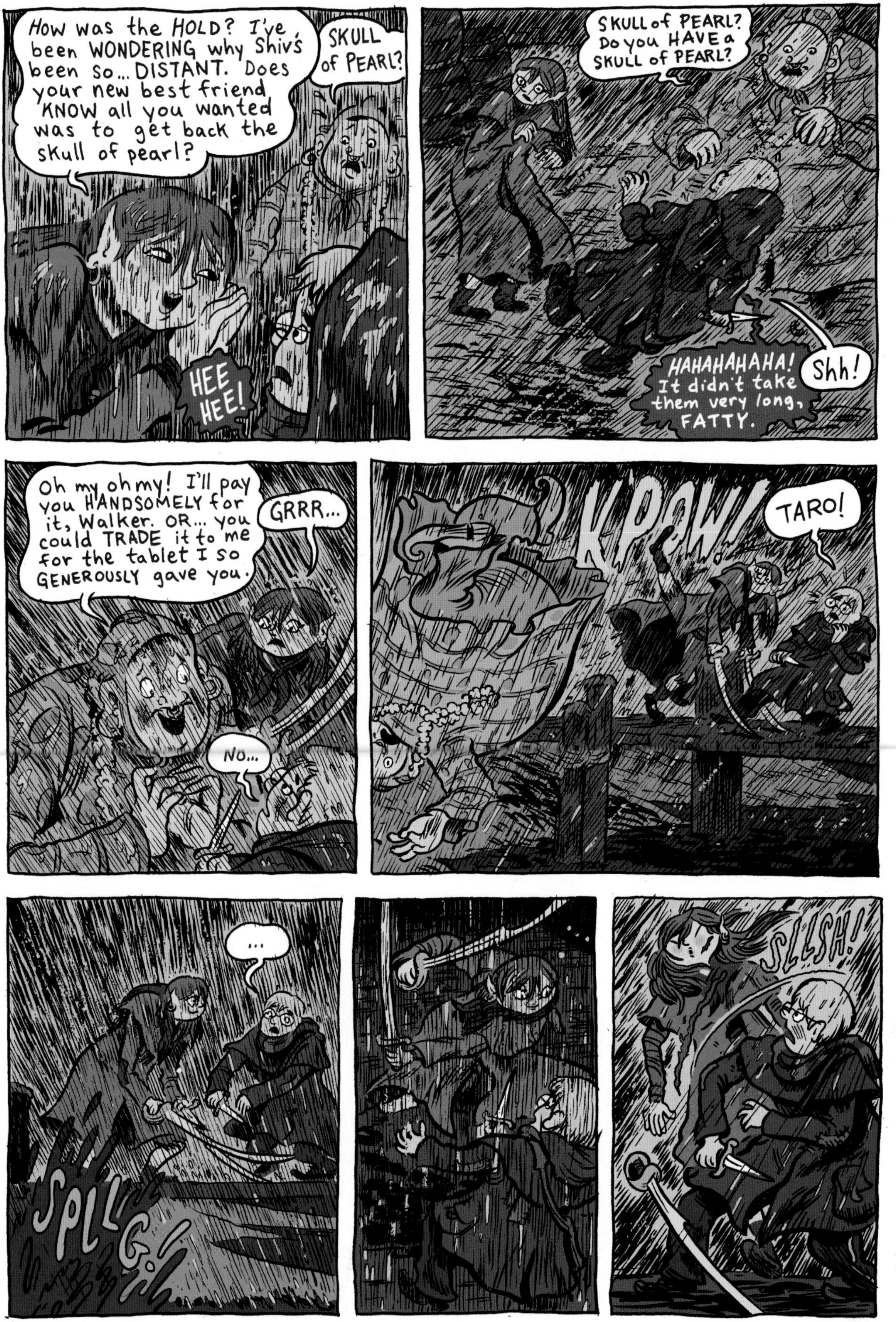
How was the HOLD? I've, been WONDERING why Shiv's been so... DISTANT. Does your new best friend KNOW all you wanted was to get back the skull of pearl?
SKULL of PEARL?
HEE HEE!
SKULL of PEARL? Do you HAVE a SKULL of PEARL?
HAHAHAHAHA! It didn't take them very long, FATTY.
Shh!
Oh my oh my! I'll pay you HANDSOMELY for it, Walker. OR... you could TRADE it to me for the tablet I so GENEROUSLY gave you.
GRRR...
NO...
KPOW!
TARO!
...
SPLG!
SLLSH!

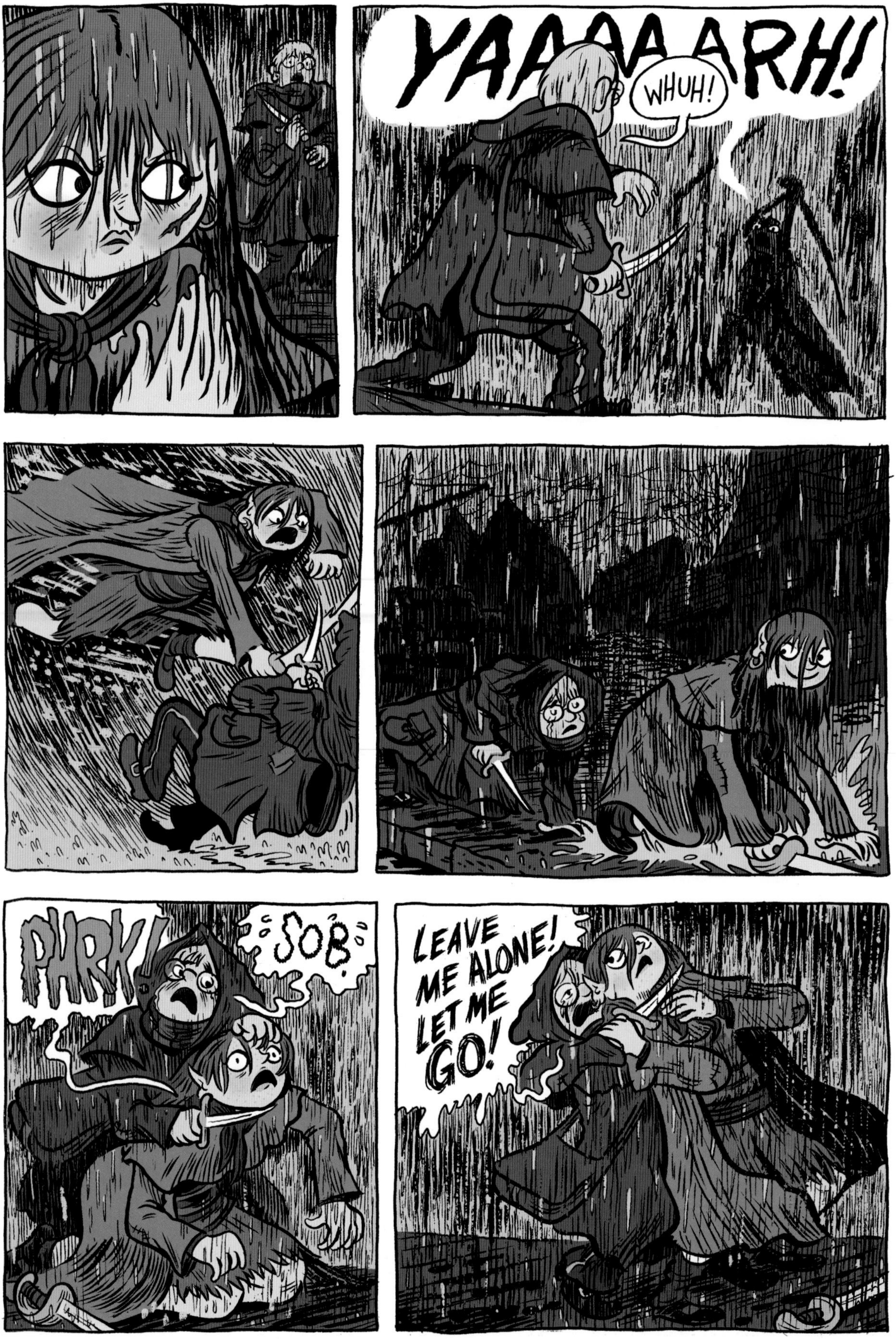
YAAAAARH!
WHUH!
PHRK!
SOB
LEAVE ME ALONE! LET ME GO!

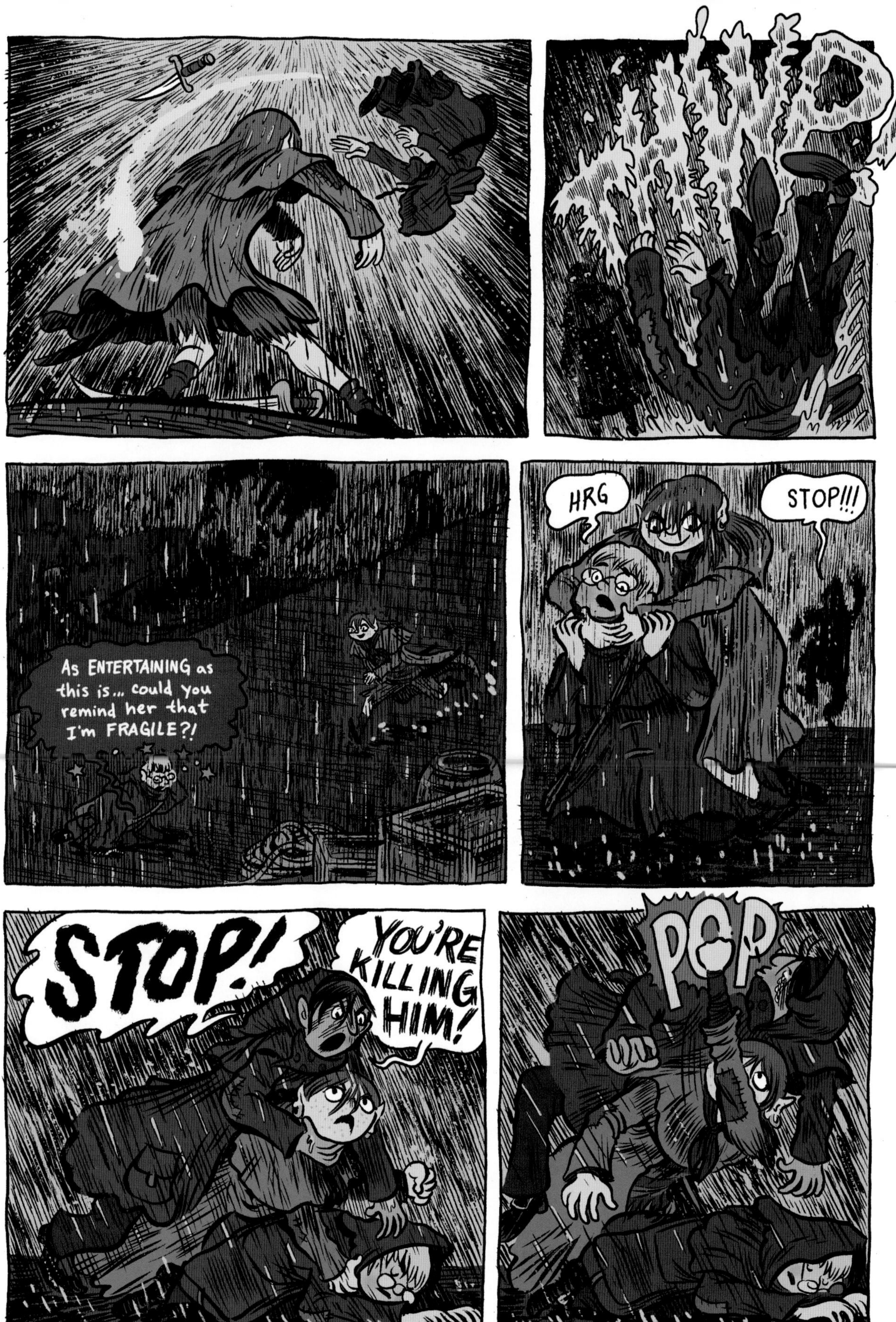
THWP!
As ENTERTAINING as this is... could you remind her that I'm FRAGILE?!
HRG
STOP!!!
STOP!
YOU'RE KILLING HIM!
POP

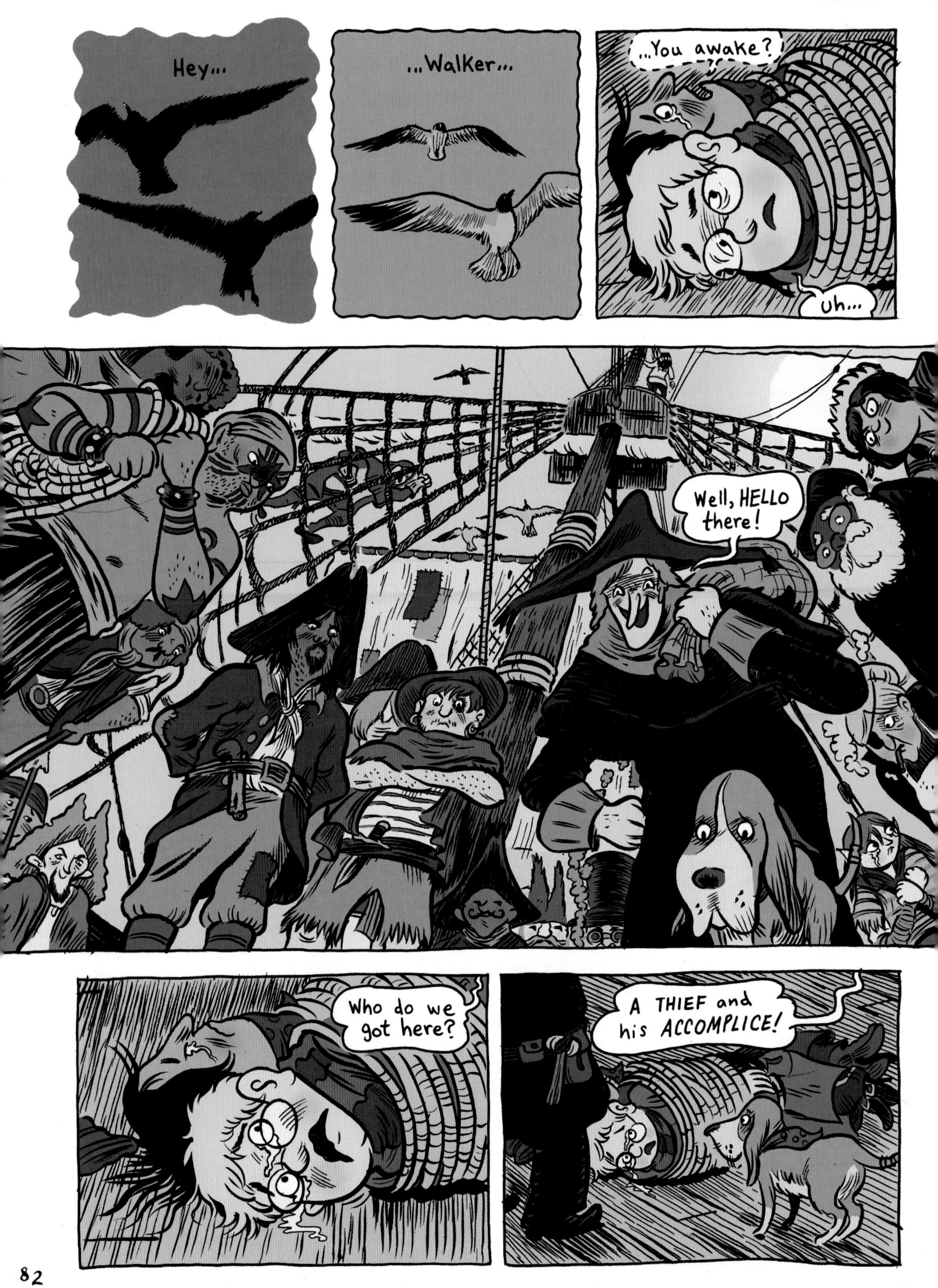

Hey...
...Walker...
...You awake?
Uh...
Well, HELLO there!
Who do we got here?
A THIEF and his ACCOMPLICE!

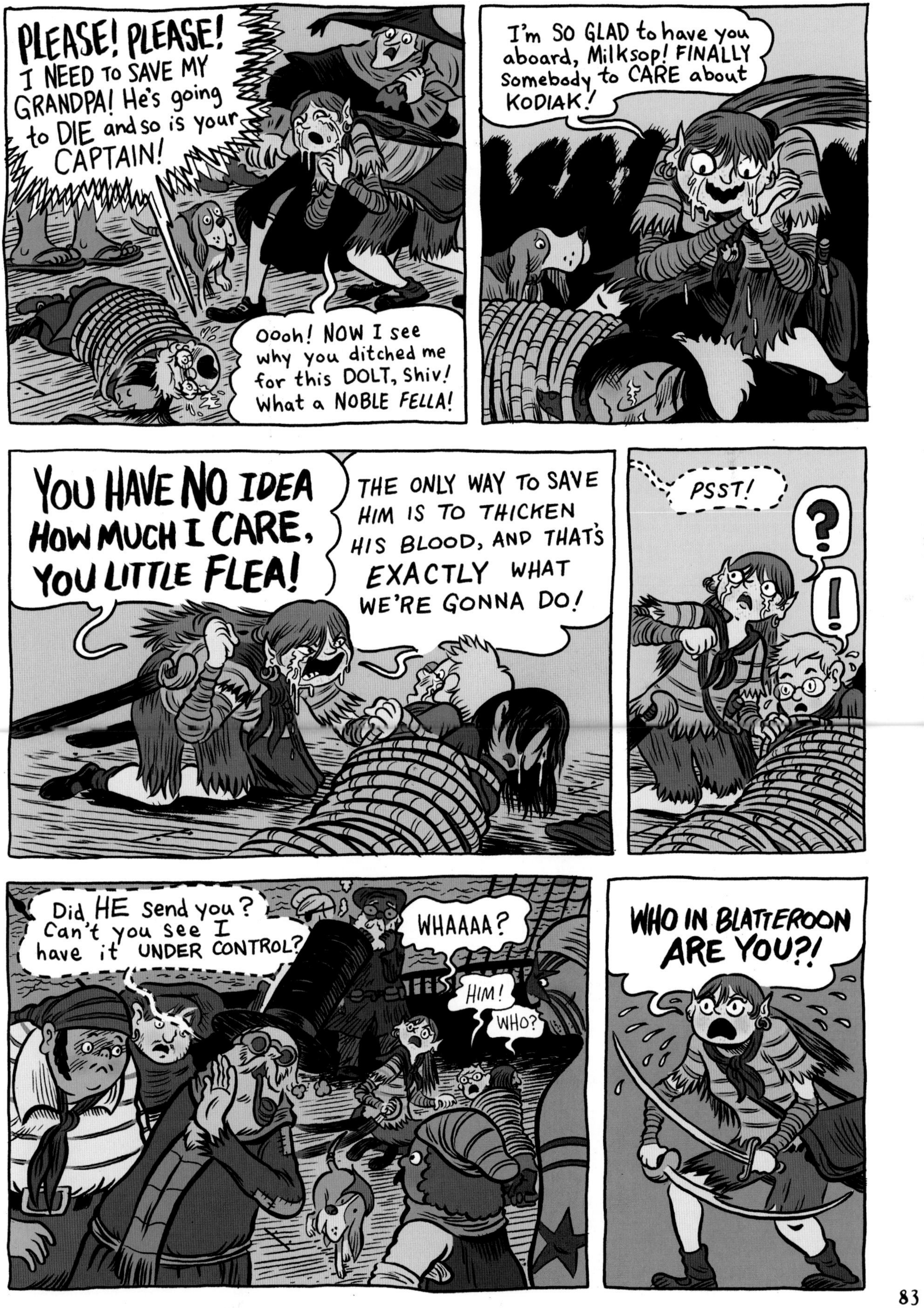
PLEASE! PLEASE! I NEED TO SAVE MY GRANDPA! He's going to DIE and so is your CAPTAIN!
Oooh! NOW I see why you ditched me for this DOLT, Shiv! What a NOBLE FELLA!
I'm SO GLAD to have you aboard, Milksop! FINALLY Somebody to CARE about KODIAK!
YOU HAVE NO IDEA HOW MUCH I CARE, YOU LITTLE FLEA!
THE ONLY WAY TO SAVE HIM IS TO THICKEN HIS BLOOD, AND THAT'S EXACTLY WHAT WE'RE GONNA DO!
PSST!
?
!
Did HE send you? Can't you see I have it UNDER CONTROL?
WHAAAA?
HIM!
WHO?
WHO IN BLATTEROON ARE YOU?!

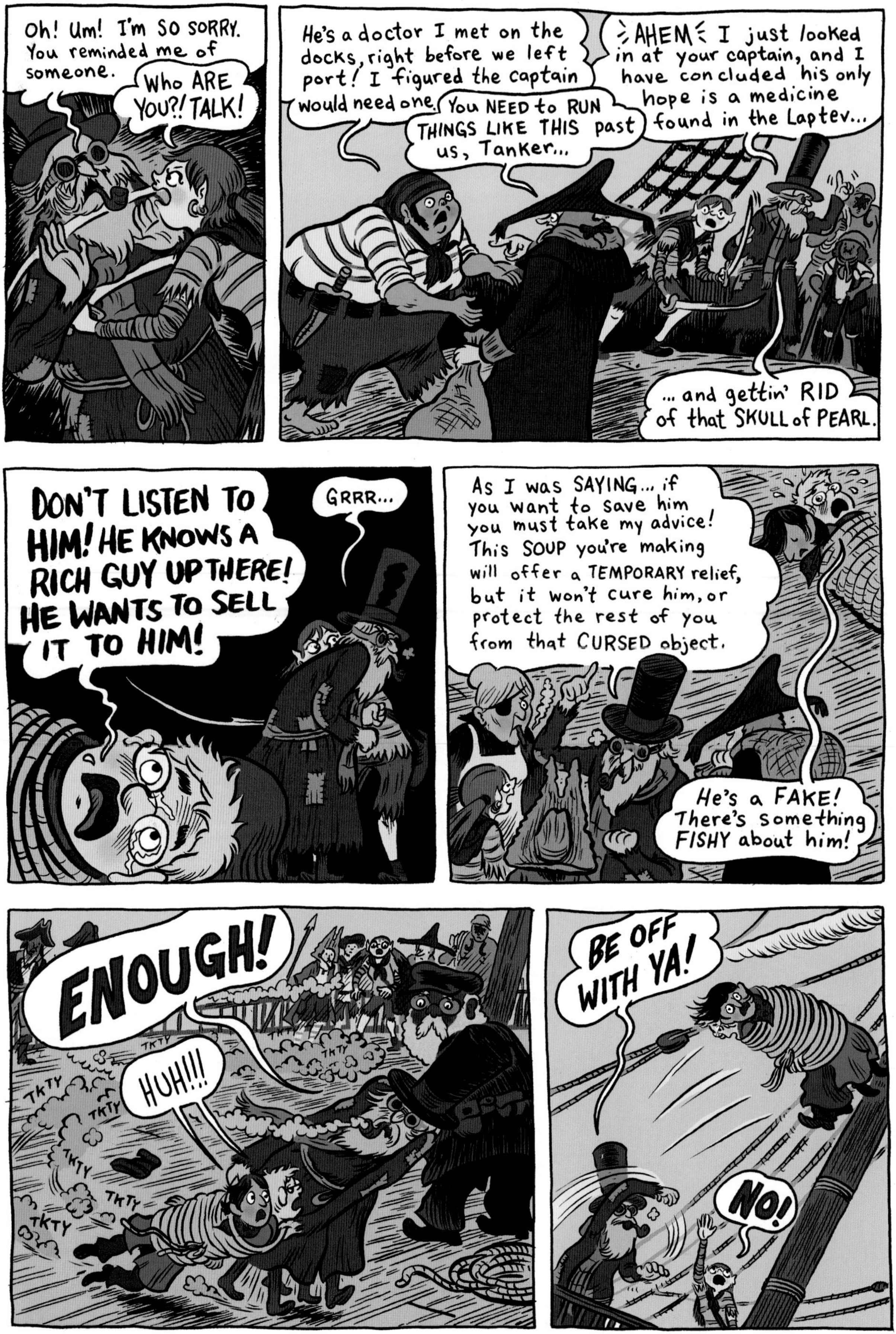
Oh! Um! I'm SO SORRY. You reminded me of someone.
Who ARE YOU?! TALK!
He's a doctor I met on the docks, right before we left port! I figured the captain would need one.
You NEED to RUN THINGS LIKE THIS past us, Tanker...
AHEM I just looked in at your captain, and I have concluded his only hope is a medicine found in the Laptev...
... and gettin' RID of that SKULL of PEARL.
DON'T LISTEN TO HIM! HE KNOWS A RICH GUY UP THERE! HE WANTS TO SELL IT TO HIM!
GRRR...
As I was SAYING... if you want to save him you must take my advice! This SOUP you're making will offer a TEMPORARY relief, but it won't cure him, or protect the rest of you from that CURSED object.
He's a FAKE! There's something FISHY about him!
ENOUGH!
HUH!!!
TKTY
TKTY
TKTY
TKTY
TKTY
TKTY
TKTY
BE OFF WITH YA!
NO!

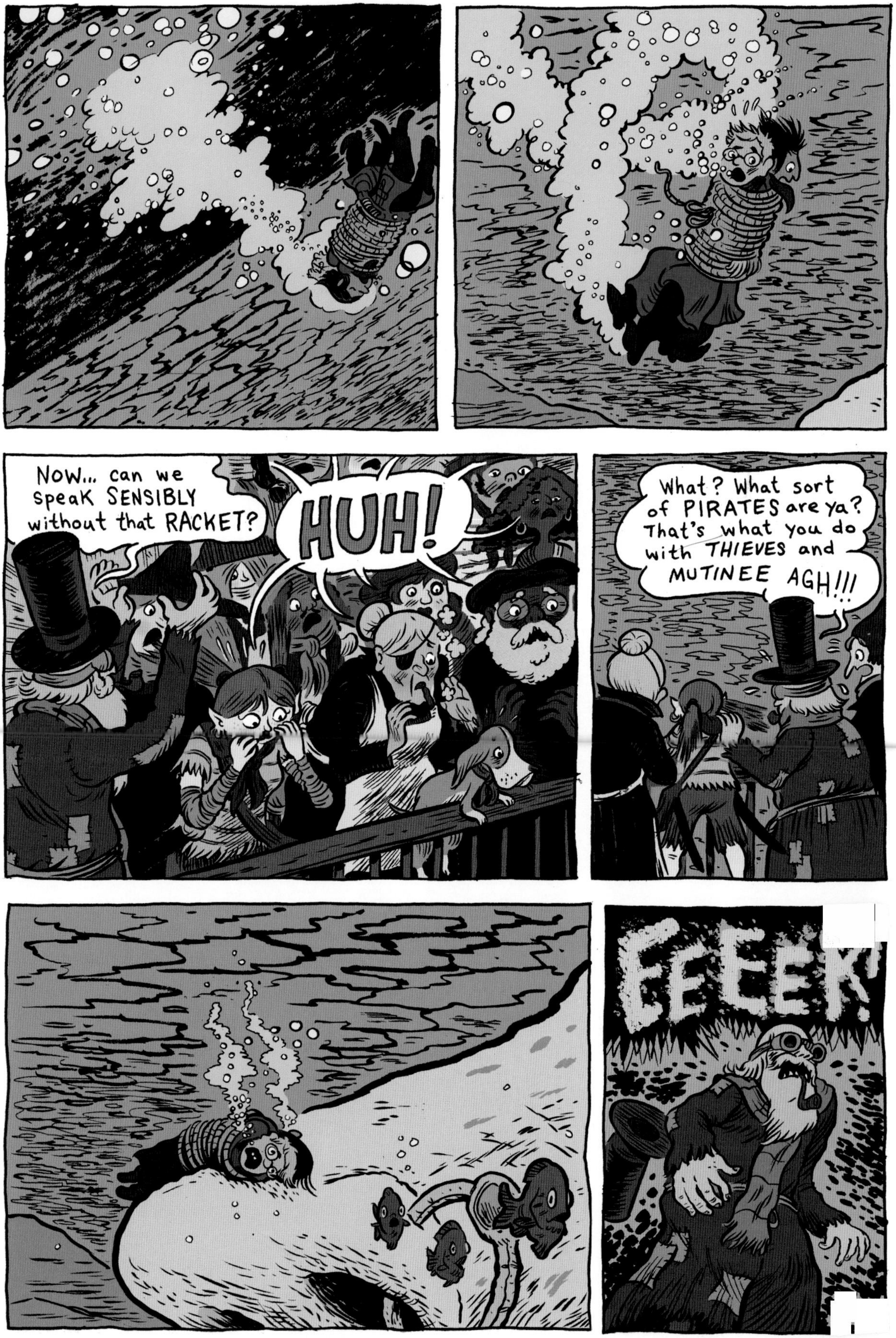

NOW... can we speak SENSIBLY without that RACKET?
HUH!
What? What sort of PIRATES are ya? That's what you do with THIEVES and MUTINEE AGH!!!
EEEEK!

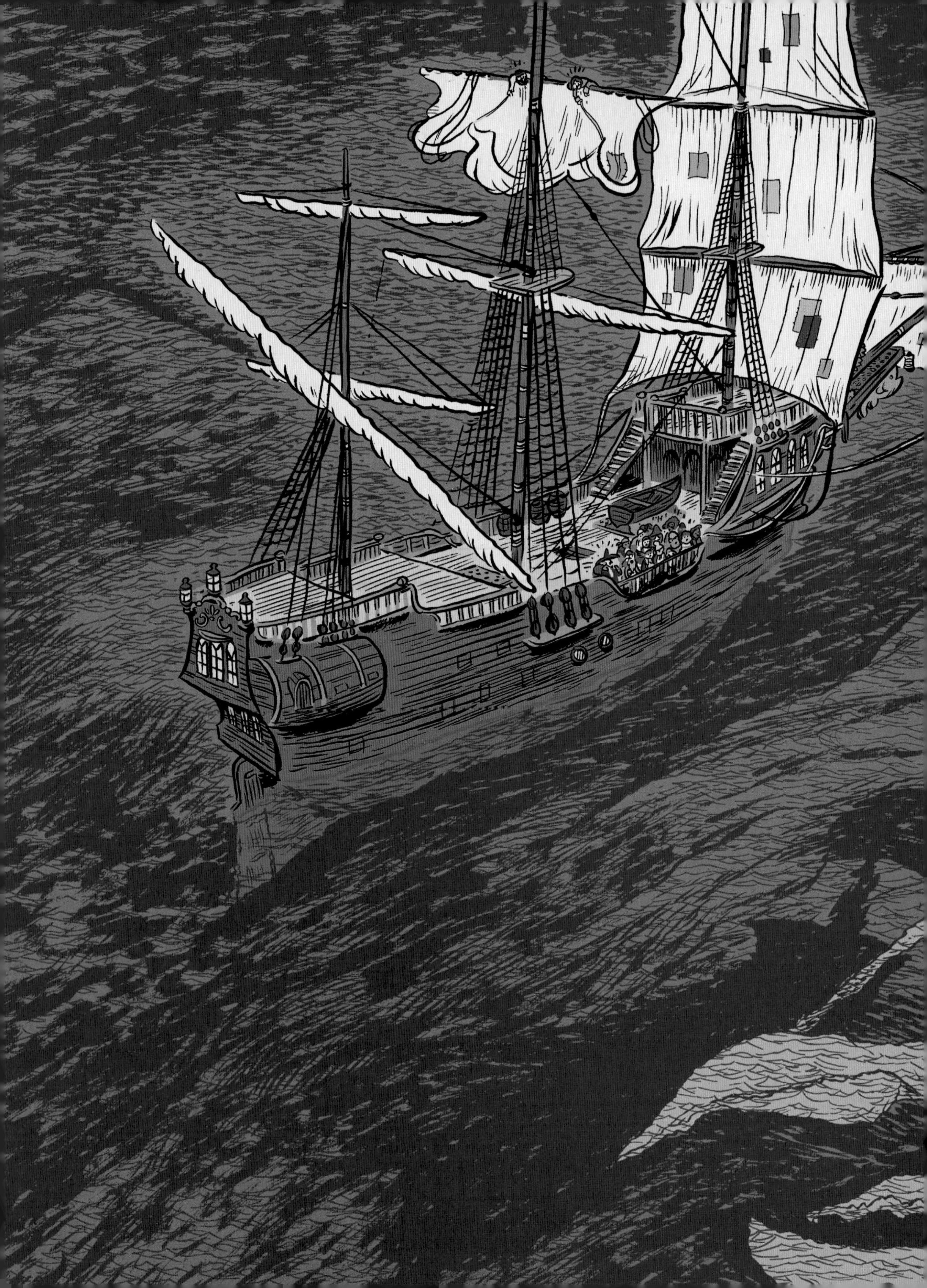

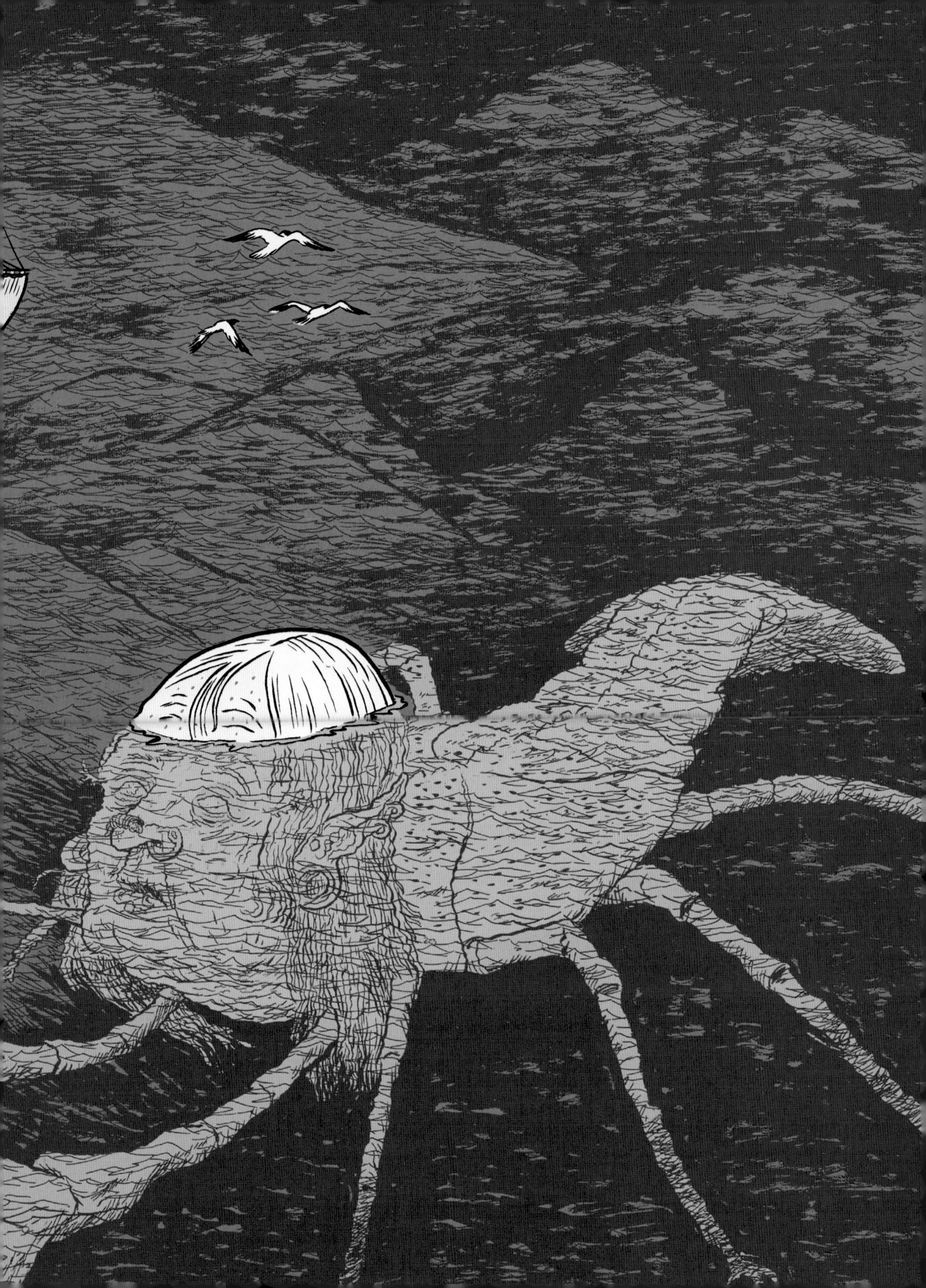

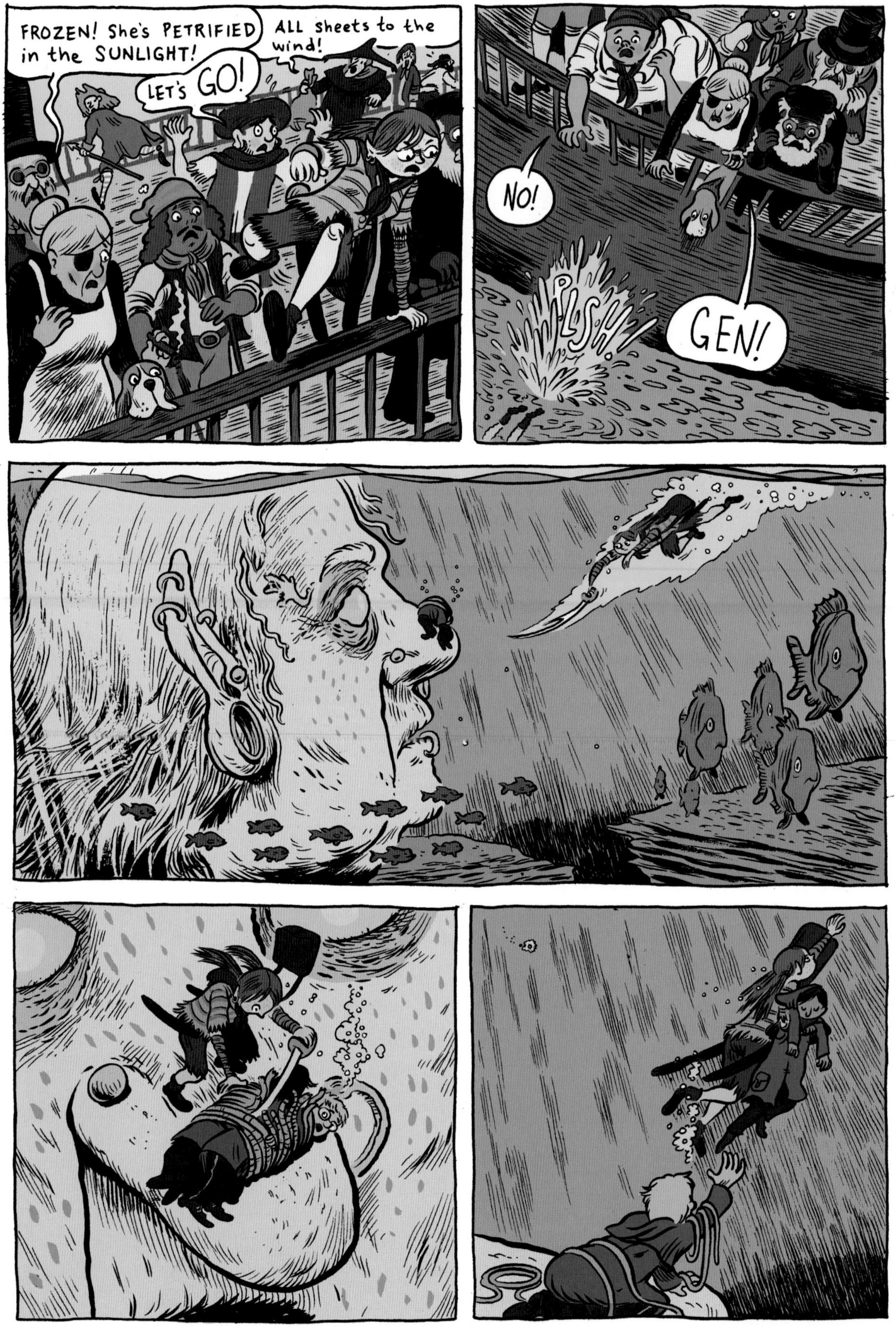
FROZEN! She's PETRIFIED in the SUNLIGHT!
ALL sheets to the wind!
LET'S GO!
NO!
PLSH!
GEN!

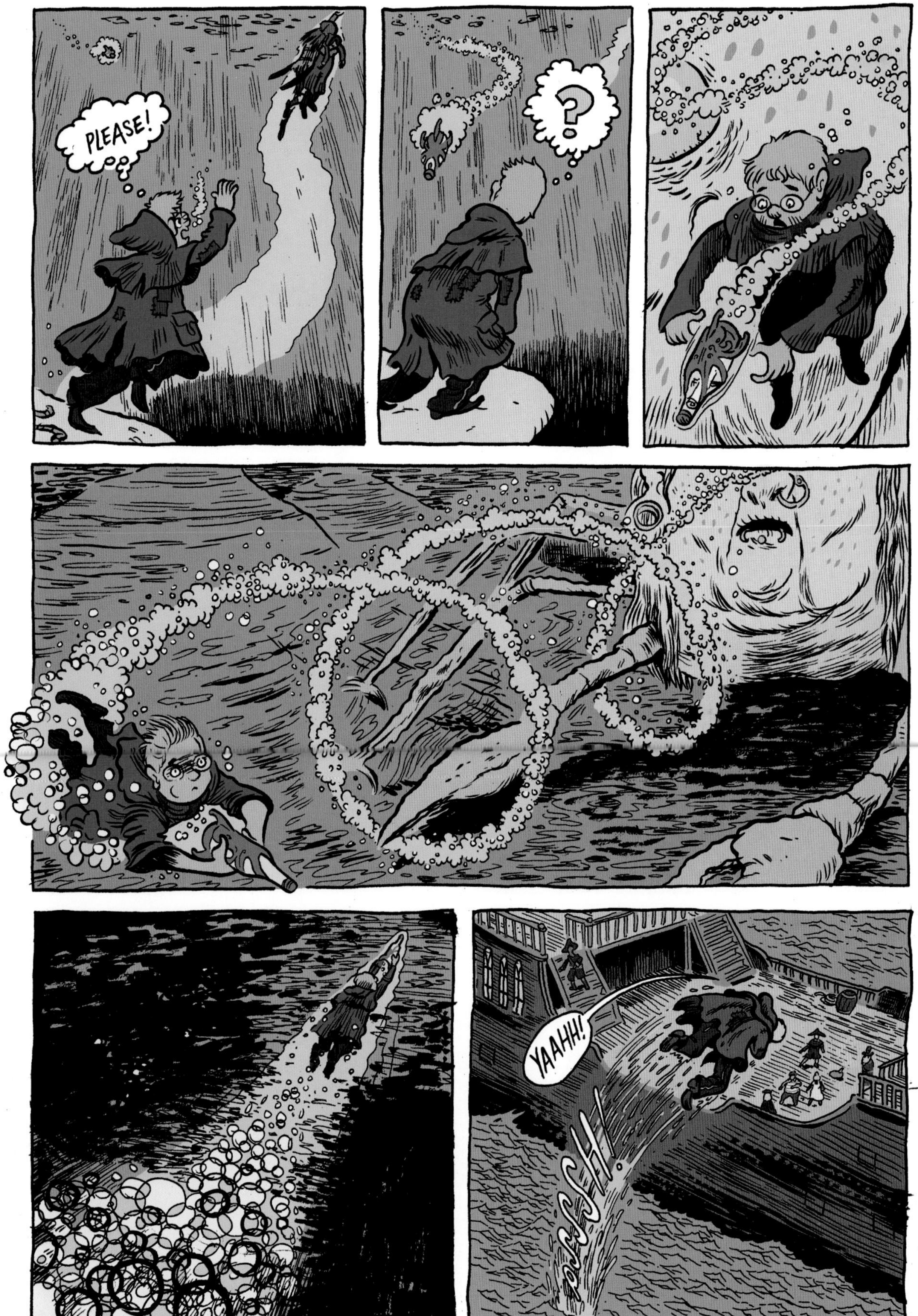
PLEASE!
?
YAAHH!
SSSSSH!

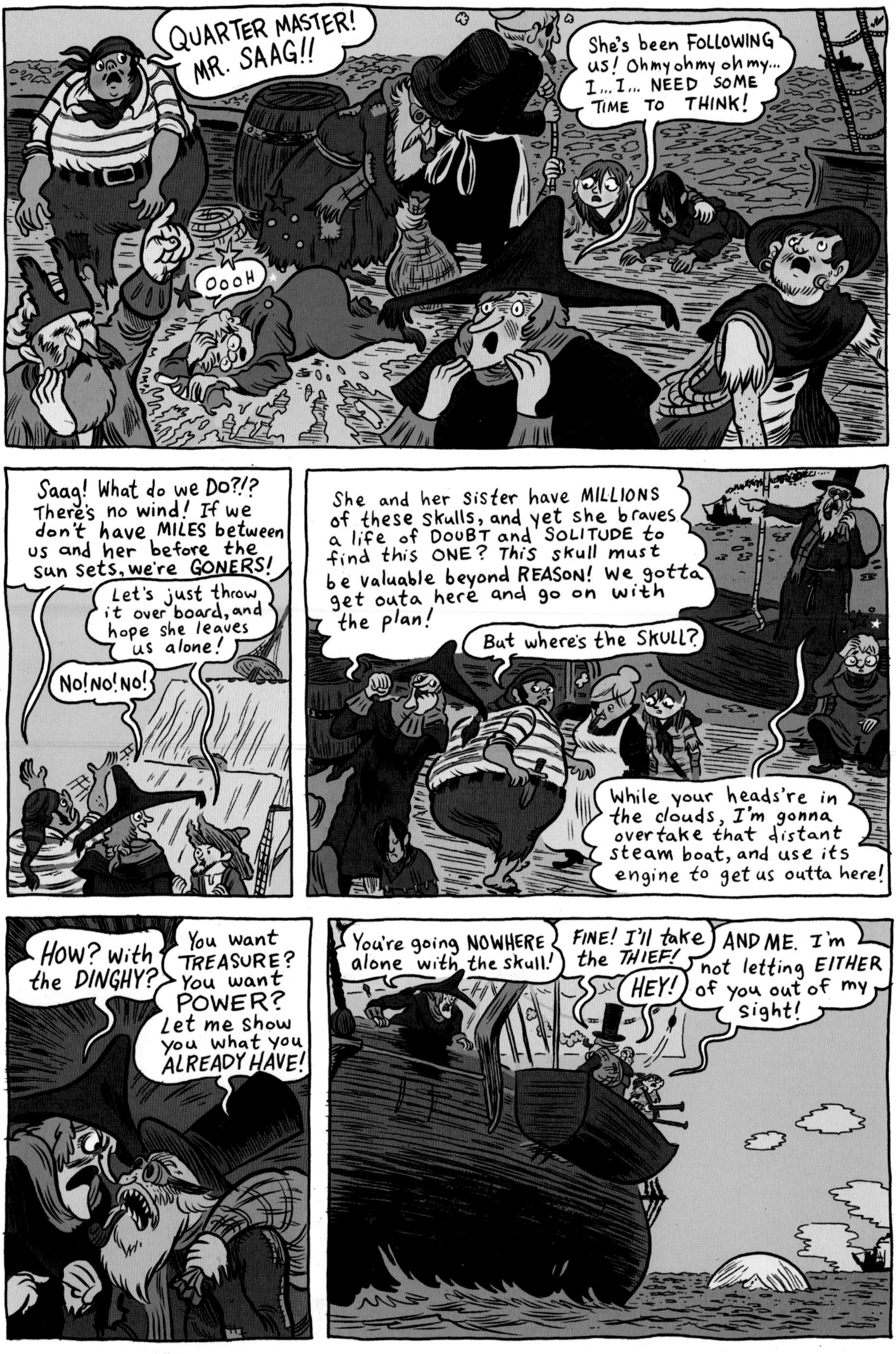
QUARTER MASTER! MR. SAAG!!
She's been FOLLOWING us! Ohmy ohmy oh my... I... I... NEED SOME TIME TO THINK!
OOOH
Saag! What do we DO?!? There's no wind! If we don't have MILES between us and her before the sun sets, we're GONERS!
Let's just throw it over board, and hope she leaves us alone!
No! No! No!
She and her sister have MILLIONS of these skulls, and yet she braves a life of DOUBT and SOLITUDE to find this ONE? This skull must be valuable beyond REASON! We gotta get outa here and go on with the plan!
But where's the SKULL?
While your heads're in the clouds, I'm gonna overtake that distant steam boat, and use its engine to get us outta here!
HOW? With the DINGHY?
You want TREASURE? You want POWER? Let me show you what you ALREADY HAVE!
You're going NOWHERE alone with the skull!
FINE! I'll take the THIEF!
HEY!
AND ME. I'm not letting EITHER of you out of my sight!

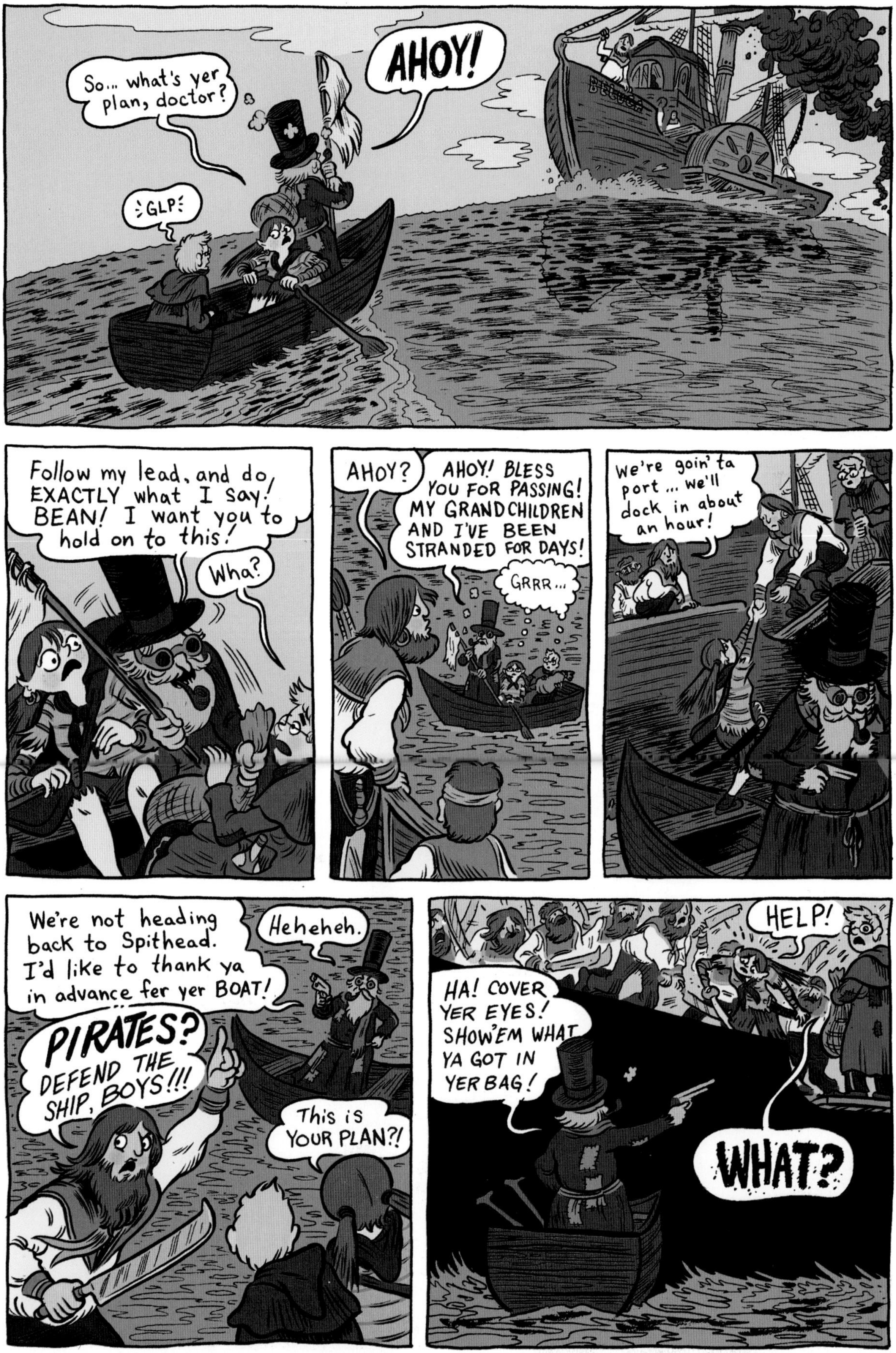
So... what's yer plan, doctor?
AHOY!
GLP
Follow my lead, and do, EXACTLY what I say! BEAN! I want you to hold on to this!
Wha?
AHOY?
AHOY! BLESS YOU FOR PASSING! MY GRANDCHILDREN AND I'VE BEEN STRANDED FOR DAYS!
GRRR...
We're goin' ta port ... we'll dock in about an hour!
We're not heading back to Spithead. I'd like to thank ya in advance fer yer BOAT!
Heheheh.
PIRATES? DEFEND THE SHIP, BOYS!!!
This is YOUR PLAN?!
HELP!
HA! COVER YER EYES! SHOW'EM WHAT YA GOT IN YER BAG!
WHAT?

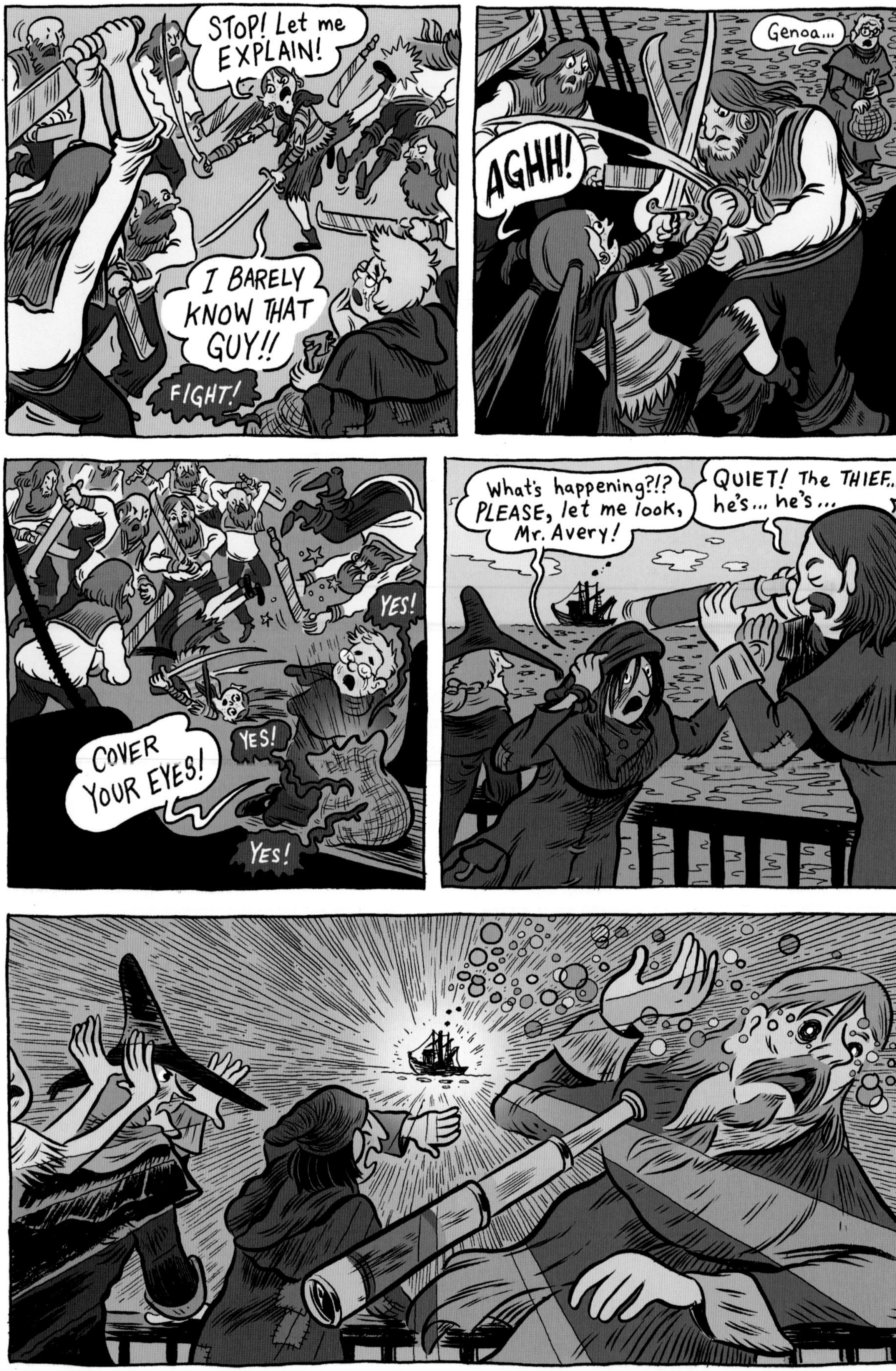
STOP! Let me EXPLAIN!
I BARELY KNOW THAT GUY!!
FIGHT!
Genoa...
AGHH!
YES!
COVER YOUR EYES!
YES!
YES!
What's happening?!? PLEASE, let me look, Mr. Avery!
QUIET! The THIEF... he's... he's...

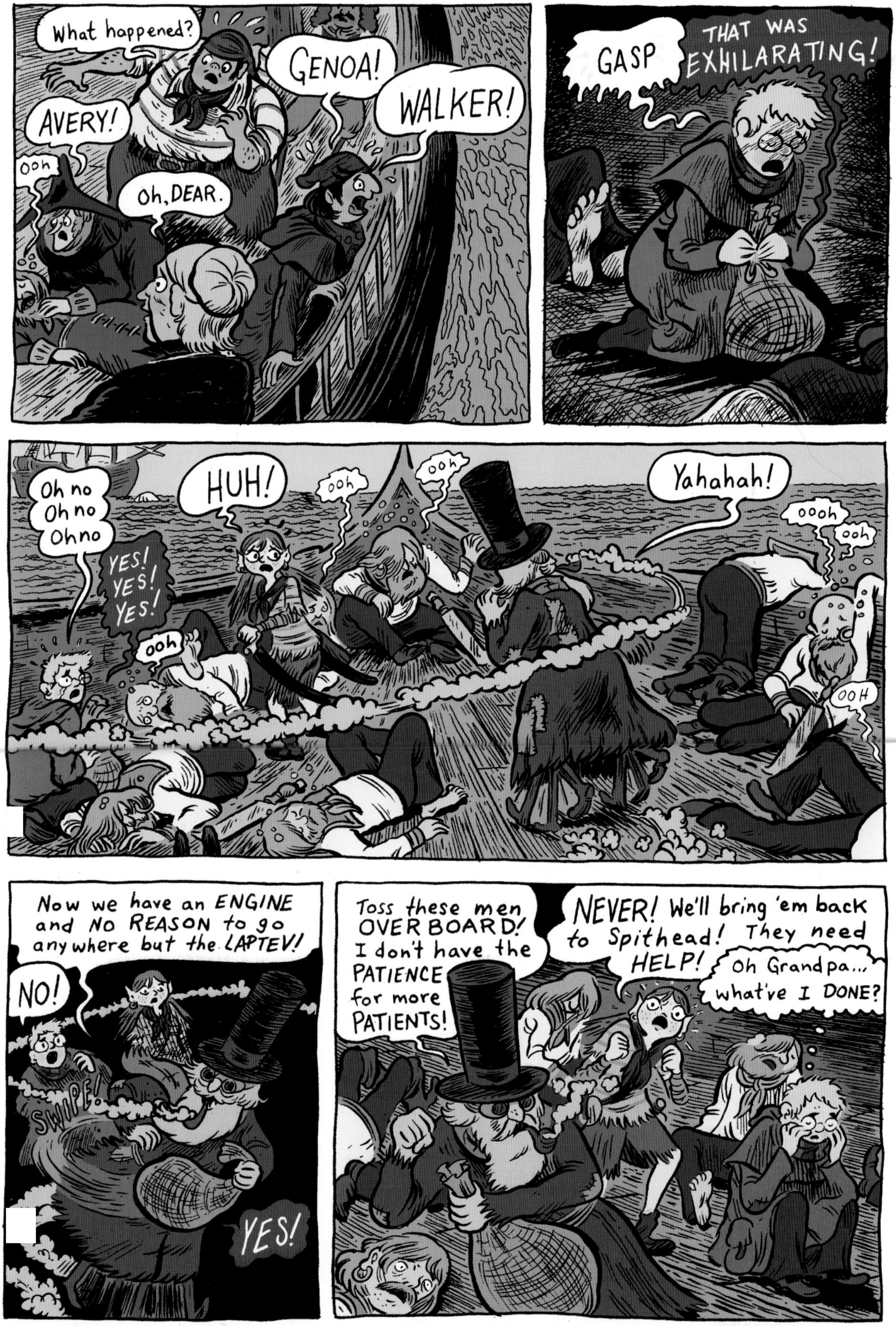
What happened?
AVERY!
GENOA!
WALKER!
ooh
Oh, DEAR.
GASP
THAT WAS EXHILARATING!
Oh no Oh no Ohno
HUH!
ooh
ooh
Yahahah!
oooh
ooh
YES! YES! YES!
ooh
OOH
Now we have an ENGINE and NO REASON to go anywhere but the LAPTEV!
NO!
SWIPE!
YES!
Toss these men OVERBOARD! I don't have the PATIENCE for more PATIENTS!
NEVER! We'll bring 'em back to Spithead! They need HELP!
Oh Grandpa... what've I DONE?

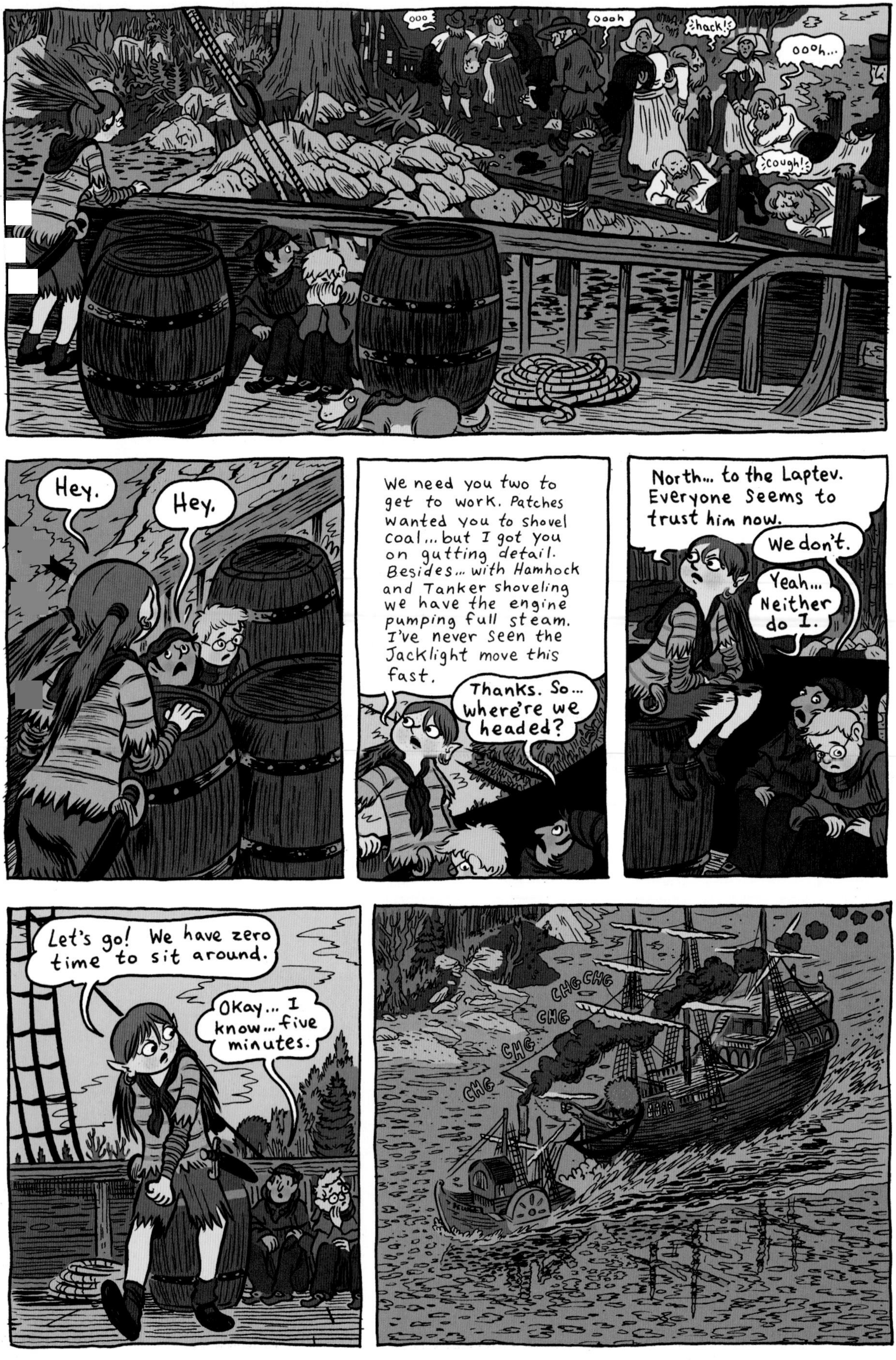
ooo
oooh
hack!
oooh...
cough!
Hey.
Hey.
We need you two to get to work. Patches wanted you to shovel coal... but I got you on gutting detail. Besides... with Hamhock and Tanker shoveling we have the engine pumping full steam. I've never seen the Jacklight move this fast.
Thanks. So... where're we headed?
North... to the Laptev. Everyone seems to trust him now.
We don't.
Yeah... Neither do I.
Let's go! We have zero time to sit around.
Okay... I know... five minutes.
CHG CHG
CHG
CHG
CHG

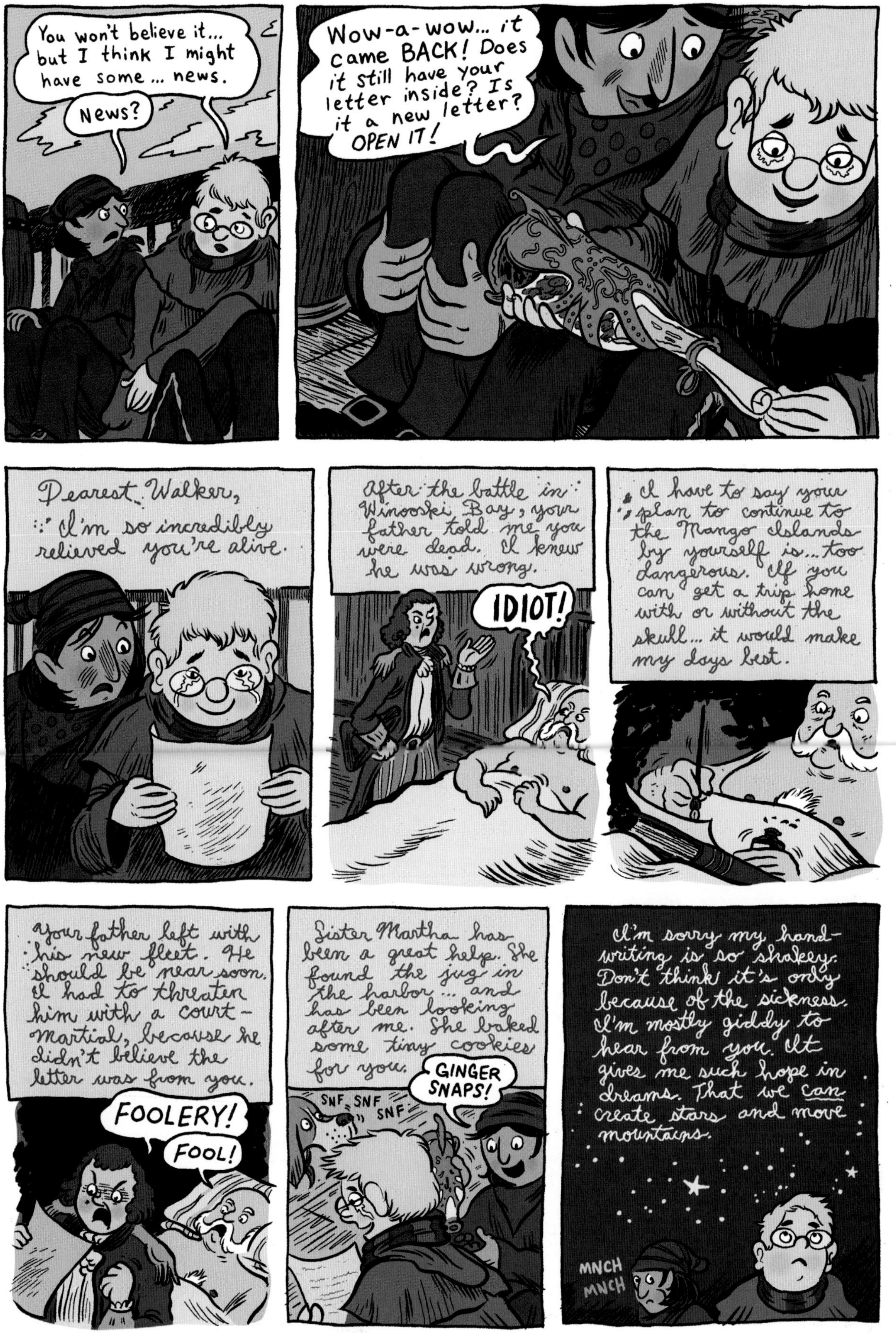

You won't believe it... but I think I might have some... news.
News?
Wow-a-wow... it came BACK! Does it still have your letter inside? Is it a new letter? OPEN IT!
Dearest Walker,
I'm so incredibly relieved you're alive.
After the battle in Winooski Bay, your father told me you were dead. I knew he was wrong.
IDIOT!
I have to say your plan to continue to the Mango Islands by yourself is... too dangerous. If you can get a trip home with or without the skull... it would make my days best.
Your father left with his new fleet. He should be near soon. I had to threaten him with a court-martial, because he didn't believe the letter was from you.
FOOLERY!
FOOL!
Sister Martha has been a great help. She found the jug in the harbor... and has been looking after me. She baked some tiny cookies for you.
GINGER SNAPS!
SNF SNF SNF
I'm sorry my handwriting is so shakey. Don't think it's only because of the sickness. I'm mostly giddy to hear from you. It gives me such hope in dreams. That we can create stars and move mountains.
MNCH MNCH

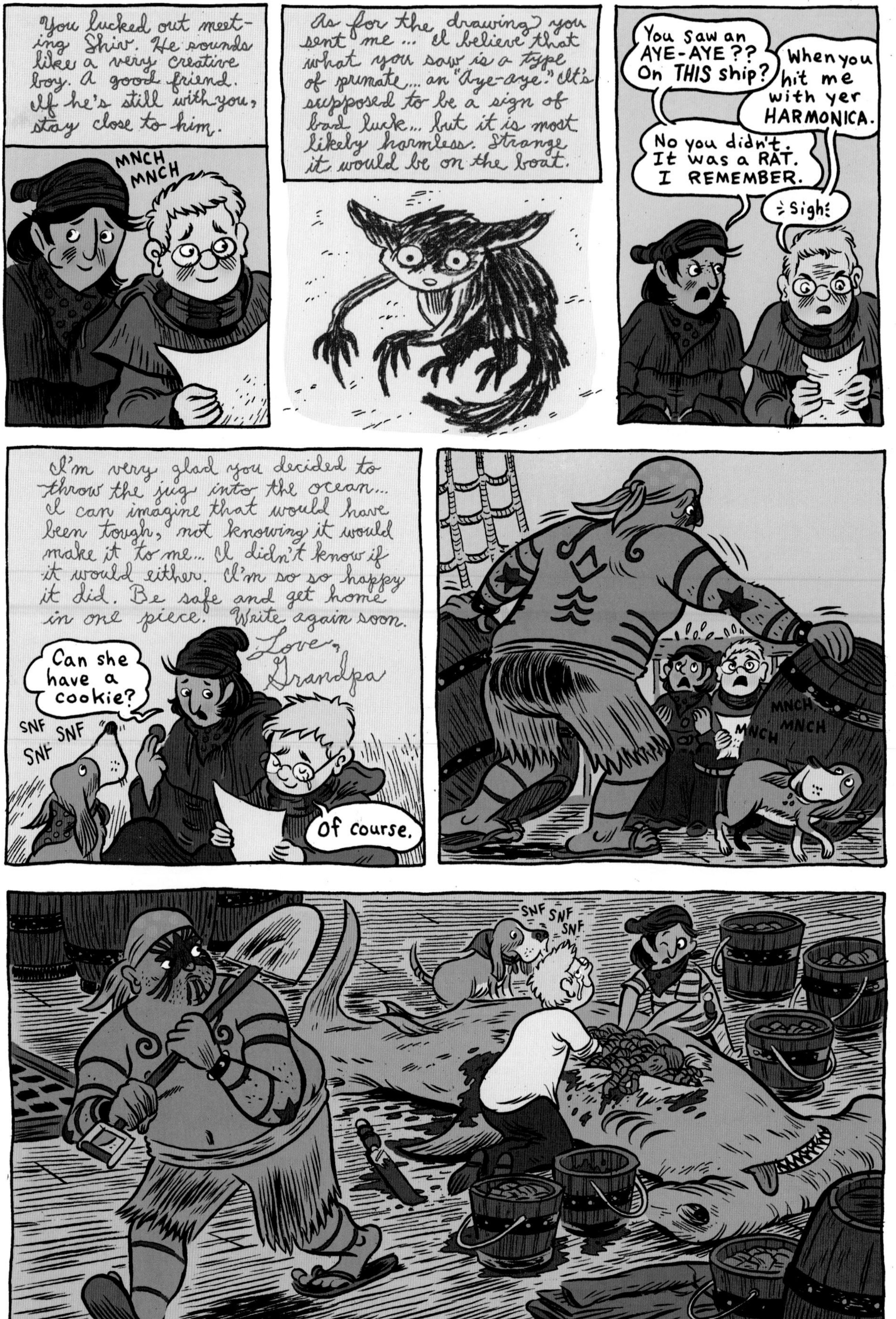
You lucked out meeting Shiv. He sounds like a very creative boy. A good friend. If he's still with you, stay close to him.
MNCH MNCH
As for the drawing you sent me... I believe that what you saw is a type of primate... an "Aye-aye." It's supposed to be a sign of bad luck... but it is most likely harmless. Strange it would be on the boat.
You saw an AYE-AYE?? On THIS ship?
When you hit me with yer HARMONICA.
No you didn't. It was a RAT. I REMEMBER.
Sigh
I'm very glad you decided to throw the jug into the ocean... I can imagine that would have been tough, not knowing it would make it to me... I didn't know if it would either. I'm so so happy it did. Be safe and get home in one piece. Write again soon.
Love,
Grandpa
Can she have a cookie?
SNF SNF SNF
Of course.
MNCH MNCH MNCH
SNF SNF SNF

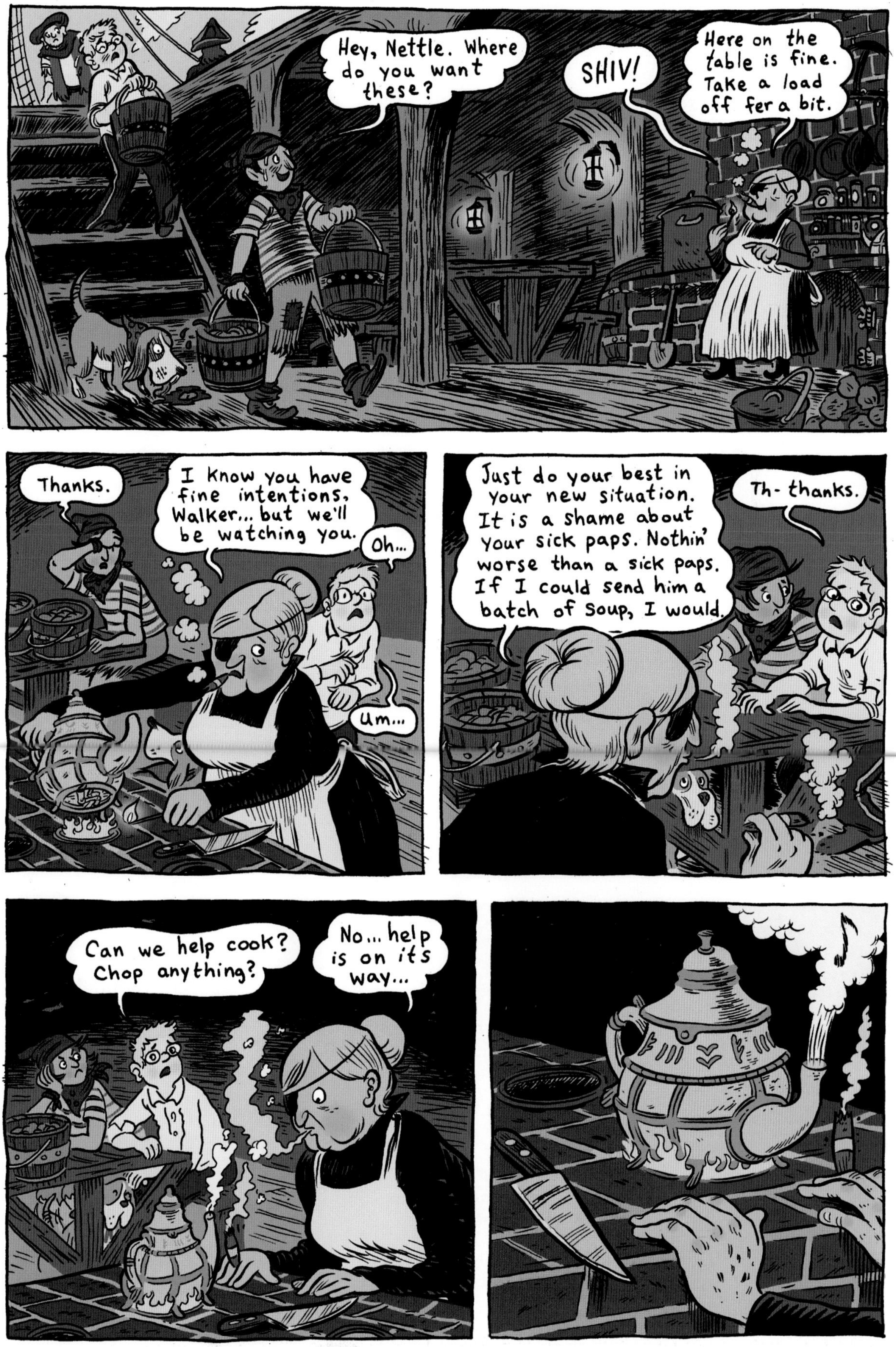
Hey, Nettle. Where do you want these?
SHIV!
Here on the table is fine. Take a load off fer a bit.
Thanks.
I know you have fine intentions, Walker... but we'll be watching you.
Oh...
Um...
Just do your best in your new situation. It is a shame about your sick paps. Nothin' worse than a sick paps. If I could send him a batch of soup, I would.
Th-thanks.
Can we help cook? Chop anything?
No... help is on its way...

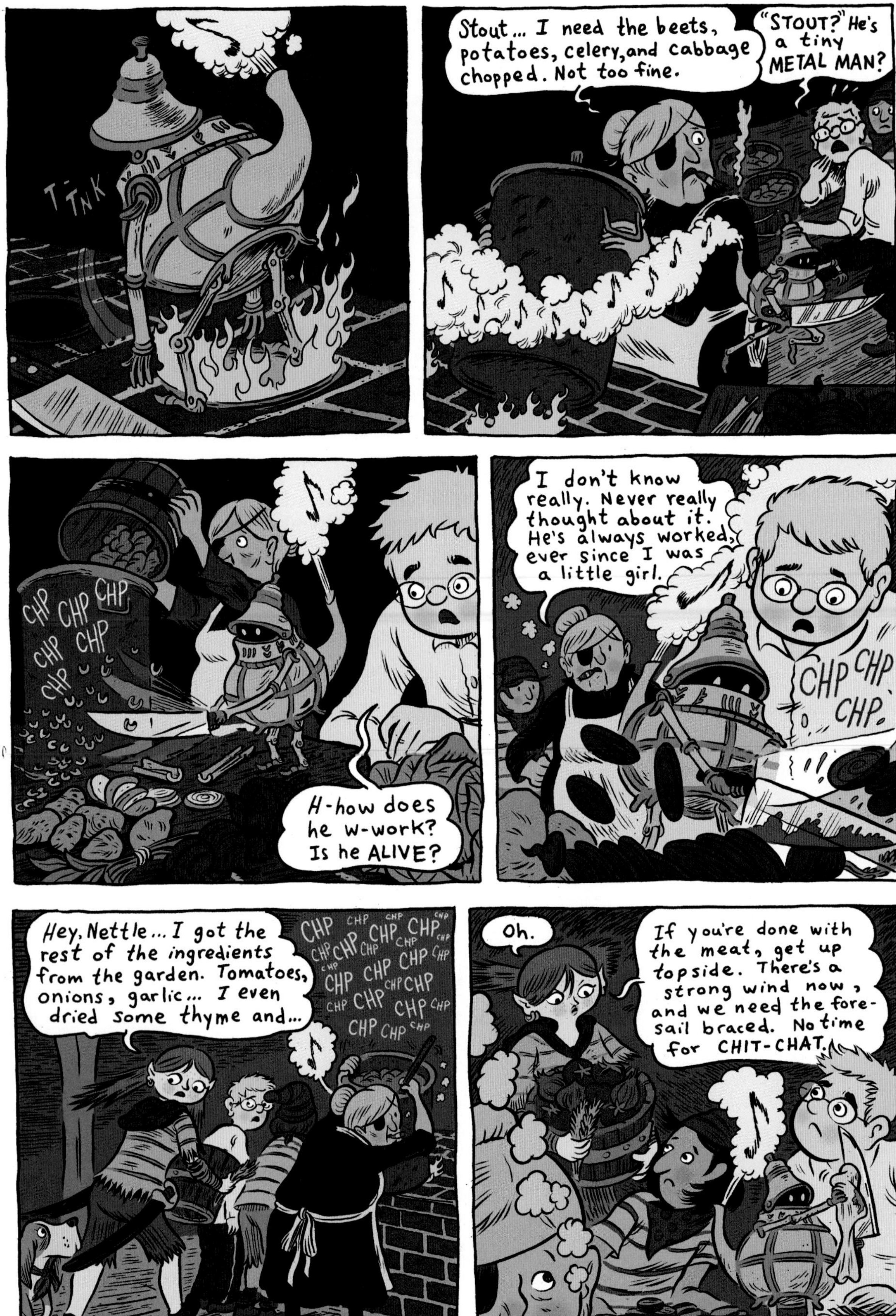
T-TNK
Stout... I need the beets, potatoes, celery, and cabbage chopped. Not too fine.
"STOUT?" He's a tiny METAL MAN?
CHP CHP CHP CHP CHP CHP
H-how does he w-work? Is he ALIVE?
I don't know really. Never really thought about it. He's always worked, ever since I was a little girl.
CHP CHP CHP
Hey, Nettle... I got the rest of the ingredients from the garden. Tomatoes, onions, garlic... I even dried some thyme and...
CHP CHP CHP CHP CHP CHP CHP CHP CHP CHP CHP CHP CHP
Oh.
If you're done with the meat, get up topside. There's a strong wind now, and we need the fore-sail braced. No time for CHIT-CHAT.

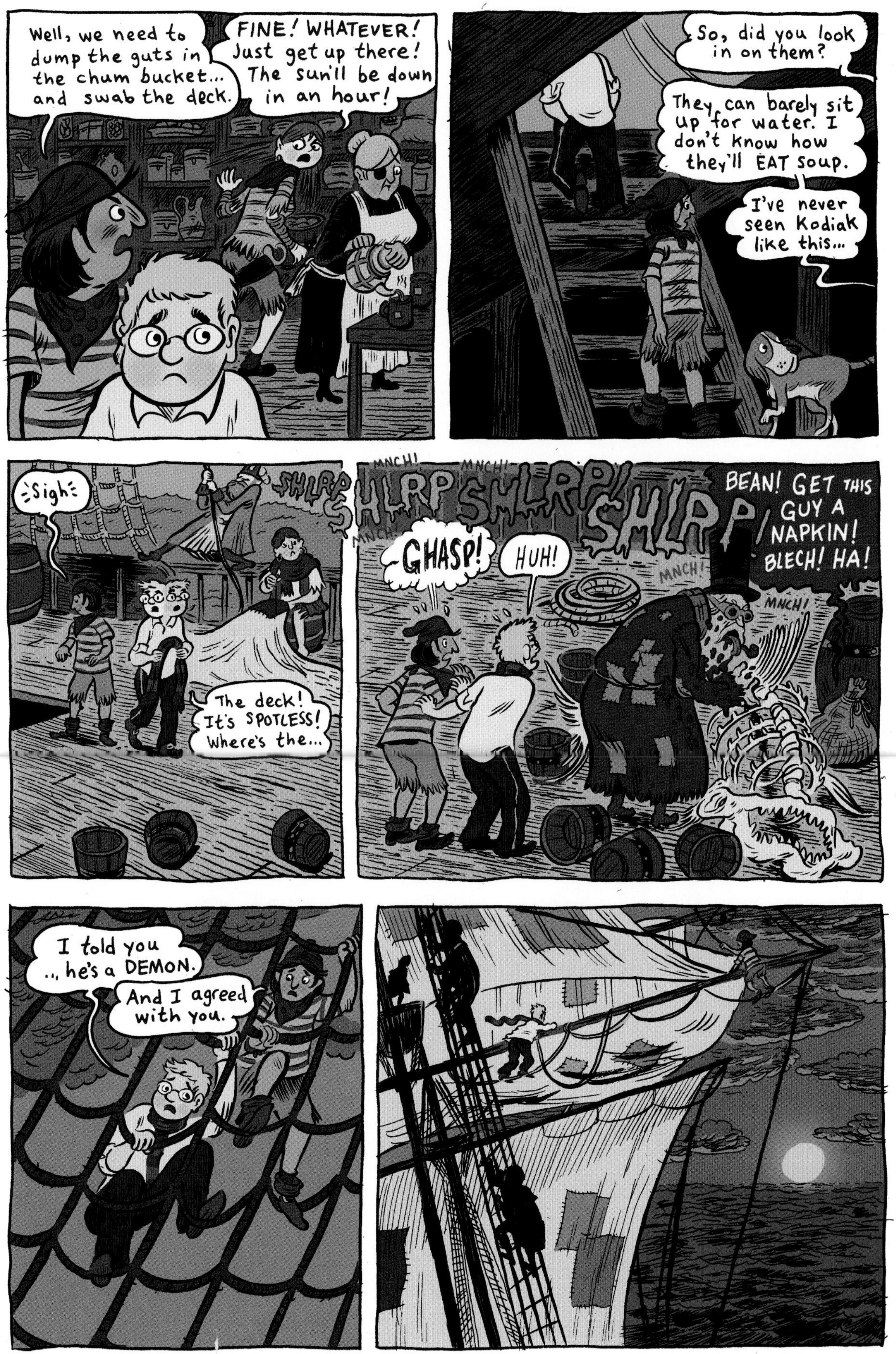

Well, we need to dump the guts in the chum bucket... and swab the deck.
FINE! WHATEVER! Just get up there! The sun'll be down in an hour!
So, did you look in on them?
They can barely sit up for water. I don't know how they'll EAT soup.
I've never seen Kodiak like this...
Sigh
The deck! It's SPOTLESS! Where's the...
SHLRP SHLRP SHLRP SHLRP!
MNCH! MNCH! MNCH!
GHASP!
HUH!
BEAN! GET THIS GUY A NAPKIN! BLECH! HA!
MNCH! MNCH!
I told you .., he's a DEMON.
And I agreed with you.

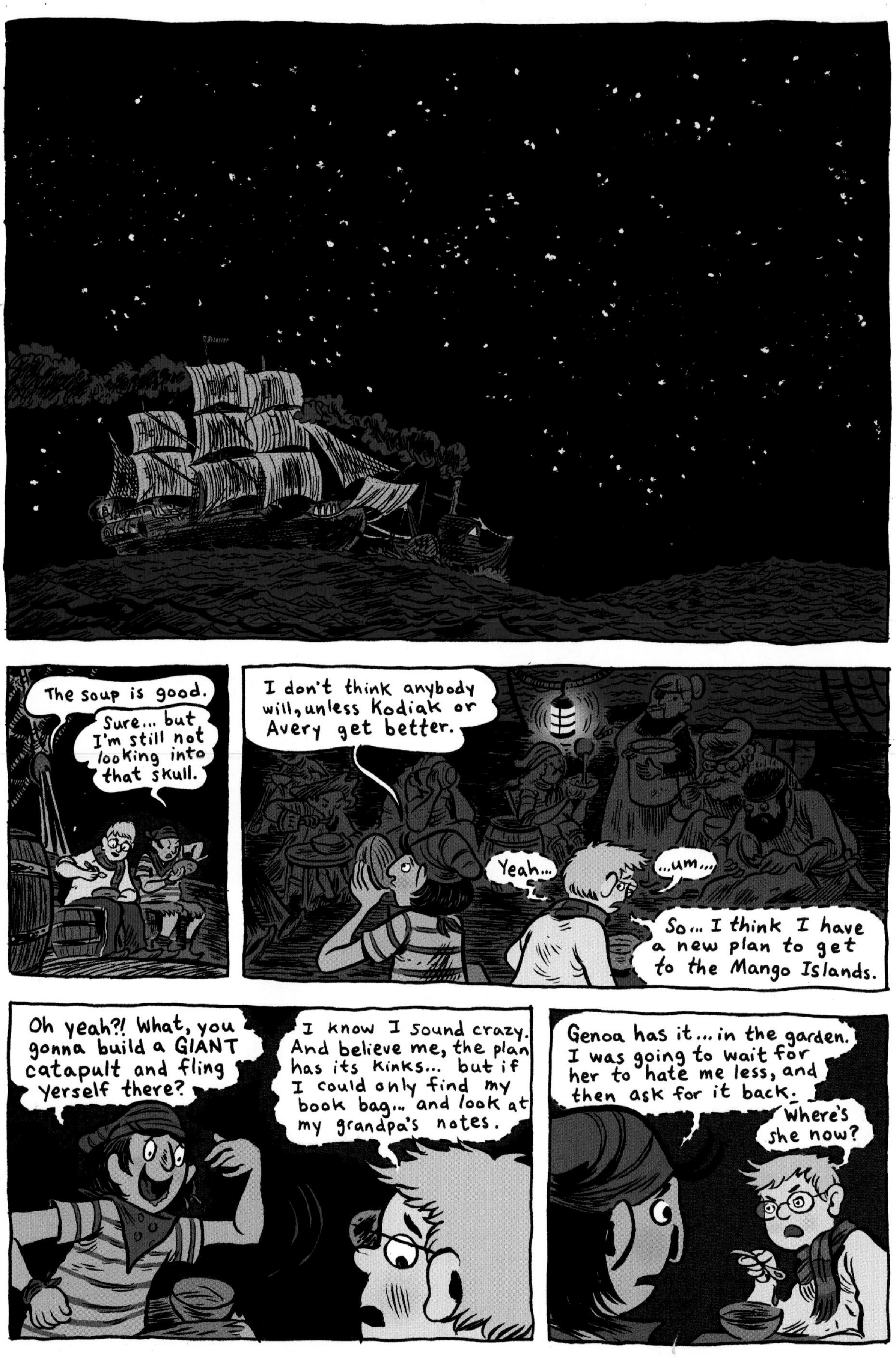
The soup is good.
Sure... but I'm still not looking into that skull.
I don't think anybody will, unless Kodiak or Avery get better.
Yeah...
...um...
So... I think I have a new plan to get to the Mango Islands.
Oh yeah?! What, you gonna build a GIANT catapult and fling yerself there?
I know I sound crazy. And believe me, the plan has its kinks... but if I could only find my book bag... and look at my grandpa's notes.
Genoa has it... in the garden. I was going to wait for her to hate me less, and then ask for it back.
Where's she now?

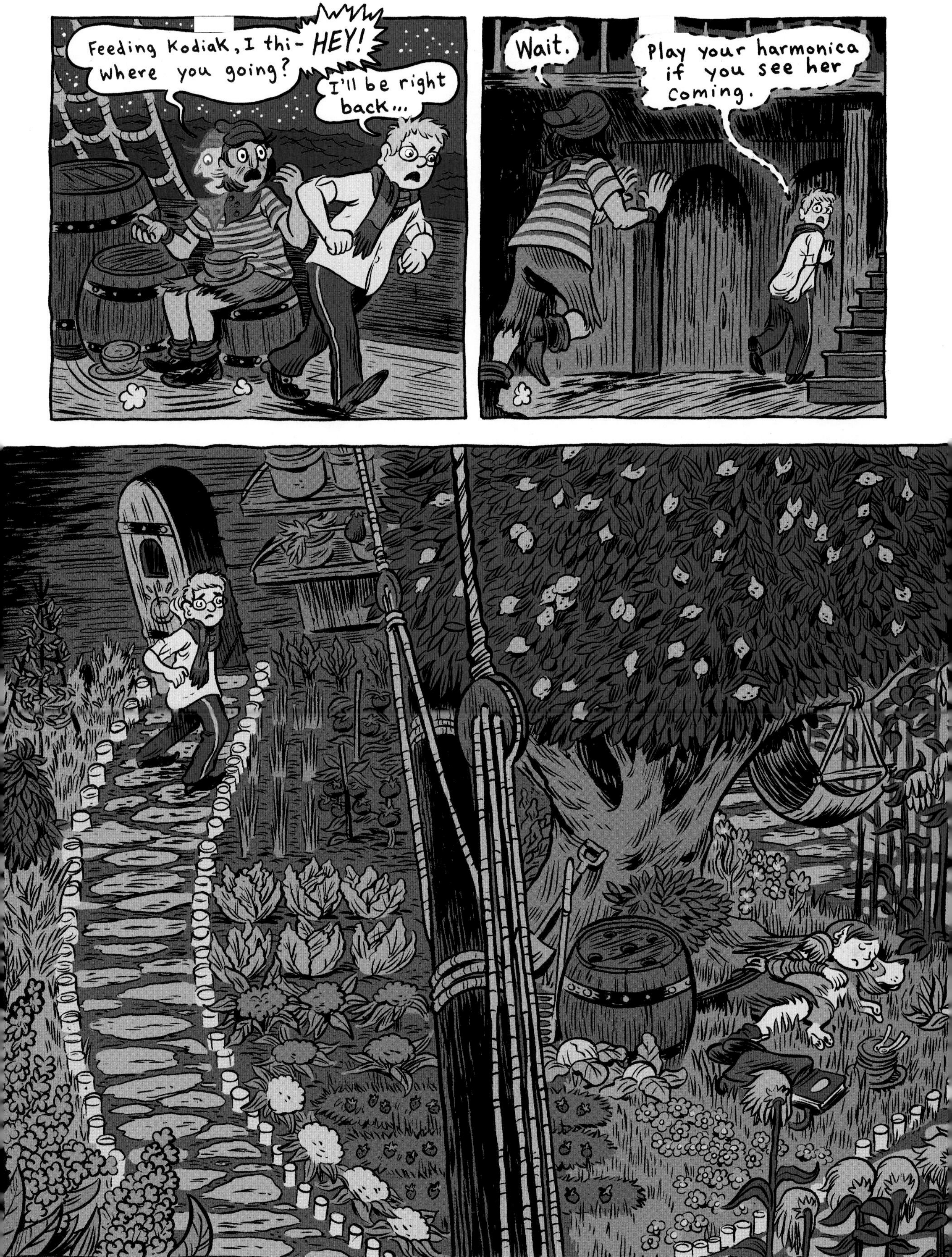
Feeding Kodiak, I thi- HEY! Where you going?
I'll be right back...
Wait.
Play your harmonica if you see her coming.

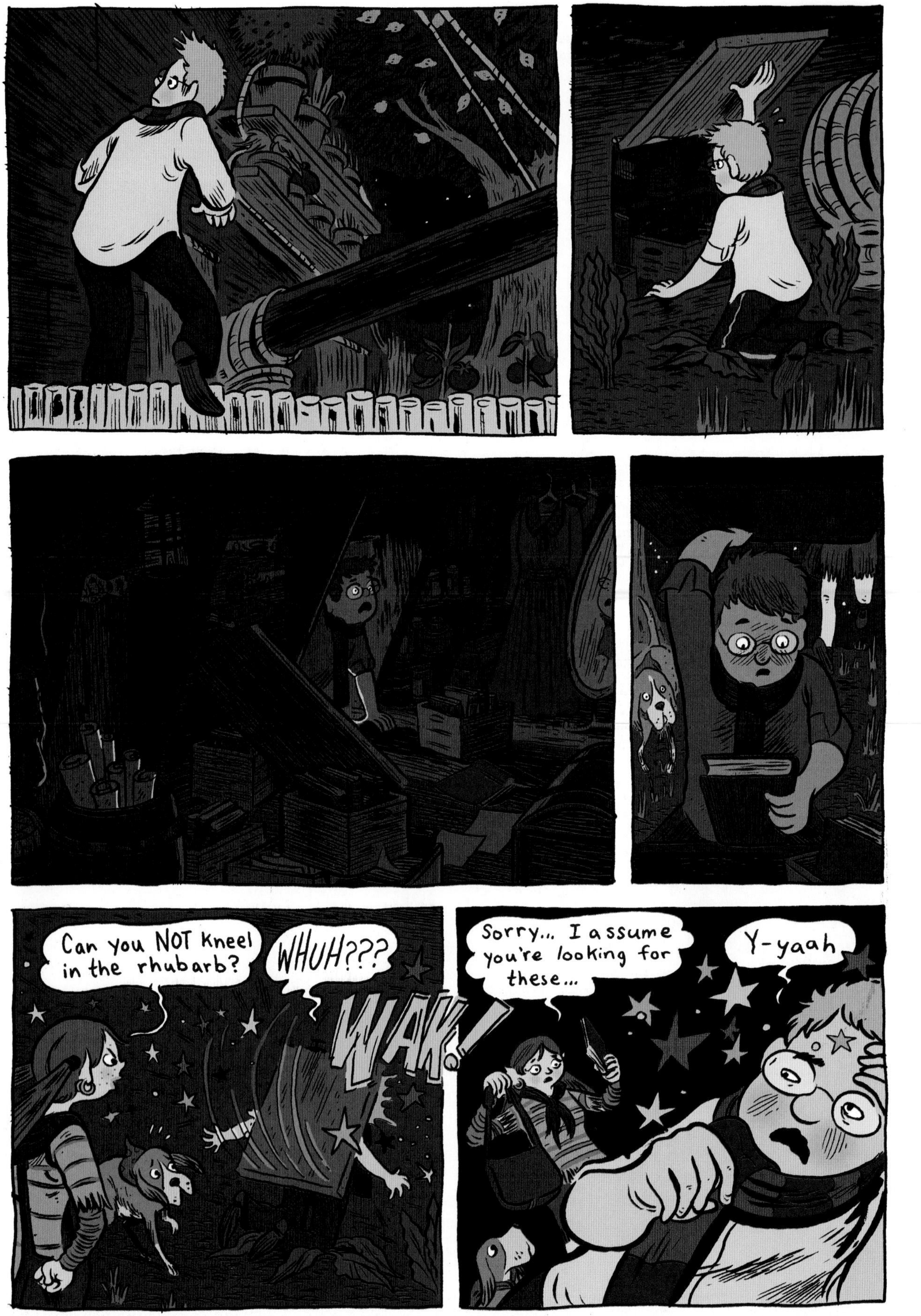

Can you NOT kneel in the rhubarb?
WHUH???
WAK!
Sorry... I assume you're looking for these...
Y-yaah

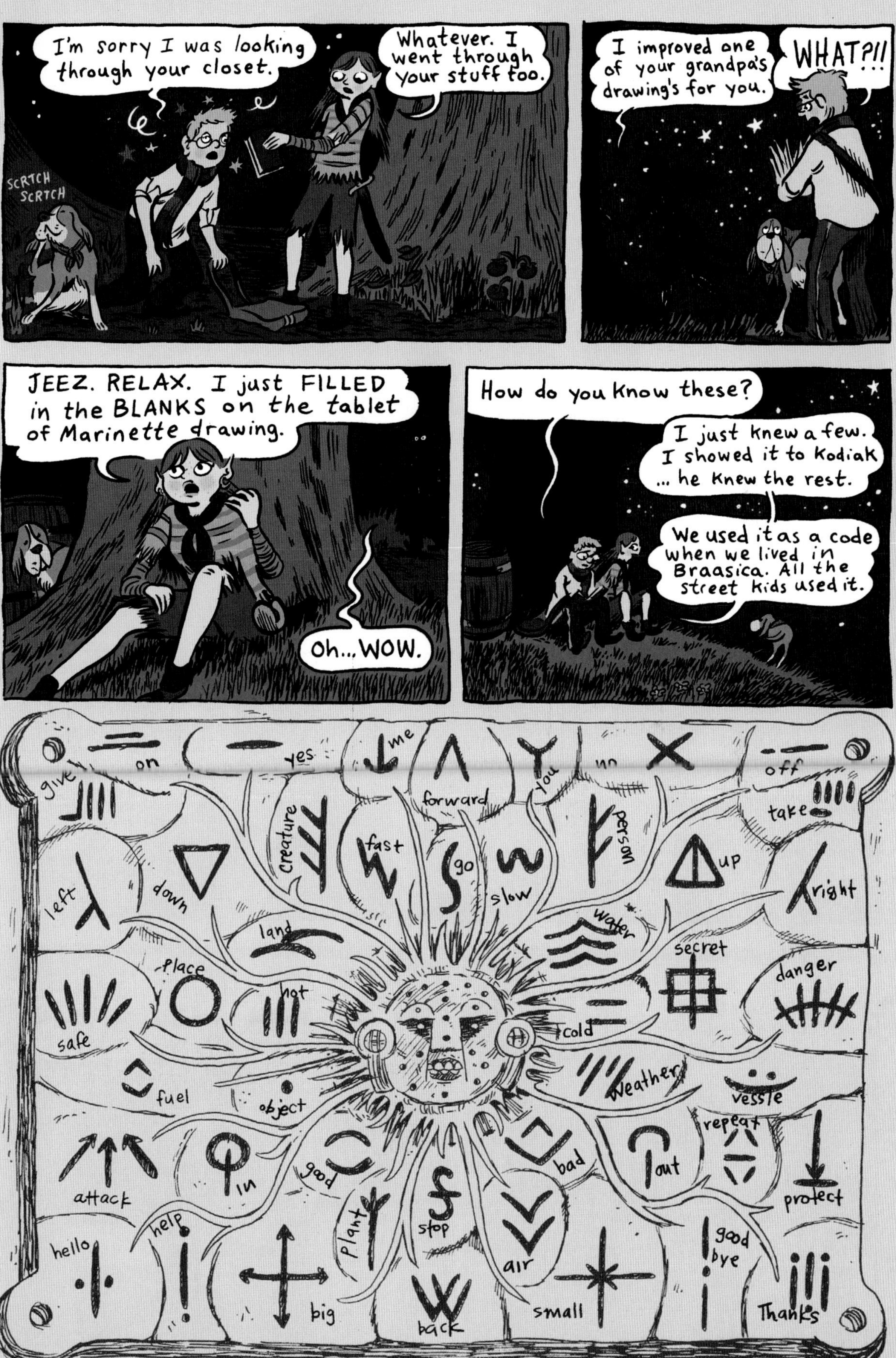
I'm sorry I was looking through your closet.
Whatever. I went through your stuff too.
SCRTCH SCRTCH
I improved one of your grandpa's drawing's for you.
WHAT?!! ...
JEEZ. RELAX. I just FILLED in the BLANKS on the tablet of Marinette drawing.
Oh... WOW.
How do you know these?
I just knew a few. I showed it to Kodiak ... he knew the rest.
We used it as a code when we lived in Braasica. All the street kids used it.
on
yes
me
no
off
give
take
forward
you
creature
fast
go
person
left
down
slow
up
right
land
water
secret
place
hot
danger
safe
cold
fuel
object
weather
vessle
repeat
attack
in
good
bad
out
protect
help
plant
stop
hello
air
good bye
big
back
small
Thanks

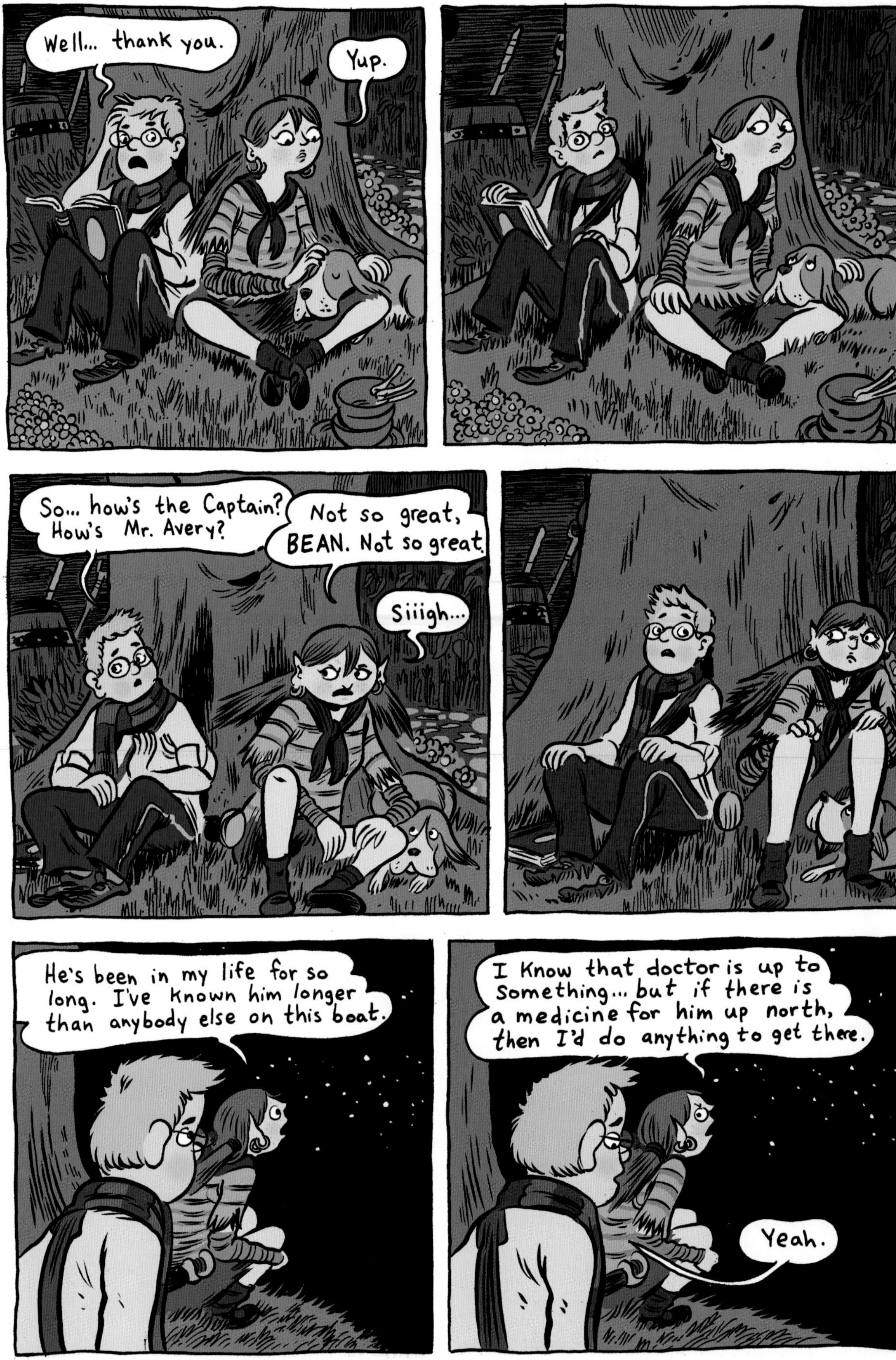
Well... thank you.
Yup.
So... how's the Captain? How's Mr. Avery?
Not so great, BEAN. Not so great.
Siiigh...
He's been in my life for so long. I've known him longer than anybody else on this boat.
I know that doctor is up to something... but if there is a medicine for him up north, then I'd do anything to get there.
Yeah.

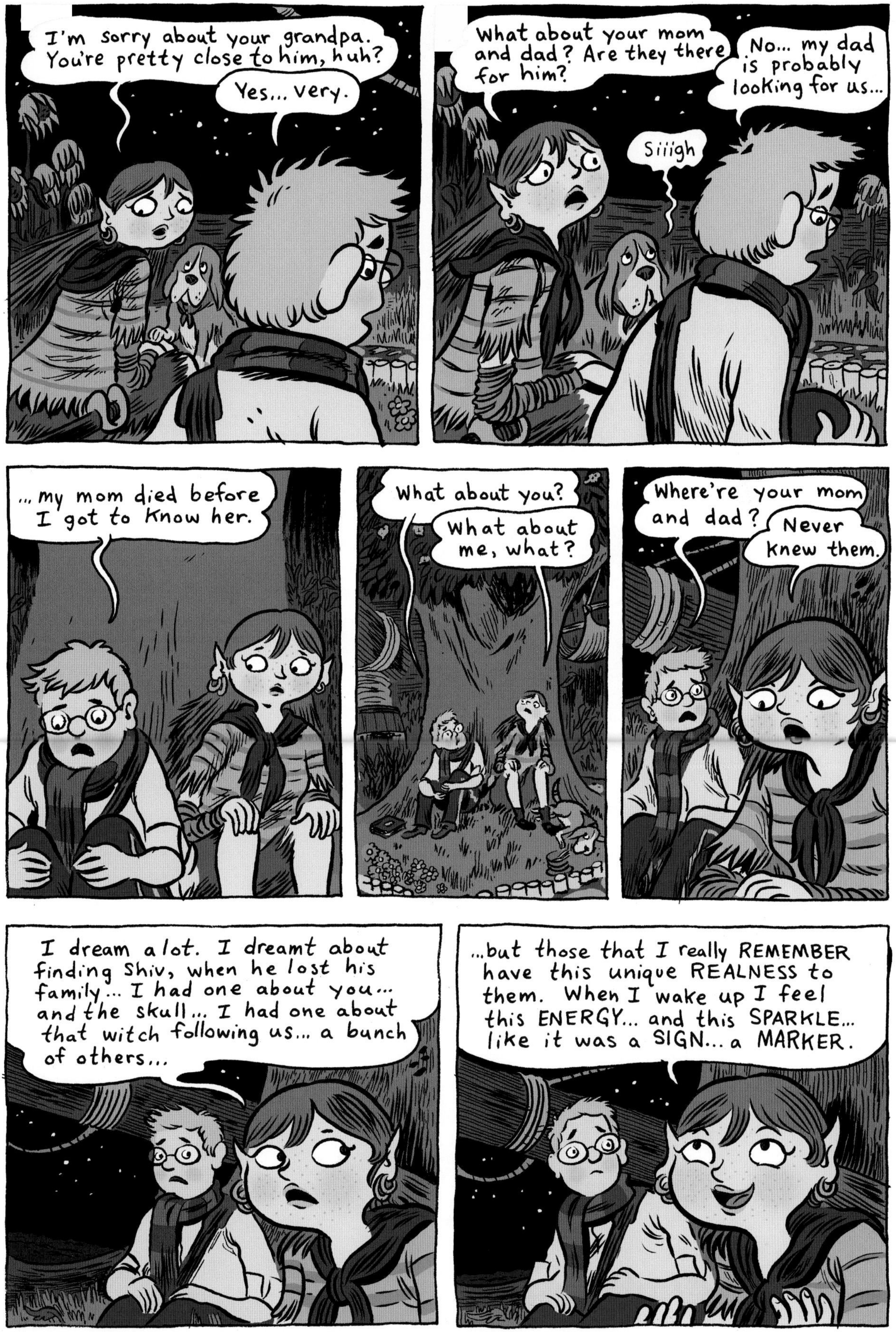
I'm sorry about your grandpa. You're pretty close to him, huh?
Yes... very.
What about your mom and dad? Are they there for him?
No... my dad is probably looking for us...
Siiigh
...my mom died before I got to know her.
What about you?
What about me, what?
Where're your mom and dad?
Never knew them.
I dream a lot. I dreamt about finding Shiv, when he lost his family... I had one about you... and the skull... I had one about that witch following us... a bunch of others...
...but those that I really REMEMBER have this unique REALNESS to them. When I wake up I feel this ENERGY... and this SPARKLE... like it was a SIGN... a MARKER.

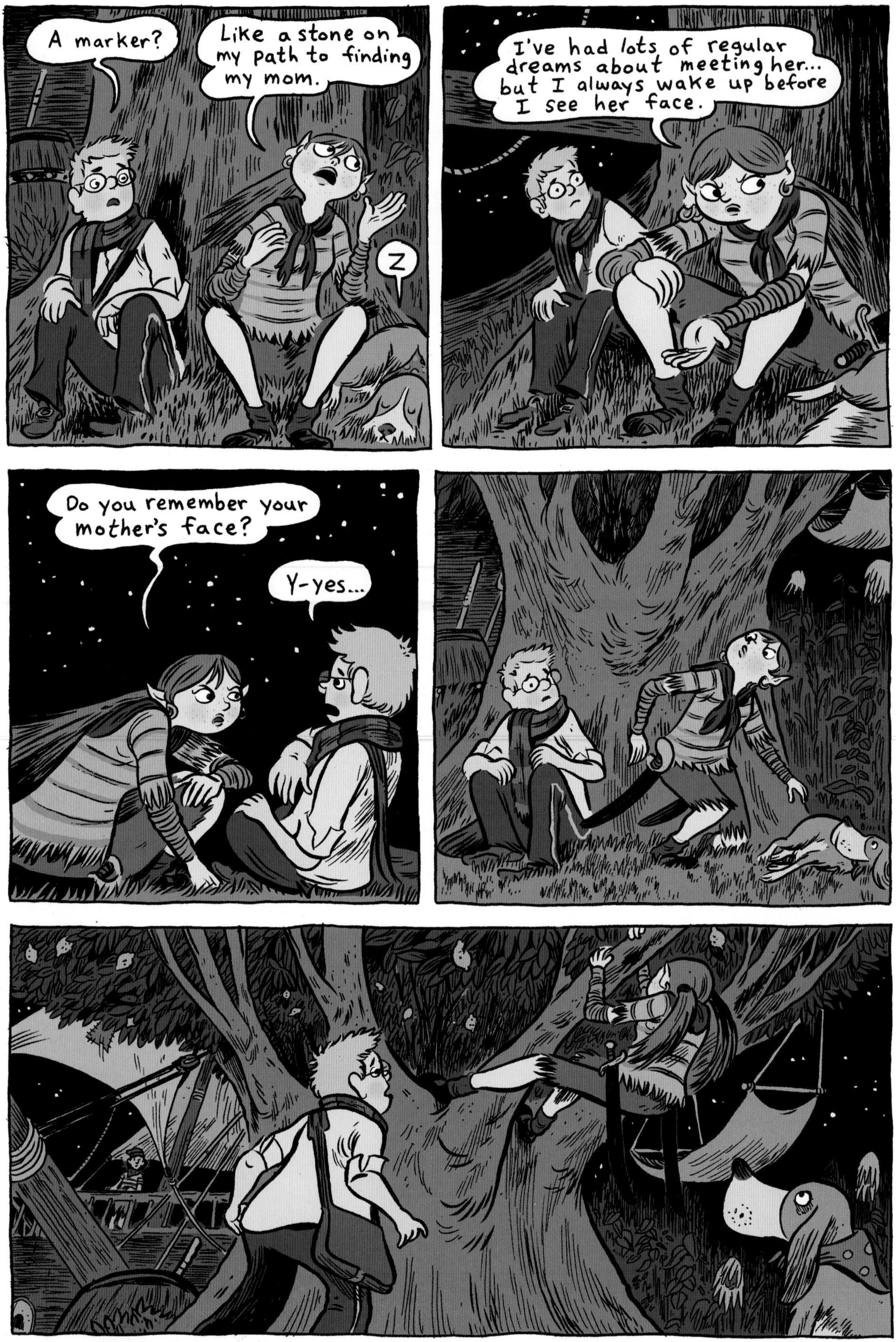
A marker?
Like a stone on my path to finding my mom.
Z
I've had lots of regular dreams about meeting her... but I always wake up before I see her face.
Do you remember your mother's face?
Y-yes...

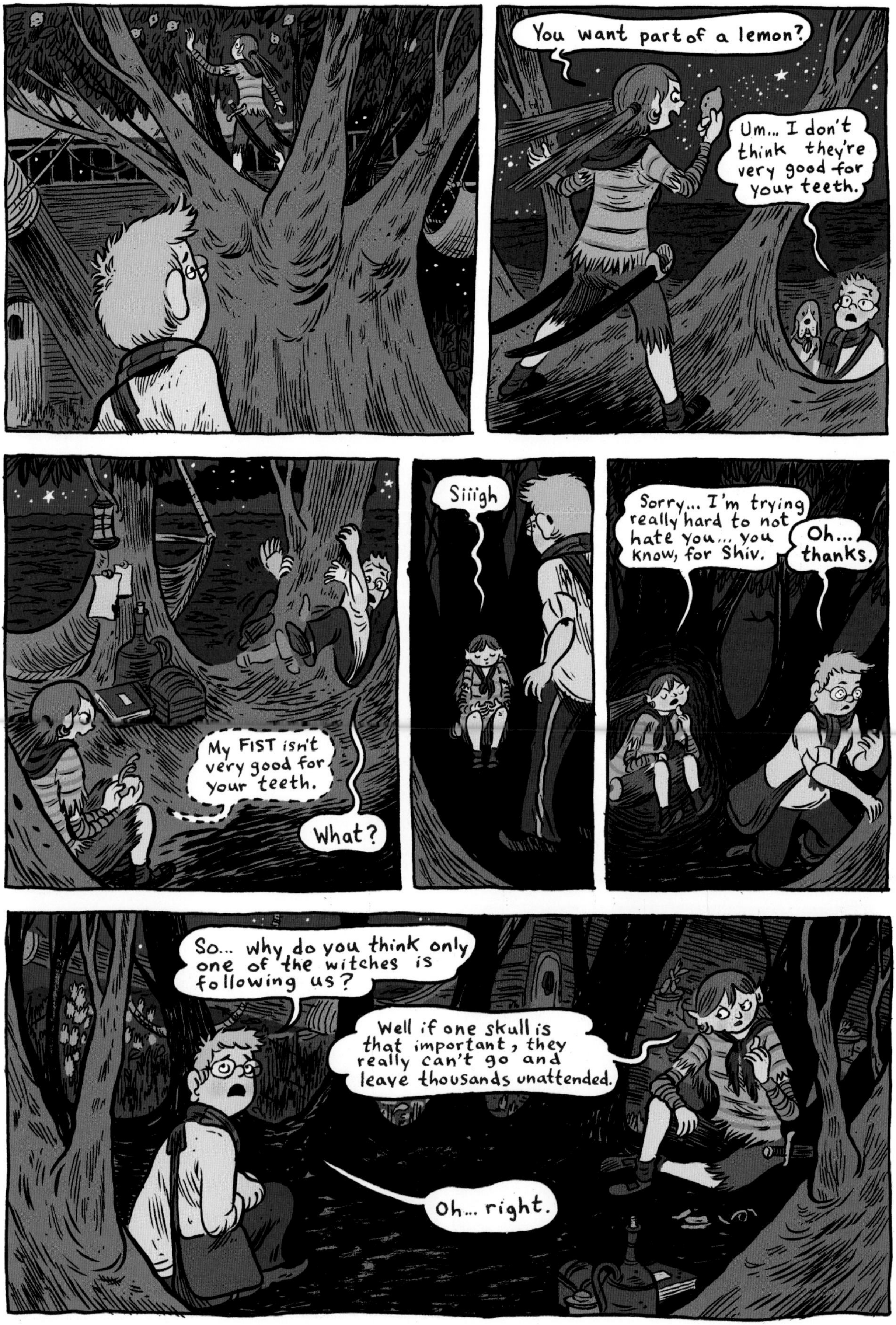
You want part of a lemon?
Um... I don't think they're very good for your teeth.
My FIST isn't very good for your teeth.
What?
Siiigh
Sorry... I'm trying really hard to not hate you... you know, for Shiv.
Oh... thanks.
So... why do you think only one of the witches is following us?
Well if one skull is that important, they really can't go and leave thousands unattended.
Oh... right.

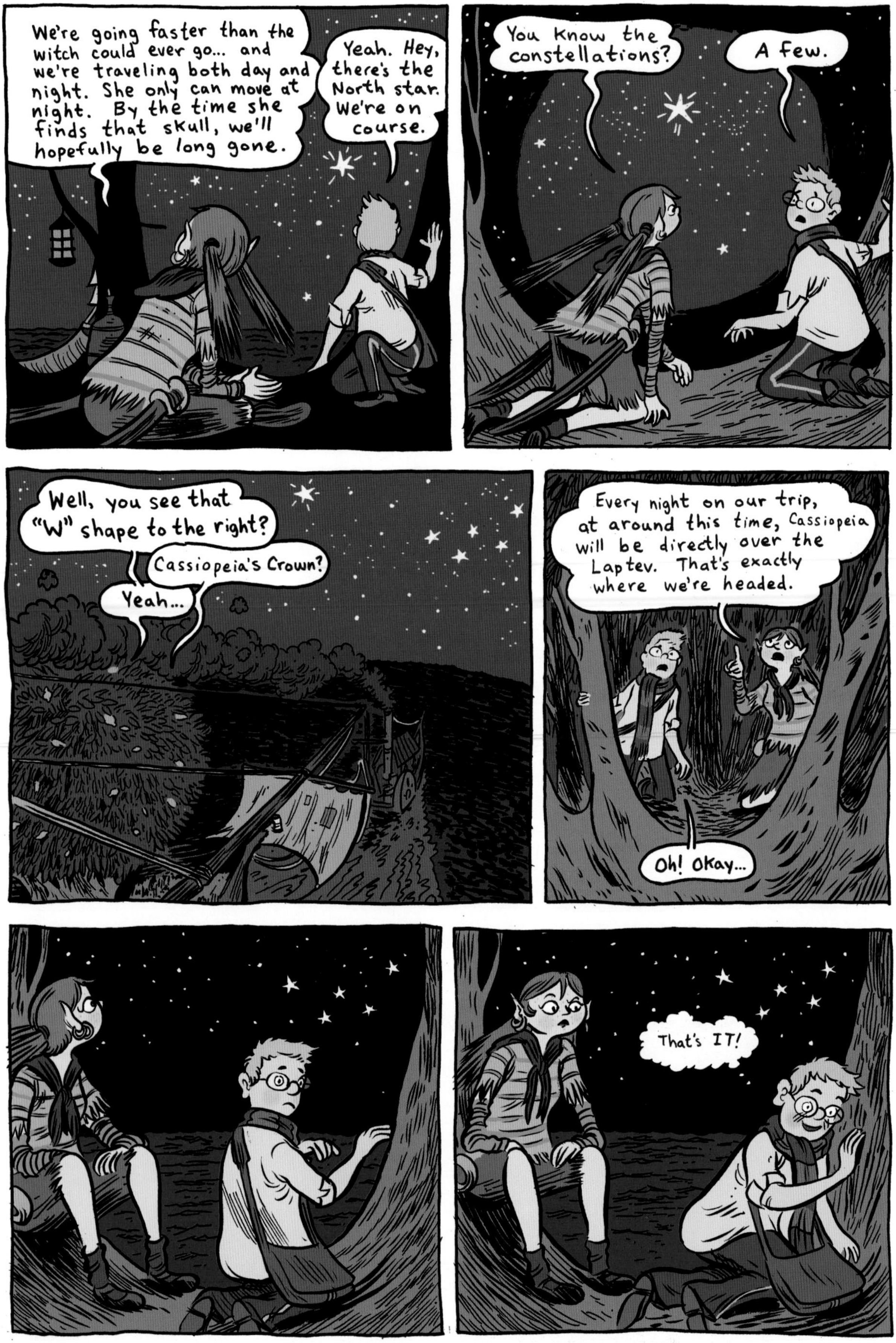
We're going faster than the witch could ever go... and we're traveling both day and night. She only can move at night. By the time she finds that skull, we'll hopefully be long gone.
Yeah. Hey, there's the North star. We're on course.
You know the constellations?
A few.
Well, you see that "W" shape to the right?
Cassiopeia's Crown?
Yeah...
Every night on our trip, at around this time, Cassiopeia will be directly over the Laptev. That's exactly where we're headed.
Oh! Okay...
That's IT!

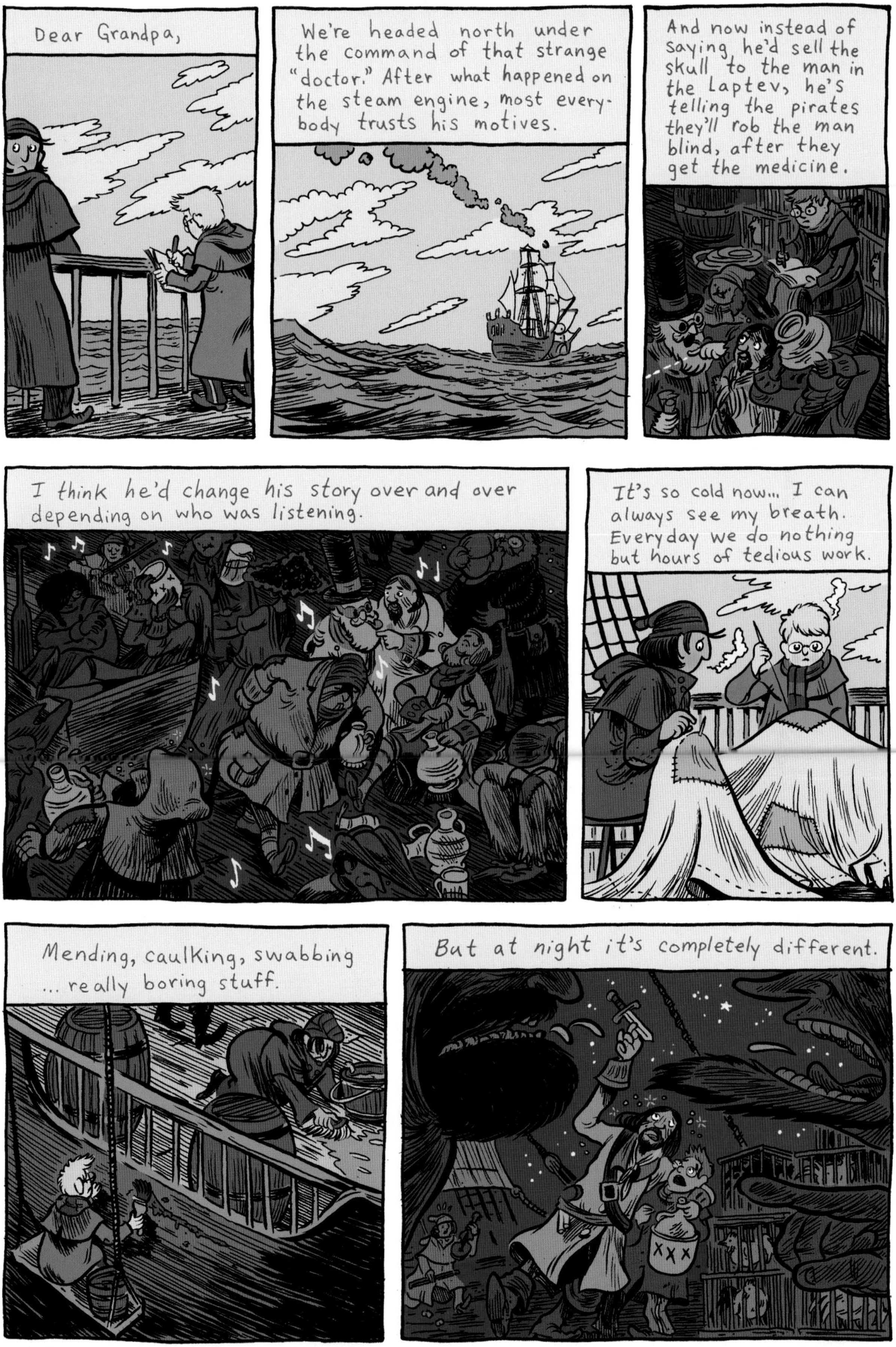

Dear Grandpa,
We're headed north under the command of that strange "doctor." After what happened on the steam engine, most every-body trusts his motives.
And now instead of saying he'd sell the skull to the man in the Laptev, he's telling the pirates they'll rob the man blind, after they get the medicine.
I think he'd change his story over and over depending on who was listening.
It's so cold now... I can always see my breath. Everyday we do nothing but hours of tedious work.
Mending, caulking, swabbing ... really boring stuff.
But at night it's completely different.
XXX

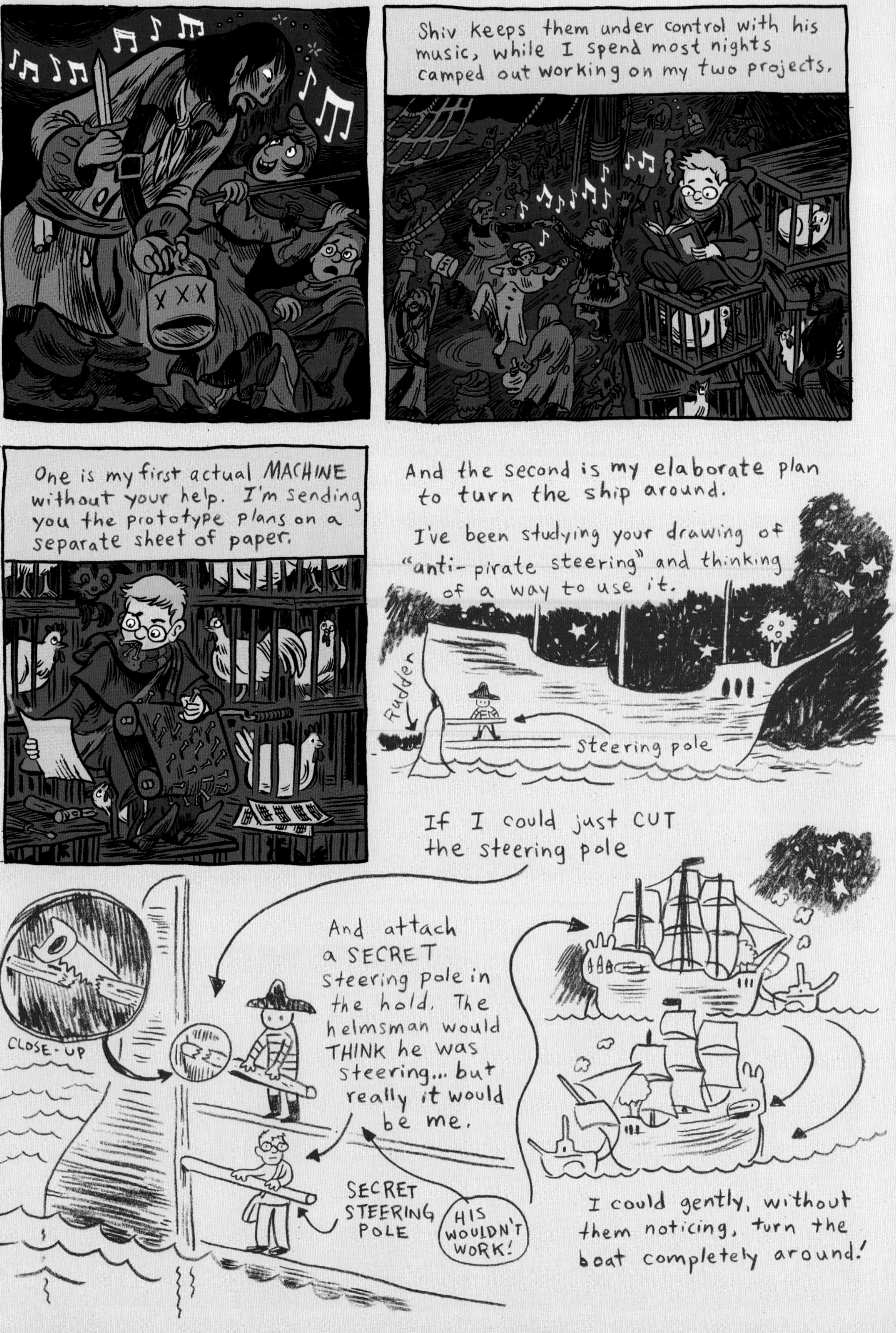
Shiv keeps them under control with his music, while I spend most nights camped out working on my two projects.
One is my first actual MACHINE without your help. I'm sending you the prototype plans on a separate sheet of paper.
And the second is my elaborate plan to turn the ship around.
I've been studying your drawing of "anti-pirate steering" and thinking of a way to use it.
Rudder
steering pole
If I could just CUT the steering pole
CLOSE-UP
And attach a SECRET steering pole in the hold. The helmsman would THINK he was steering... but really it would be me.
SECRET STEERING POLE
HIS WOULDN'T WORK!
I could gently, without them noticing, turn the boat completely around!

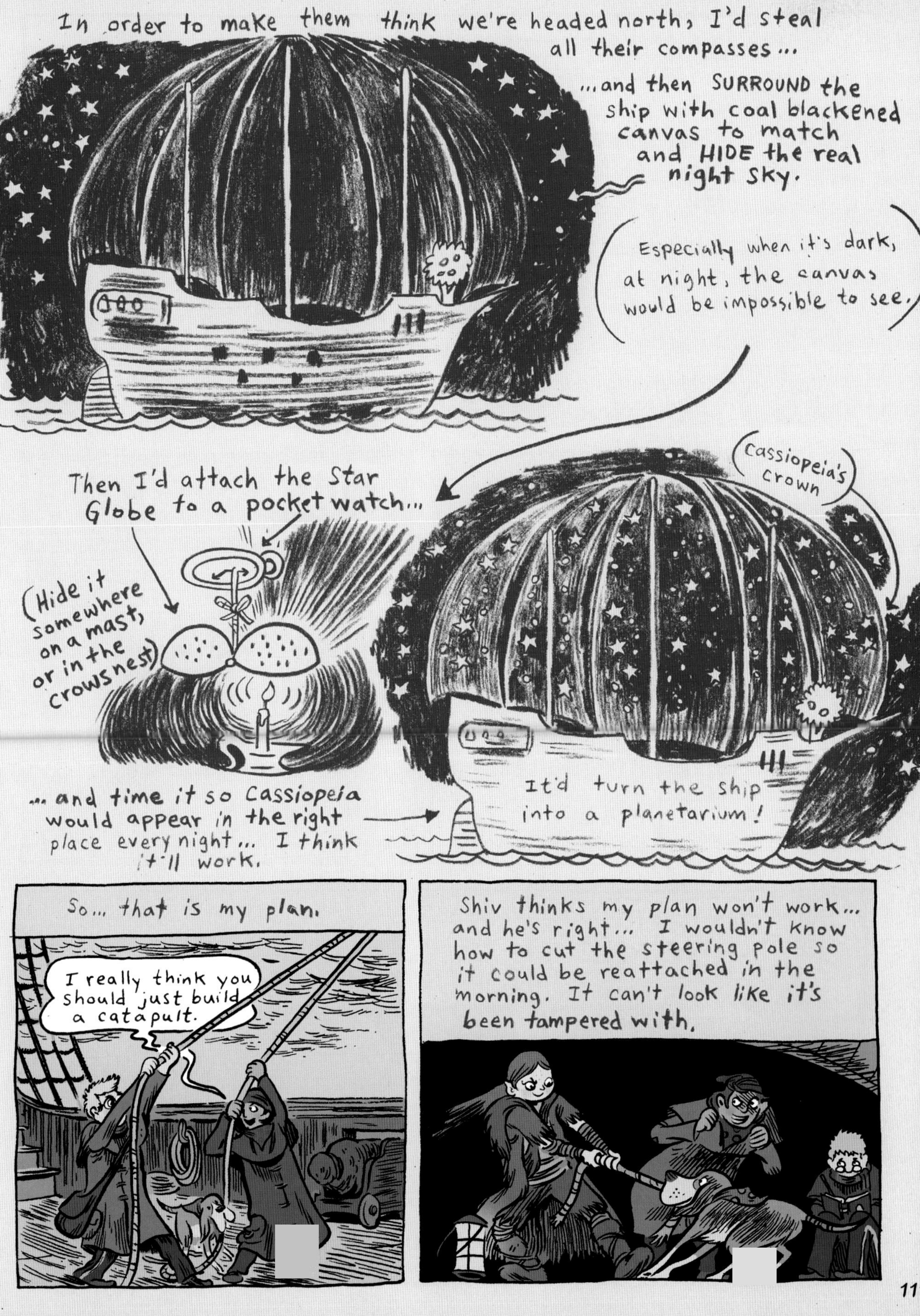

In order to make them think we're headed north, I'd steal all their compasses...
...and then SURROUND the ship with coal blackened canvas to match and HIDE the real night sky.
Especially when it's dark, at night, the canvas would be impossible to see.
Then I'd attach the Star Globe to a pocket watch...
(Hide it somewhere on a mast, or in the crowsnest)
(Cassiopeia's Crown)
...and time it so Cassiopeia would appear in the right place every night... I think it'll work.
It'd turn the ship into a planetarium!
So... that is my plan.
I really think you should just build a catapult.
Shiv thinks my plan won't work... and he's right... I wouldn't know how to cut the steering pole so it could be reattached in the morning. It can't look like it's been tampered with.

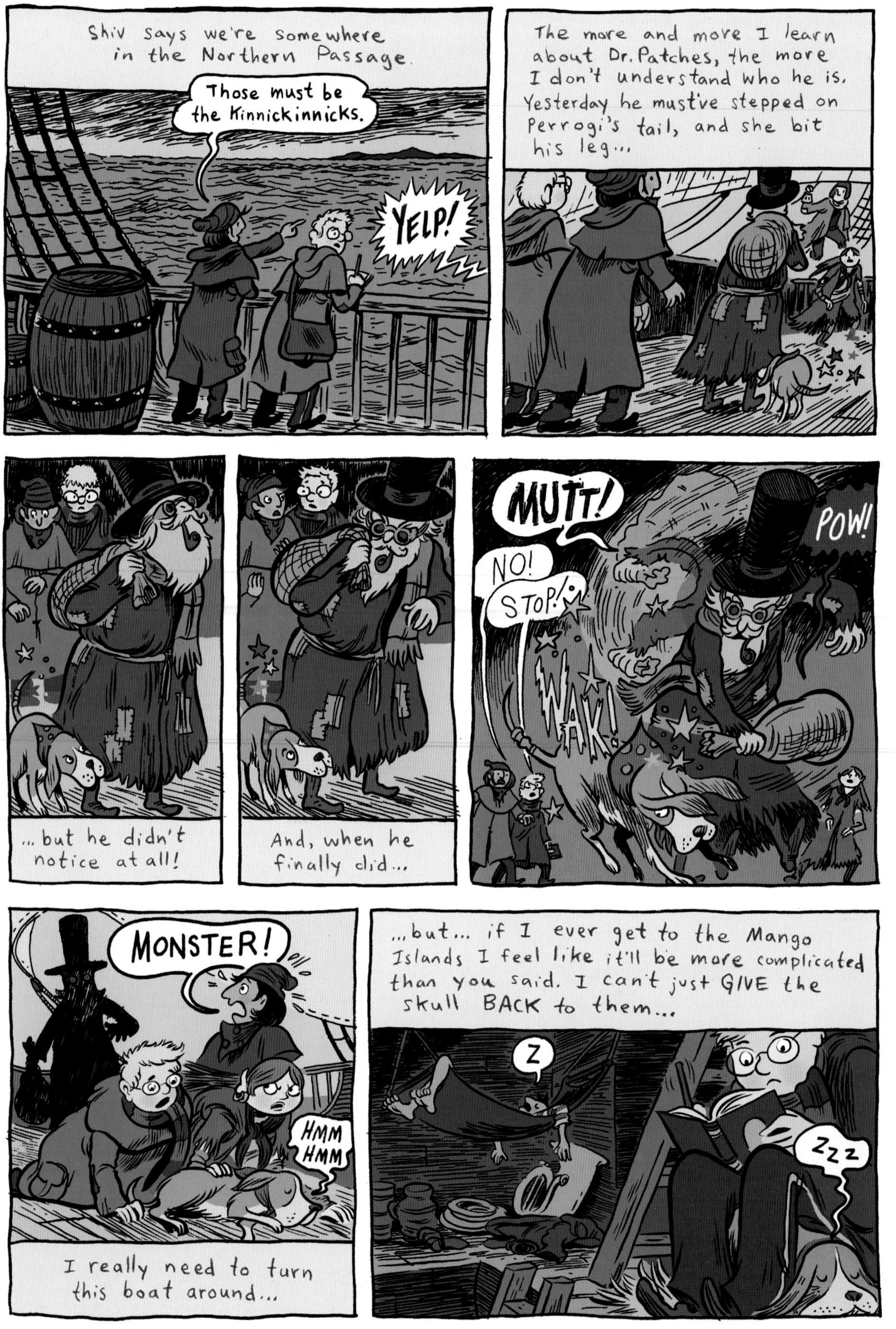
Shiv says we're somewhere in the Northern Passage.
Those must be the Kinnickinnicks.
YELP!
The more and more I learn about Dr. Patches, the more I don't understand who he is. Yesterday he must've stepped on Perrogi's tail, and she bit his leg...
...but he didn't notice at all!
And, when he finally did...
MUTT!
POW!
NO! STOP!
WAK!
MONSTER!
HMM HMM
I really need to turn this boat around...
...but... if I ever get to the Mango Islands I feel like it'll be more complicated than you said. I can't just GIVE the skull BACK to them...
Z
Z Z Z

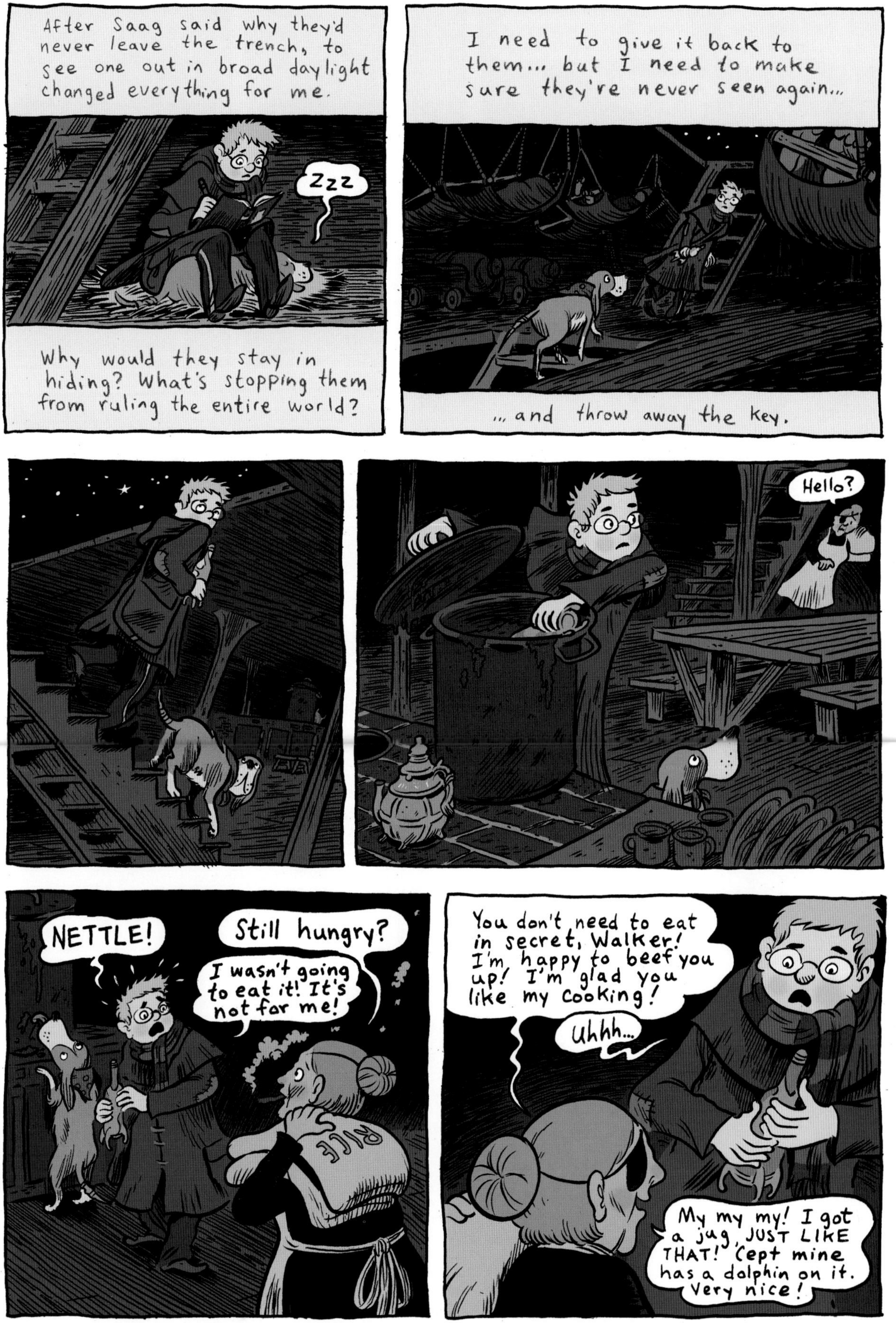
After Saag said why they'd never leave the trench, to see one out in broad daylight changed everything for me.
ZZZ
Why would they stay in hiding? What's stopping them from ruling the entire world?
I need to give it back to them... but I need to make sure they're never seen again...
... and throw away the key.
Hello?
NETTLE!
Still hungry?
I wasn't going to eat it! It's not for me!
RICE
You don't need to eat in secret, Walker! I'm happy to beef you up! I'm glad you like my cooking!
Uhhh...
My my my! I got a jug, JUST LIKE THAT! 'Cept mine has a dolphin on it. Very nice!

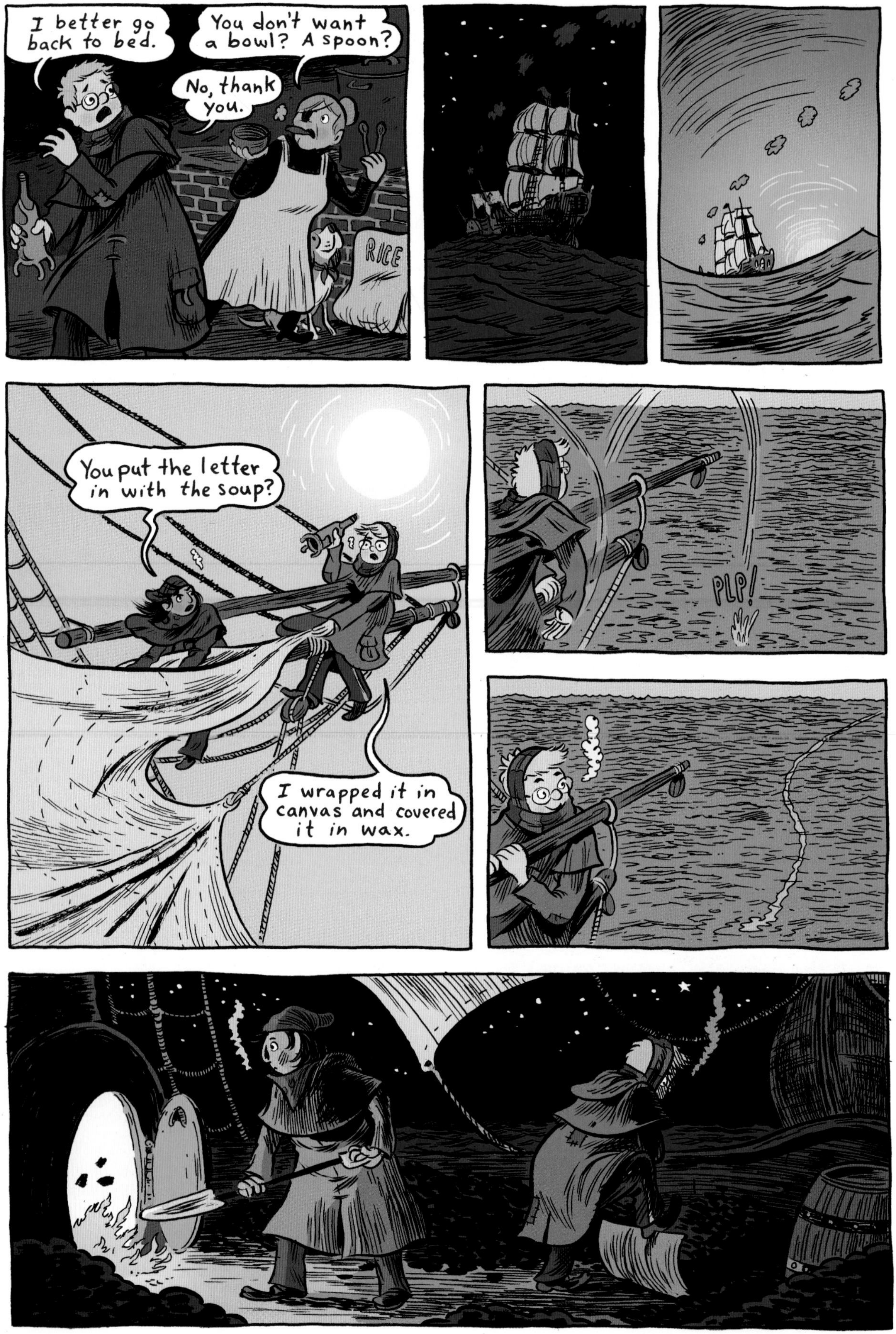
I better go back to bed.
You don't want a bowl? A spoon?
No, thank you.
RICE
You put the letter in with the soup?
I wrapped it in canvas and covered it in wax.
PLP!

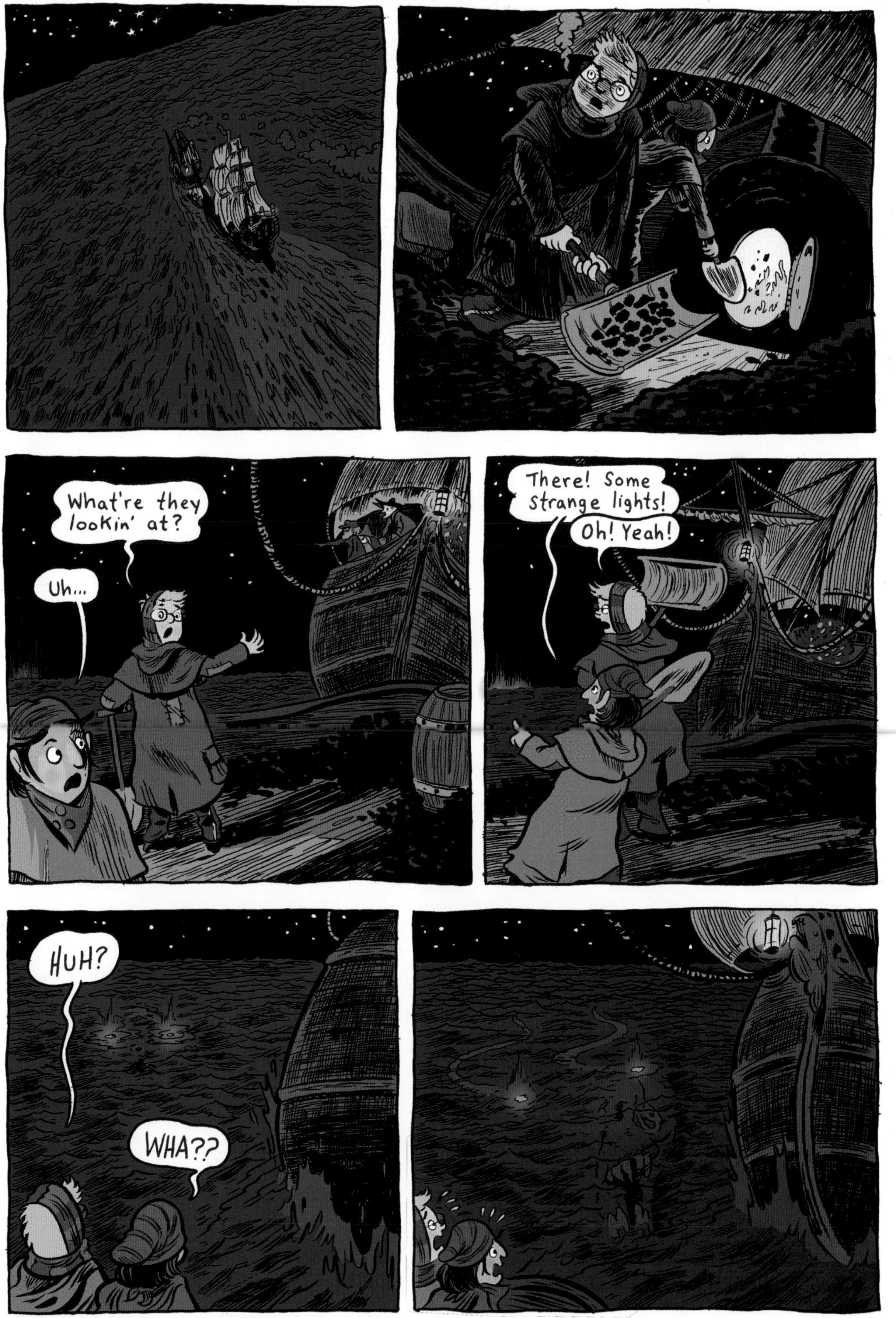
What're they lookin' at?
Uh...
There! Some strange lights!
Oh! Yeah!
HUH?
WHA??

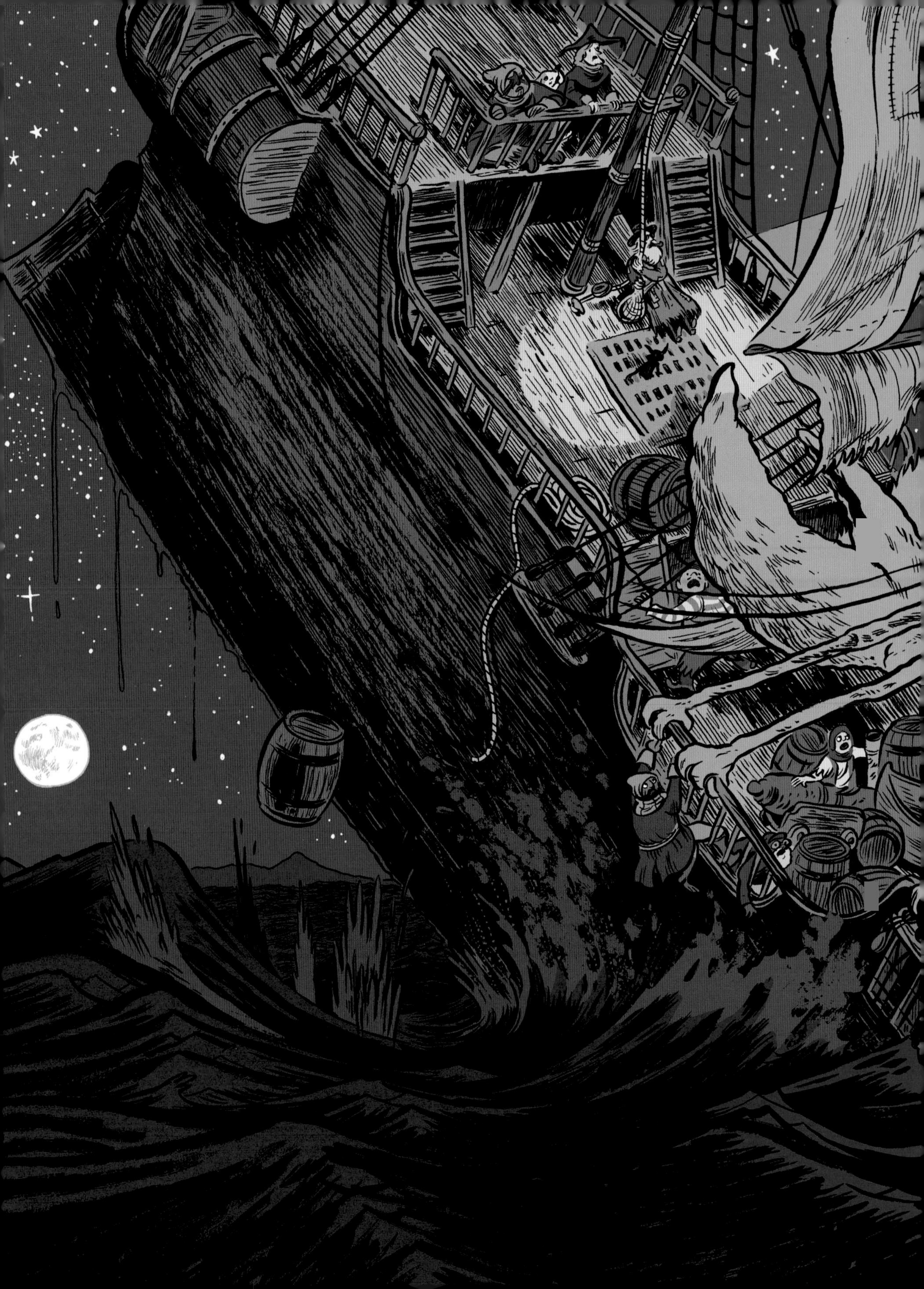

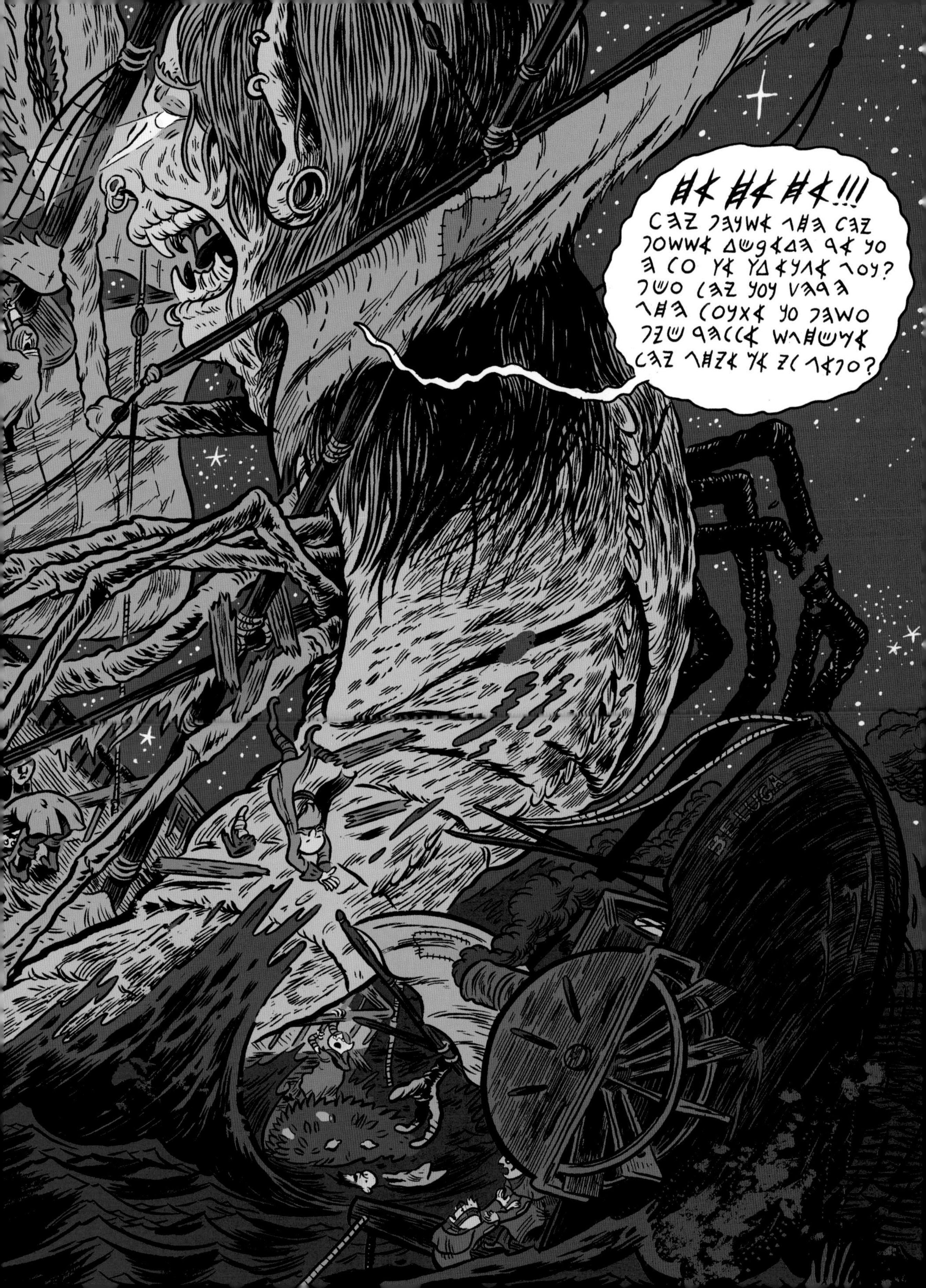

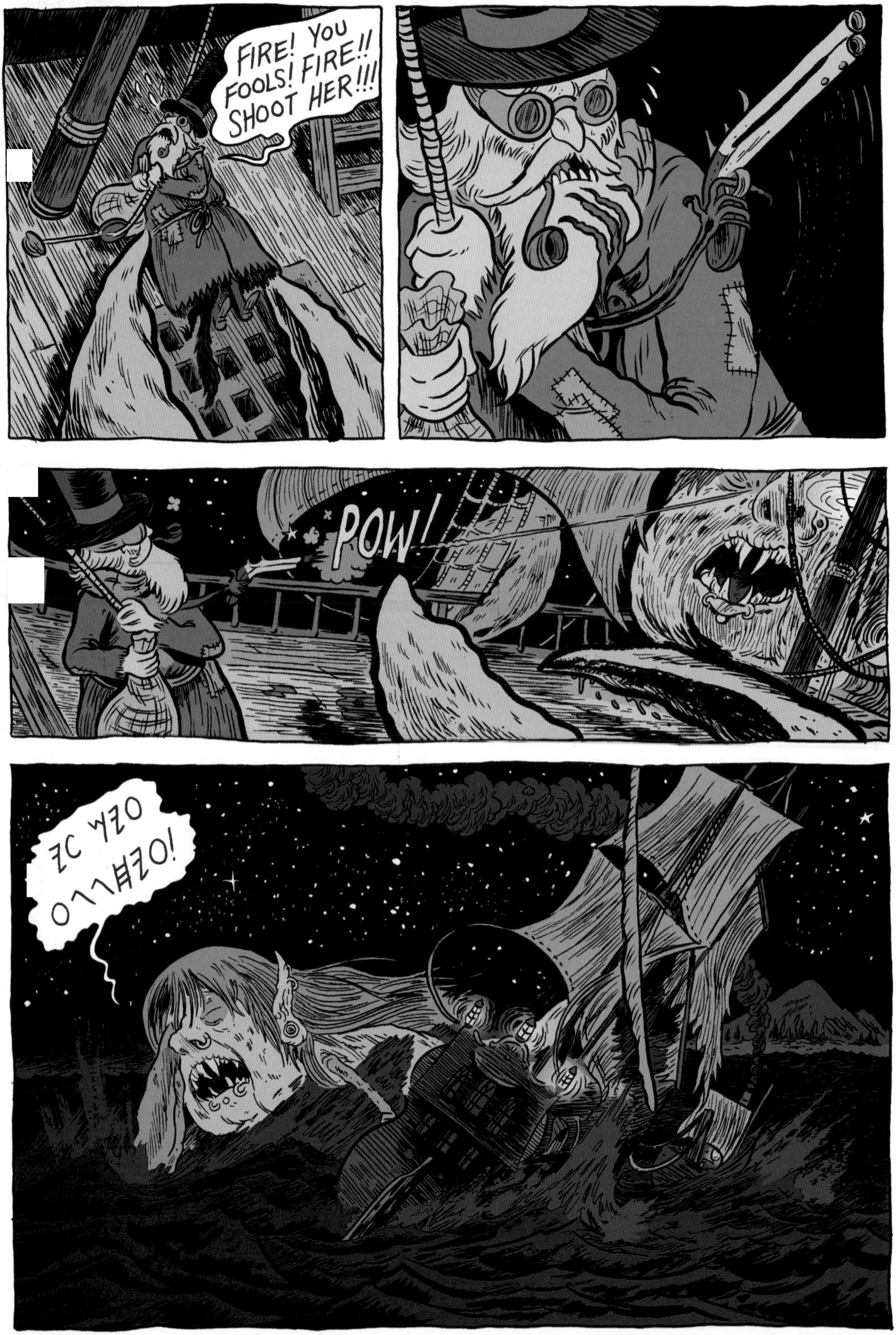
FIRE! YOU FOOLS! FIRE!! SHOOT HER!!!
POW!

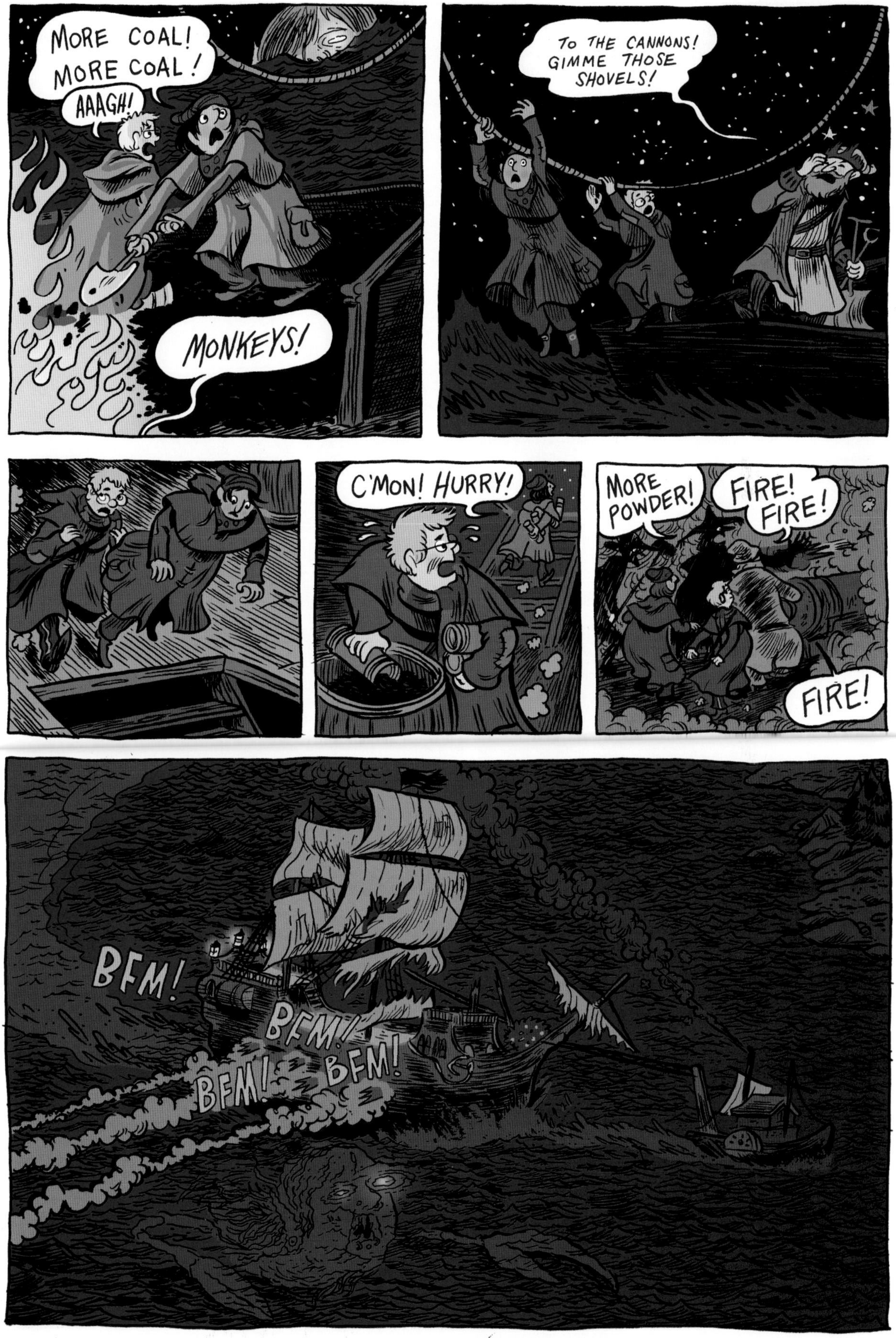

MORE COAL! MORE COAL!
AAAGH!
MONKEYS!
TO THE CANNONS! GIMME THOSE SHOVELS!
C'MON! HURRY!
MORE POWDER!
FIRE! FIRE!
FIRE!
BFM!
BFM!
BFM!
BFM!

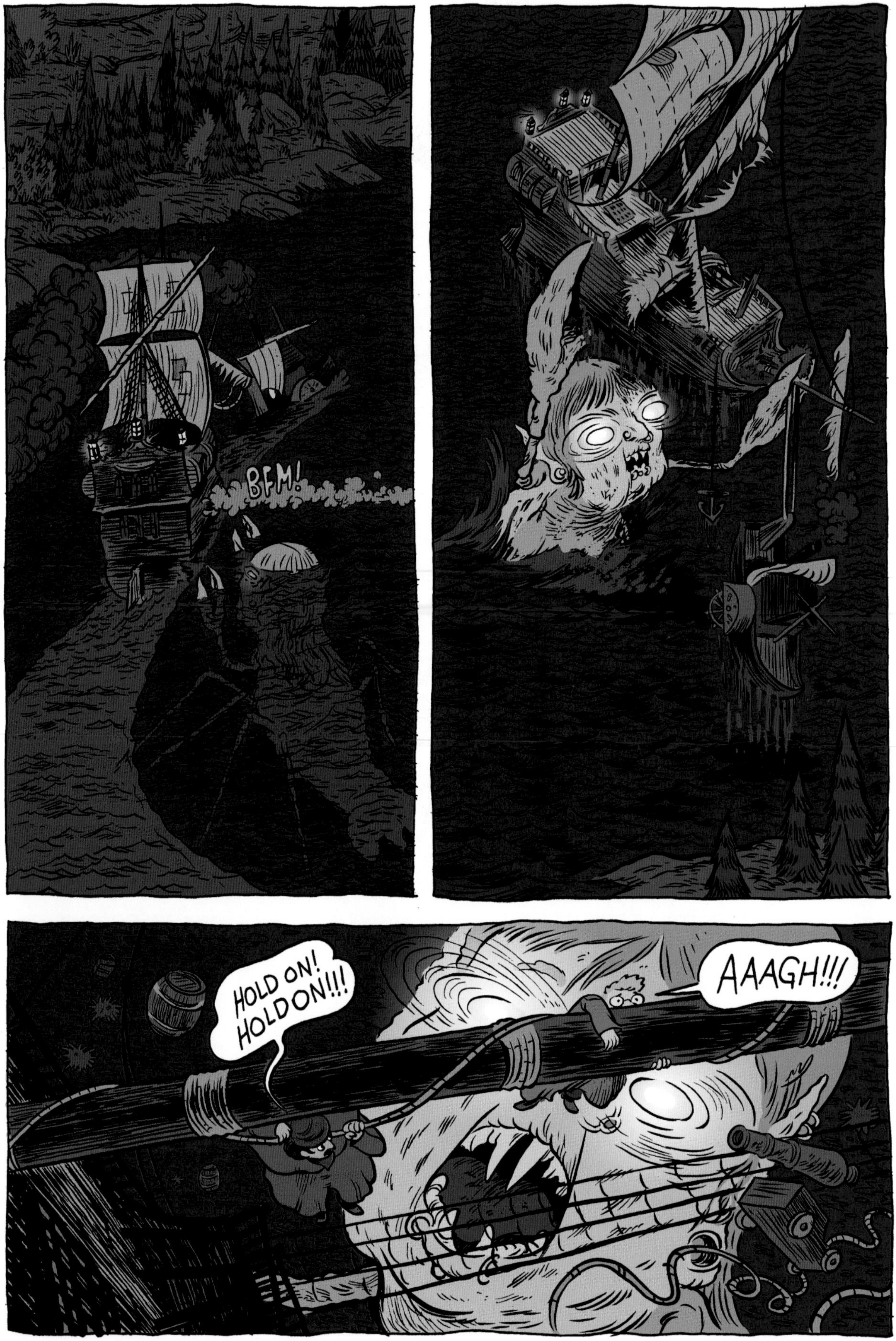
BFM!
HOLD ON! HOLD ON!!!
AAAGH!!!

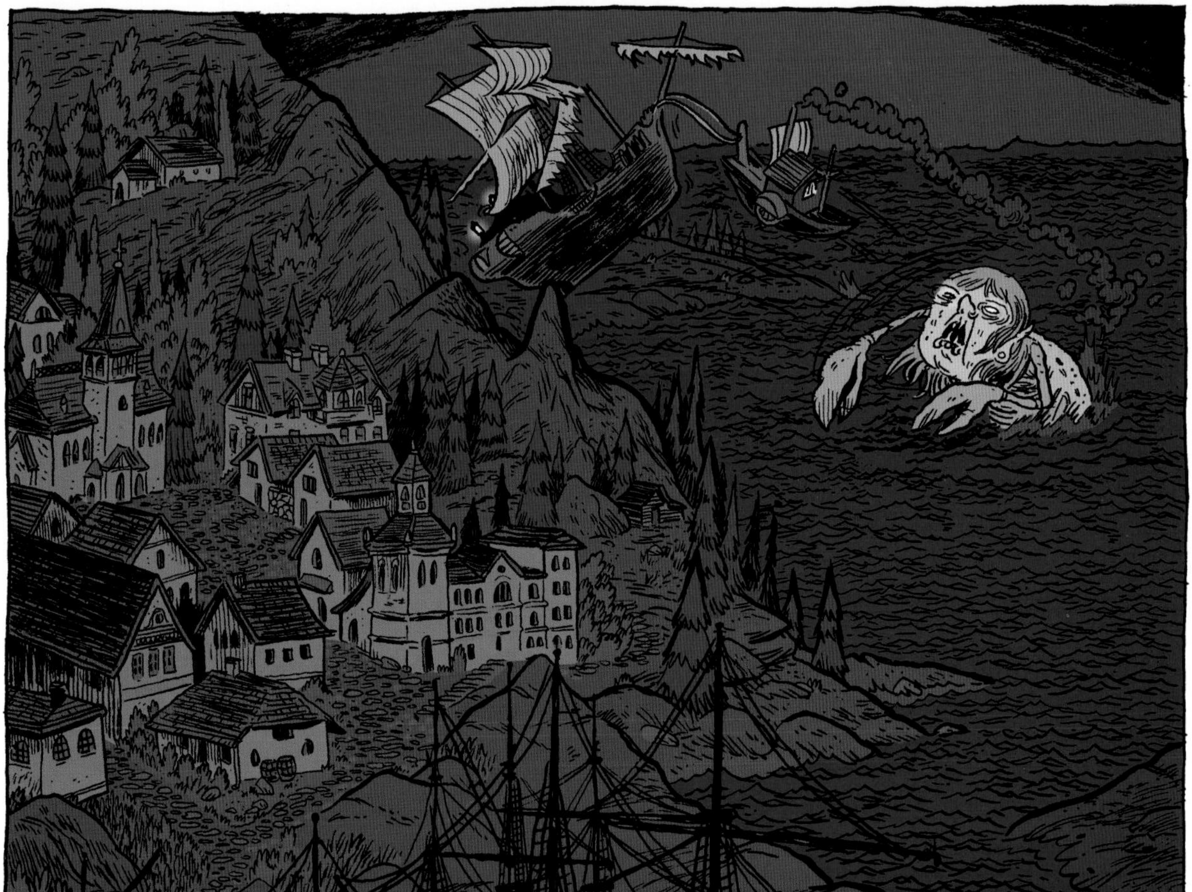

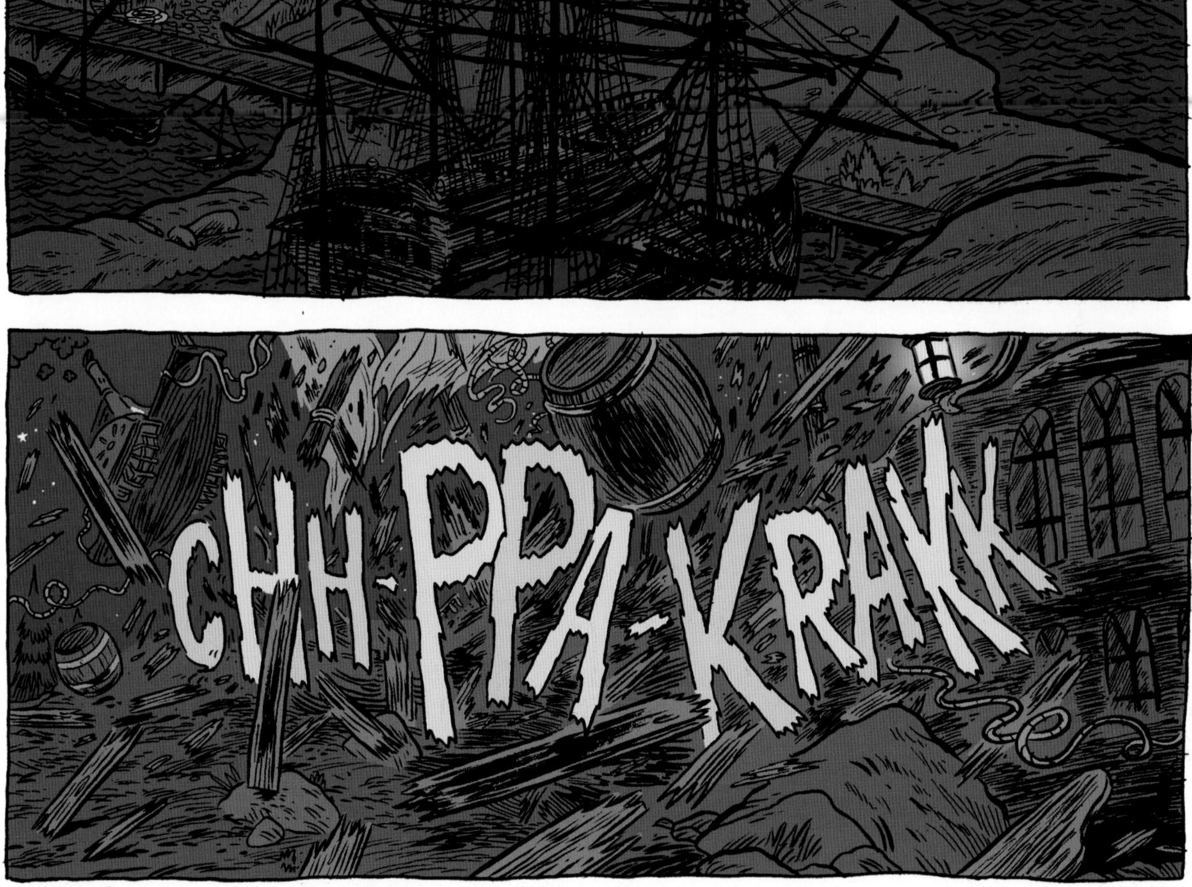
CHH-PPA-KRAKK

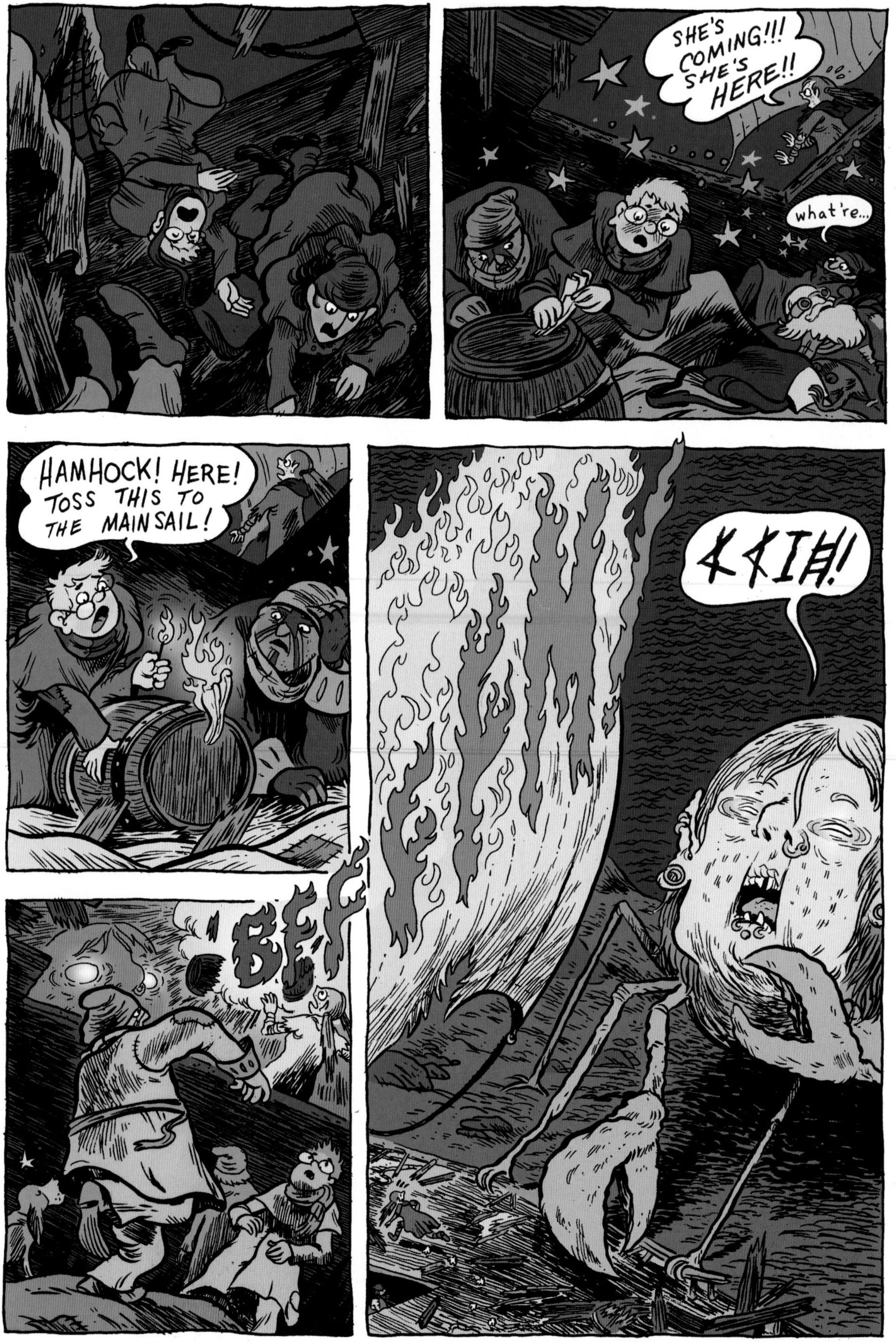
SHE'S COMING!!! SHE'S HERE!!
what're...
HAMHOCK! HERE! TOSS THIS TO THE MAINSAIL!

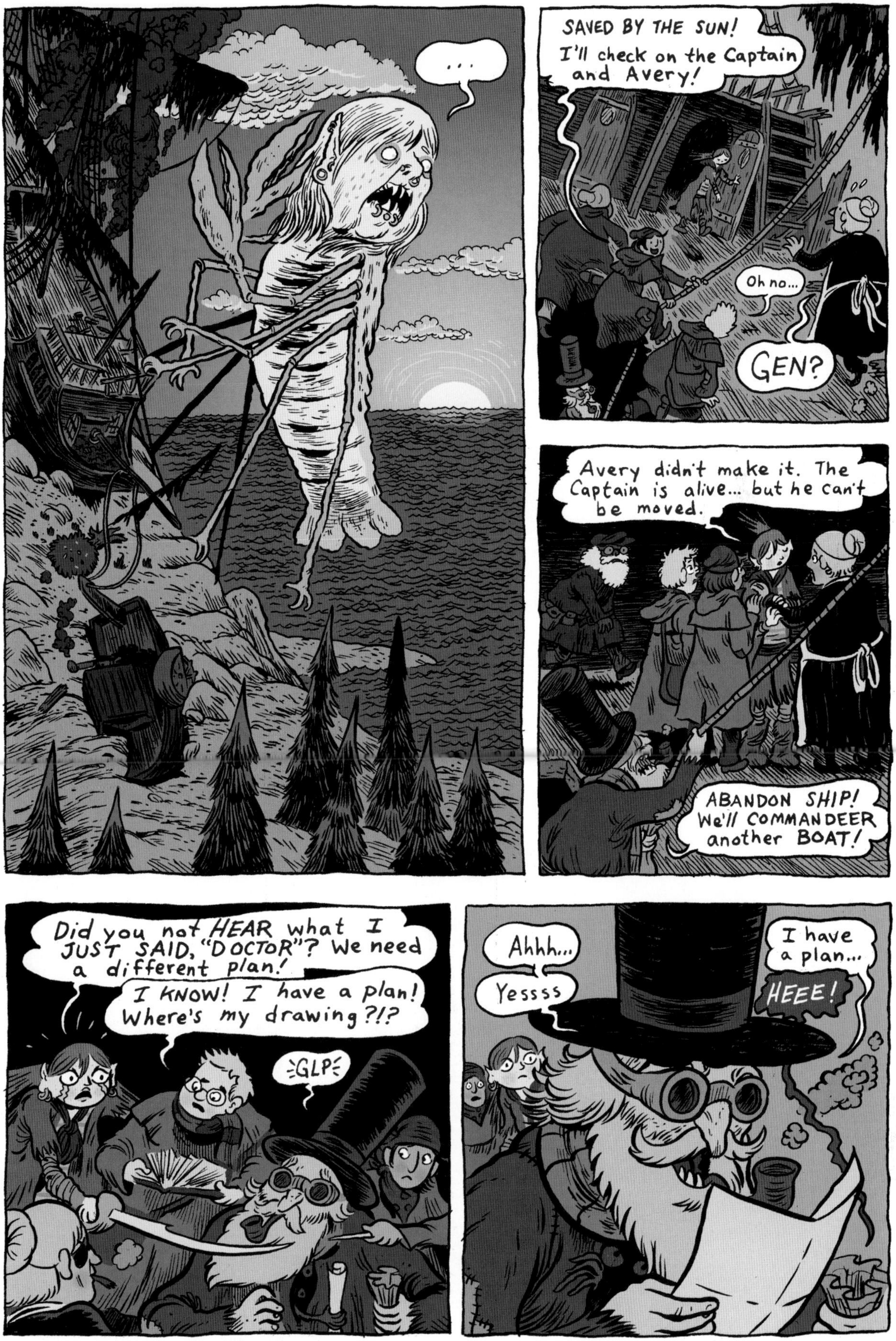
...
SAVED BY THE SUN!
I'll check on the Captain and Avery!
Oh no...
GEN?
Avery didn't make it. The Captain is alive... but he can't be moved.
ABANDON SHIP! We'll COMMANDEER another BOAT!
Did you not HEAR what I JUST SAID, "DOCTOR"? We need a different plan!
I KNOW! I have a plan! Where's my drawing?!?
GLP
Ahhh...
Yessss
I have a plan...
HEEE!

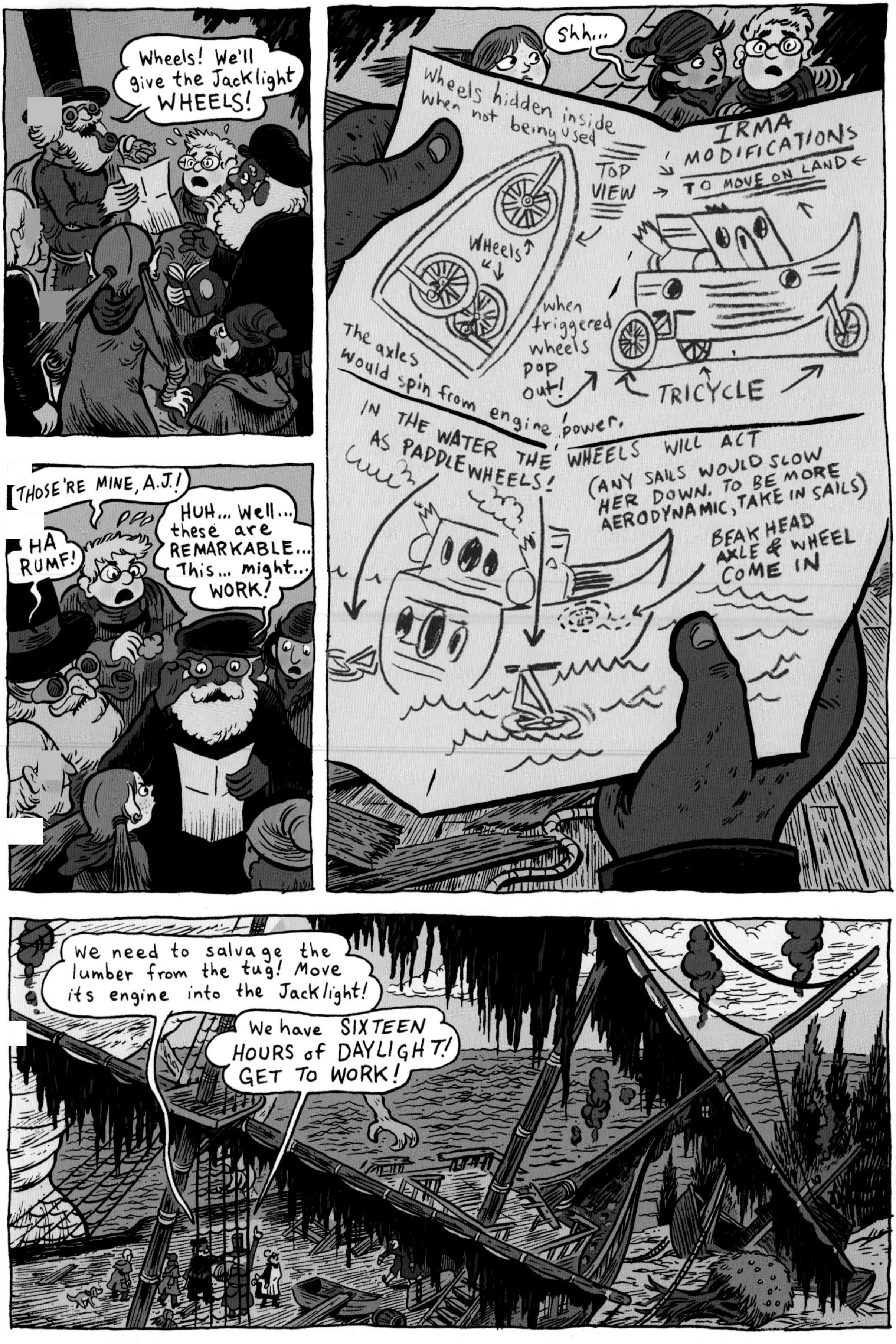
Wheels! We'll give the Jacklight WHEELS!
Shh...
Wheels hidden inside when not being used
IRMA MODIFICATIONS TO MOVE ON LAND
TOP VIEW
WHEELS
when triggered wheels pop out!
The axles would spin from engine power.
TRICYCLE
IN THE WATER THE WHEELS WILL ACT AS PADDLEWHEELS!
(ANY SAILS WOULD SLOW HER DOWN. TO BE MORE AERODYNAMIC, TAKE IN SAILS)
BEAK HEAD AXLE & WHEEL COME IN
THOSE'RE MINE, A.J.!
HA RUMF!
HUH... Well... these are REMARKABLE... This... might... WORK!
We need to salvage the lumber from the tug! Move its engine into the Jacklight!
We have SIXTEEN HOURS of DAYLIGHT! GET TO WORK!

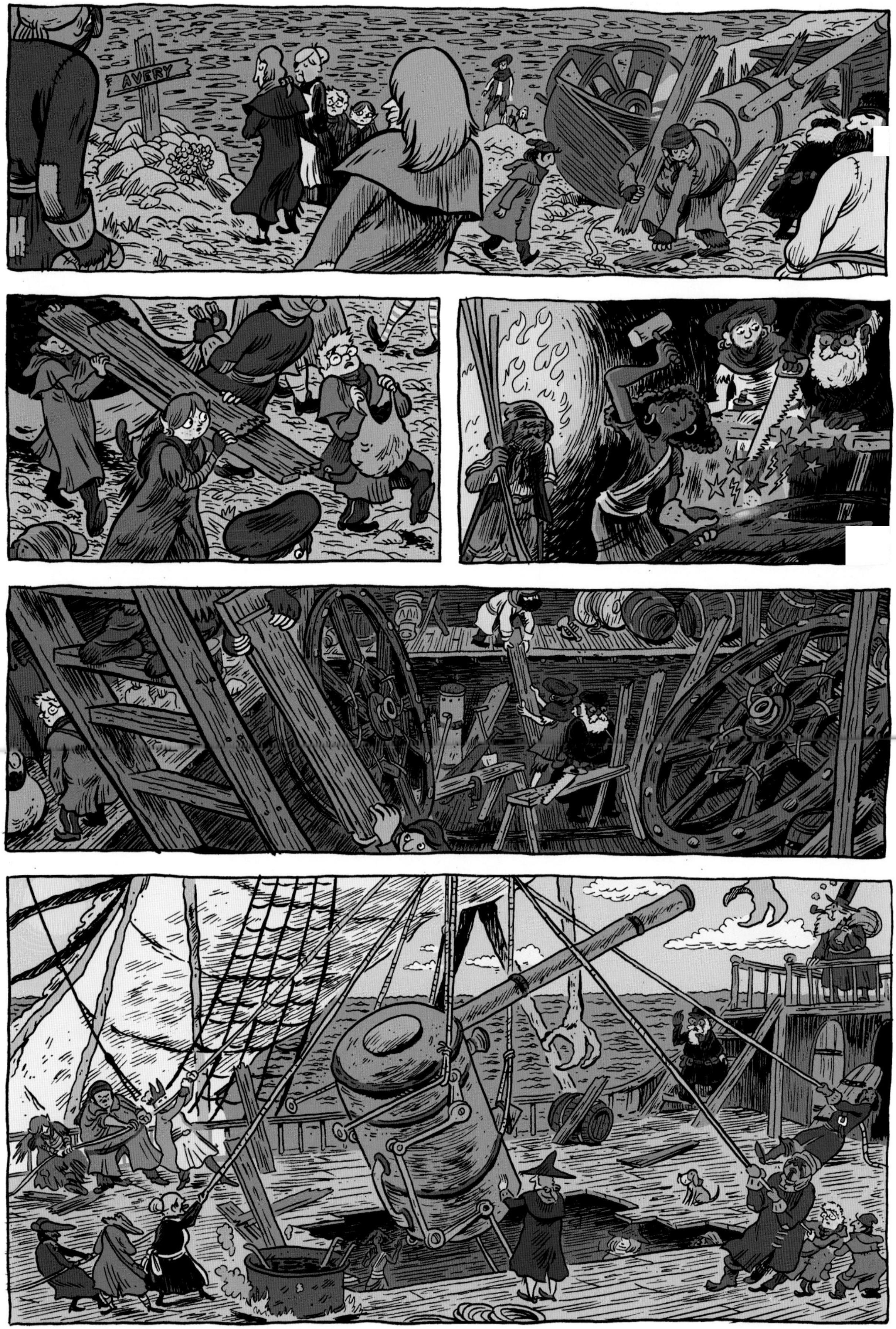
AVERY

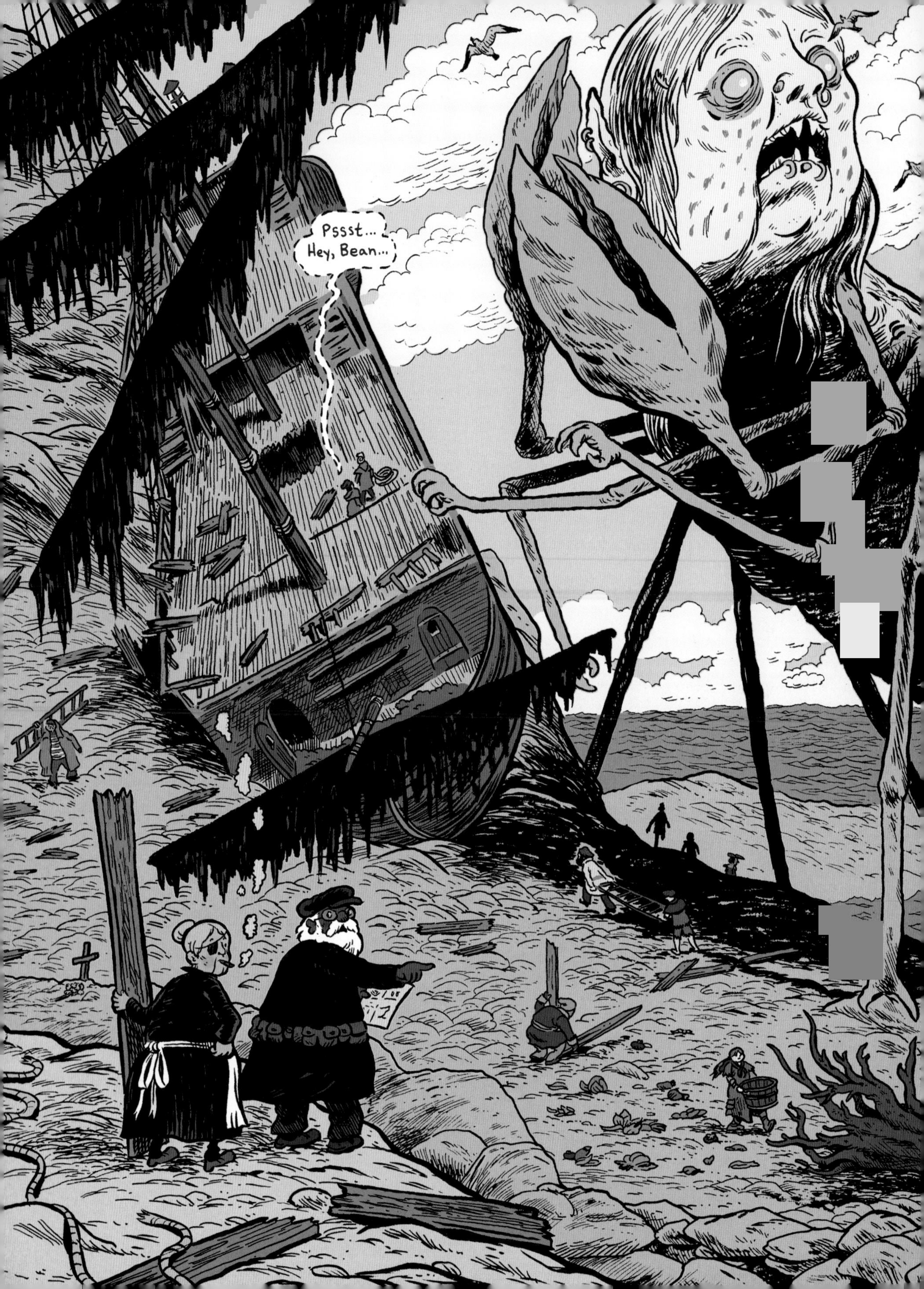
Pssst... Hey, Bean...

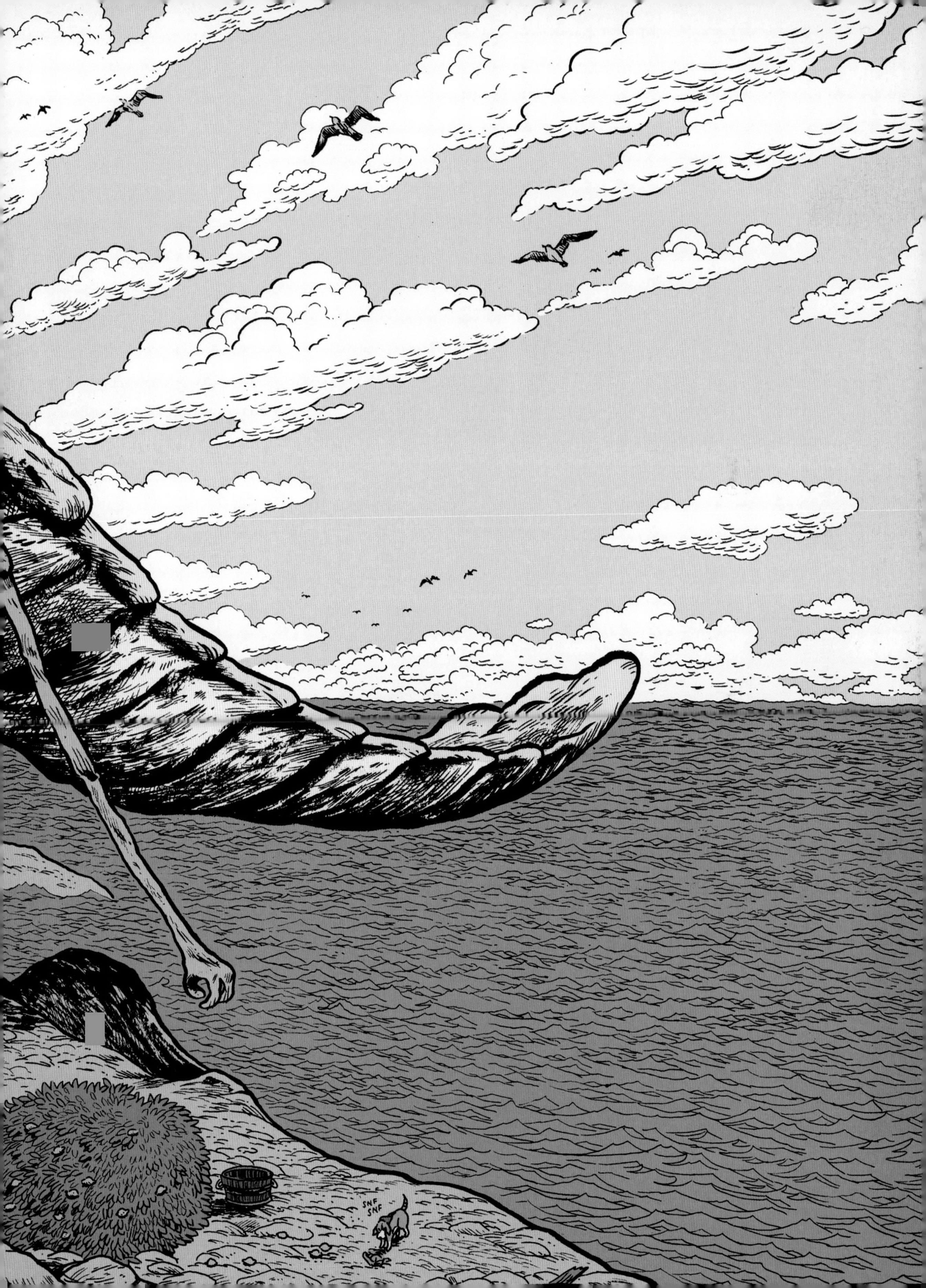
SNF
SNF

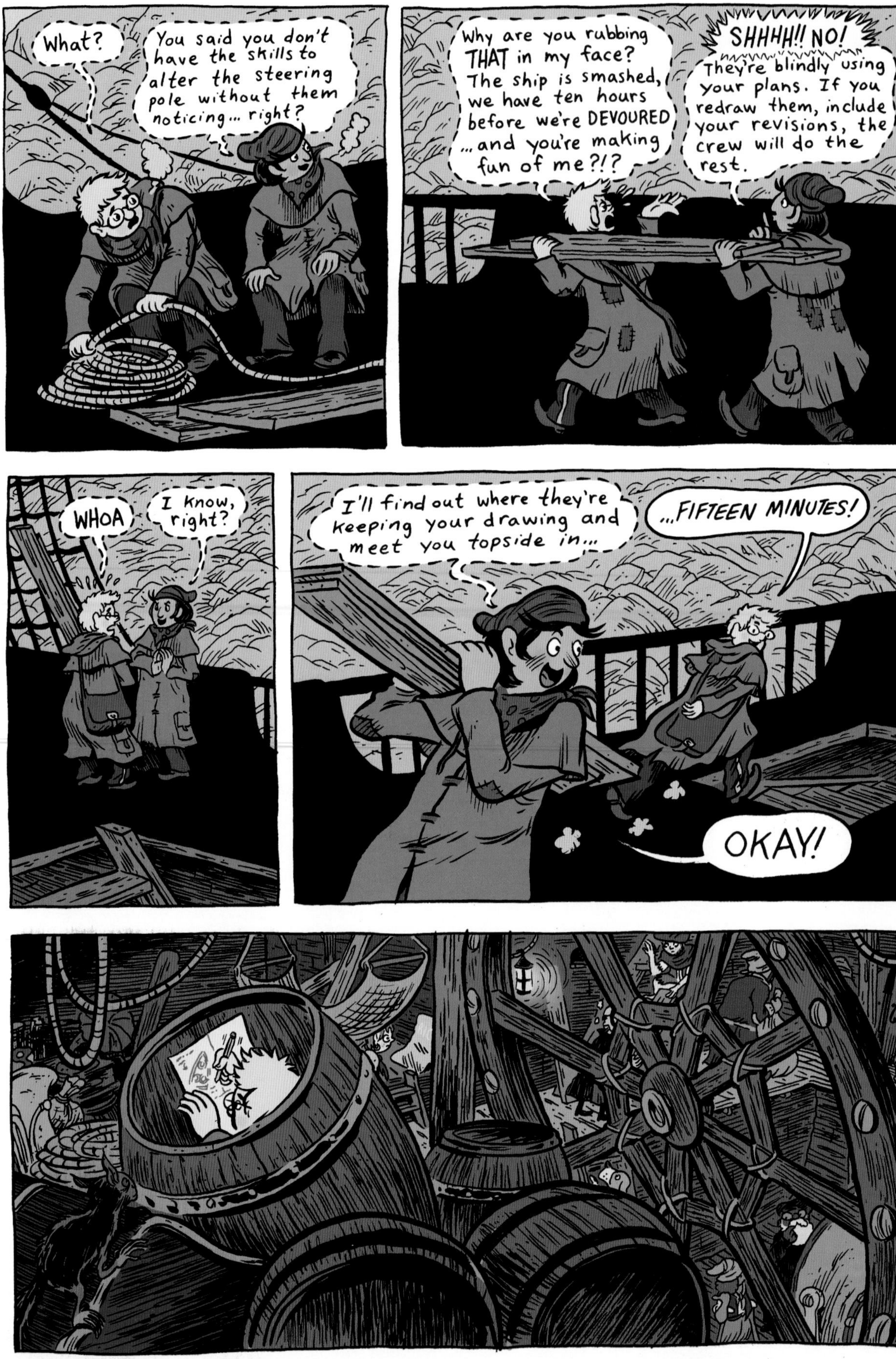

What?
You said you don't have the skills to alter the steering pole without them noticing... right?
Why are you rubbing THAT in my face? The ship is smashed, we have ten hours before we're DEVOURED ...and you're making fun of me?!?
SHHHH!! NO!
They're blindly using your plans. If you redraw them, include your revisions, the crew will do the rest.
WHOA
I know, right?
I'll find out where they're keeping your drawing and meet you topside in...
...FIFTEEN MINUTES!
OKAY!

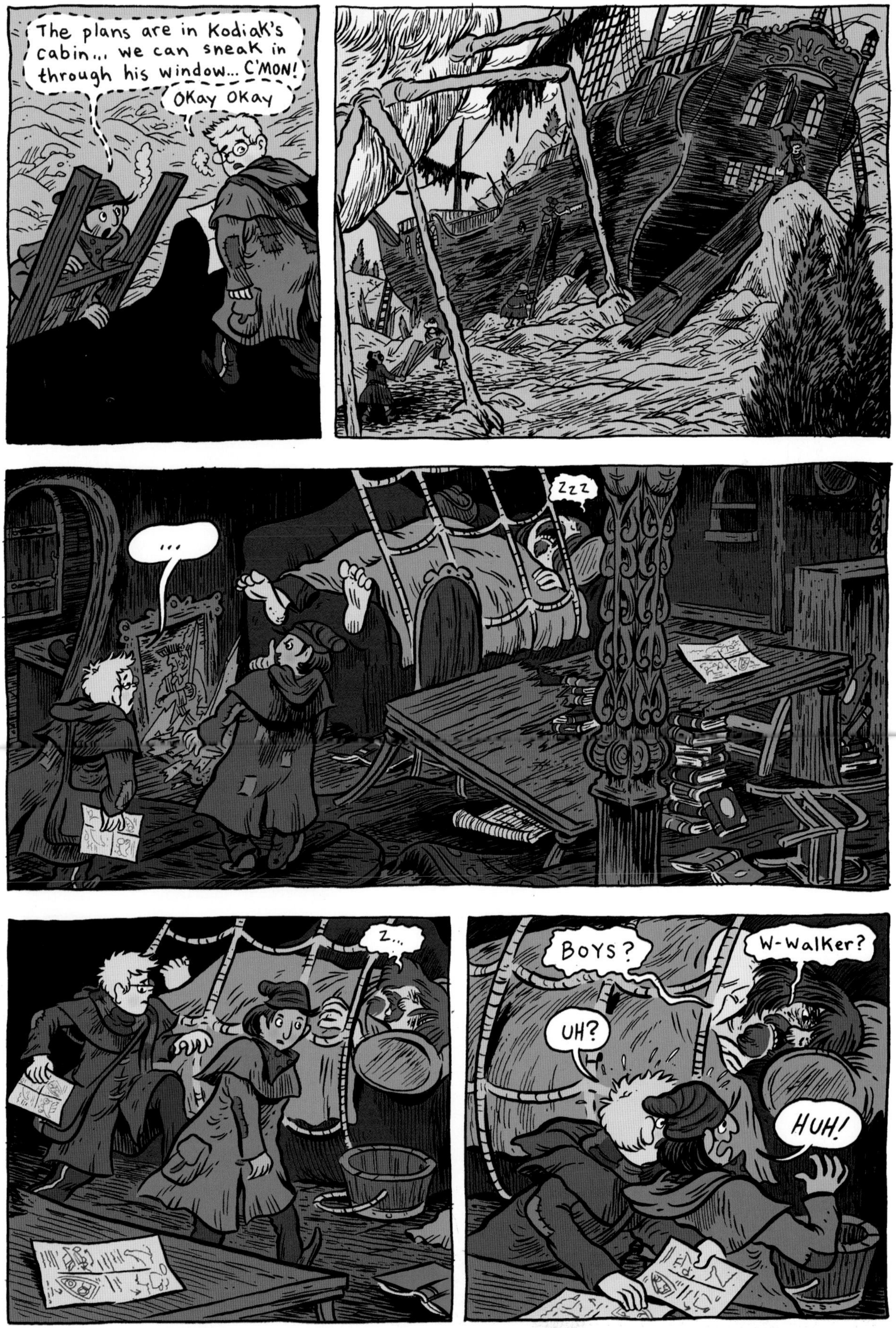
The plans are in Kodiak's cabin... we can sneak in through his window... C'MON!
OKay OKay
...
Zzz
Z...
BOYS?
W-Walker?
UH?
HUH!

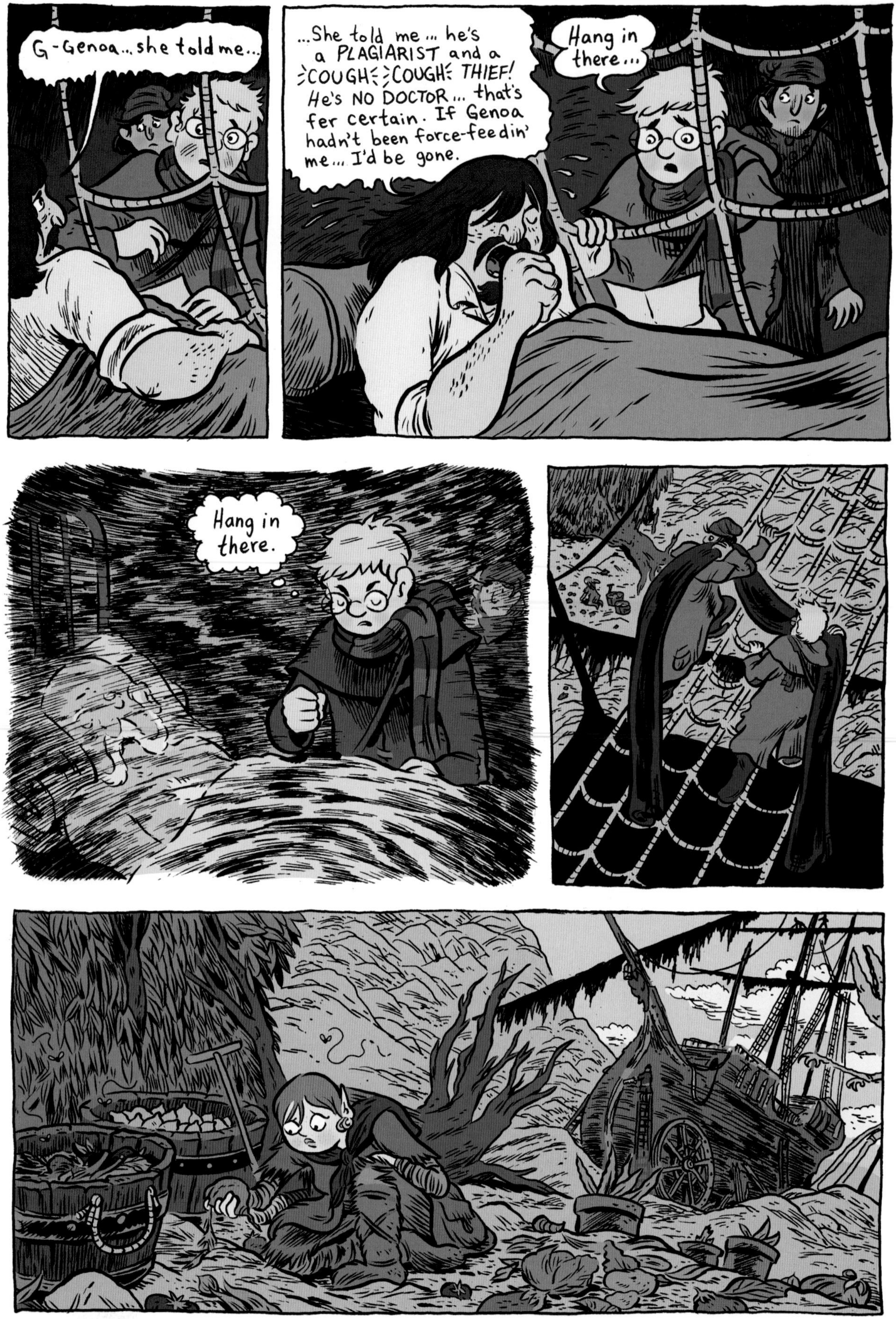
G-Genoa... she told me...
...She told me... he's a PLAGIARIST and a COUGH COUGH THIEF! He's NO DOCTOR... that's fer certain. If Genoa hadn't been force-feedin' me... I'd be gone.
Hang in there...
Hang in there.

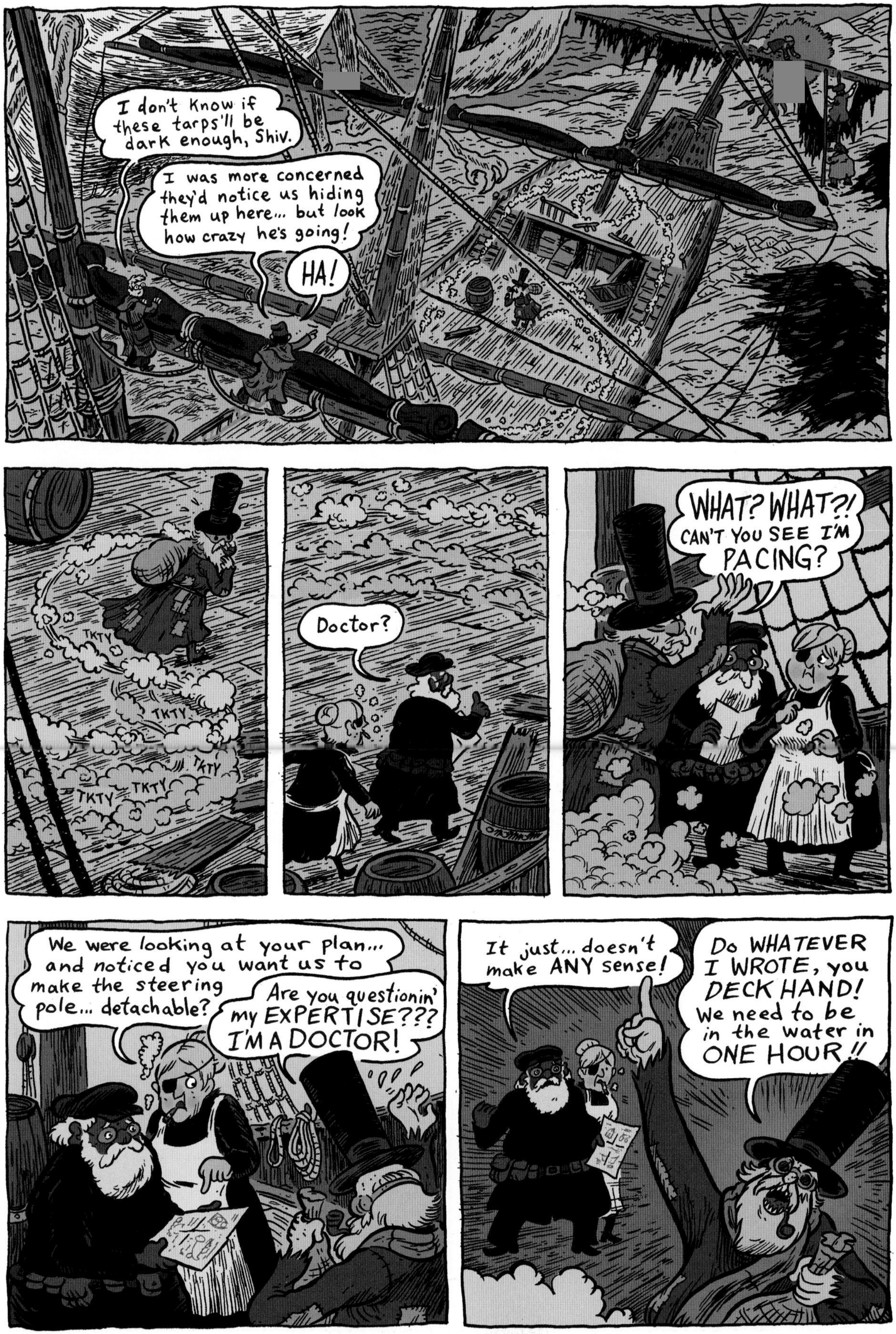
I don't know if these tarps'll be dark enough, Shiv.
I was more concerned they'd notice us hiding them up here... but look how crazy he's going!
HA!
TKTY
TKTY
TKTY
TKTY
TKTY
Doctor?
WHAT? WHAT?! CAN'T YOU SEE I'M PACING?
We were looking at your plan... and noticed you want us to make the steering pole... detachable?
Are you questionin' my EXPERTISE??? I'M A DOCTOR!
It just... doesn't make ANY sense!
Do WHATEVER I WROTE, you DECK HAND! We need to be in the water in ONE HOUR!!

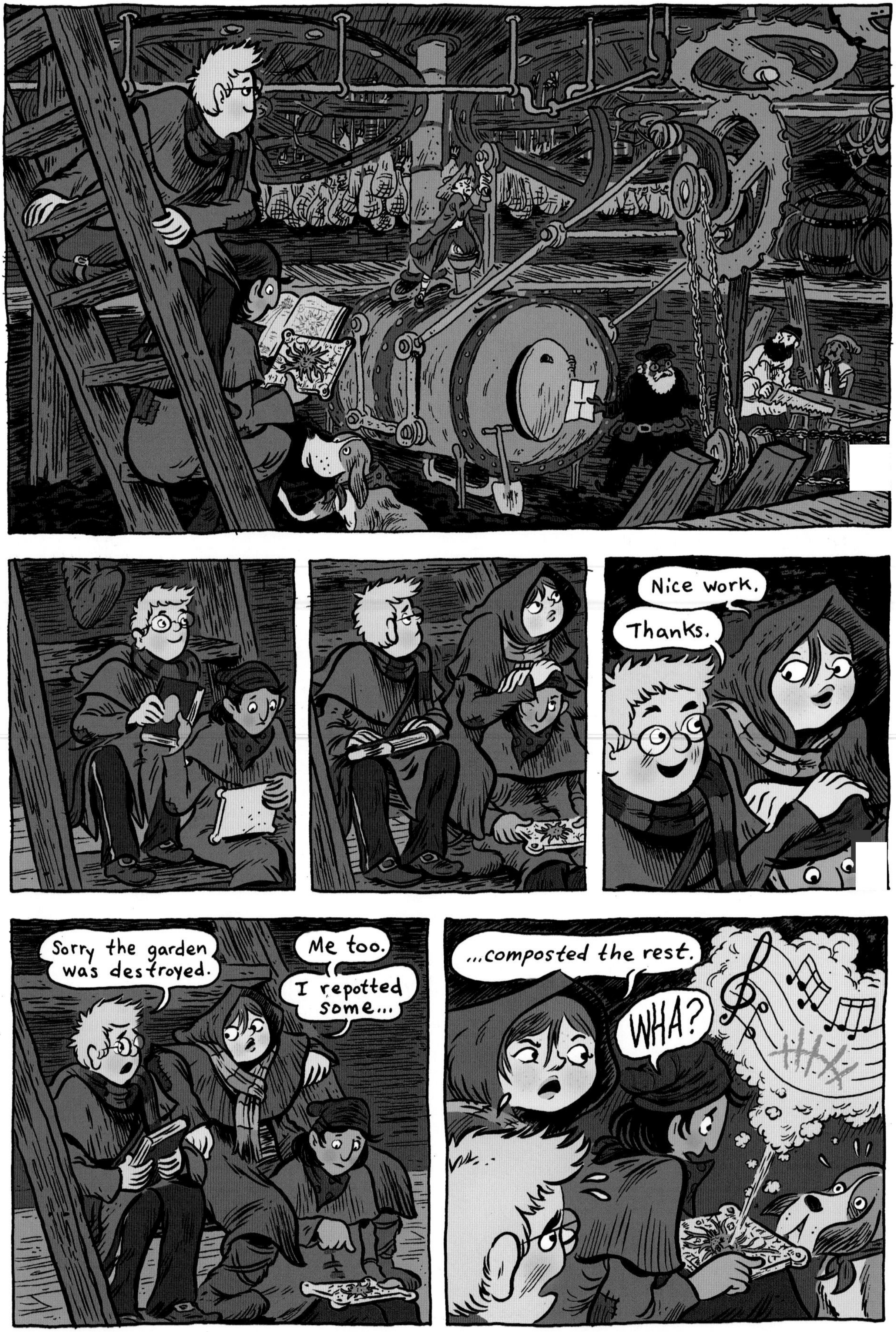
Nice work.
Thanks.
Sorry the garden was destroyed.
Me too.
I repotted some...
...composted the rest.
WHA?

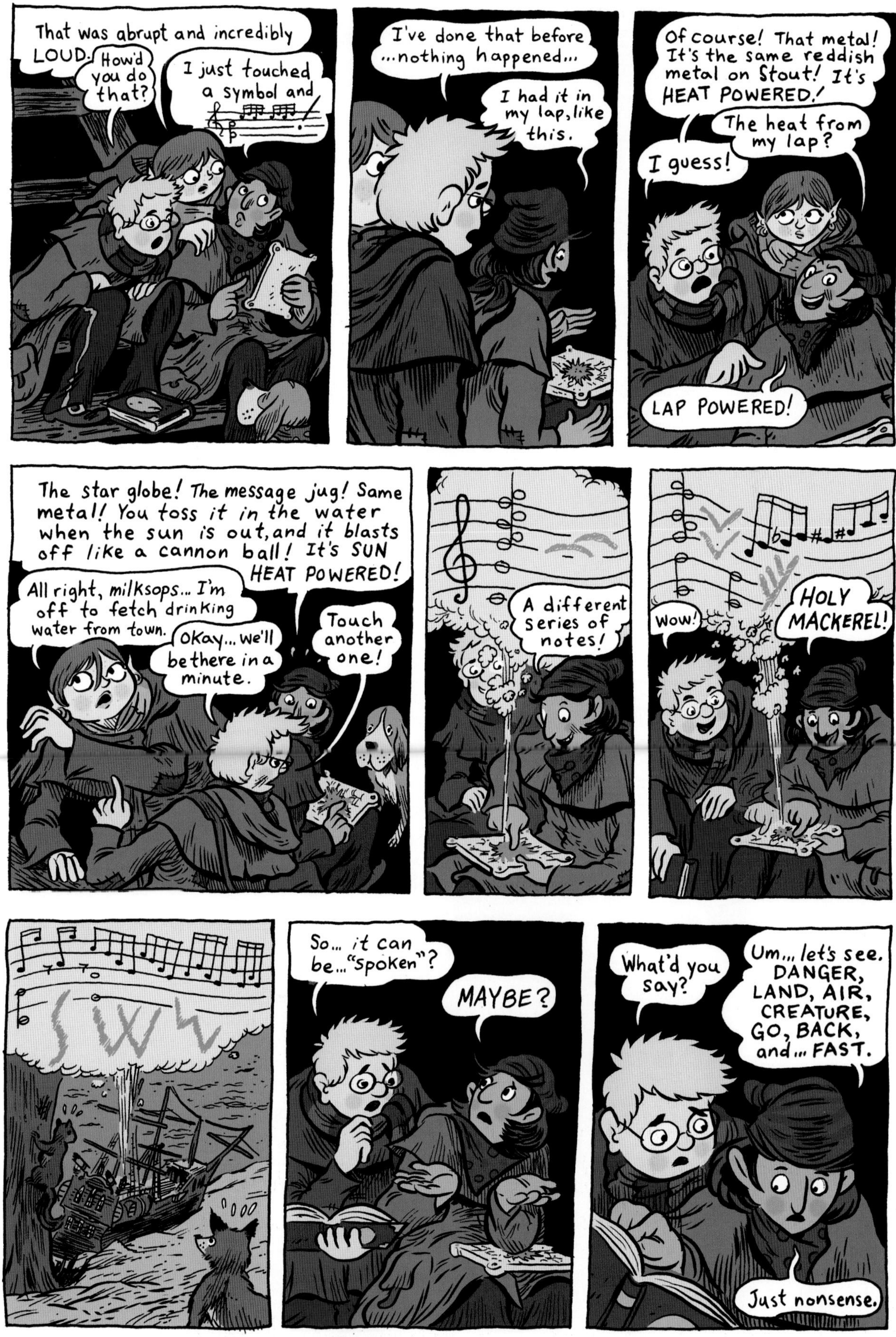

That was abrupt and incredibly LOUD.
How'd you do that?
I just touched a symbol and
I've done that before ...nothing happened...
I had it in my lap, like this.
Of course! That metal! It's the same reddish metal on Stout! It's HEAT POWERED!
I guess!
The heat from my lap?
LAP POWERED!
The star globe! The message jug! Same metal! You toss it in the water when the sun is out, and it blasts off like a cannon ball! It's SUN HEAT POWERED!
All right, milksops... I'm off to fetch drinking water from town.
Okay... we'll be there in a minute.
Touch another one!
A different series of notes!
Wow!
HOLY MACKEREL!
So... it can be... "spoken"?
MAYBE?
What'd you say?
Um... let's see. DANGER, LAND, AIR, CREATURE, GO, BACK, and... FAST.
Just nonsense.

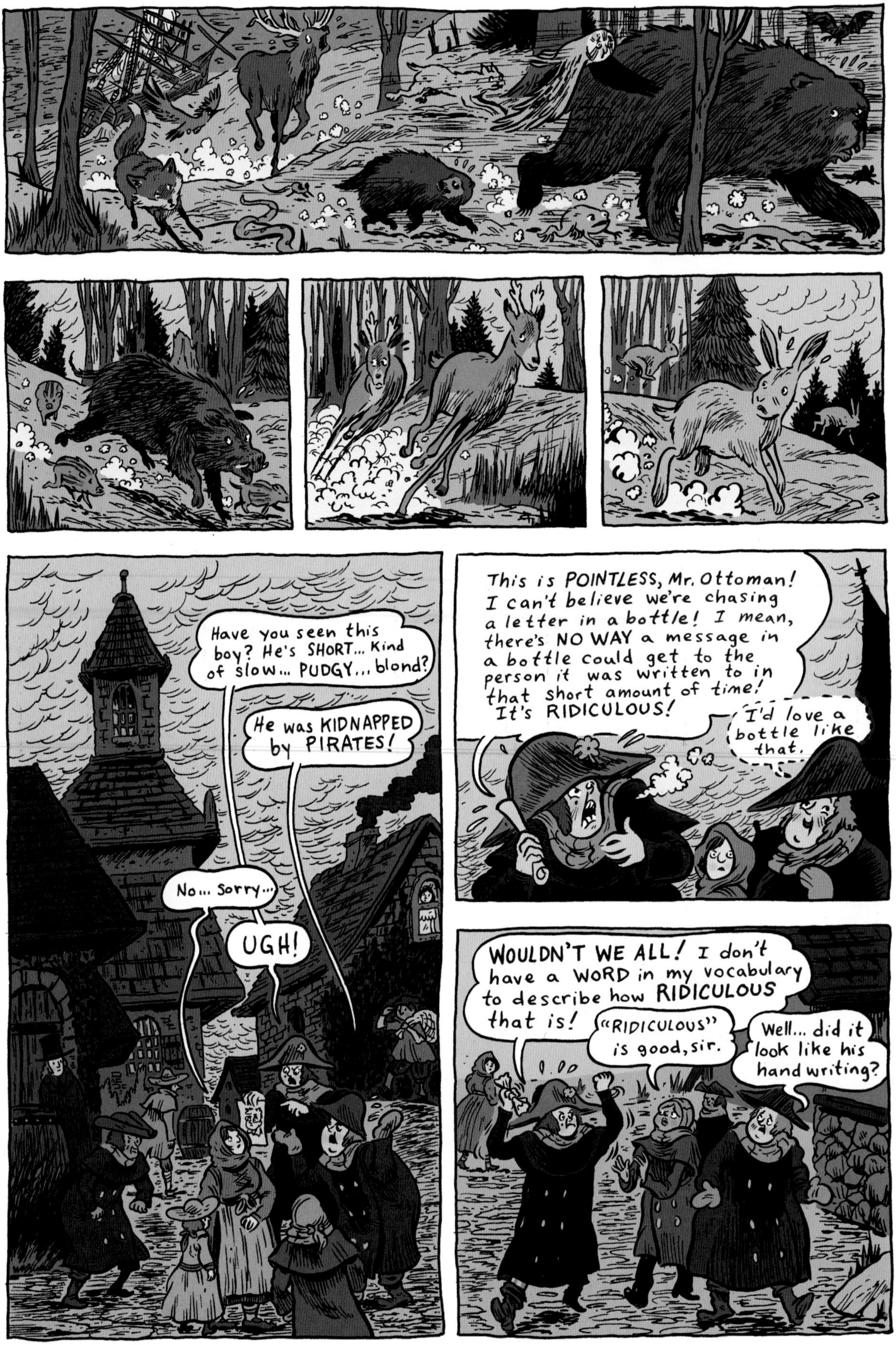

Have you seen this boy? He's SHORT... Kind of slow... PUDGY... blond?
He was KIDNAPPED by PIRATES!
No... sorry...
UGH!
This is POINTLESS, Mr. Ottoman! I can't believe we're chasing a letter in a bottle! I mean, there's NO WAY a message in a bottle could get to the person it was written to in that short amount of time! It's RIDICULOUS!
I'd love a bottle like that.
WOULDN'T WE ALL! I don't have a WORD in my vocabulary to describe how RIDICULOUS that is!
"RIDICULOUS" is good, sir.
Well... did it look like his handwriting?

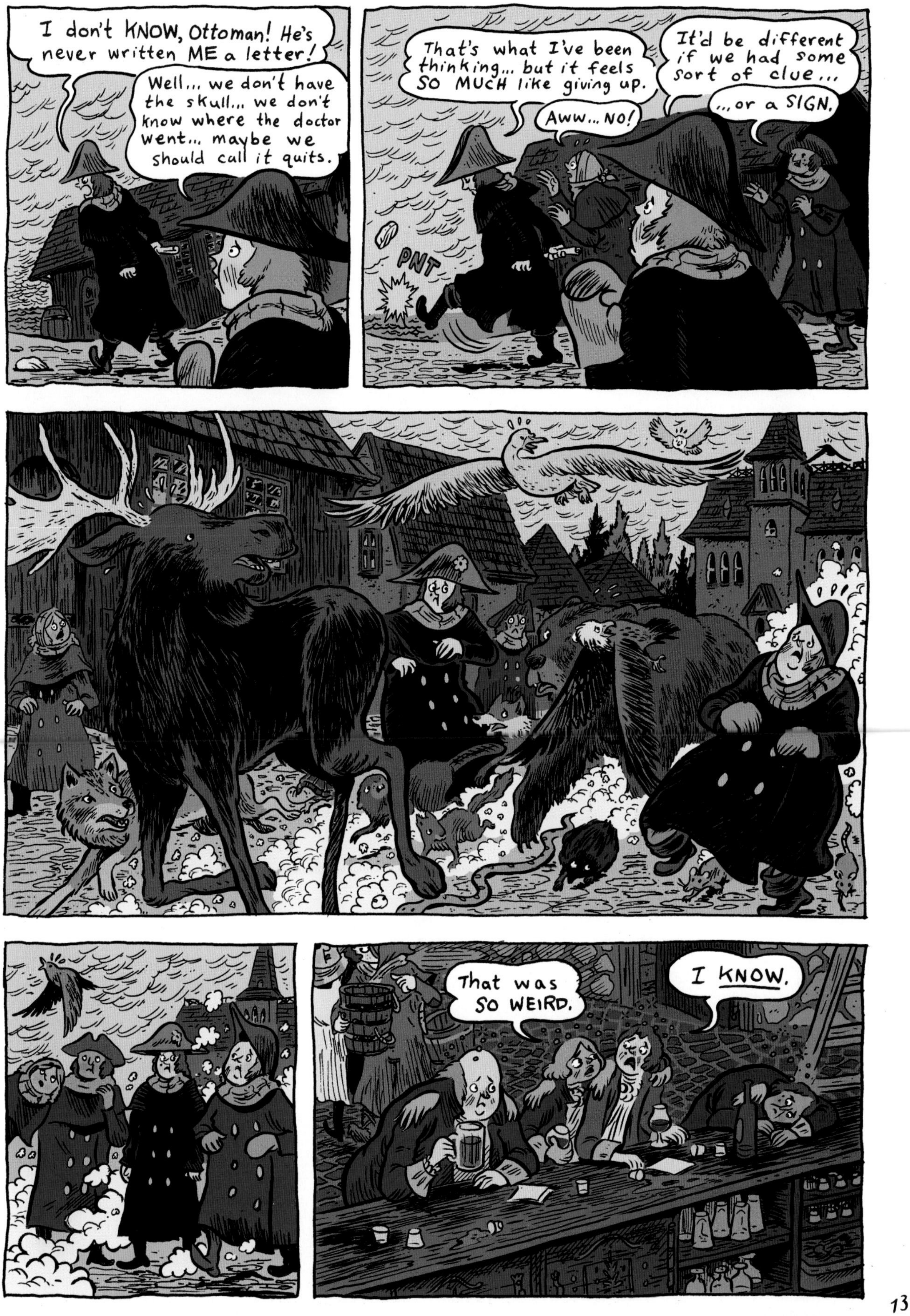
I don't KNOW, Ottoman! He's never written ME a letter!
Well... we don't have the skull... we don't know where the doctor went... maybe we should call it quits.
That's what I've been thinking... but it feels SO MUCH like giving up.
It'd be different if we had some sort of clue...
Aww... NO!
...or a SIGN.
PNT
That was SO WEIRD.
I KNOW.

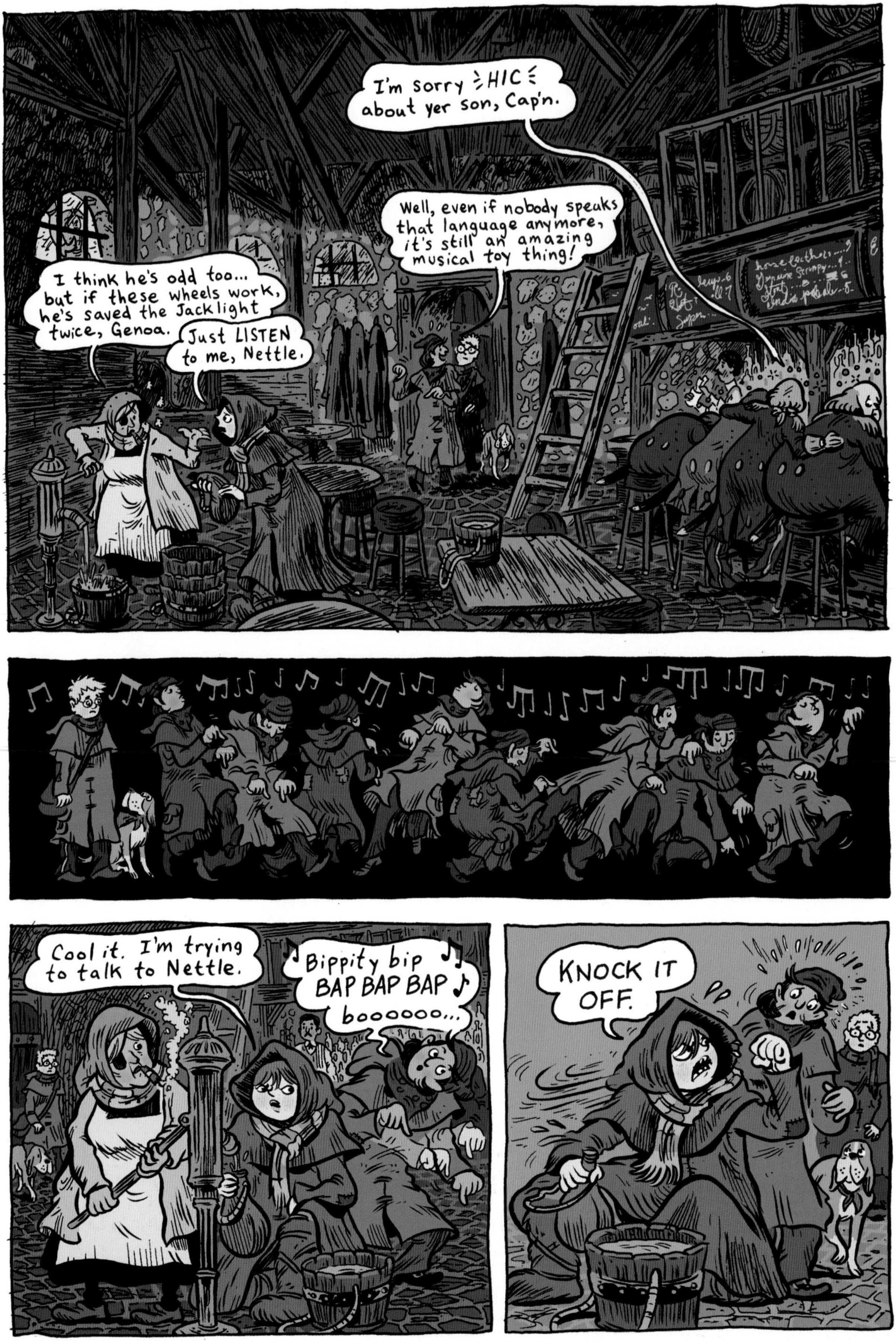
I'm sorry HIC about yer son, Cap'n.
I think he's odd too... but if these wheels work, he's saved the Jacklight twice, Genoa.
Just LISTEN to me, Nettle.
Well, even if nobody speaks that language anymore, it's still an amazing musical toy thing!
Cool it. I'm trying to talk to Nettle.
Bippity bip BAP BAP BAP boooooo...
KNOCK IT OFF.

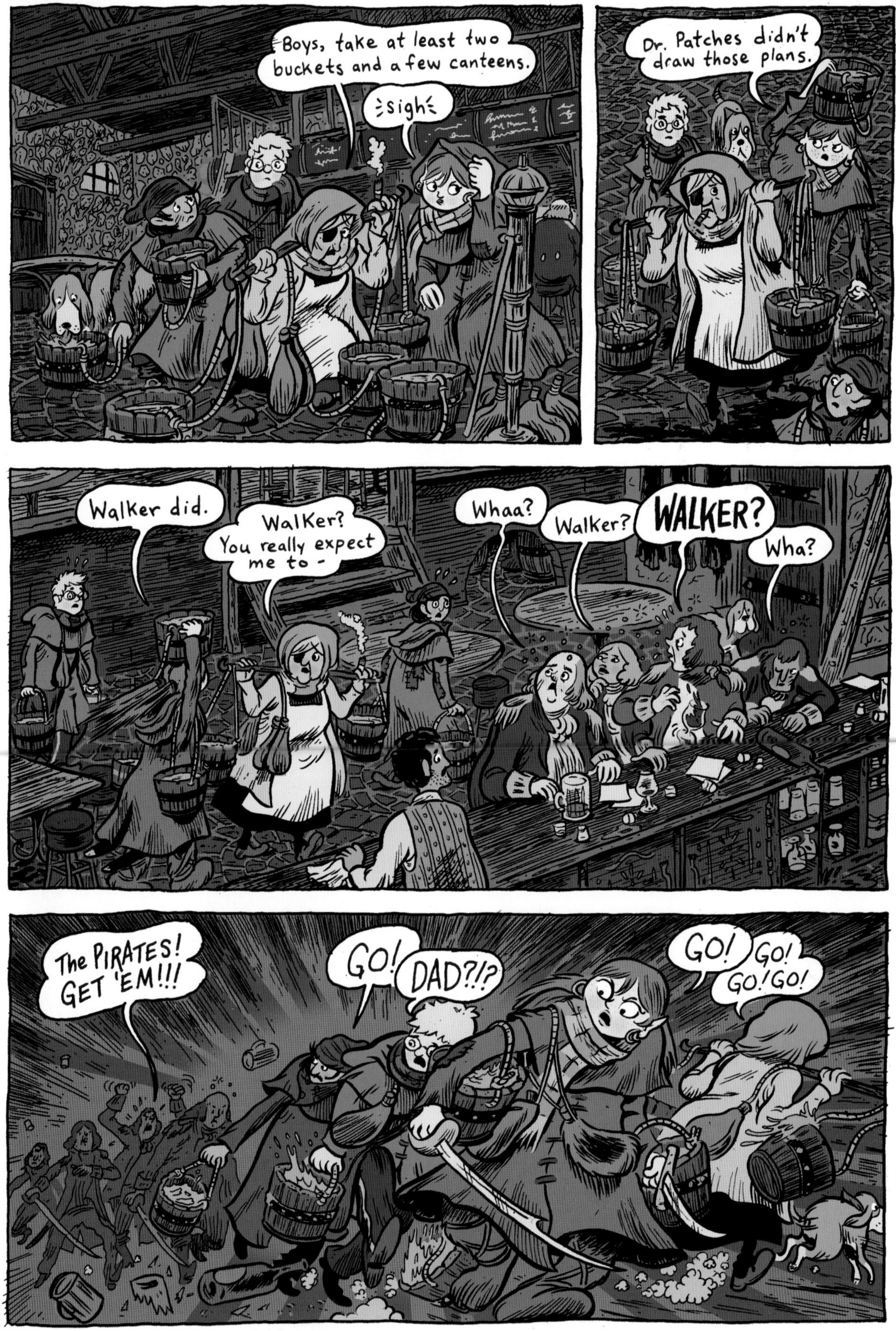
Boys, take at least two buckets and a few canteens.
sigh
Dr. Patches didn't draw those plans.
Walker did.
Walker? You really expect me to -
Whaa?
Walker?
WALKER?
Wha?
The PIRATES! GET 'EM!!!
GO!
DAD?!?
GO!
GO! GO! GO!

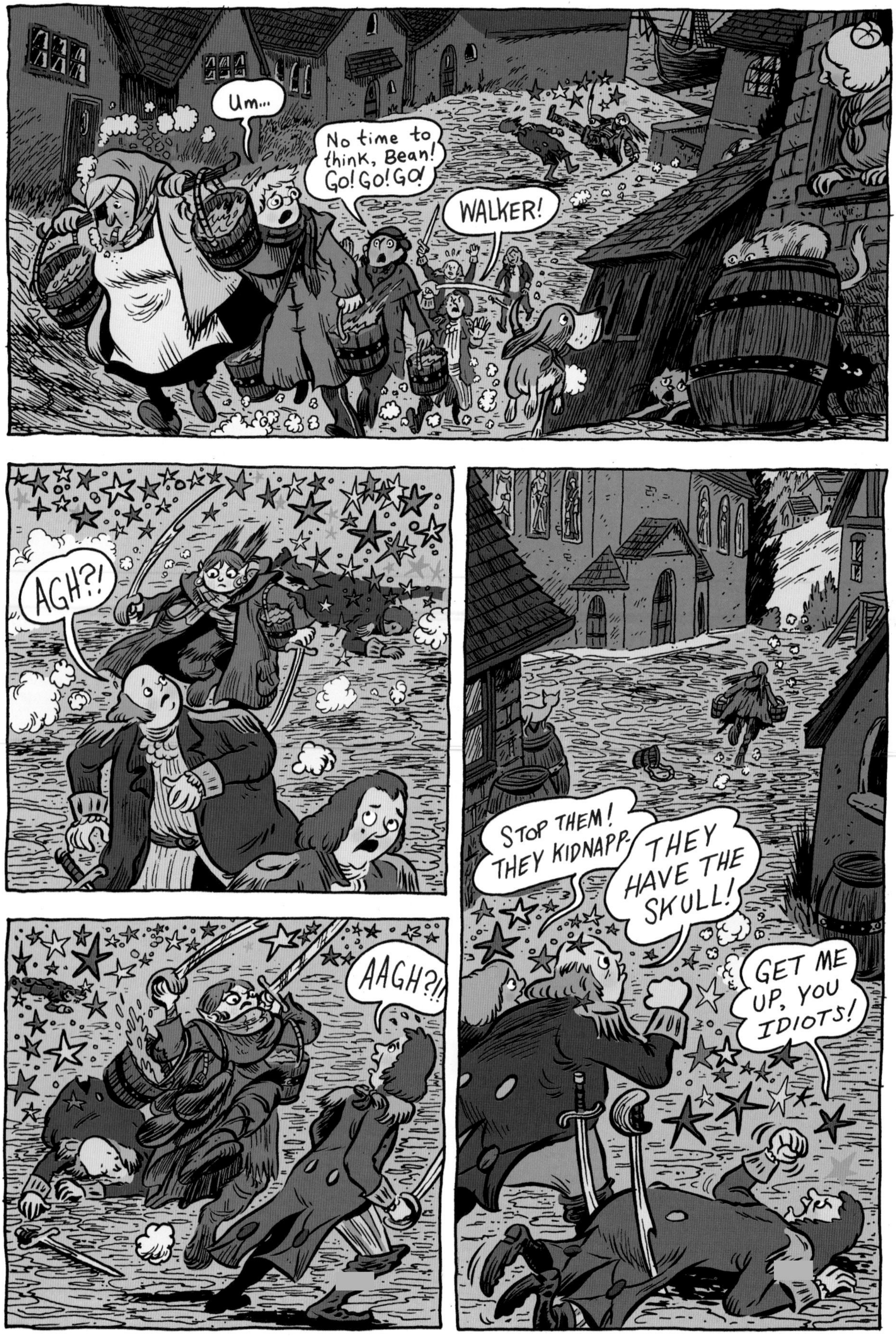
Um...
No time to think, Bean! GO! GO! GO!
WALKER!
AGH?!
AAGH?!!
STOP THEM! THEY KIDNAPP-
THEY HAVE THE SKULL!
GET ME UP, YOU IDIOTS!

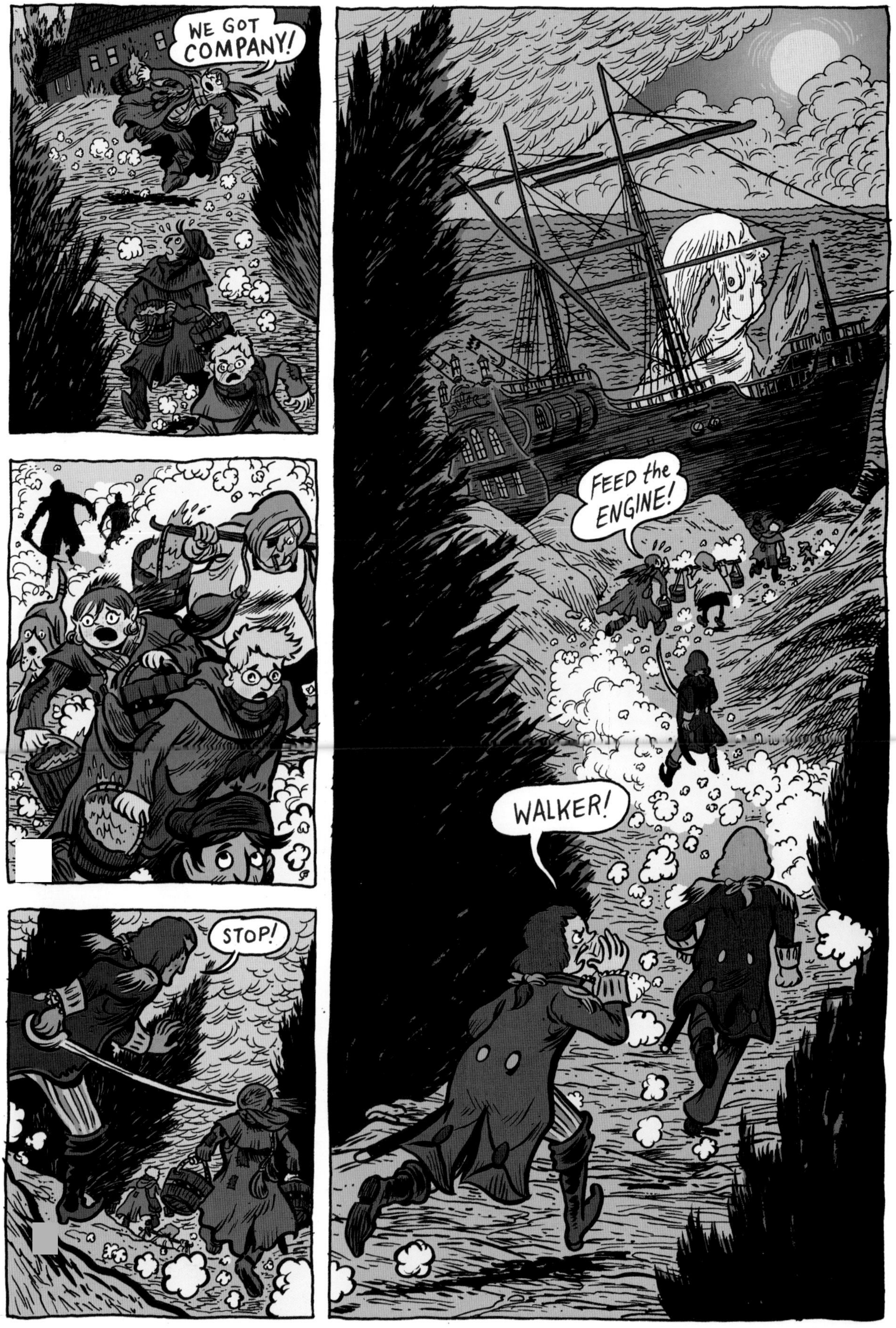

WE GOT COMPANY!
STOP!
FEED the ENGINE!
WALKER!

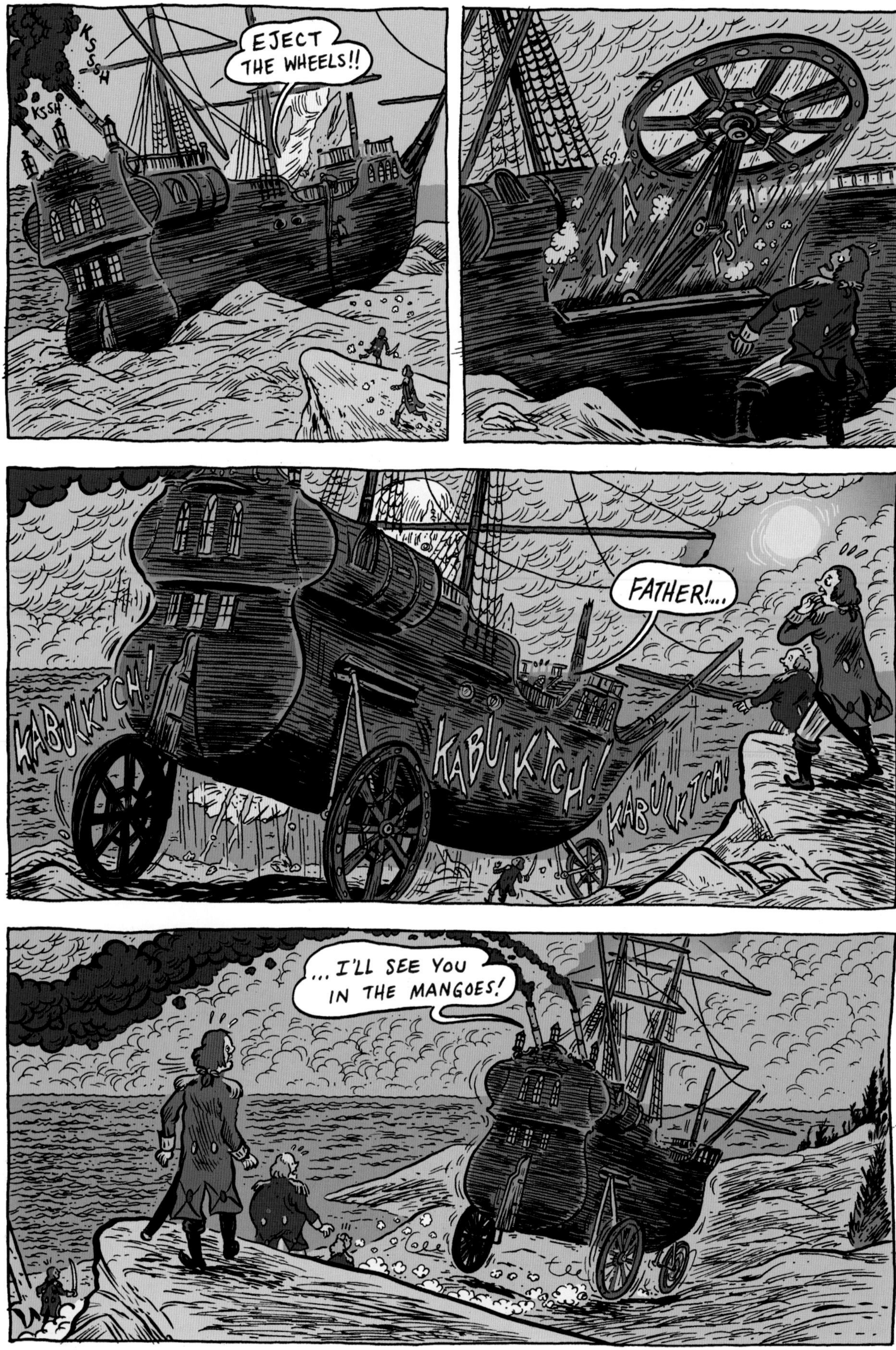
KSSSH
KSSH
EJECT THE WHEELS!!
KA-FSH!
FATHER!...
KABULKTCH!
KABULKTCH!
KABULKTCH!
...I'LL SEE YOU IN THE MANGOES!

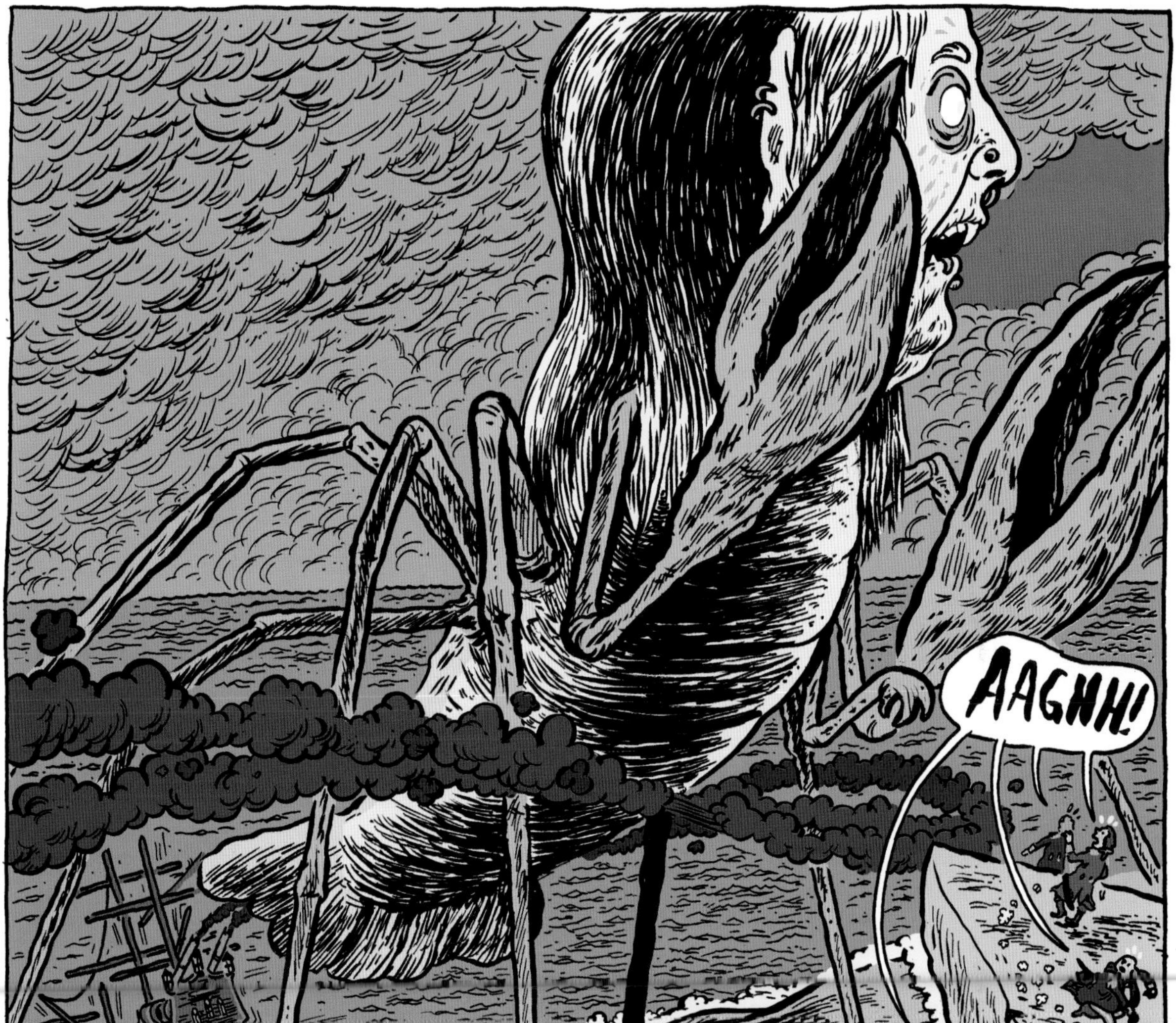
AAGNH!

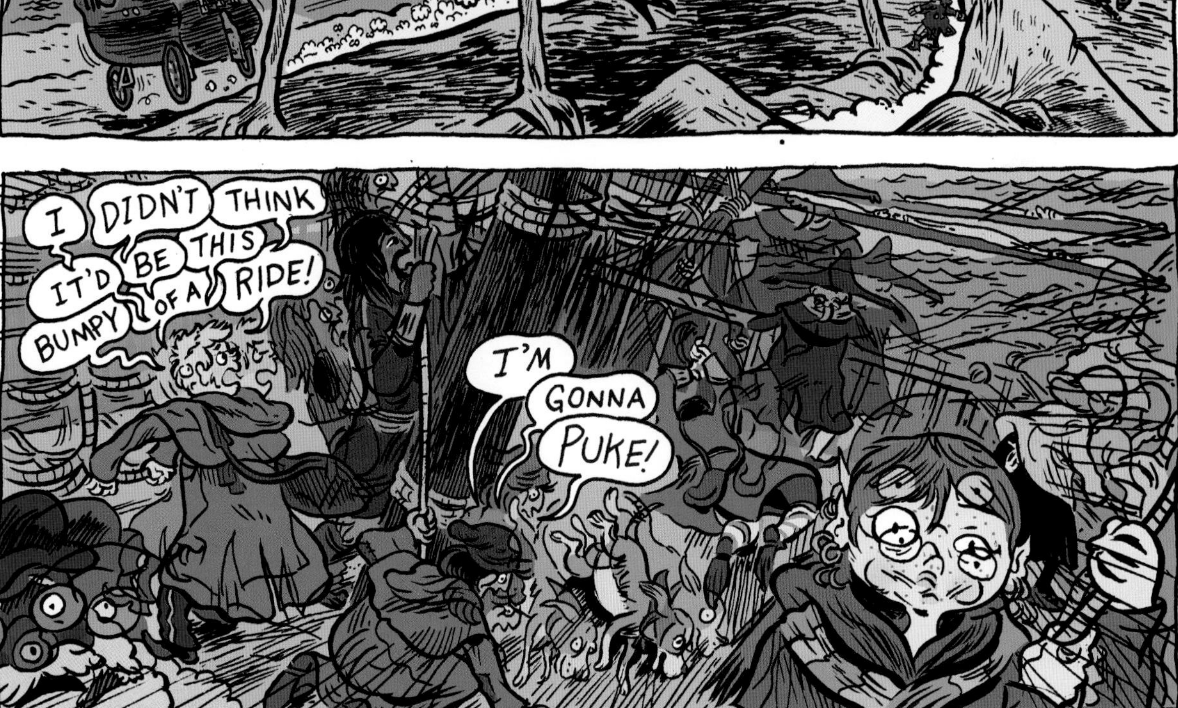
I DIDN'T THINK IT'D BE THIS BUMPY OF A RIDE!
I'M GONNA PUKE!

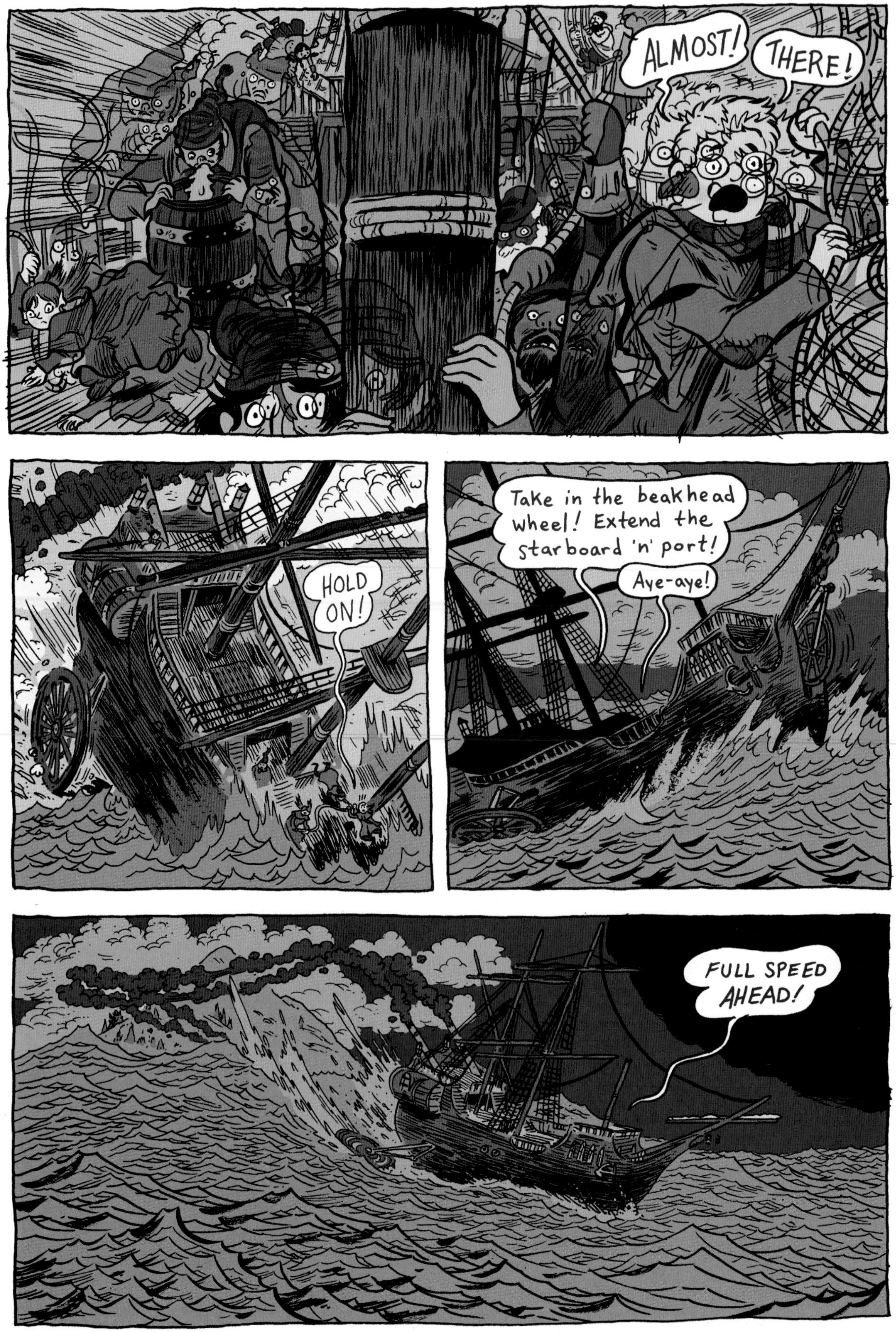
ALMOST!
THERE!
HOLD ON!
Take in the beakhead wheel! Extend the starboard 'n' port!
Aye-aye!
FULL SPEED AHEAD!

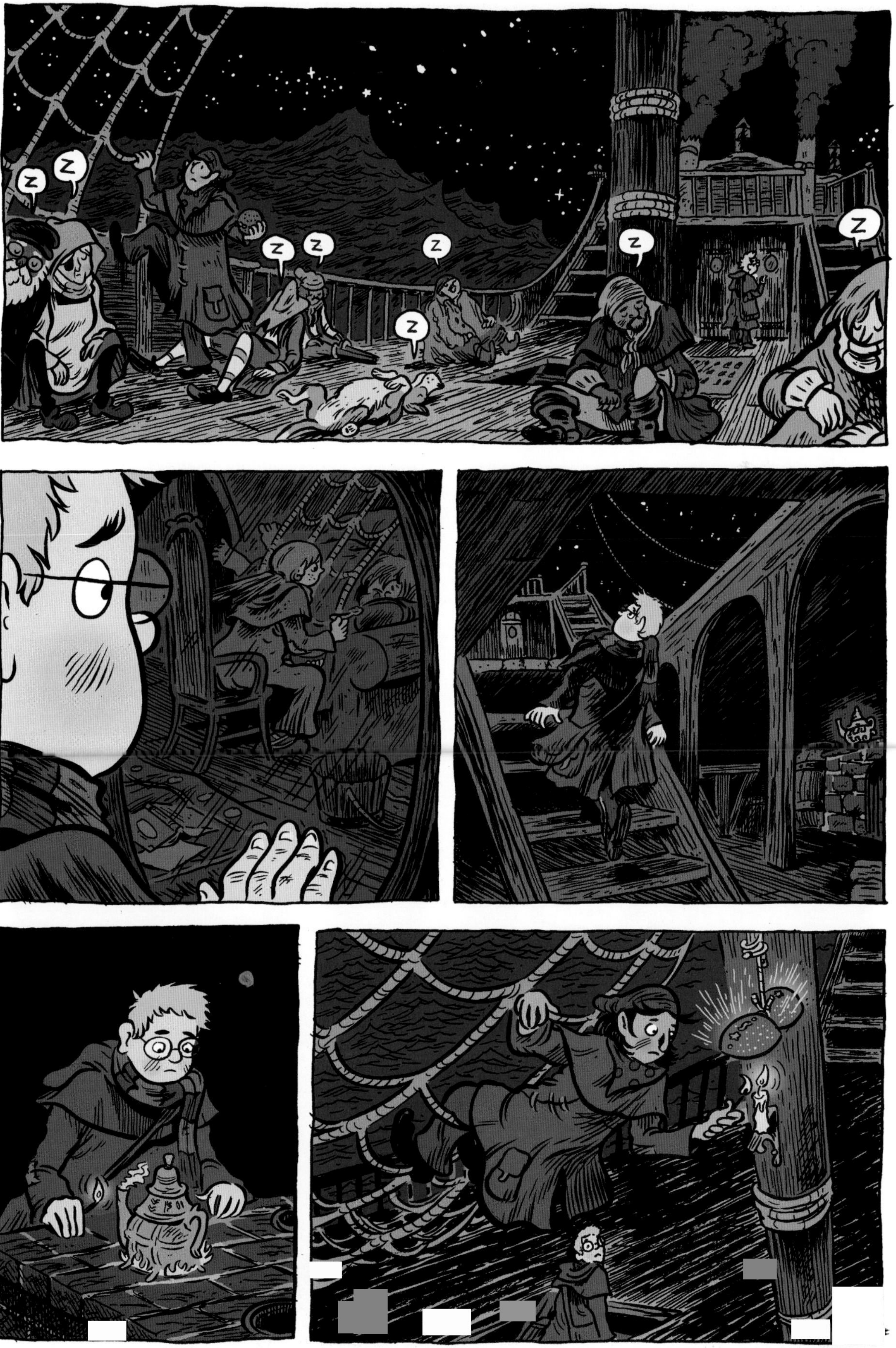
Z
Z
Z
Z
Z
Z
Z
Z

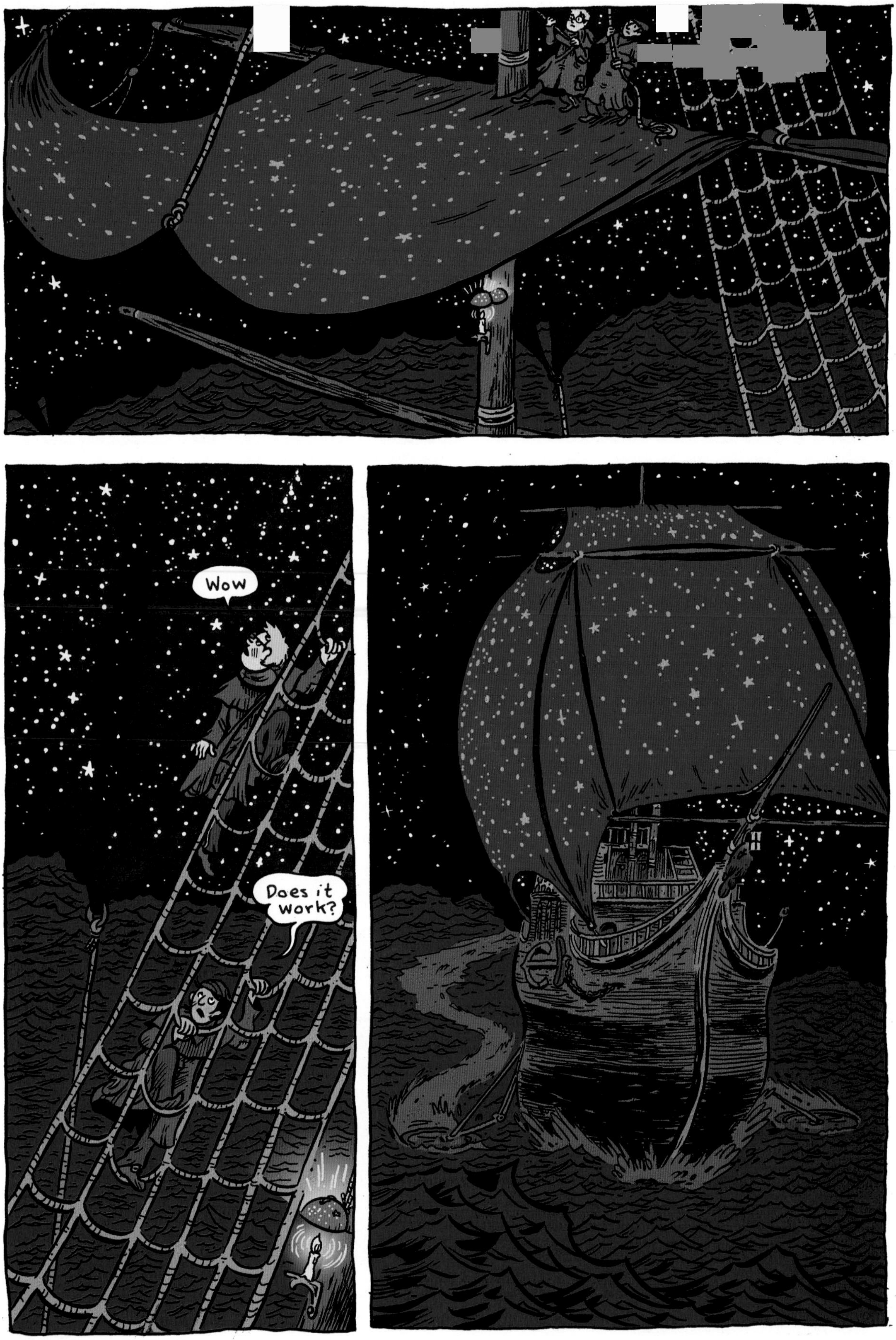
Wow
Does it work?

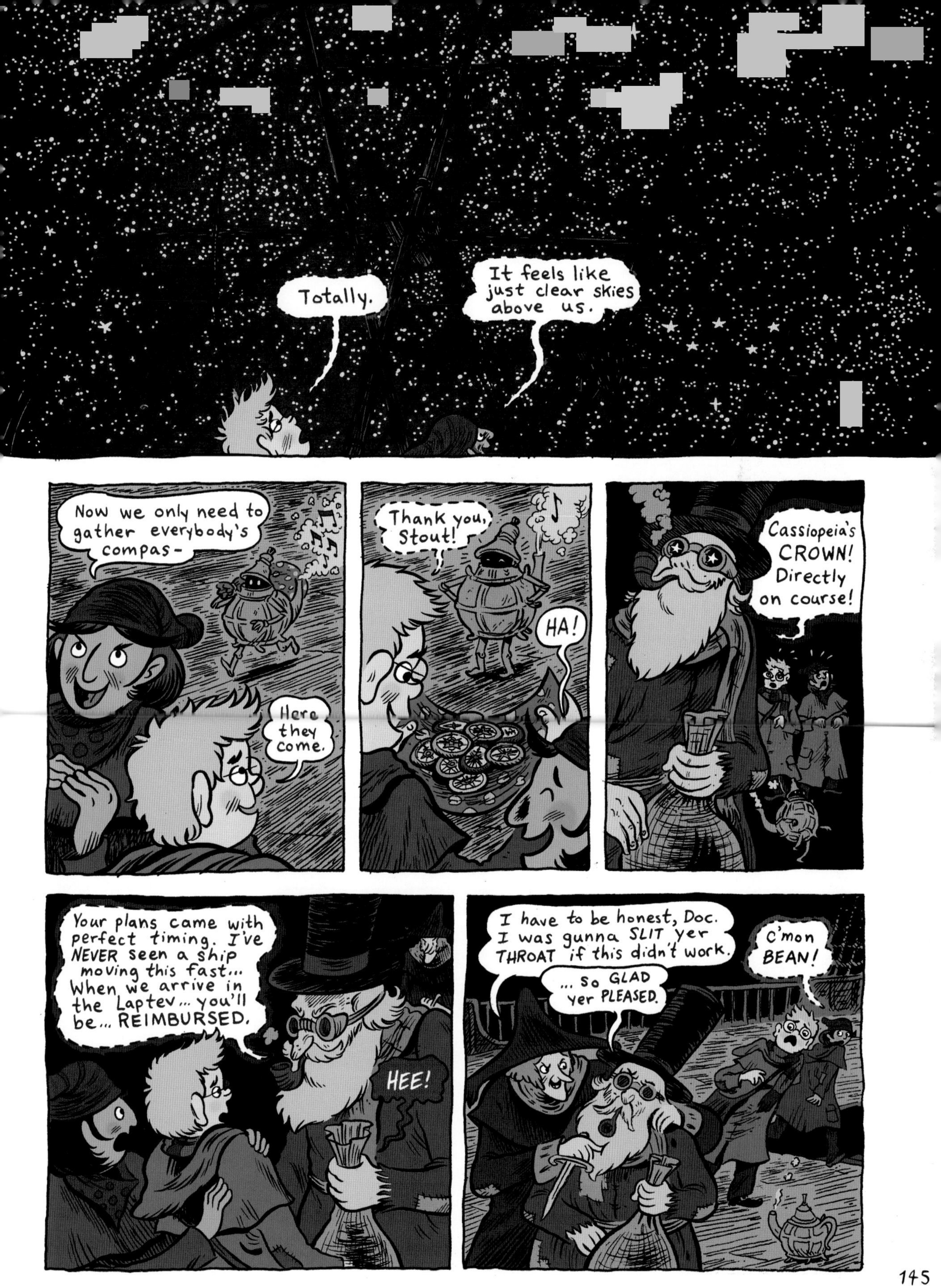
It feels like just clear skies above us.
Totally.
Now we only need to gather everybody's compas-
Here they come.
Thank you, Stout!
HA!
Cassiopeia's CROWN! Directly on course!
Your plans came with perfect timing. I've NEVER seen a ship moving this fast... When we arrive in the Laptev... you'll be... REIMBURSED.
HEE!
I have to be honest, Doc. I was gunna SLIT yer THROAT if this didn't work.
... so GLAD yer PLEASED.
C'mon BEAN!

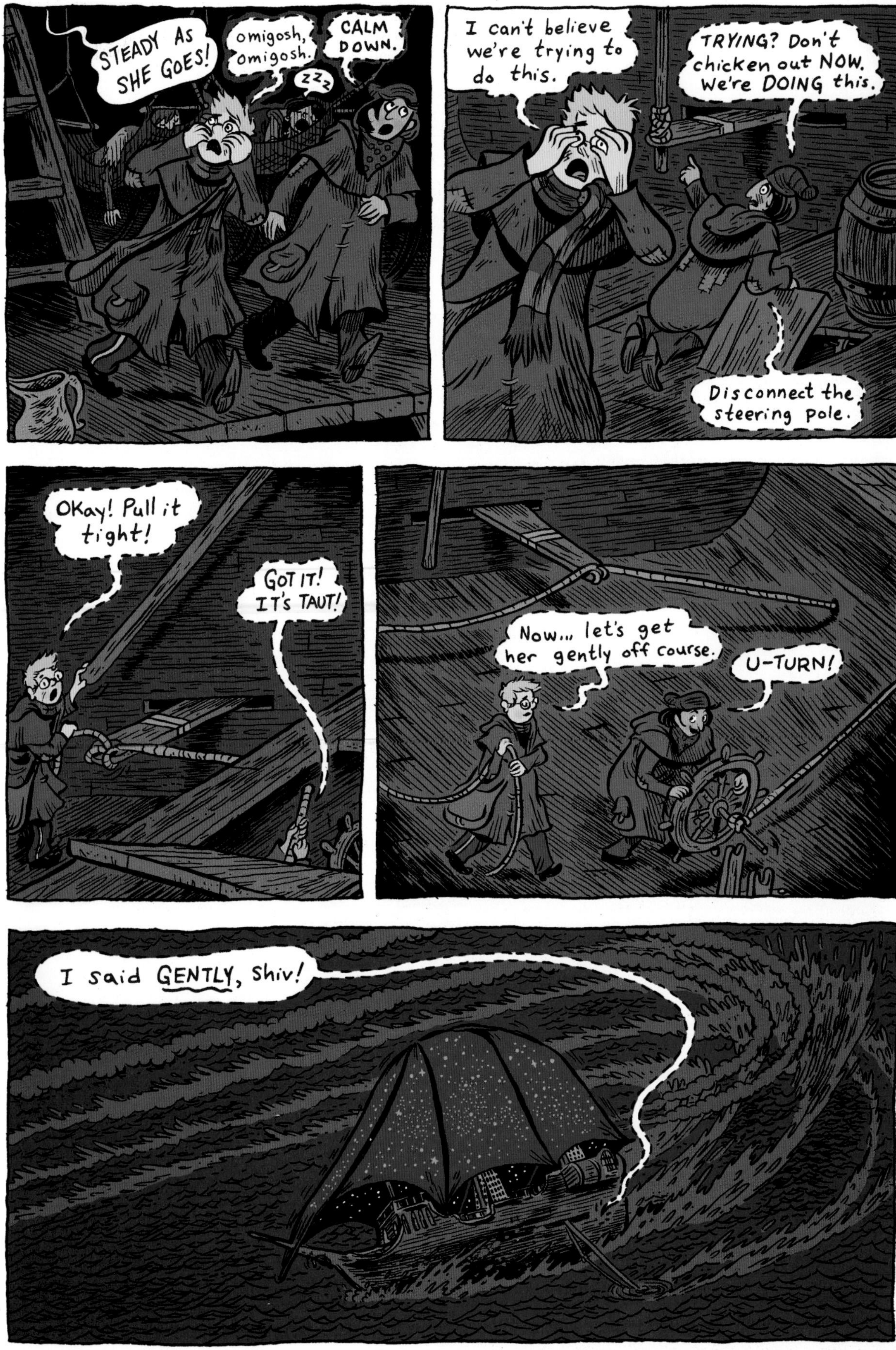
STEADY AS SHE GOES!
omigosh, omigosh.
CALM DOWN.
zzz
I can't believe we're trying to do this.
TRYING? Don't chicken out NOW. We're DOING this.
Disconnect the steering pole.
OKay! Pull it tight!
GOT IT! IT'S TAUT!
Now... let's get her gently off course.
U-TURN!
I said GENTLY, shiv!

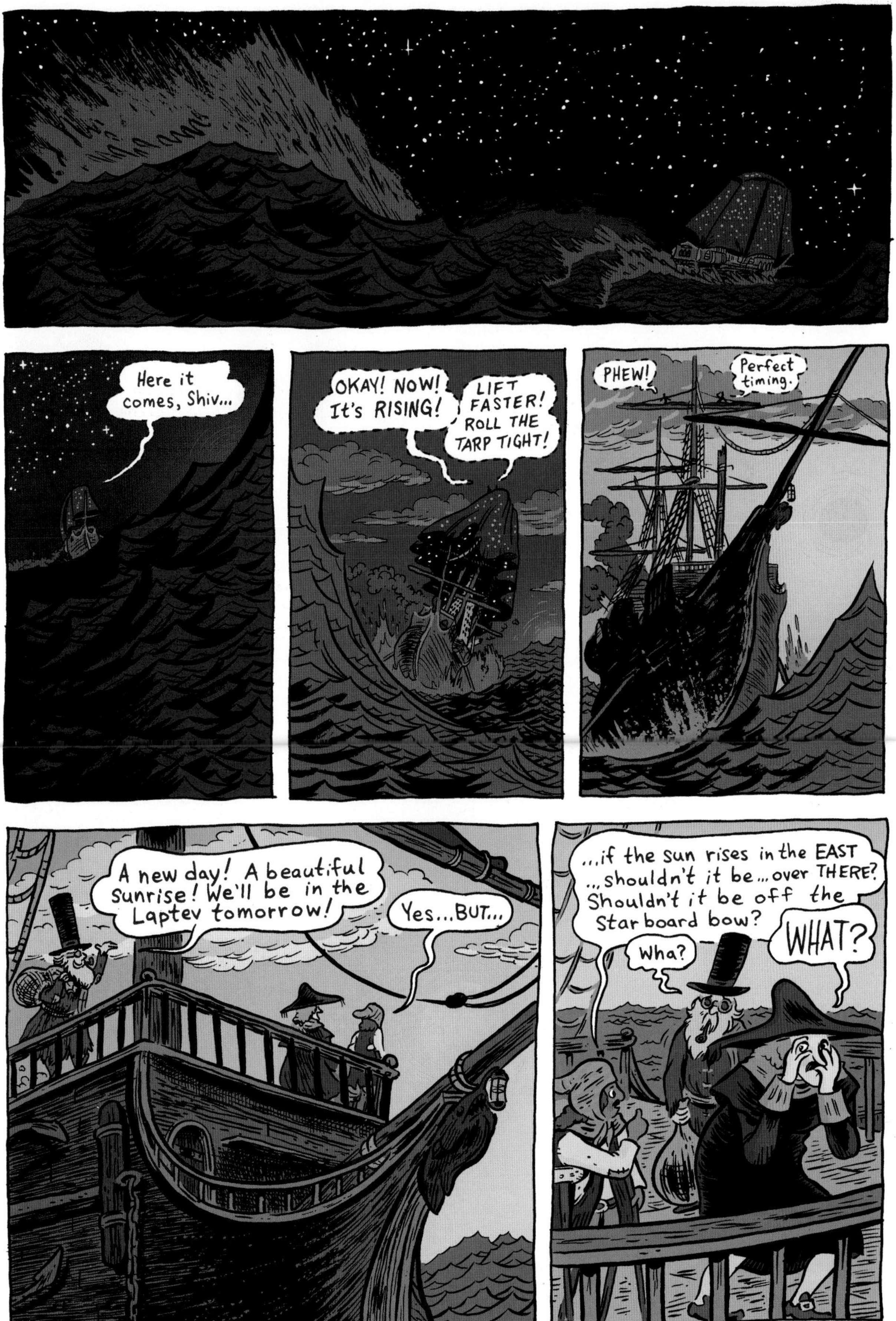
Here it comes, Shiv...
OKAY! NOW! It's RISING!
LIFT FASTER! ROLL THE TARP TIGHT!
PHEW!
Perfect timing.
A new day! A beautiful sunrise! We'll be in the Laptev tomorrow!
Yes...BUT...
...if the sun rises in the EAST ...shouldn't it be... over THERE? Shouldn't it be off the Starboard bow?
Wha?
WHAT?

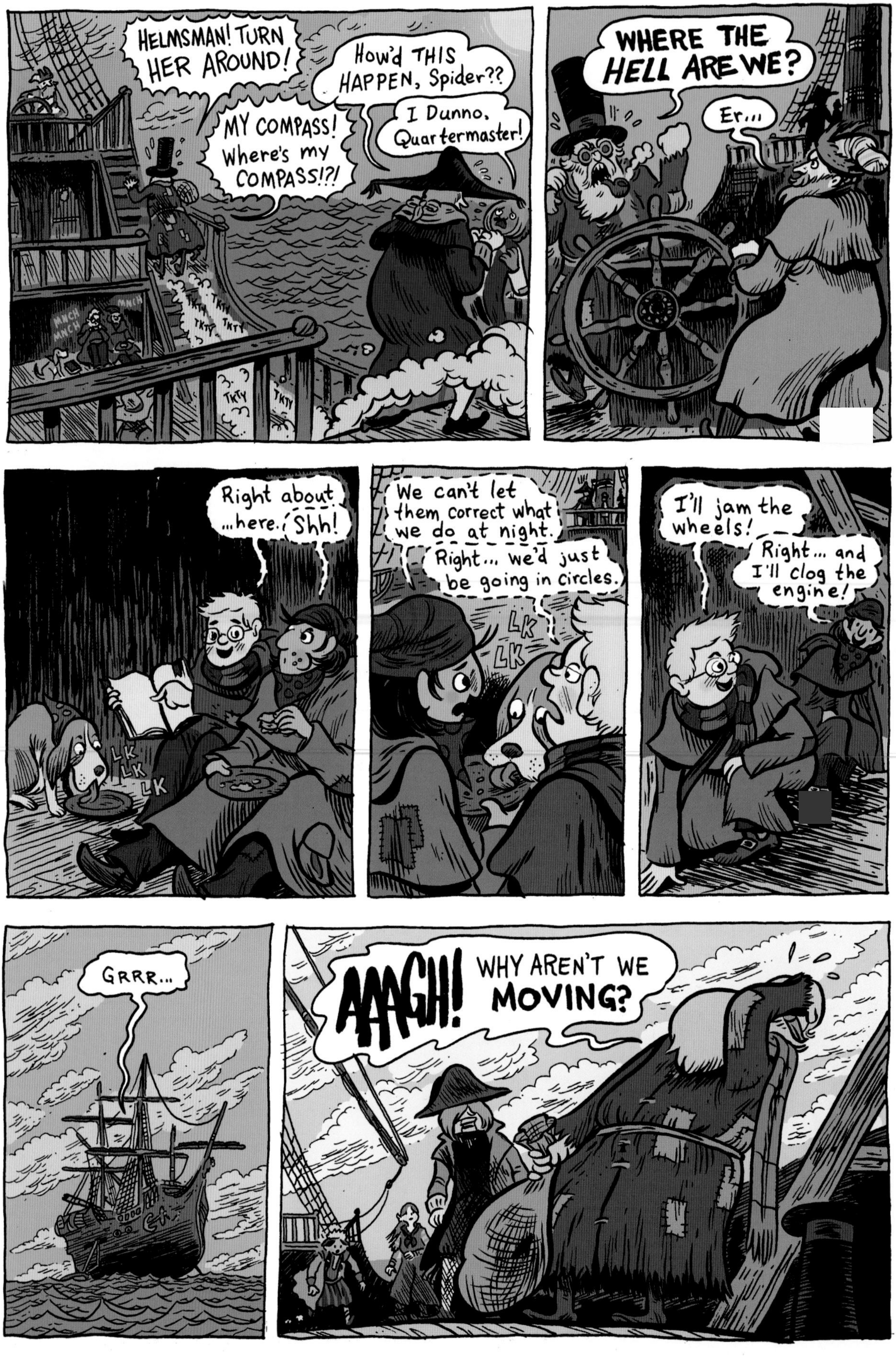
HELMSMAN! TURN HER AROUND!
How'd THIS HAPPEN, Spider??
MY COMPASS! Where's my COMPASS!?!
I Dunno, Quartermaster!
MNCH MNCH
MNCH
TKTY TKTY
TKTY TKTY
TKTY TKTY
WHERE THE HELL ARE WE?
Er...
Right about ...here.
Shh!
LK LK LK
We can't let them correct what we do at night.
Right... we'd just be going in circles.
LK LK
I'll jam the wheels!
Right... and I'll clog the engine!
GRRR...
AAAGH! WHY AREN'T WE MOVING?

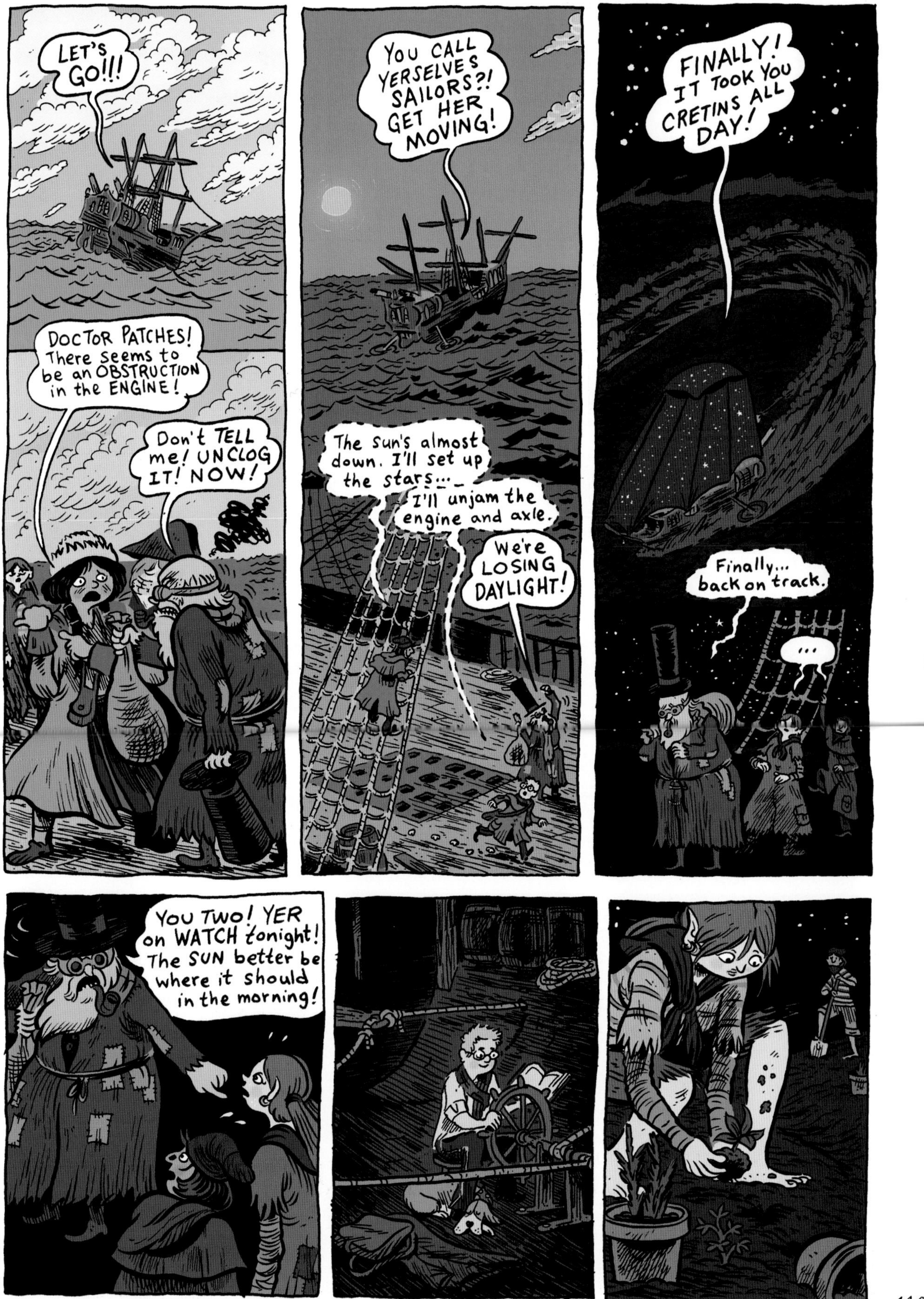
LET'S GO!!!
DOCTOR PATCHES! There seems to be an OBSTRUCTION in the ENGINE!
Don't TELL me! UNCLOG IT! NOW!
YOU CALL YERSELVES SAILORS?! GET HER MOVING!
The sun's almost down. I'll set up the stars...
I'll unjam the engine and axle.
We're LOSING DAYLIGHT!
FINALLY! IT TOOK YOU CRETINS ALL DAY!
Finally... back on track.
...
YOU TWO! YER on WATCH tonight! The SUN better be where it should in the morning!

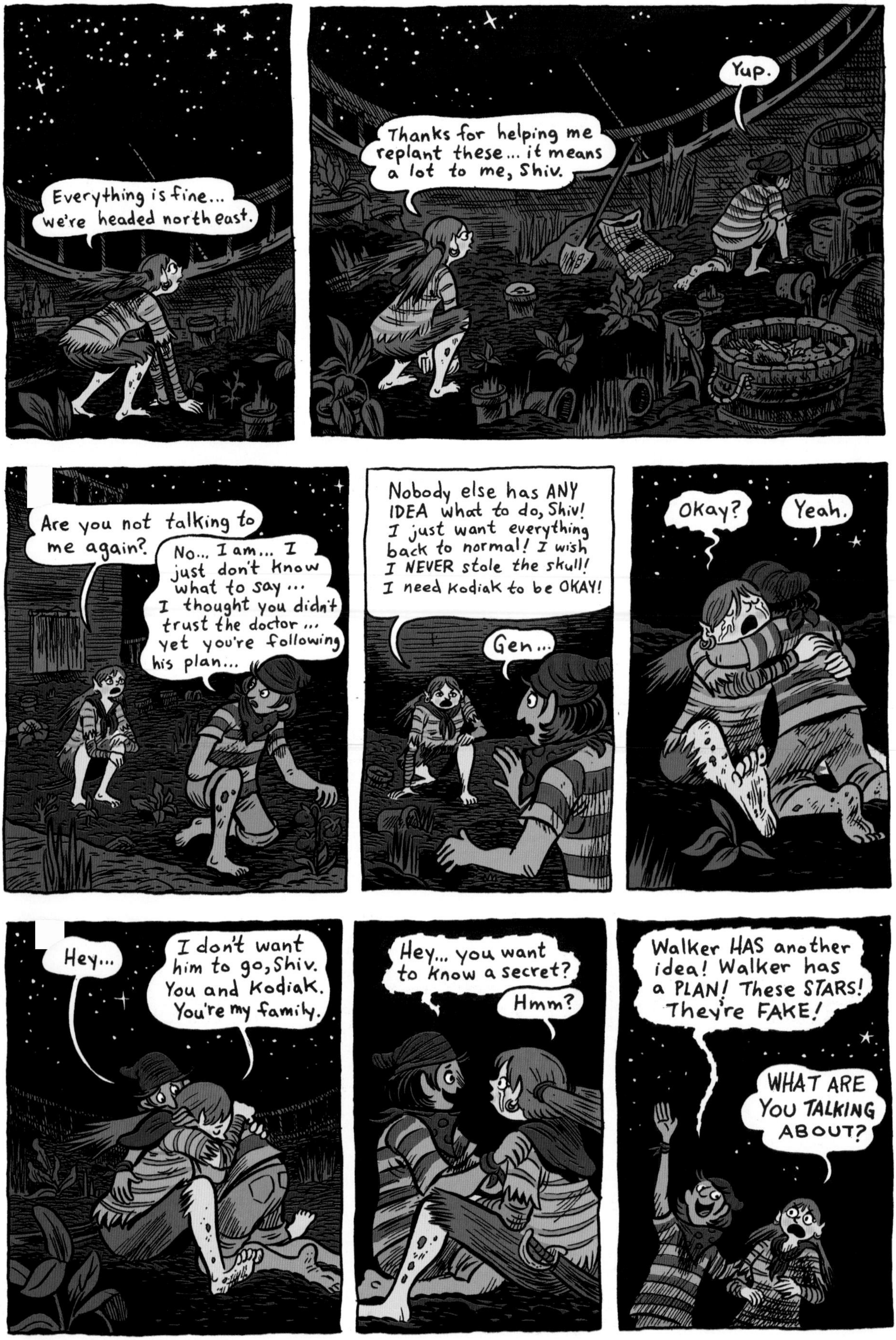
Everything is fine... we're headed northeast.
Thanks for helping me replant these... it means a lot to me, Shiv.
Yup.
Are you not talking to me again?
No... I am... I just don't know what to say... I thought you didn't trust the doctor... yet you're following his plan...
Nobody else has ANY IDEA what to do, Shiv! I just want everything back to normal! I wish I NEVER stole the skull! I need Kodiak to be OKAY!
Gen...
Okay?
Yeah.
Hey...
I don't want him to go, Shiv. You and Kodiak. You're my family.
Hey... you want to know a secret?
Hmm?
Walker HAS another idea! Walker has a PLAN! These STARS! They're FAKE!
WHAT ARE YOU TALKING ABOUT?

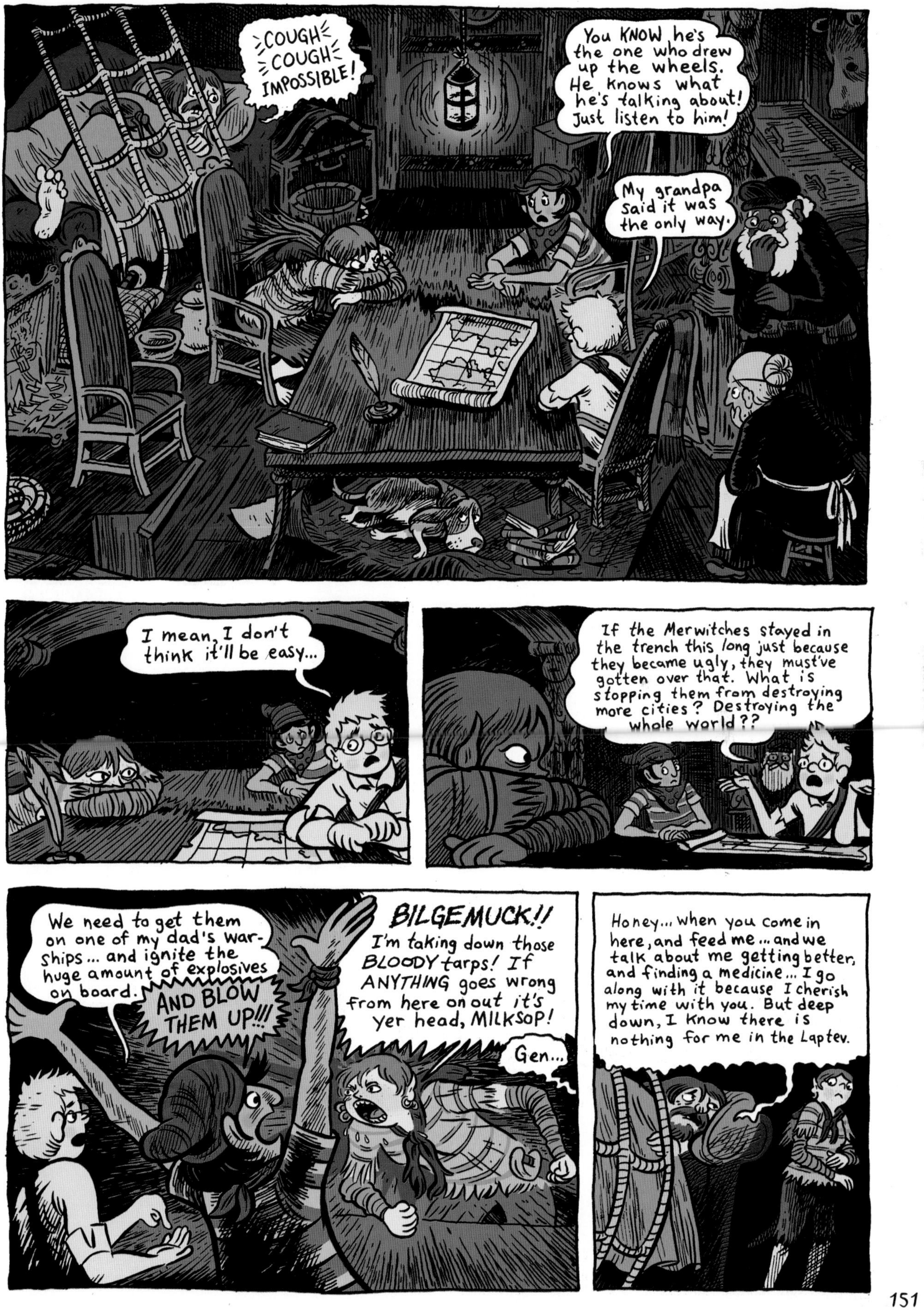
COUGH COUGH IMPOSSIBLE!
You KNOW he's the one who drew up the wheels. He knows what he's talking about! Just listen to him!
My grandpa said it was the only way.
I mean, I don't think it'll be easy...
If the Merwitches stayed in the trench this long just because they became ugly, they must've gotten over that. What is stopping them from destroying more cities? Destroying the whole world??
We need to get them on one of my dad's war-ships... and ignite the huge amount of explosives on board.
AND BLOW THEM UP!!!
BILGEMUCK!!
I'm taking down those BLOODY tarps! If ANYTHING goes wrong from here on out it's yer head, MILKSOP!
Gen...
Honey... when you come in here, and feed me... and we talk about me getting better, and finding a medicine... I go along with it because I cherish my time with you. But deep down, I know there is nothing for me in the Laptev.

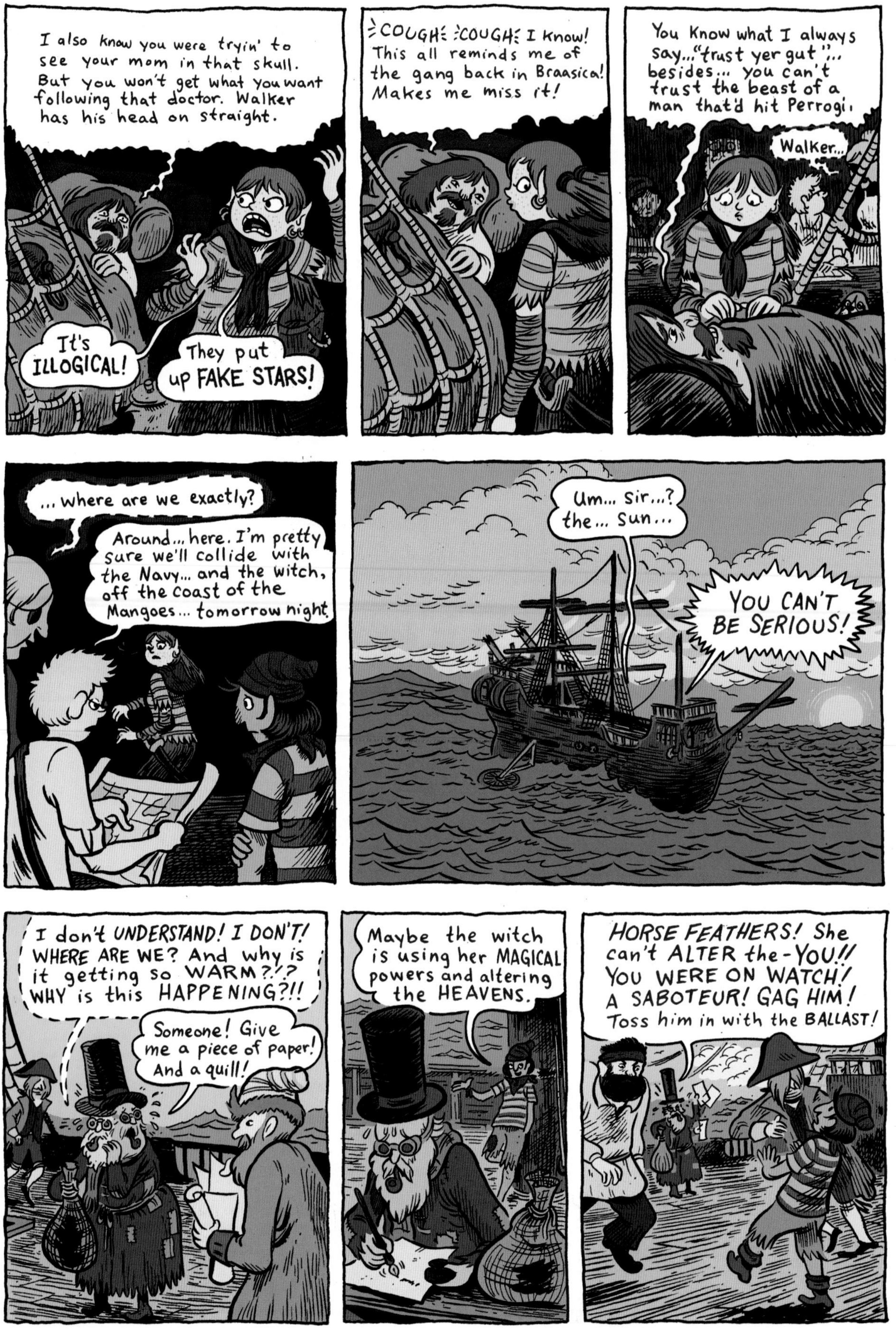
I also know you were tryin' to see your mom in that skull. But you won't get what you want following that doctor. Walker has his head on straight.
It's ILLOGICAL!
They put up FAKE STARS!
COUGH! COUGH! I know! This all reminds me of the gang back in Braasica! Makes me miss it!
You know what I always say..."trust yer gut"... besides... you can't trust the beast of a man that'd hit Perrogi.
Walker...
... where are we exactly?
Around... here. I'm pretty sure we'll collide with the Navy... and the witch, off the coast of the Mangoes... tomorrow night.
Um... sir...? the... sun...
YOU CAN'T BE SERIOUS!
I don't UNDERSTAND! I DON'T! WHERE ARE WE? And why is it getting so WARM?!? WHY is this HAPPENING?!!
Someone! Give me a piece of paper! And a quill!
Maybe the witch is using her MAGICAL powers and altering the HEAVENS.
HORSE FEATHERS! She can't ALTER the-YOU!! YOU WERE ON WATCH! A SABOTEUR! GAG HIM! Toss him in with the BALLAST!

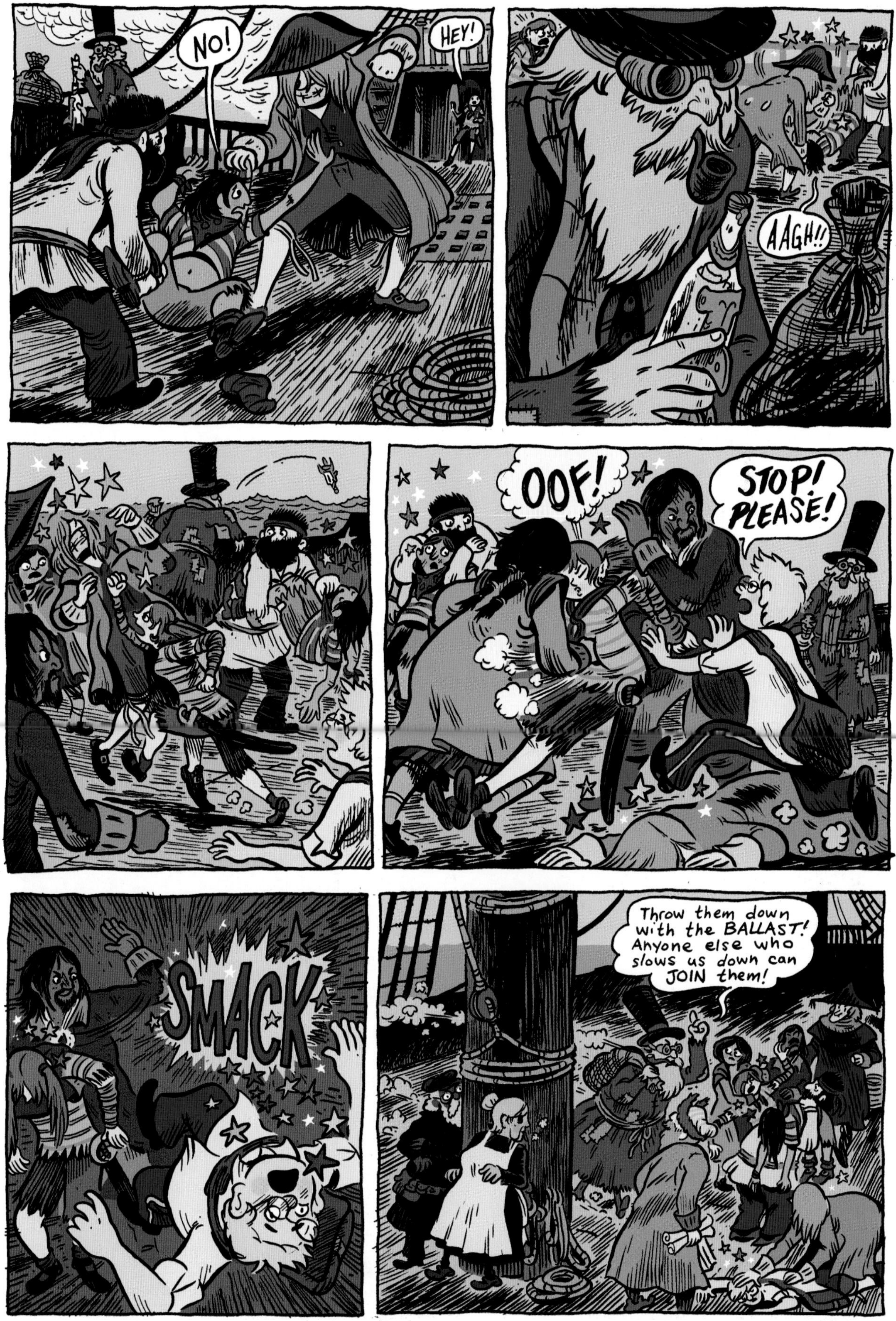
NO!
HEY!
AAGH!!
OOF!
STOP! PLEASE!
SMACK
Throw them down with the BALLAST! Anyone else who slows us down can JOIN them!

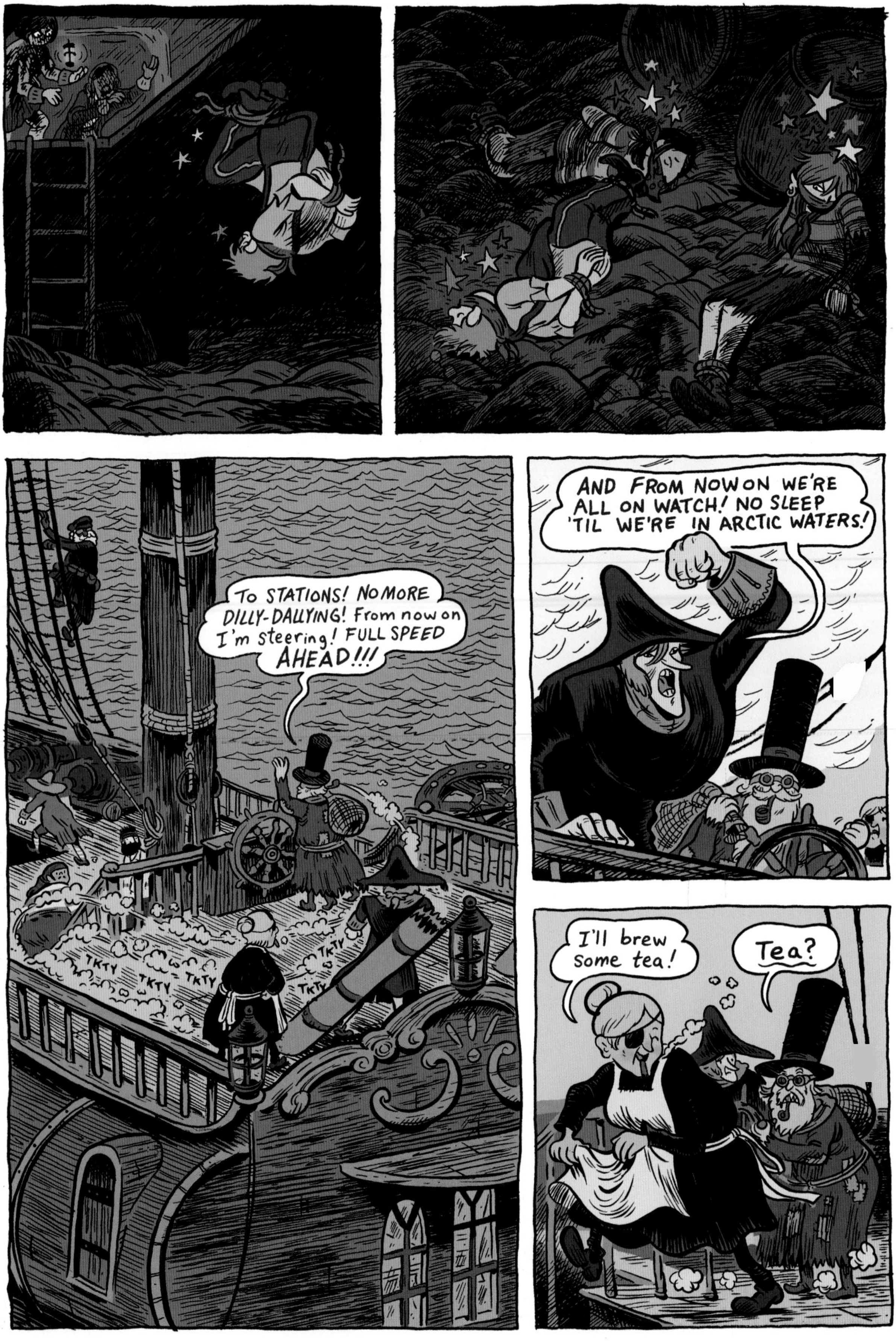
To STATIONS! NO MORE DILLY-DALLYING! From now on I'm steering! FULL SPEED AHEAD!!!
TKTY
TKTY
TKTY
TKTY
TKTY
AND FROM NOW ON WE'RE ALL ON WATCH! NO SLEEP 'TIL WE'RE IN ARCTIC WATERS!
I'll brew some tea!
Tea?

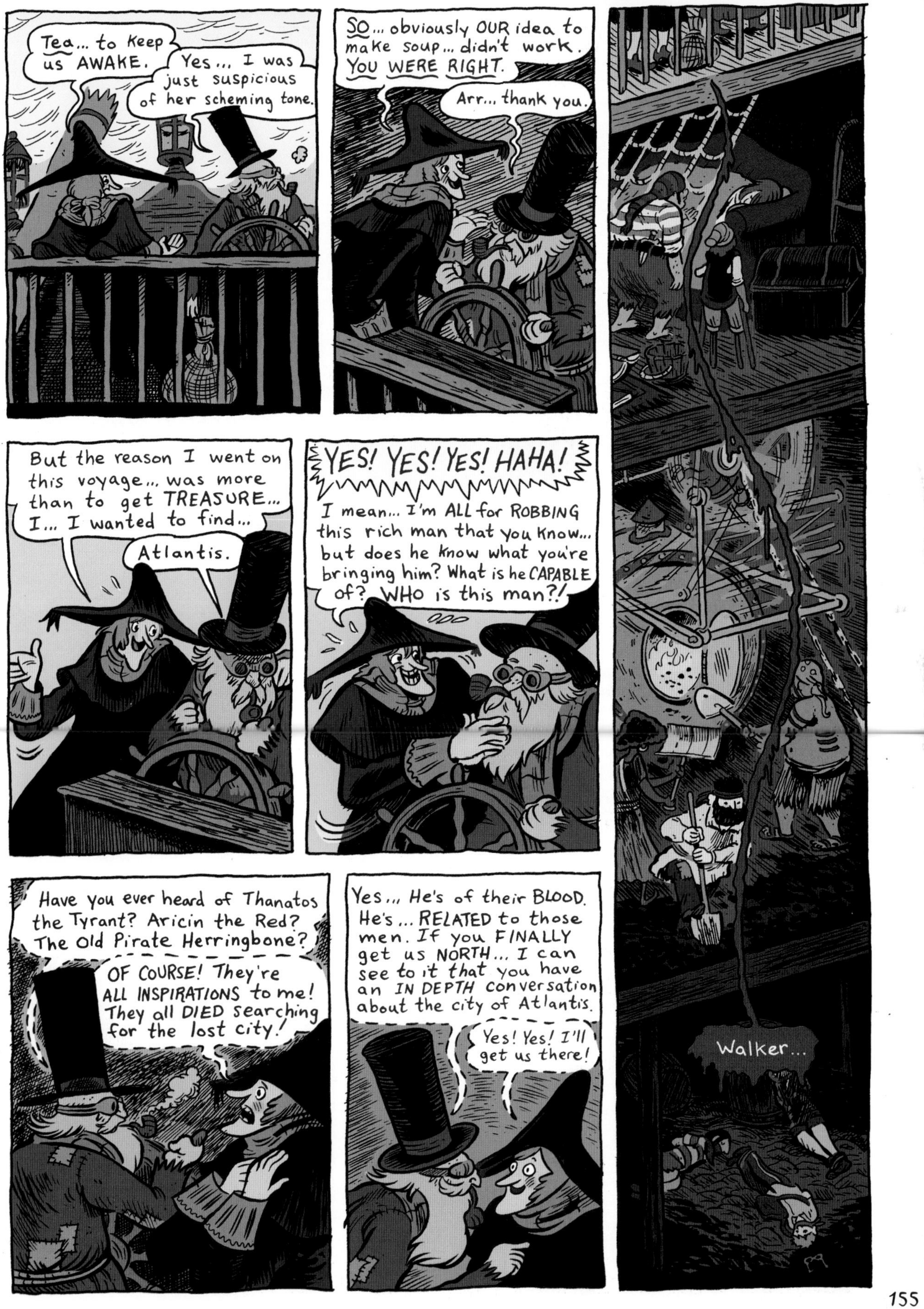

Tea... to keep us AWAKE.
Yes... I was just suspicious of her scheming tone.
SO... obviously OUR idea to make soup... didn't work. YOU WERE RIGHT.
Arr... thank you.
But the reason I went on this voyage... was more than to get TREASURE... I... I wanted to find...
Atlantis.
YES! YES! YES! HAHA!
I mean... I'm ALL for ROBBING this rich man that you know... but does he know what you're bringing him? What is he CAPABLE of? WHO is this man?!
Have you ever heard of Thanatos the Tyrant? Aricin the Red? The Old Pirate Herringbone?
OF COURSE! They're ALL INSPIRATIONS to me! They all DIED searching for the lost city!
Yes... He's of their BLOOD. He's... RELATED to those men. If you FINALLY get us NORTH... I can see to it that you have an IN DEPTH conversation about the city of Atlantis.
Yes! Yes! I'll get us there!
Walker...

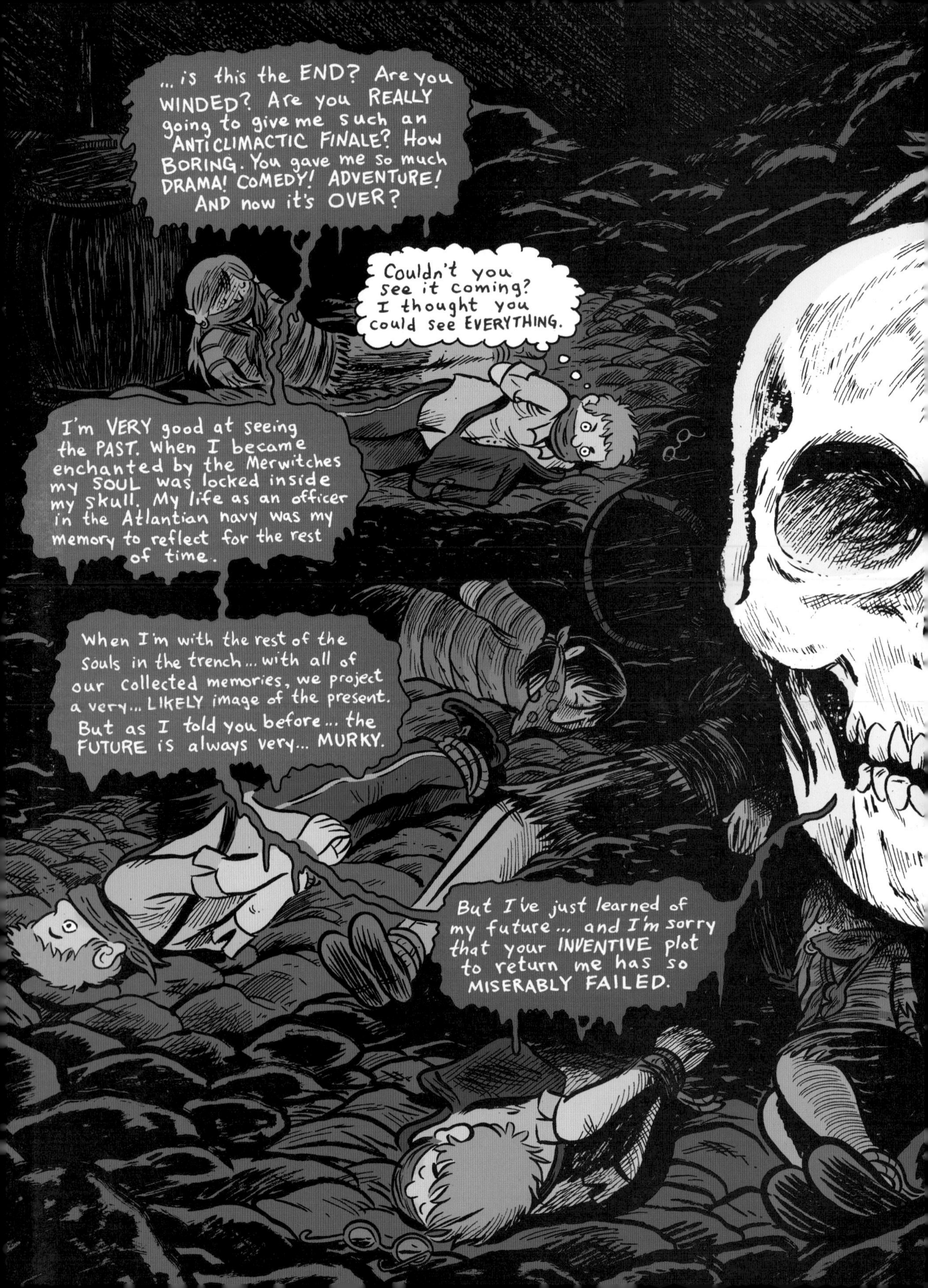
... is this the END? Are you WINDED? Are you REALLY going to give me such an ANTICLIMACTIC FINALE? How BORING. You gave me so much DRAMA! COMEDY! ADVENTURE! AND now it's OVER?
Couldn't you see it coming? I thought you could see EVERYTHING.
I'm VERY good at seeing the PAST. When I became enchanted by the Merwitches my SOUL was locked inside my skull. My life as an officer in the Atlantian navy was my memory to reflect for the rest of time.
When I'm with the rest of the souls in the trench... with all of our collected memories, we project a very... LIKELY image of the present. But as I told you before... the FUTURE is always very... MURKY.
But I've just learned of my future... and I'm sorry that your INVENTIVE plot to return me has so MISERABLY FAILED.

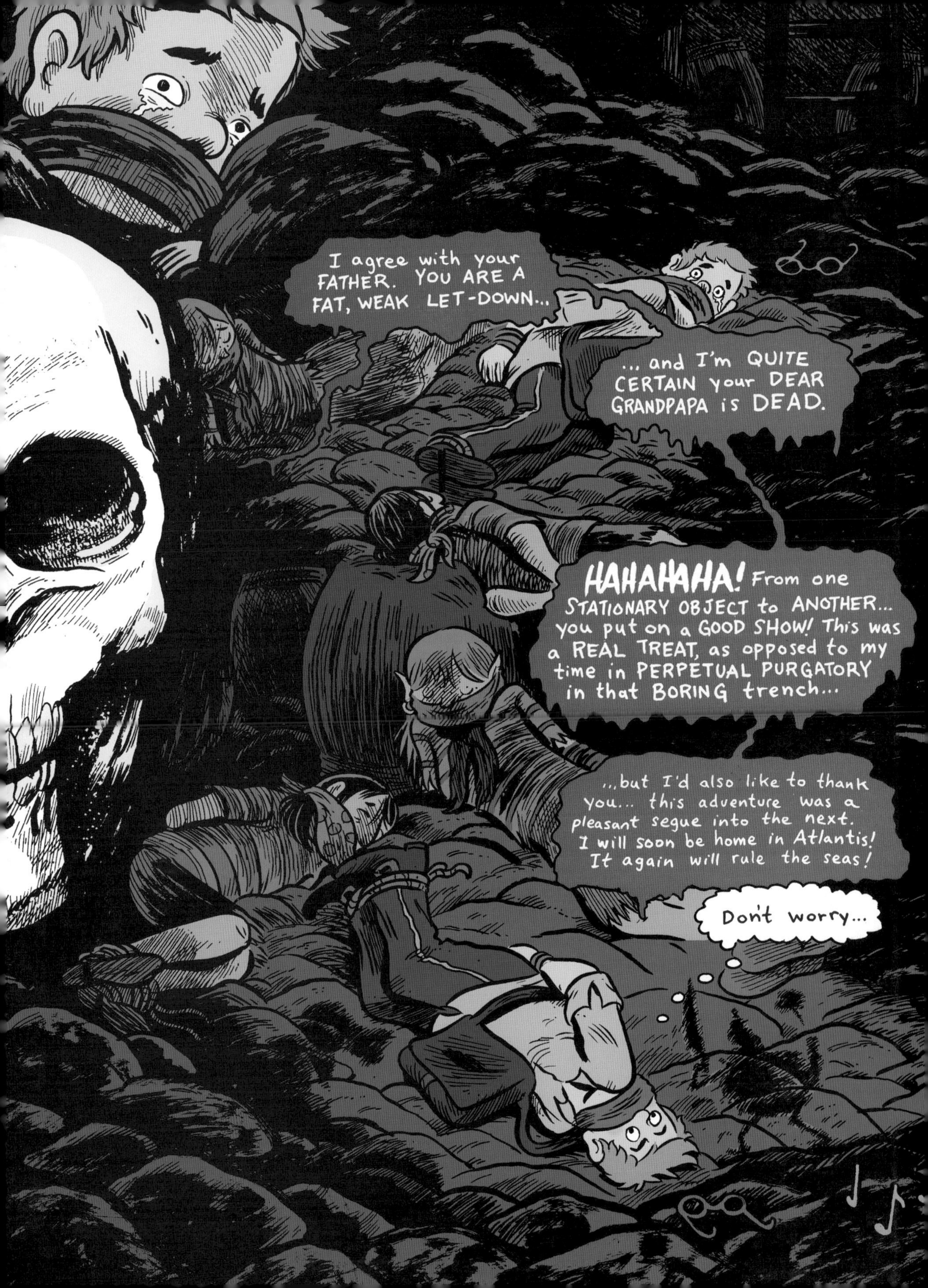
I agree with your FATHER. YOU ARE A FAT, WEAK LET-DOWN...
... and I'm QUITE CERTAIN your DEAR GRANDPAPA is DEAD.
HAHAHAHA! From one STATIONARY OBJECT to ANOTHER... you put on a GOOD SHOW! This was a REAL TREAT, as opposed to my time in PERPETUAL PURGATORY in that BORING trench...
...but I'd also like to thank you... this adventure was a pleasant segue into the next. I will soon be home in Atlantis! It again will rule the seas!
Don't worry...

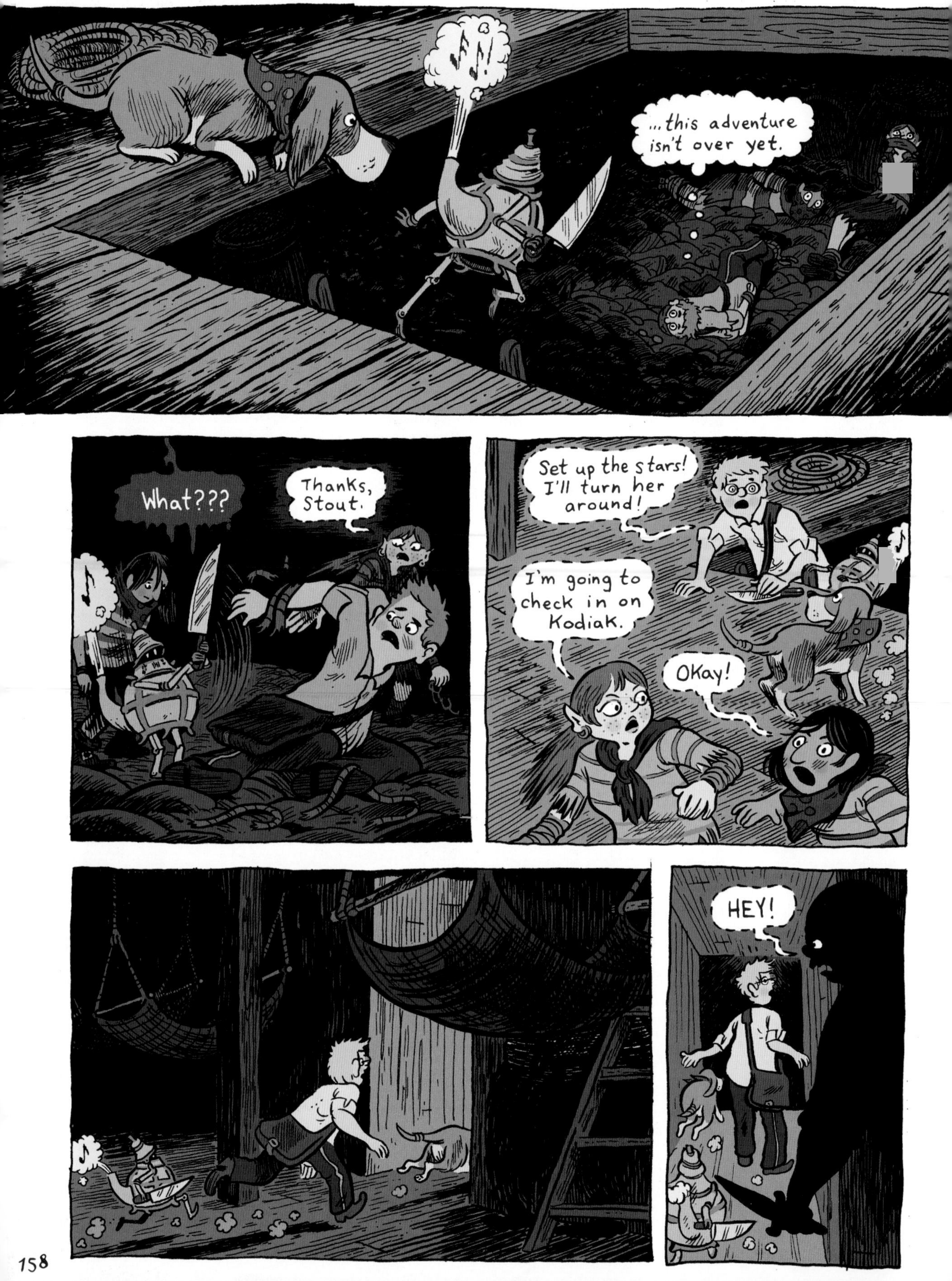
...this adventure isn't over yet.
What???
Thanks, Stout.
Set up the stars! I'll turn her around!
I'm going to check in on Kodiak.
OKay!
HEY!

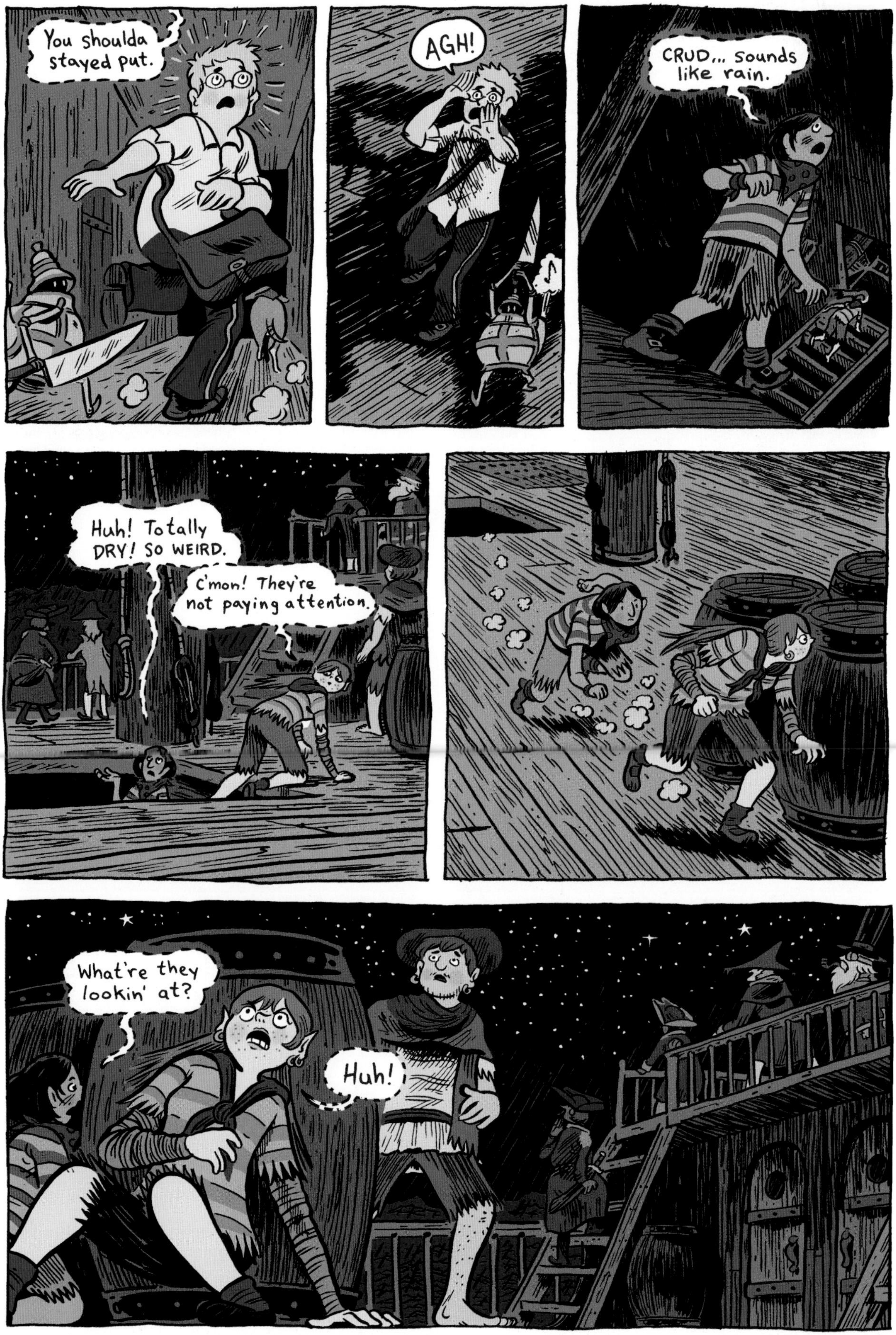
You shoulda stayed put.
AGH!
CRUD... sounds like rain.
Huh! Totally DRY! SO WEIRD.
C'mon! They're not paying attention.
What're they lookin' at?
Huh!

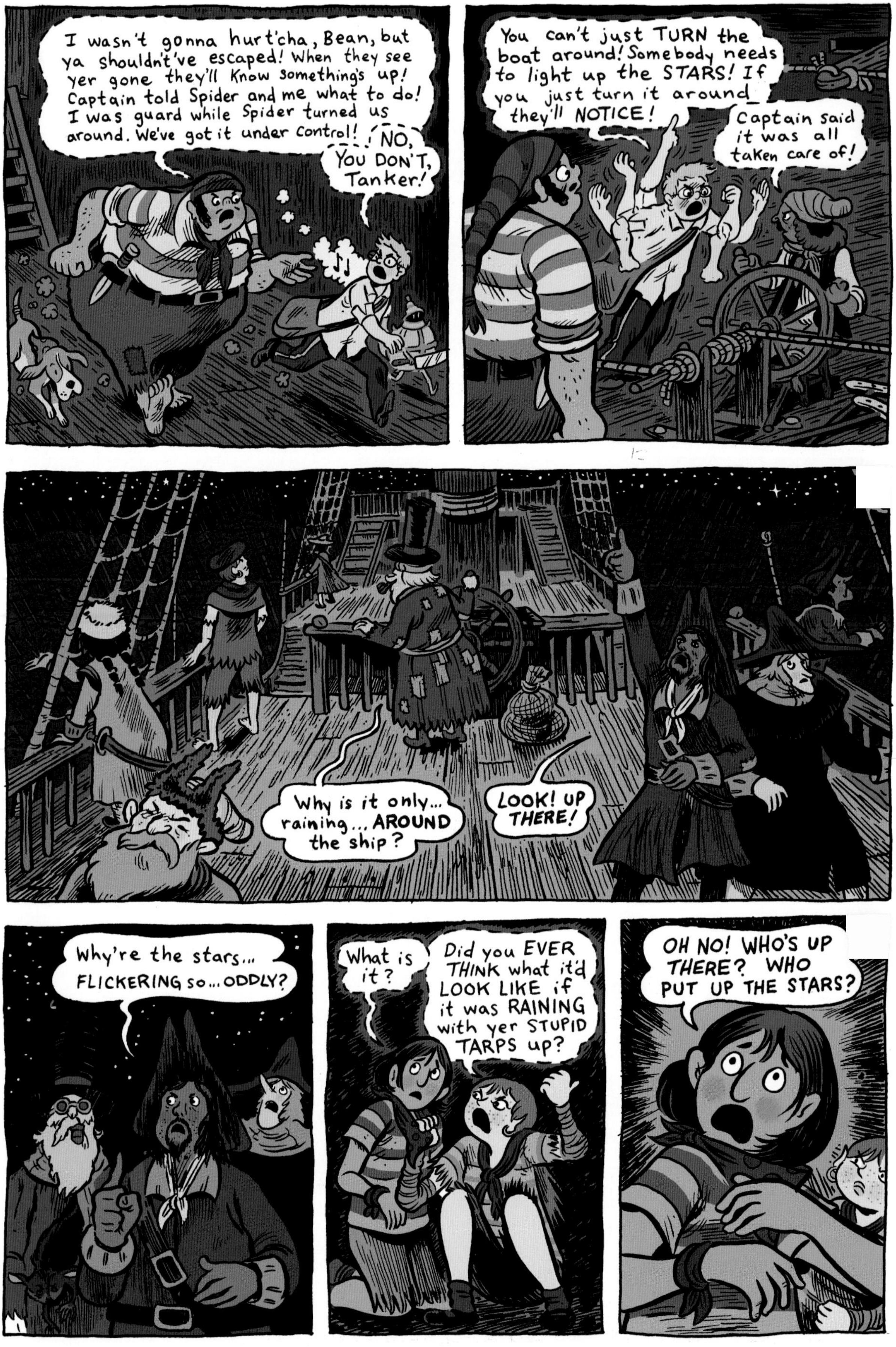
I wasn't gonna hurt'cha, Bean, but ya shouldn't've escaped! When they see yer gone they'll Know something's up! Captain told Spider and me what to do! I was guard while Spider turned us around. We've got it under control!
NO, YOU DON'T, Tanker!
You can't just TURN the boat around! Somebody needs to light up the STARS! If you just turn it around they'll NOTICE!
Captain said it was all taken care of!
Why is it only... raining... AROUND the ship?
LOOK! UP THERE!
Why're the stars... FLICKERING so... ODDLY?
What is it?
Did you EVER THINK what it'd LOOK LIKE if it was RAINING with yer STUPID TARPS up?
OH NO! WHO'S UP THERE? WHO PUT UP THE STARS?

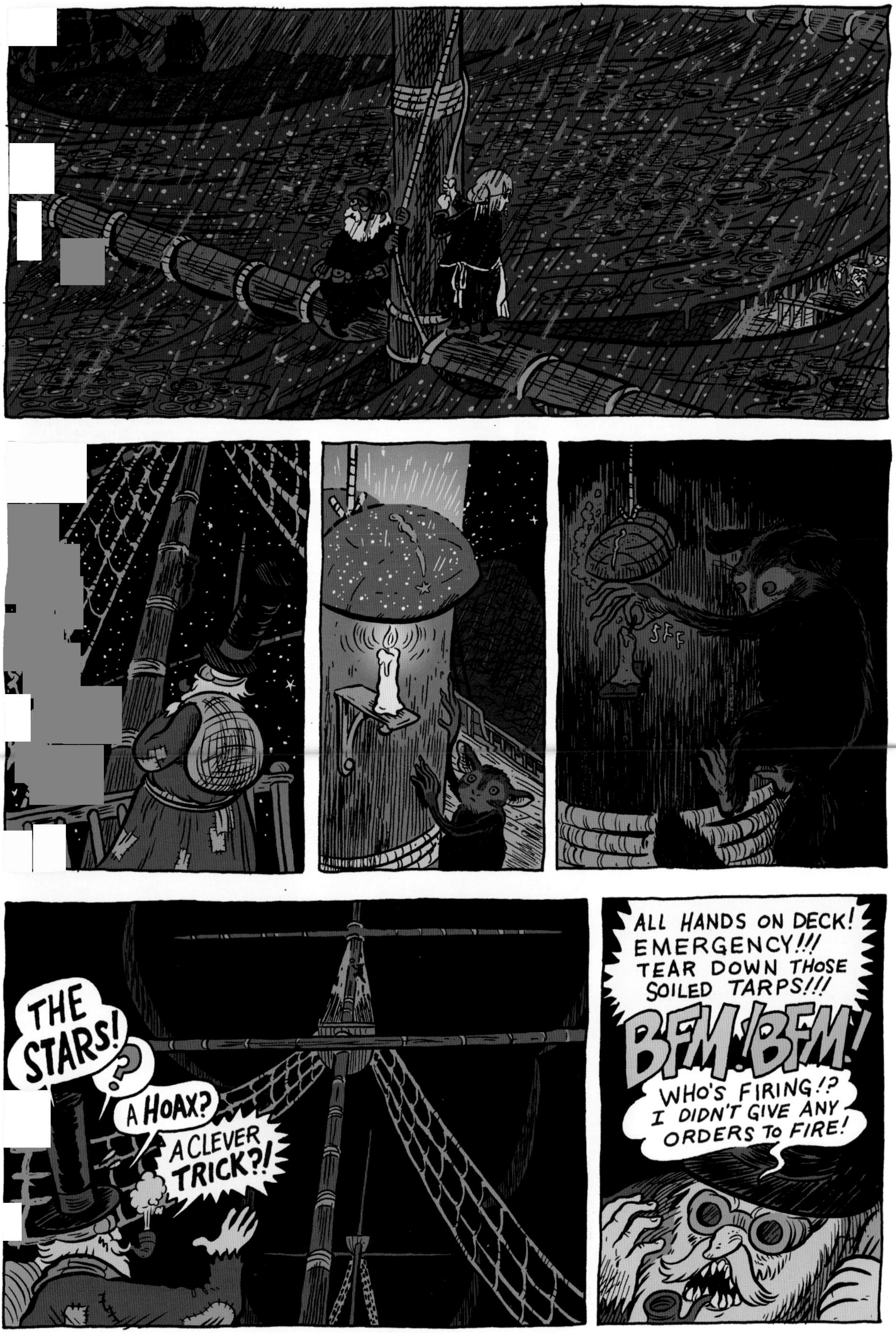
SFF
THE STARS!
?!
A HOAX?
A CLEVER TRICK?!
ALL HANDS ON DECK! EMERGENCY!!! TEAR DOWN THOSE SOILED TARPS!!!
BFM! BFM!
WHO'S FIRING!? I DIDN'T GIVE ANY ORDERS TO FIRE!

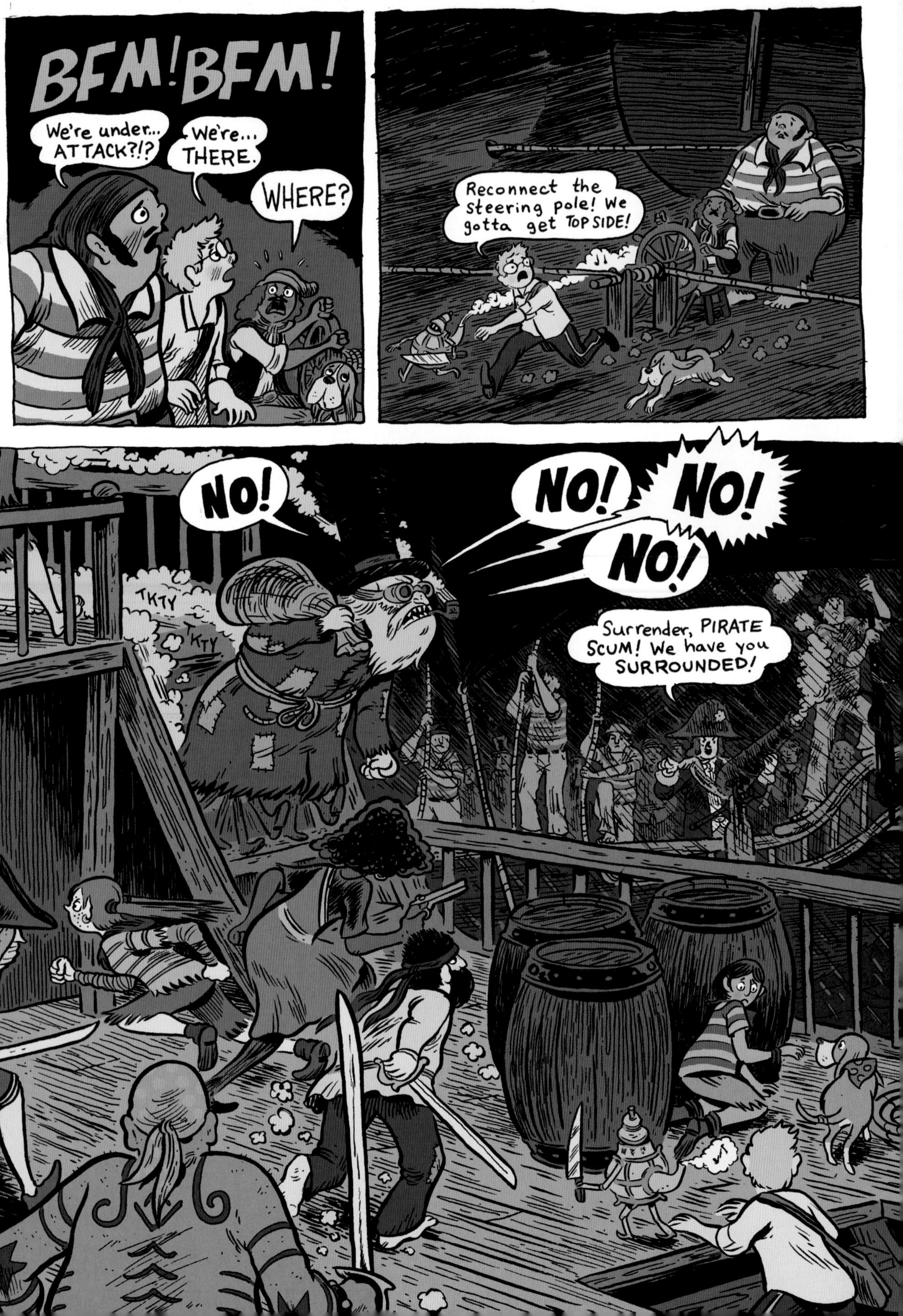
BFM! BFM!
We're under... ATTACK?!?
We're... THERE.
WHERE?
Reconnect the steering pole! We gotta get TOP SIDE!
NO!
NO!
NO!
NO!
TKTY
TKTY
Surrender, PIRATE SCUM! We have you SURROUNDED!

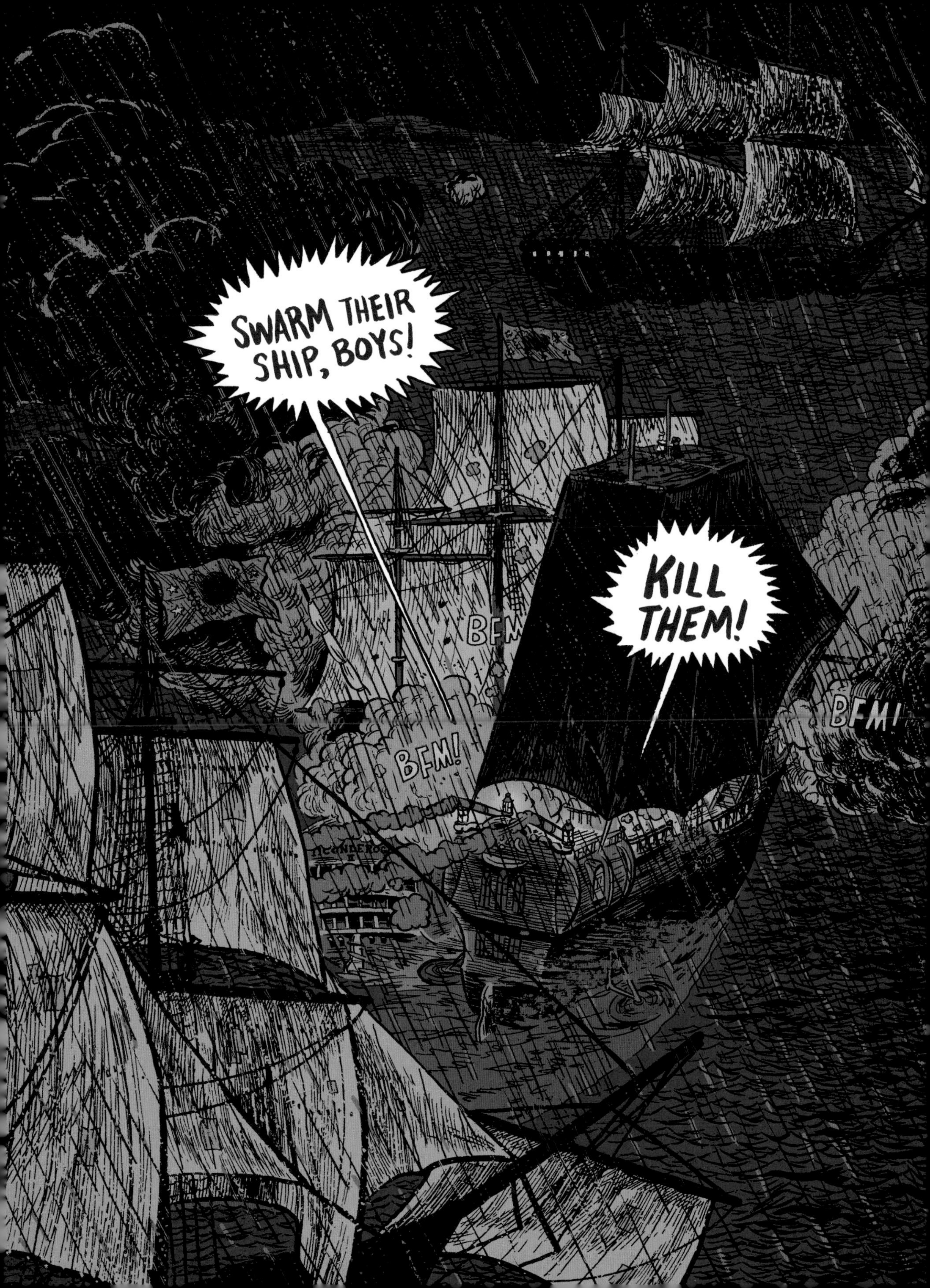
SWARM THEIR SHIP, BOYS!
BFM!
BFM!
KILL THEM!
BFM!

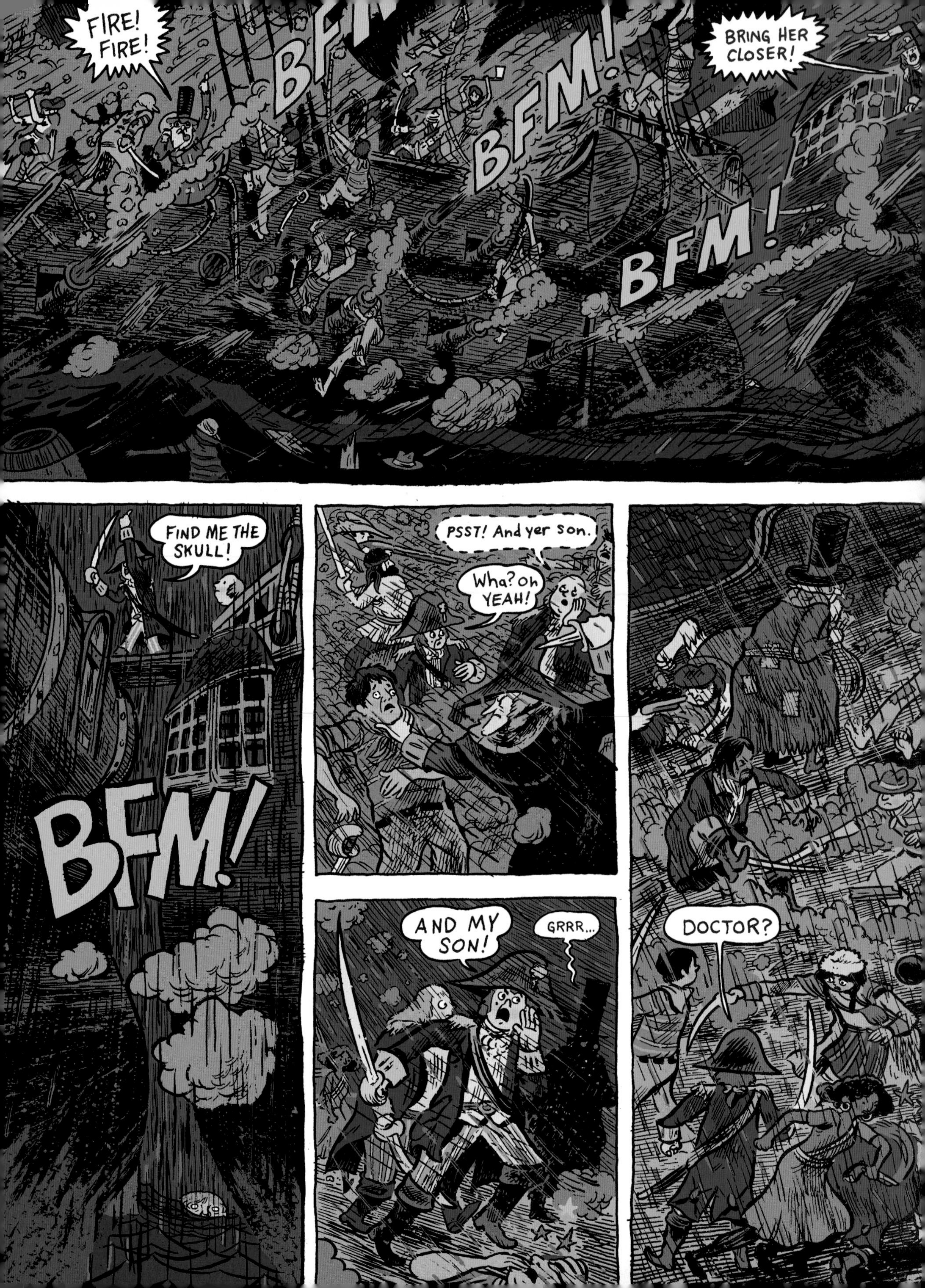
FIRE! FIRE!
BFM!
BFM!
BFM!
BRING HER CLOSER!
FIND ME THE SKULL!
BFM!
PSST! And yer son.
Wha? oh YEAH!
AND MY SON!
GRRR...
DOCTOR?

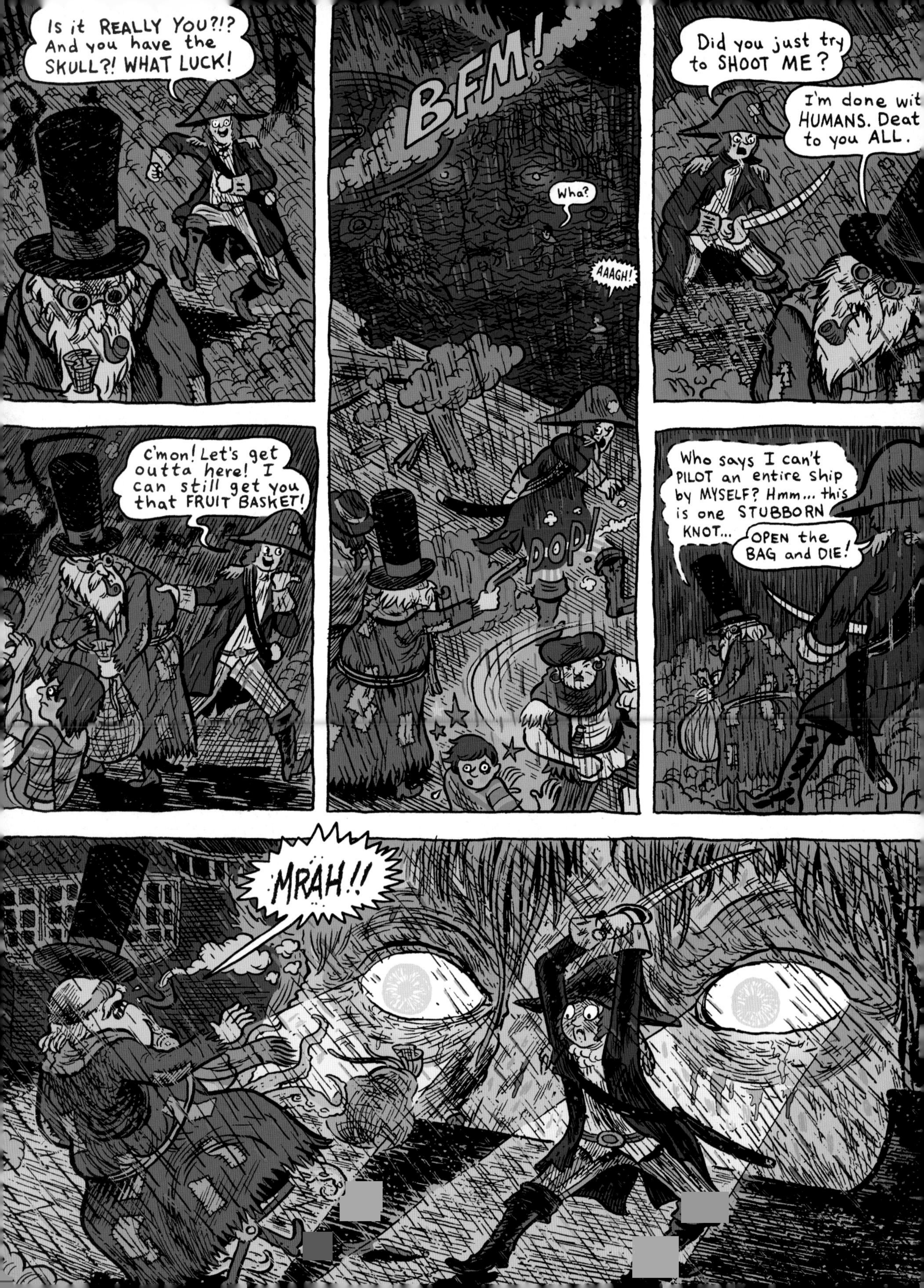
Is it REALLY YOU?!? And you have the SKULL?! WHAT LUCK!
BFM!
Wha?
AAAGH!
Did you just try to SHOOT ME?
I'm done wit HUMANS. Deat to you ALL.
C'mon! Let's get outta here! I can still get you that FRUIT BASKET!
POP!
Who says I can't PILOT an entire ship by MYSELF? Hmm... this is one STUBBORN KNOT...
OPEN the BAG and DIE!
MRAH!!

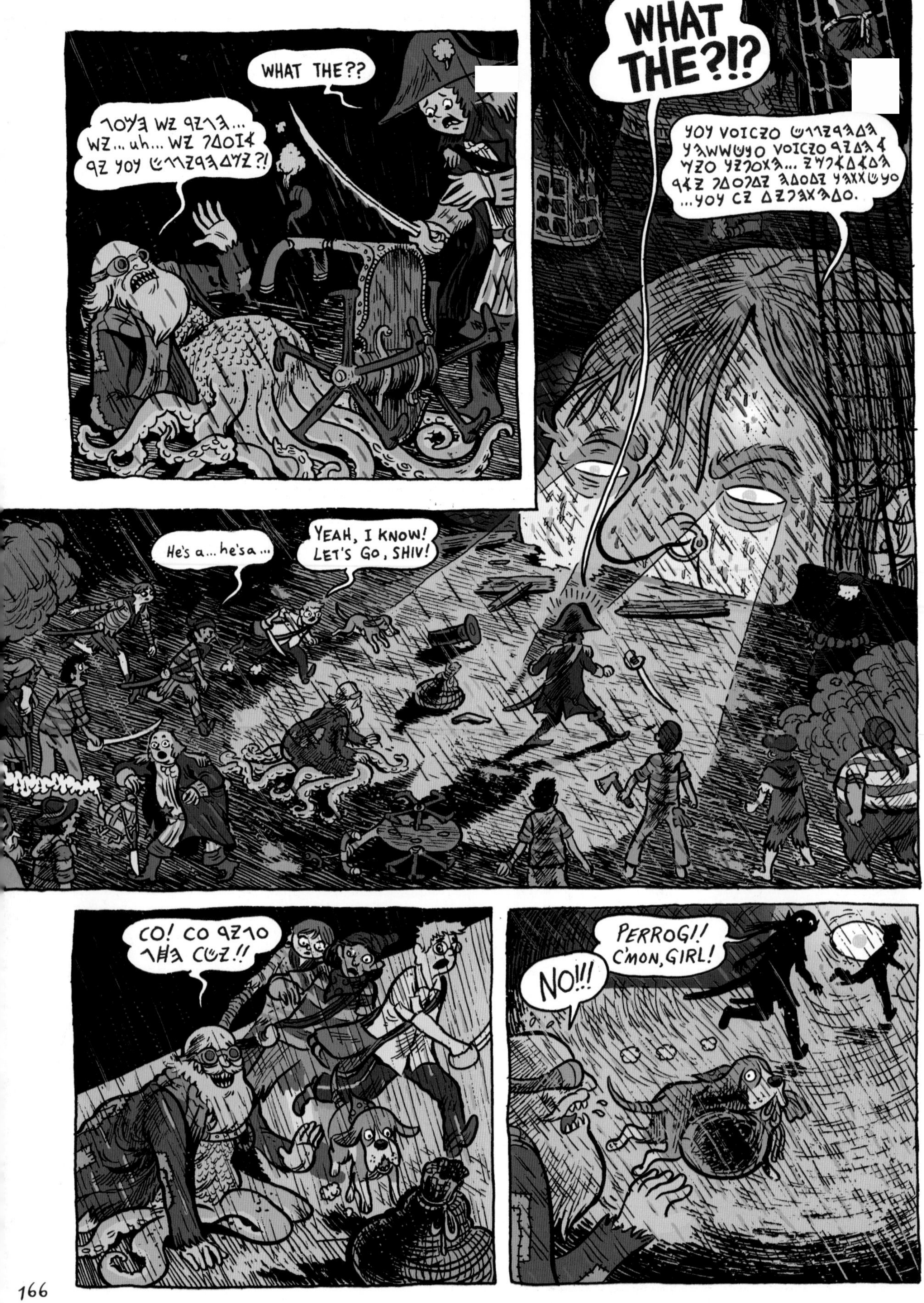
WHAT THE??
WHAT THE?!?
He's a... he's a...
YEAH, I KNOW! LET'S GO, SHIV!
PERROG!! C'MON, GIRL!
NO!!!

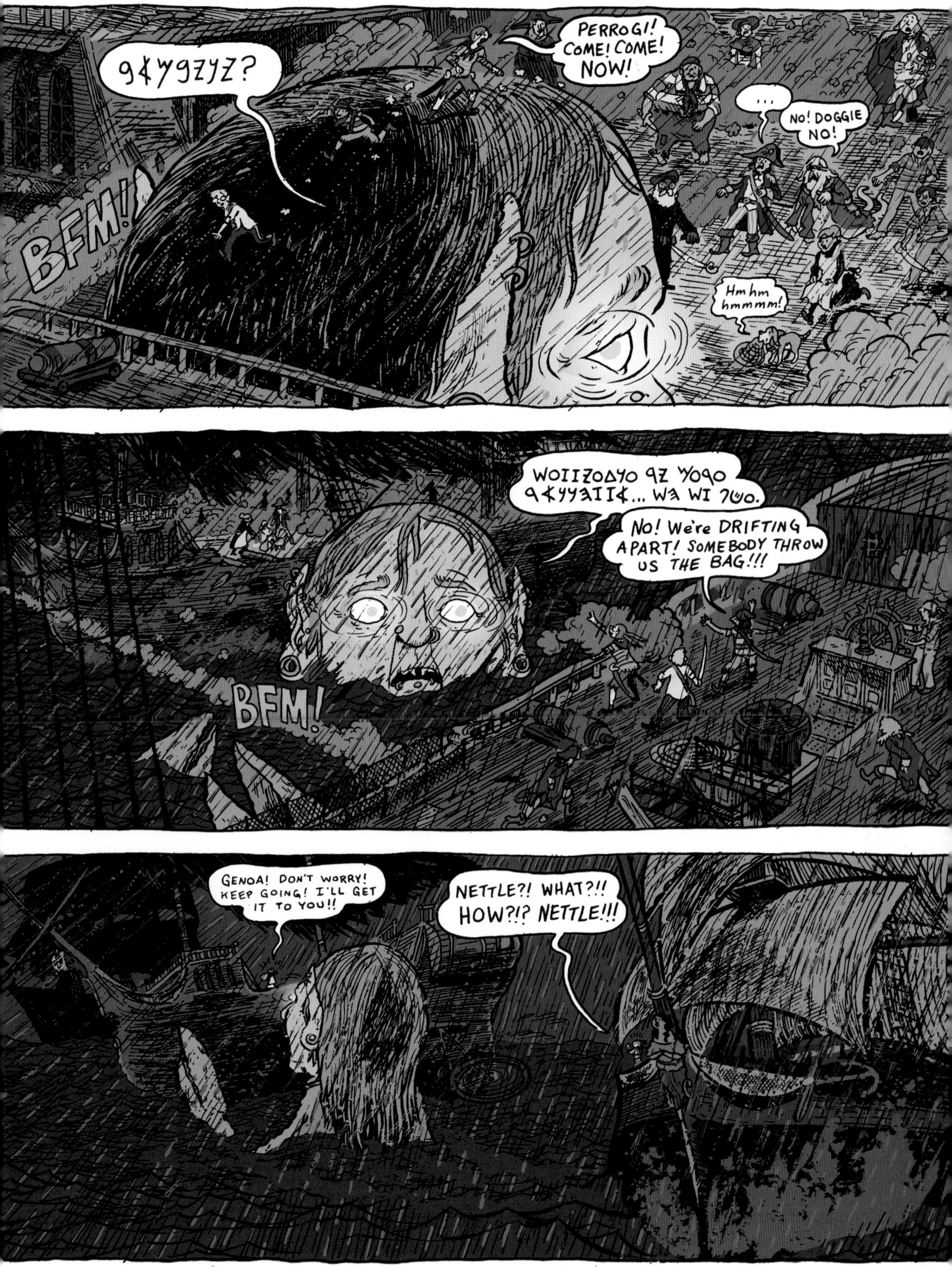

BFM!
PERROGI! COME! COME! NOW!
...
NO! DOGGIE NO!
Hmhm hmmmm!
No! We're DRIFTING APART! SOMEBODY THROW US THE BAG!!!
BFM!
GENOA! DON'T WORRY! KEEP GOING! I'LL GET IT TO YOU!!
NETTLE?! WHAT?!! HOW?!? NETTLE!!!

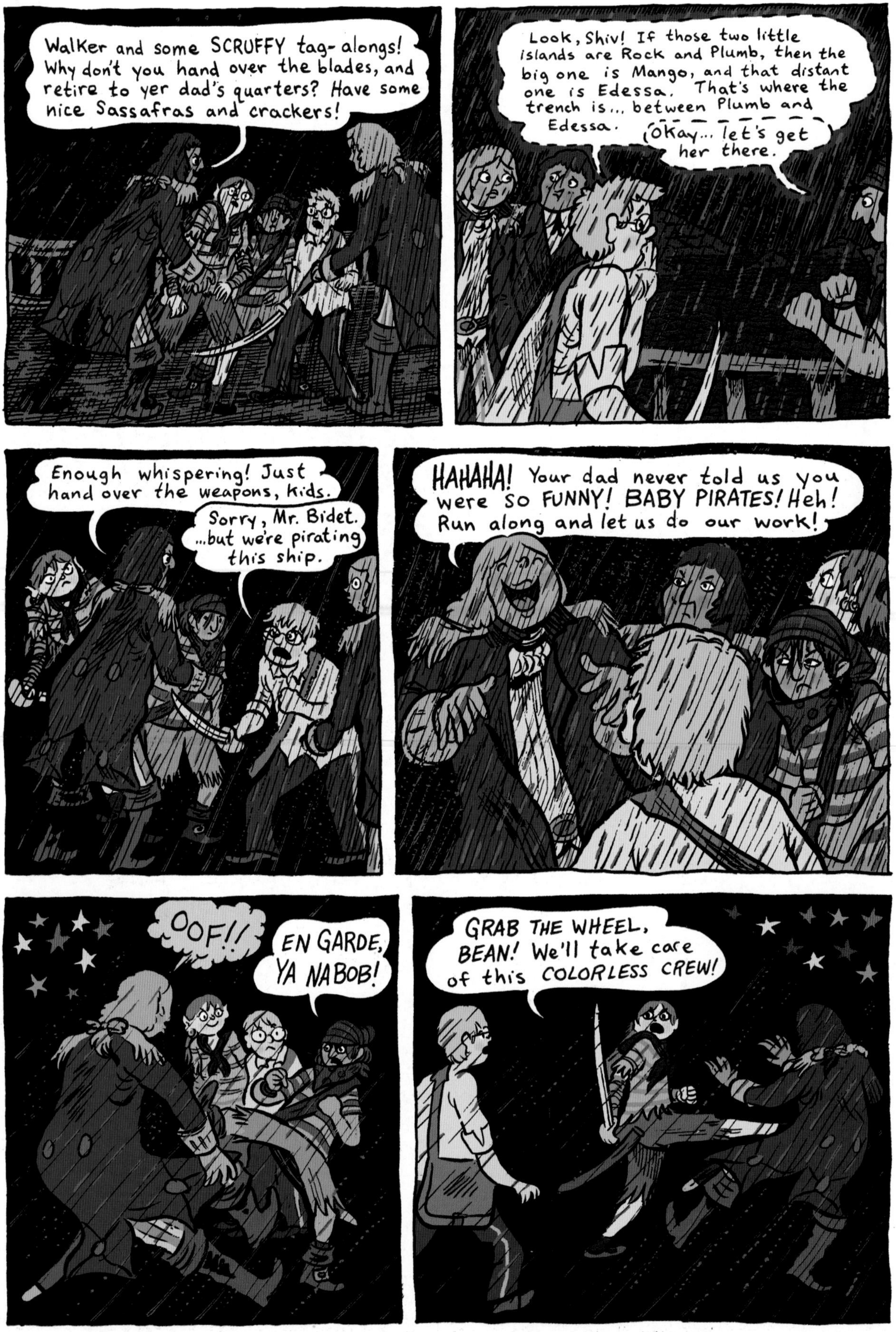
Walker and some SCRUFFY tag-alongs! Why don't you hand over the blades, and retire to yer dad's quarters? Have some nice Sassafras and crackers!
Look, Shiv! If those two little islands are Rock and Plumb, then the big one is Mango, and that distant one is Edessa. That's where the trench is... between Plumb and Edessa.
Okay... let's get her there.
Enough whispering! Just hand over the weapons, kids.
Sorry, Mr. Bidet. ...but we're pirating this ship.
HAHAHA! Your dad never told us you were so FUNNY! BABY PIRATES! Heh! Run along and let us do our work!
OOF!!
EN GARDE, YA NABOB!
GRAB THE WHEEL, BEAN! We'll take care of this COLORLESS CREW!

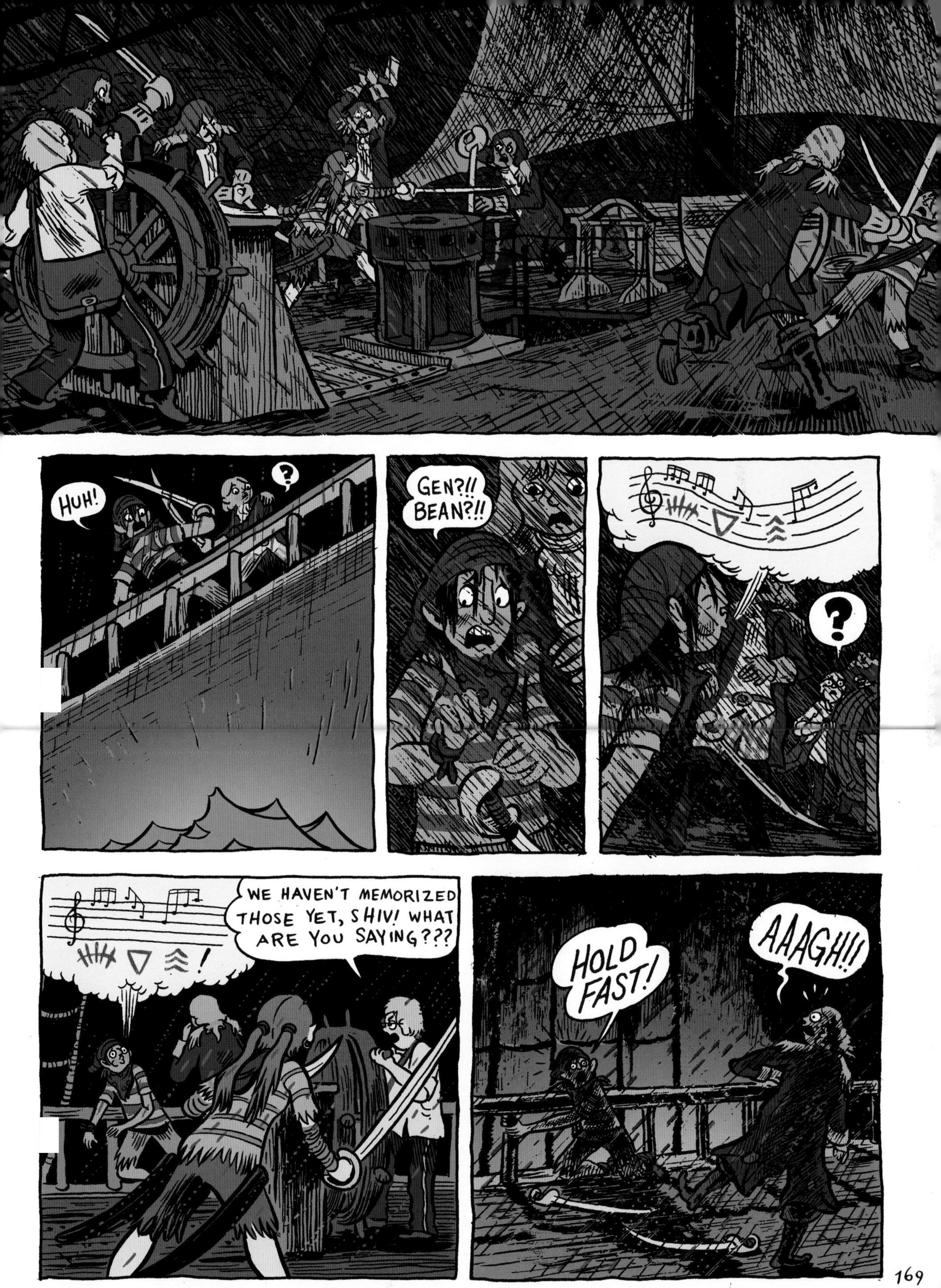
HUH!
?
GEN?!!
BEAN?!!
?
WE HAVEN'T MEMORIZED THOSE YET, SHIV! WHAT ARE YOU SAYING???
HOLD FAST!
AAAGH!!

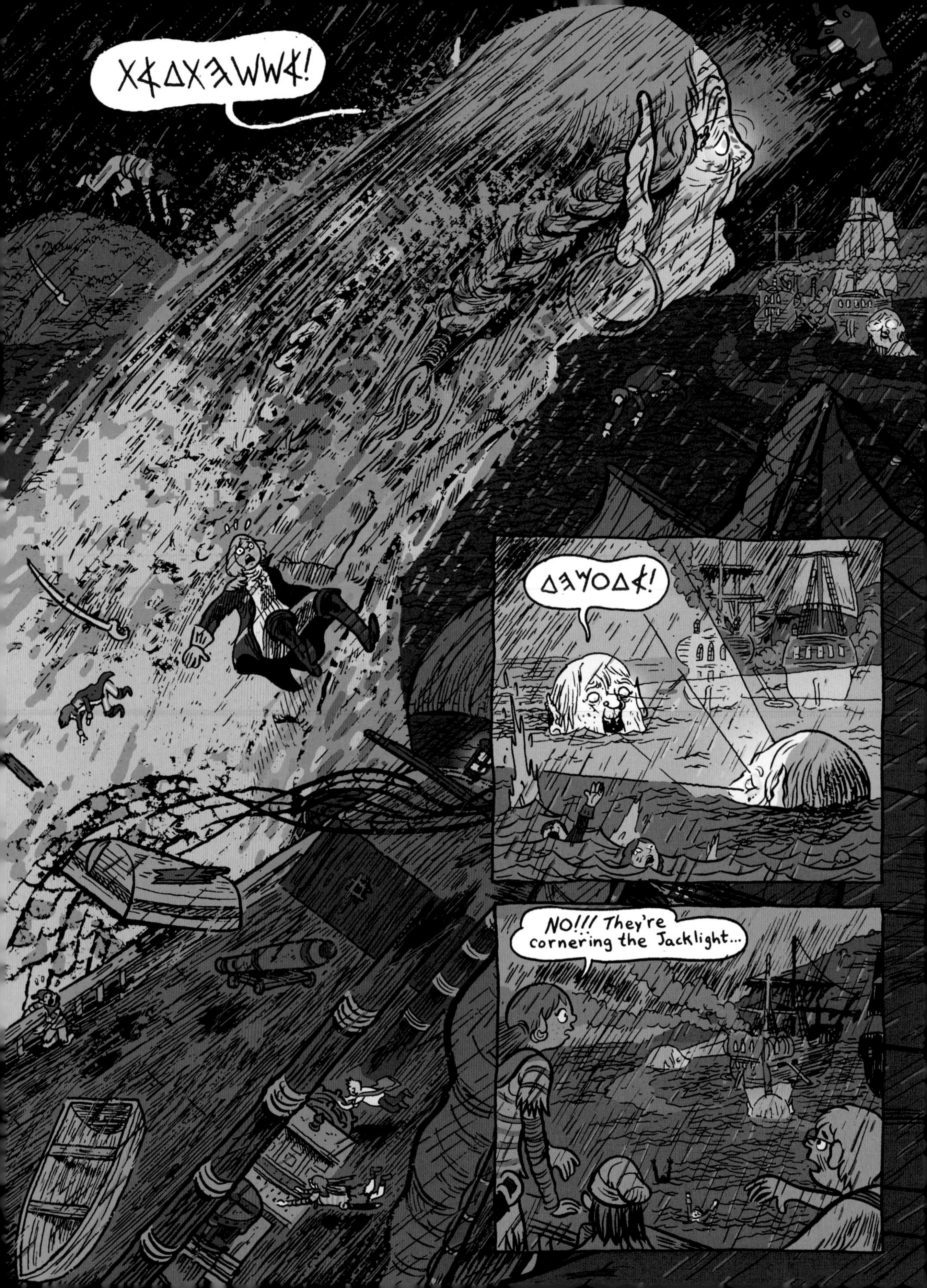
NO!!! They're cornering the Jacklight...

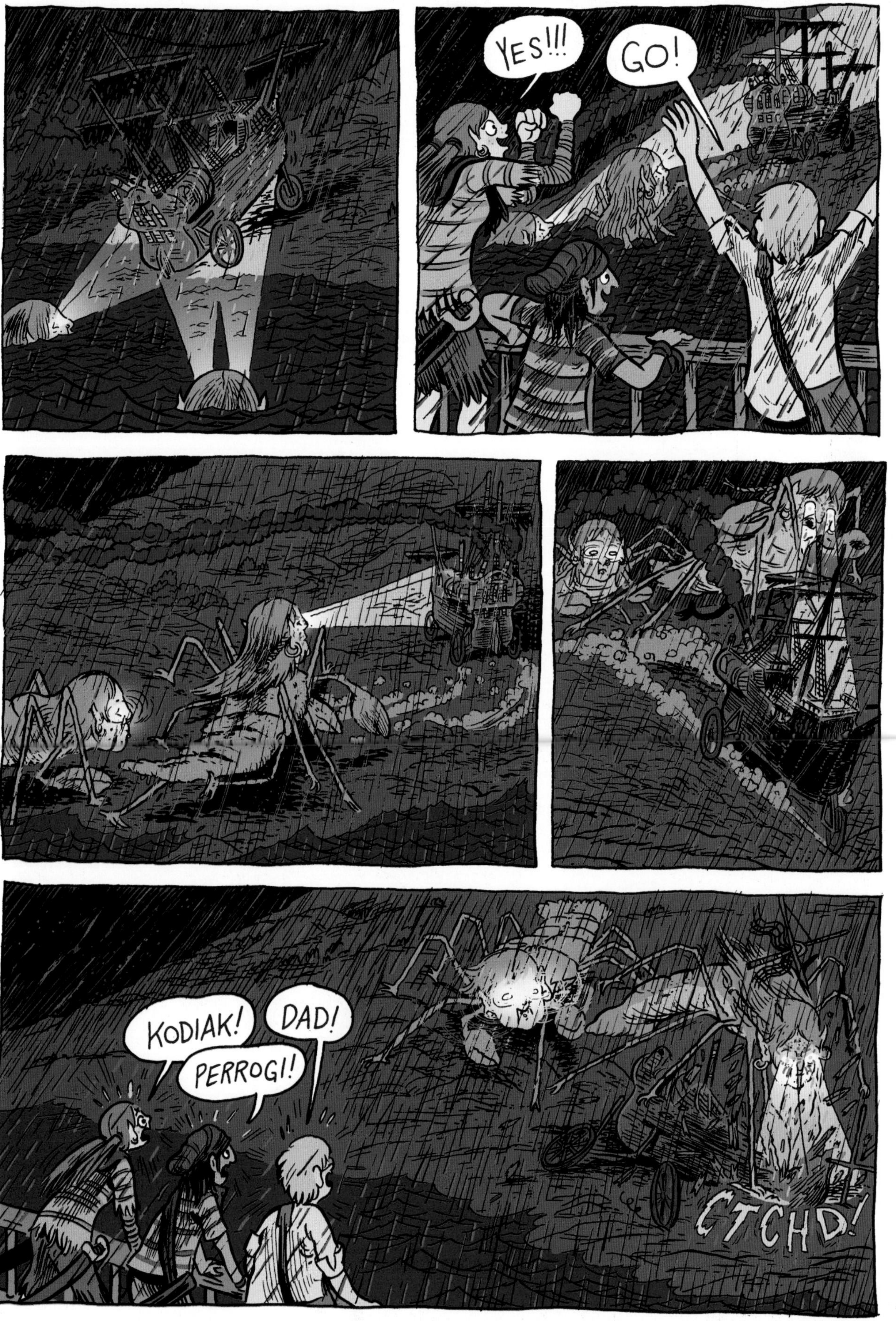
YES!!!
GO!
KODIAK!
DAD!
PERROGI!
CTCHD!

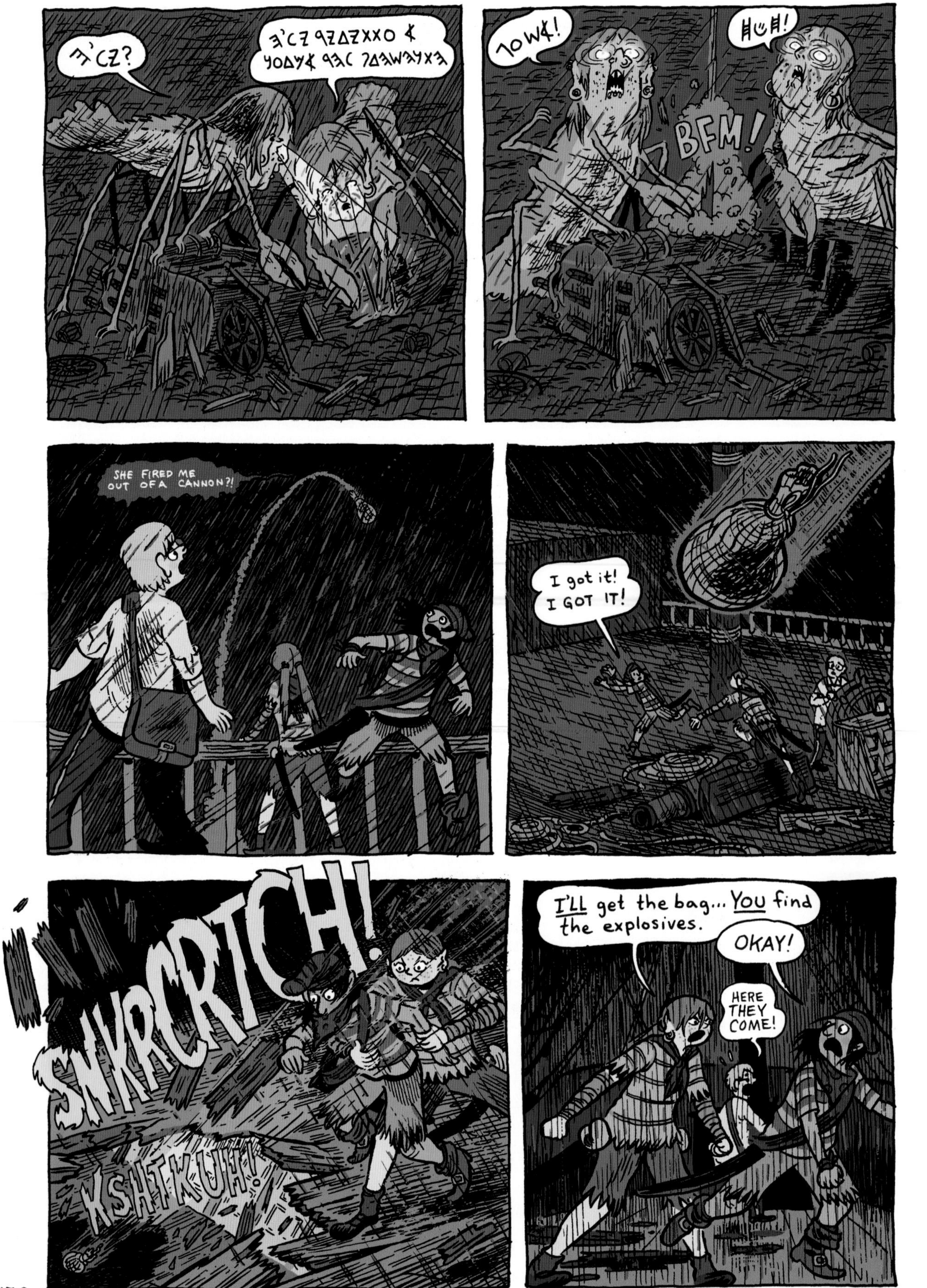
BFM!
SHE FIRED ME OUT OF A CANNON?!
I got it! I GOT IT!
SNKRCRTCH!
KSHTKUH!
I'LL get the bag... YOU find the explosives.
OKAY!
HERE THEY COME!

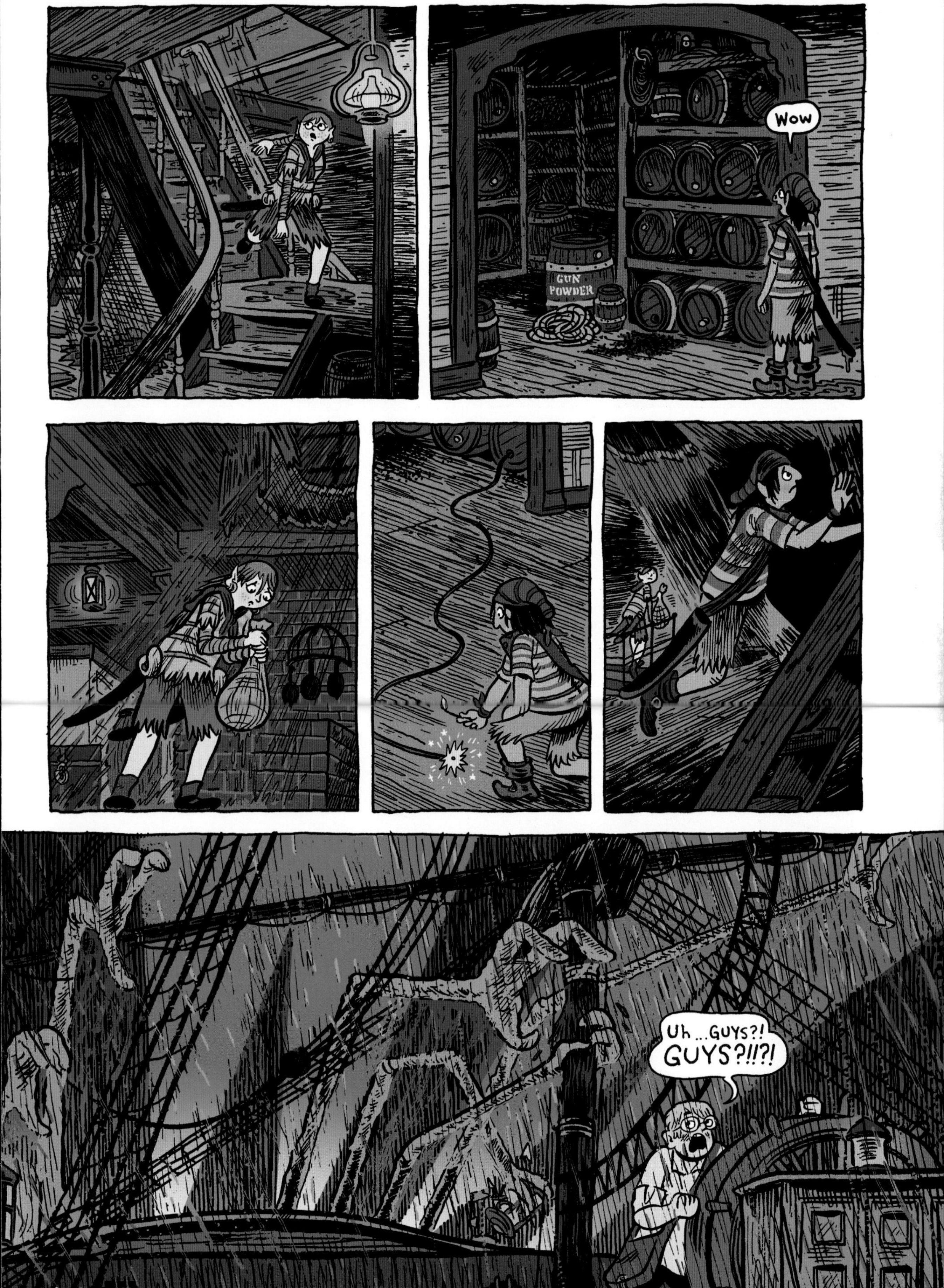
Wow
GUN POWDER
Uh ...GUYS?!
GUYS?!!?!

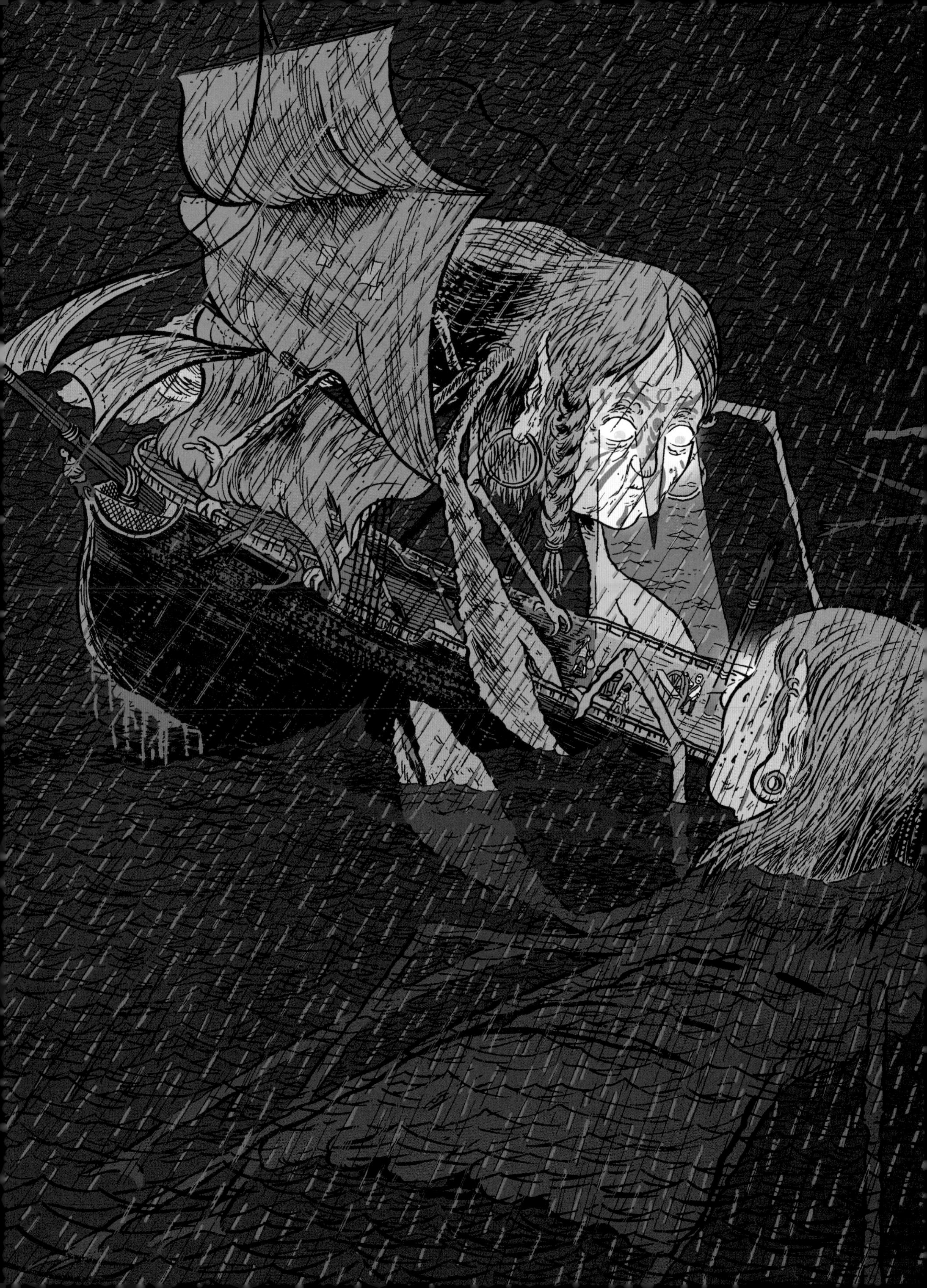

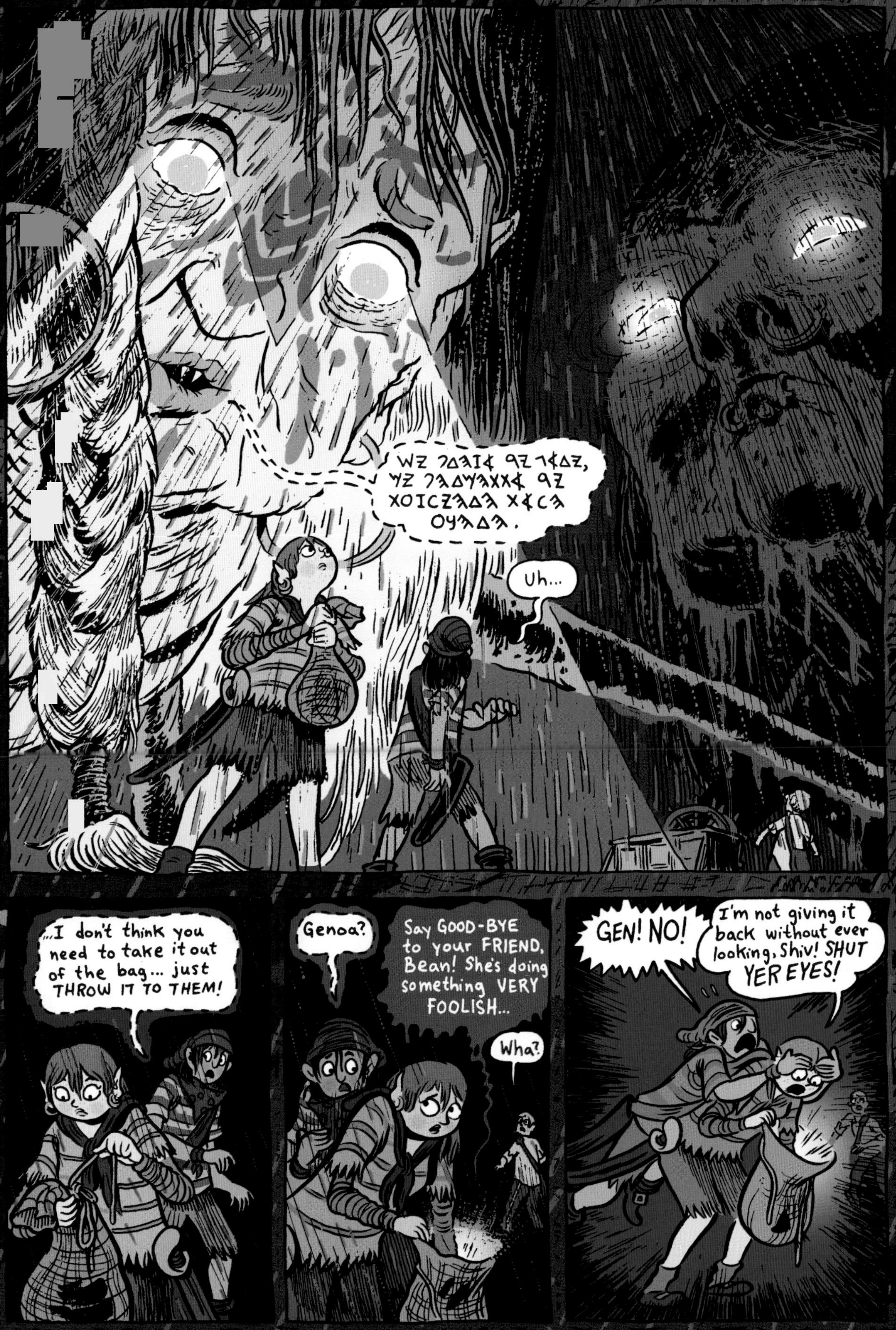
Uh...
...I don't think you need to take it out of the bag... just THROW IT TO THEM!
Genoa?
Say GOOD-BYE to your FRIEND, Bean! She's doing something VERY FOOLISH...
Wha?
GEN! NO!
I'm not giving it back without ever looking, Shiv! SHUT YER EYES!

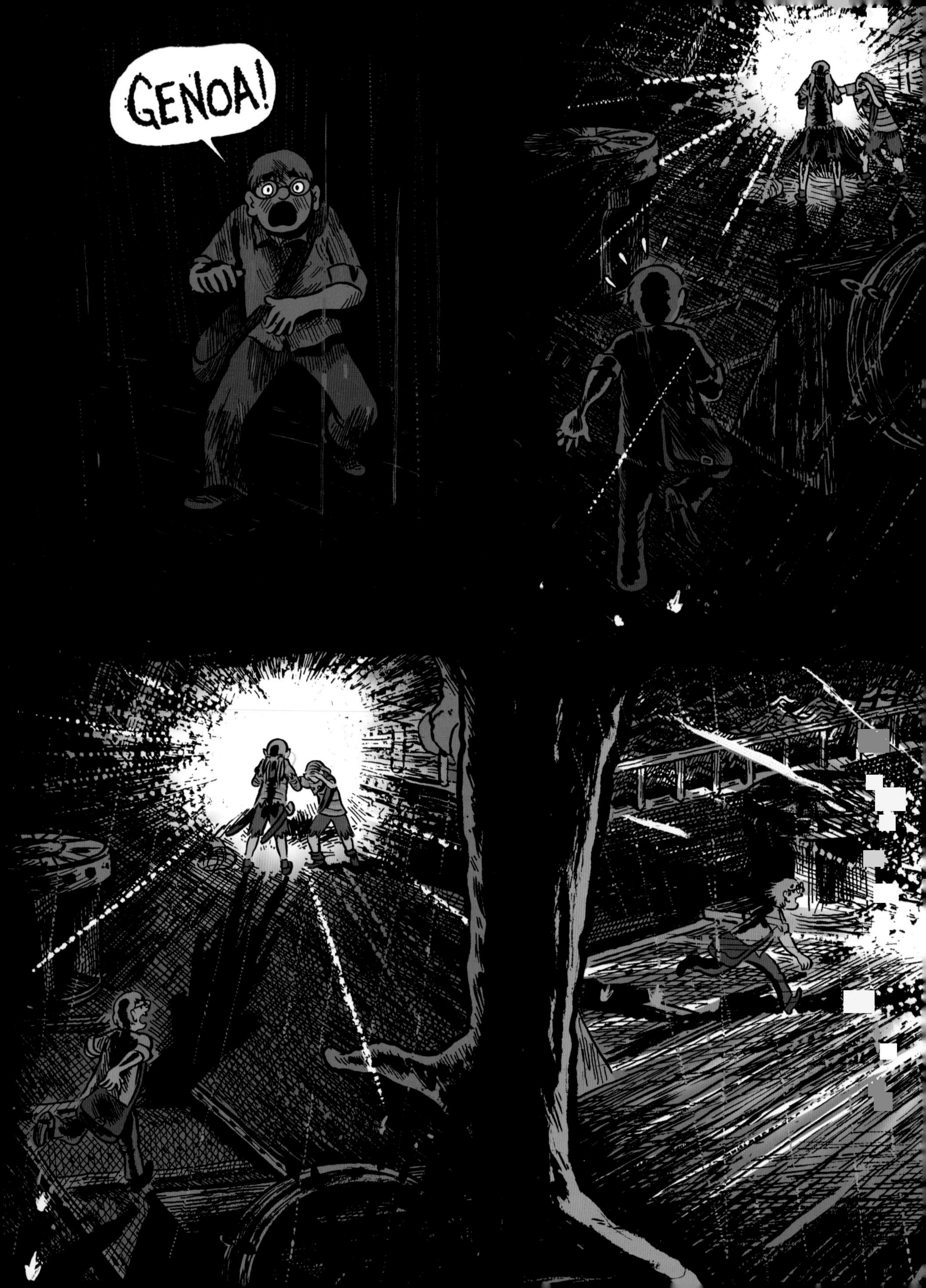
GENOA!

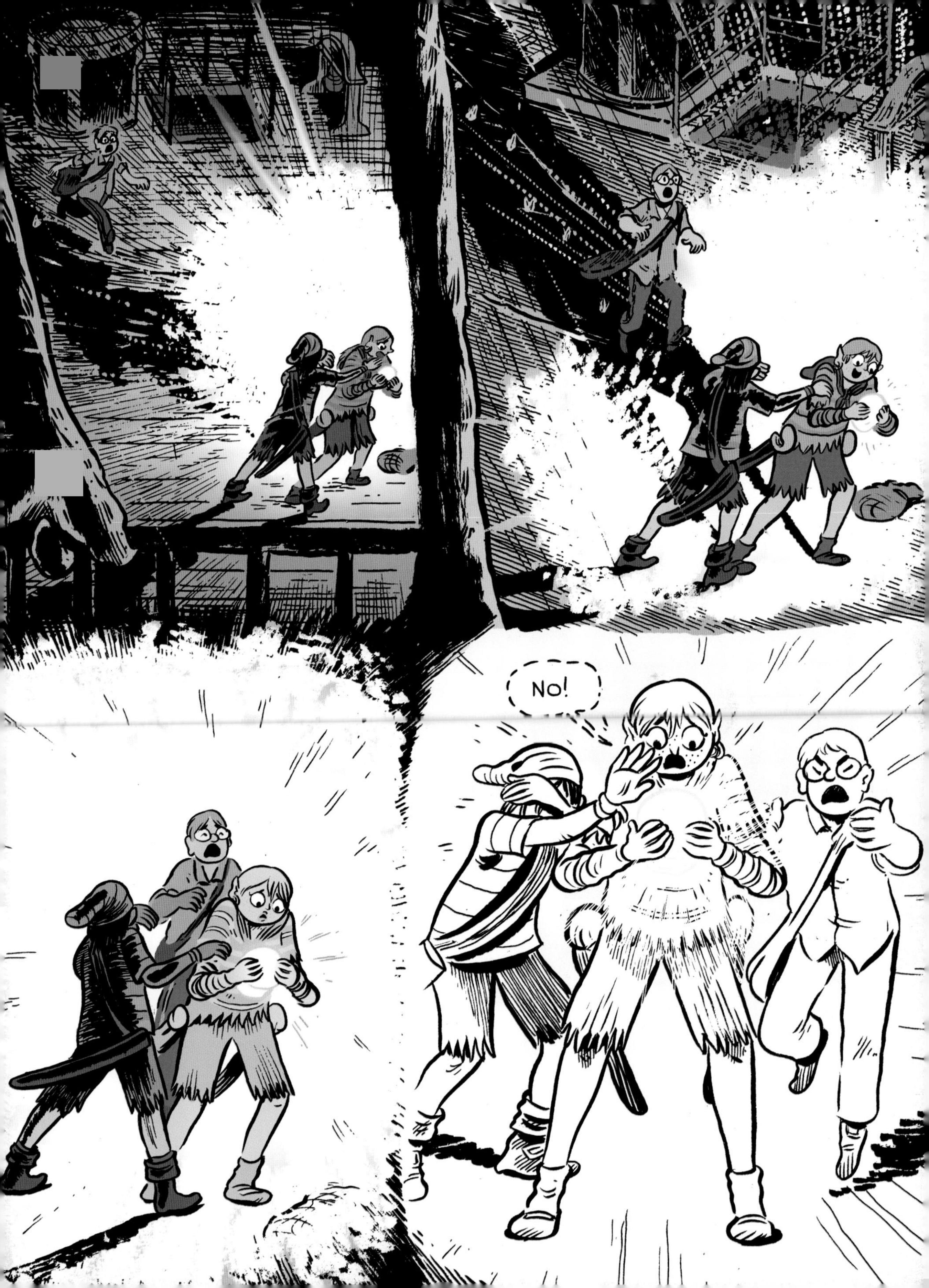
No!

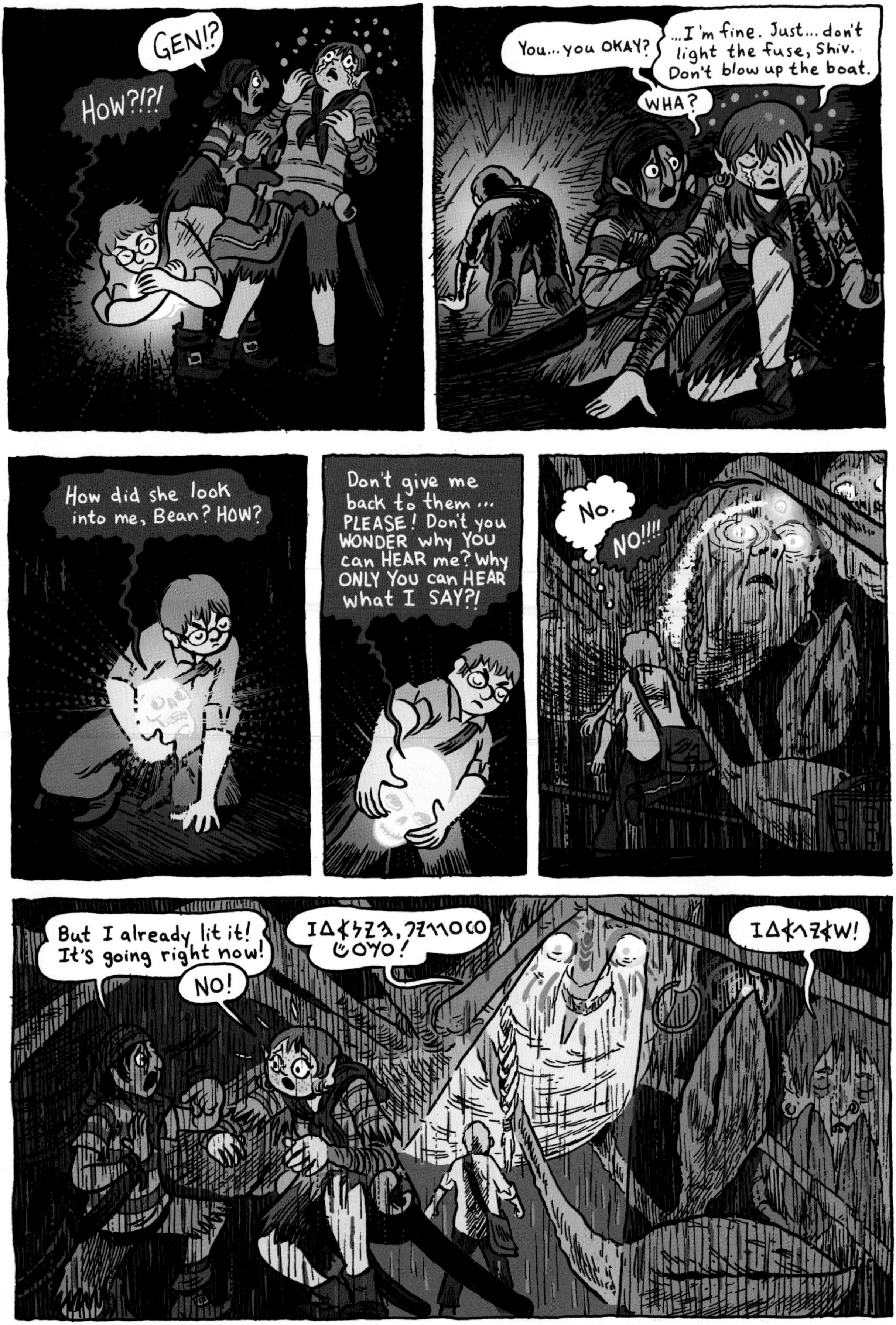
GEN!?
HOW?!?!
You... you OKAY?
...I'm fine. Just... don't light the fuse, Shiv. Don't blow up the boat.
WHA?
How did she look into me, Bean? HOW?
Don't give me back to them... PLEASE! Don't you WONDER why YOU can HEAR me? Why ONLY YOU can HEAR what I SAY?!
No.
NO!!!!
But I already lit it! It's going right now!
NO!

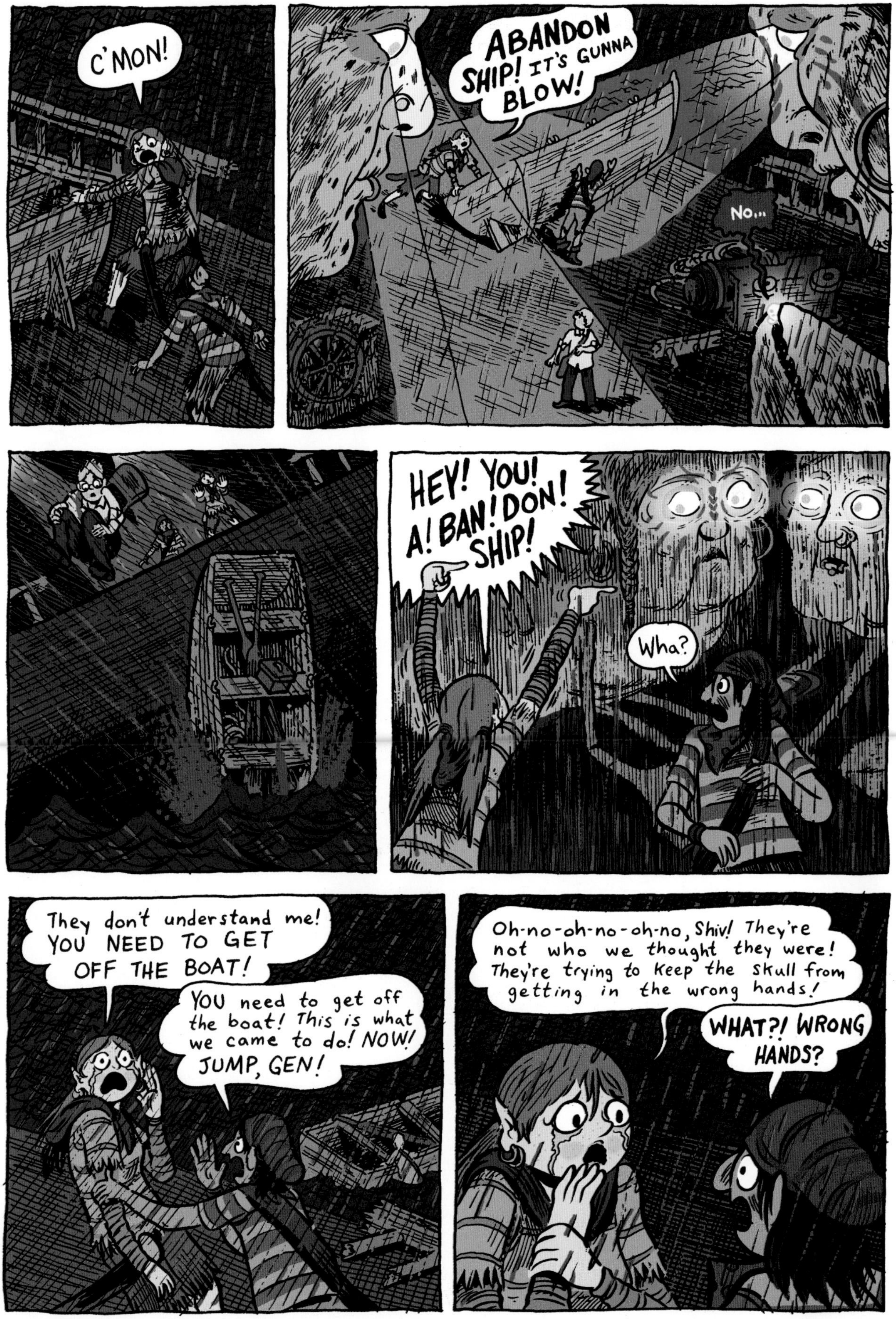
C'MON!
ABANDON SHIP! IT'S GUNNA BLOW!
No...
HEY! YOU! A! BAN! DON! SHIP!
Wha?
They don't understand me! YOU NEED TO GET OFF THE BOAT!
YOU need to get off the boat! This is what we came to do! NOW! JUMP, GEN!
Oh-no-oh-no-oh-no, Shiv! They're not who we thought they were! They're trying to keep the skull from getting in the wrong hands!
WHAT?! WRONG HANDS?

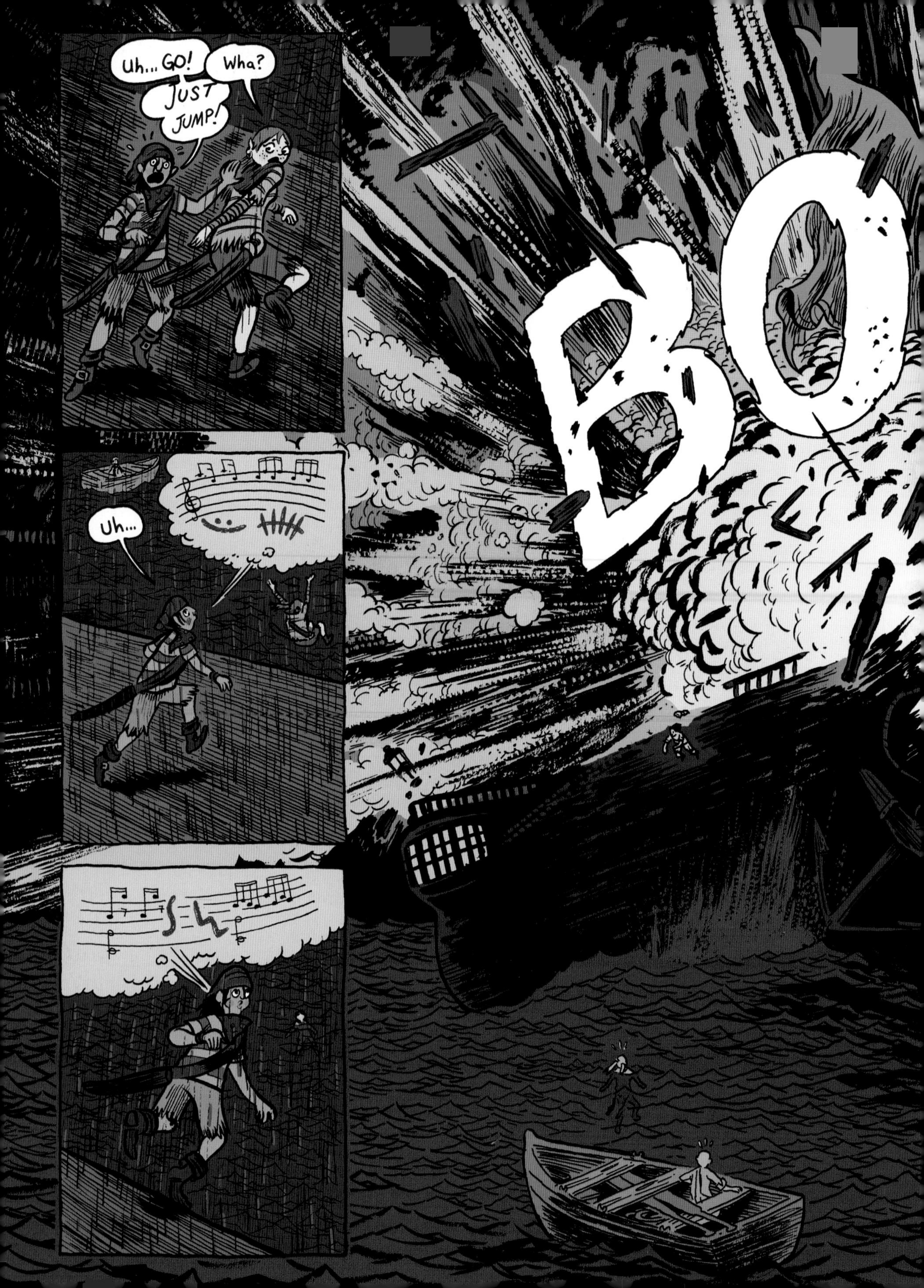
Uh... GO!
Wha?
JUST JUMP!
Uh...
BO

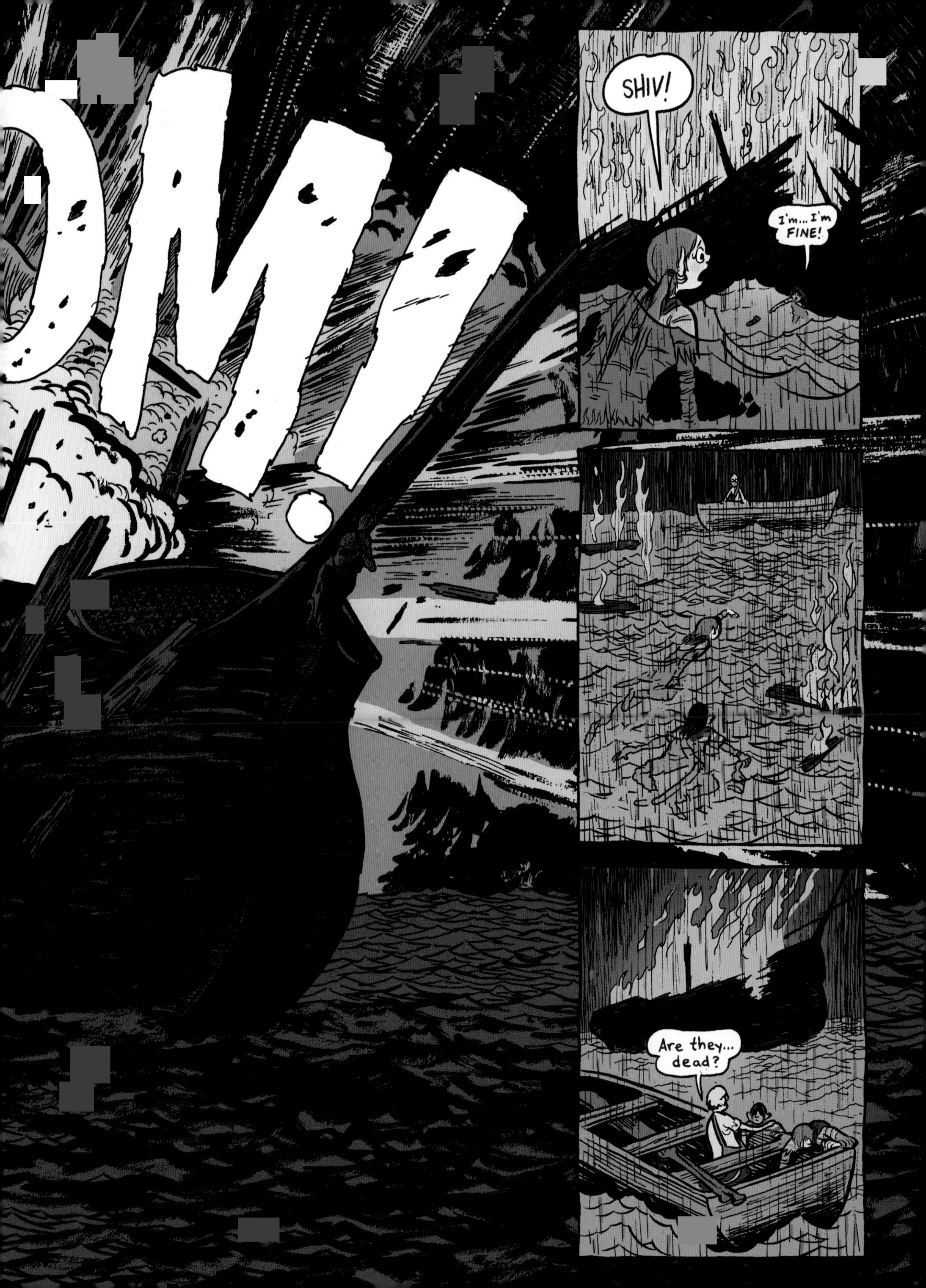
OM!
SHIV!
I'm... I'm FINE!
Are they... dead?

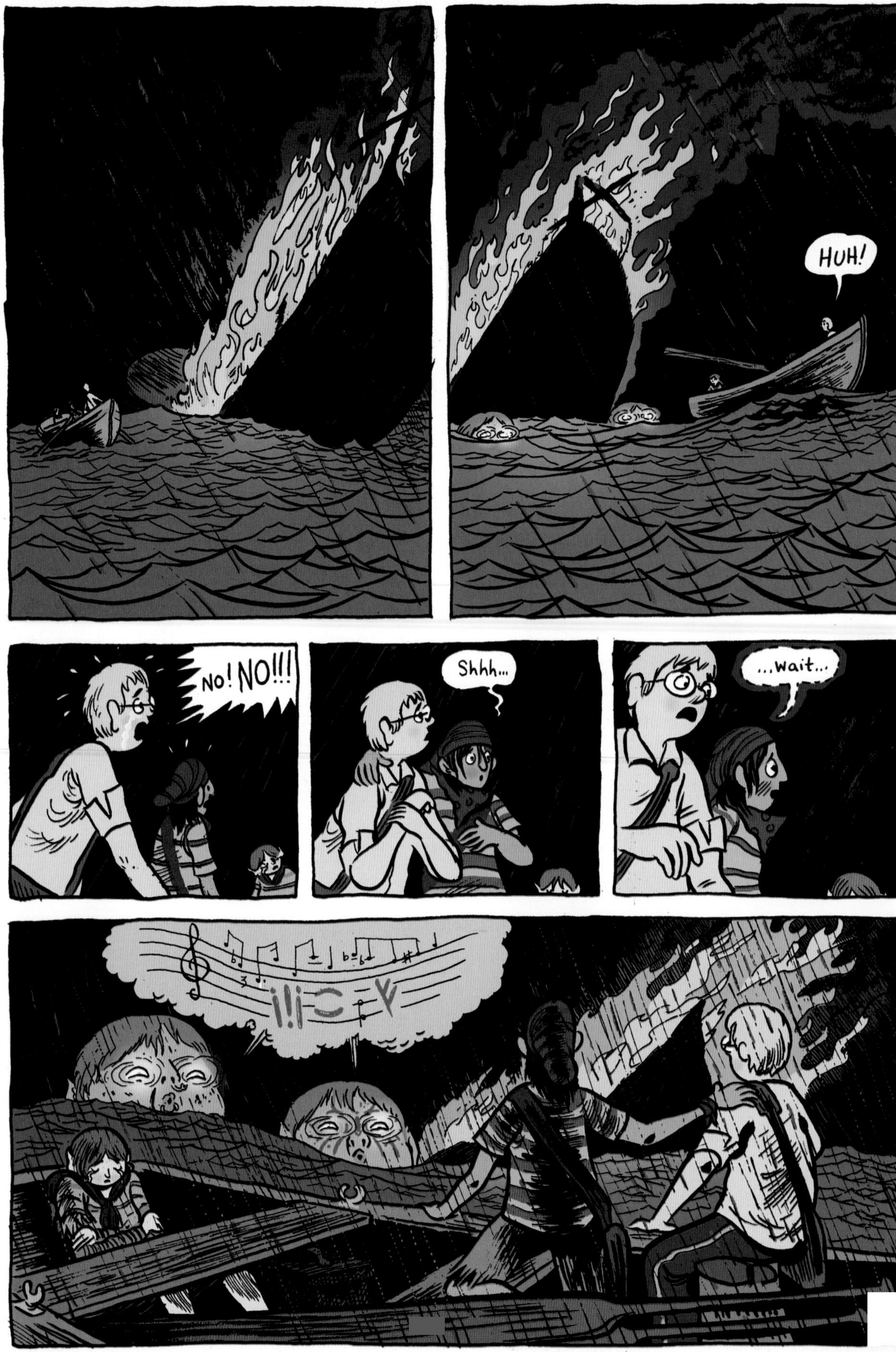
HUH!
No! NO!!!
Shhh...
...wait...

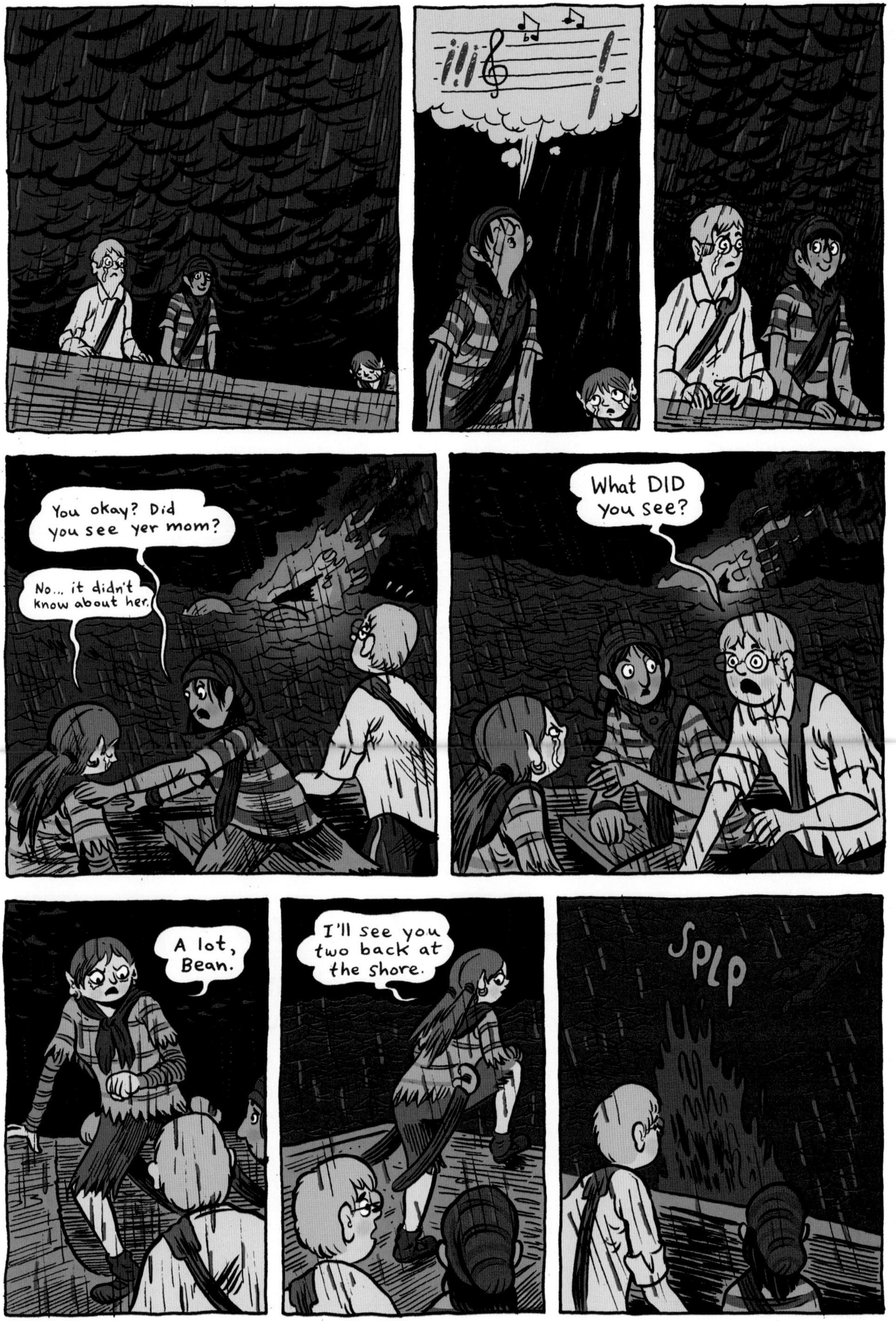
!!
You okay? Did you see yer mom?
No... it didn't know about her.
What DID you see?
A lot, Bean.
I'll see you two back at the shore.
SPLP

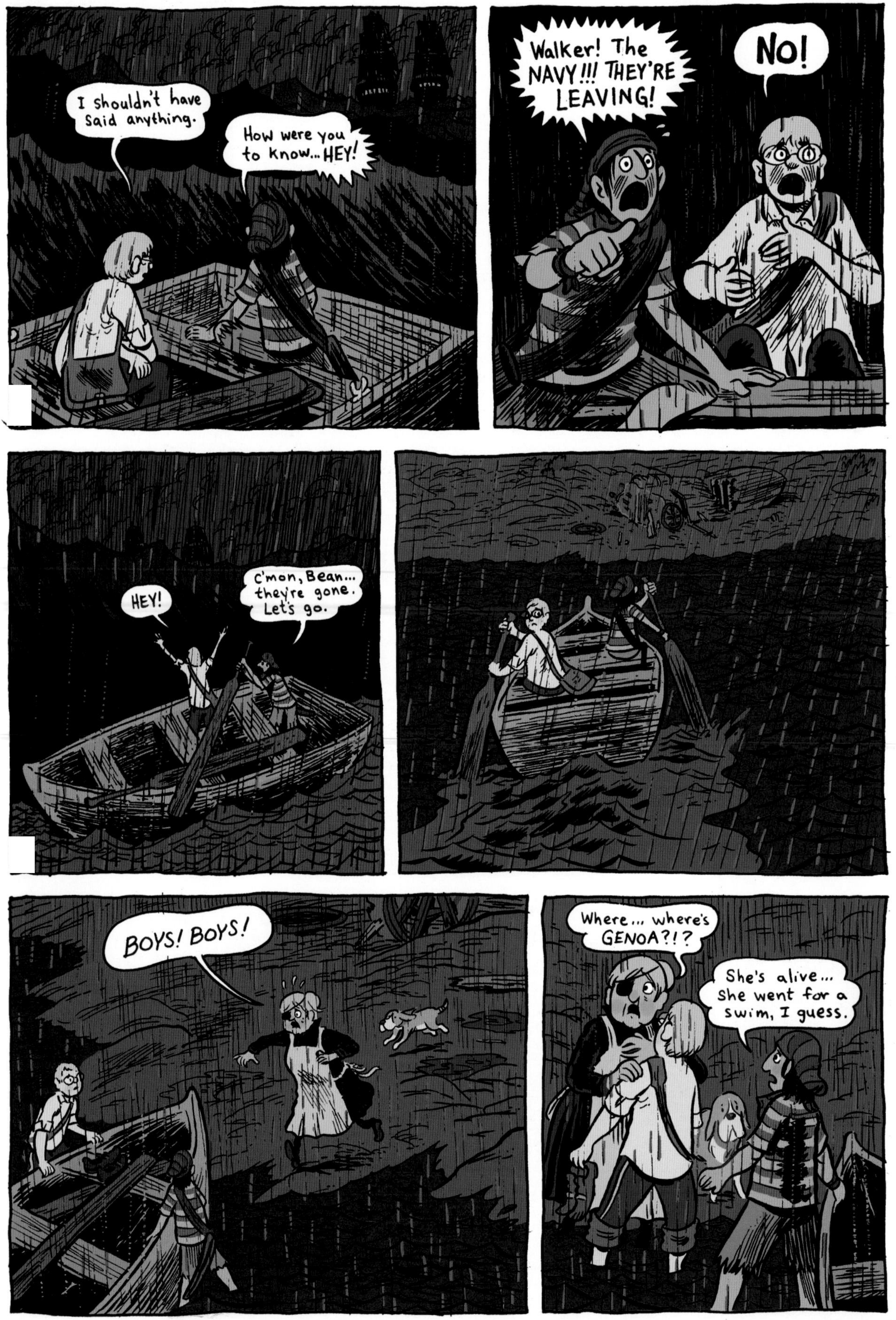
I shouldn't have said anything.
How were you to know... HEY!
Walker! The NAVY!!! THEY'RE LEAVING!
NO!
HEY!
C'mon, Bean... they're gone. Let's go.
BOYS! BOYS!
Where... where's GENOA?!?
She's alive... she went for a swim, I guess.

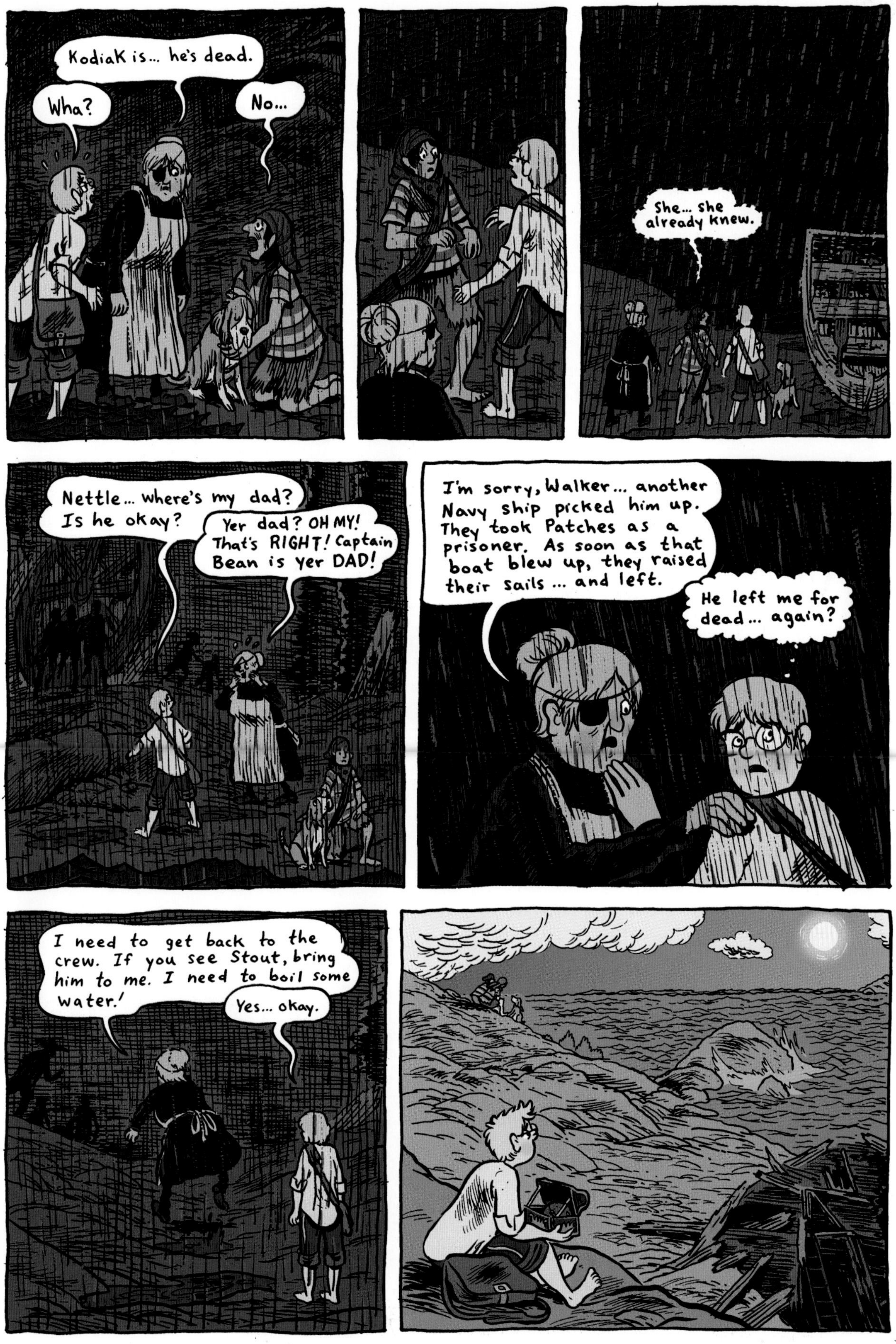
Kodiak is... he's dead.
Wha?
No...
She... she already knew.
Nettle... where's my dad? Is he okay?
Yer dad? OH MY! That's RIGHT! Captain Bean is yer DAD!
I'm sorry, Walker... another Navy ship picked him up. They took Patches as a prisoner. As soon as that boat blew up, they raised their sails ... and left.
He left me for dead... again?
I need to get back to the crew. If you see Stout, bring him to me. I need to boil some water!
Yes... okay.

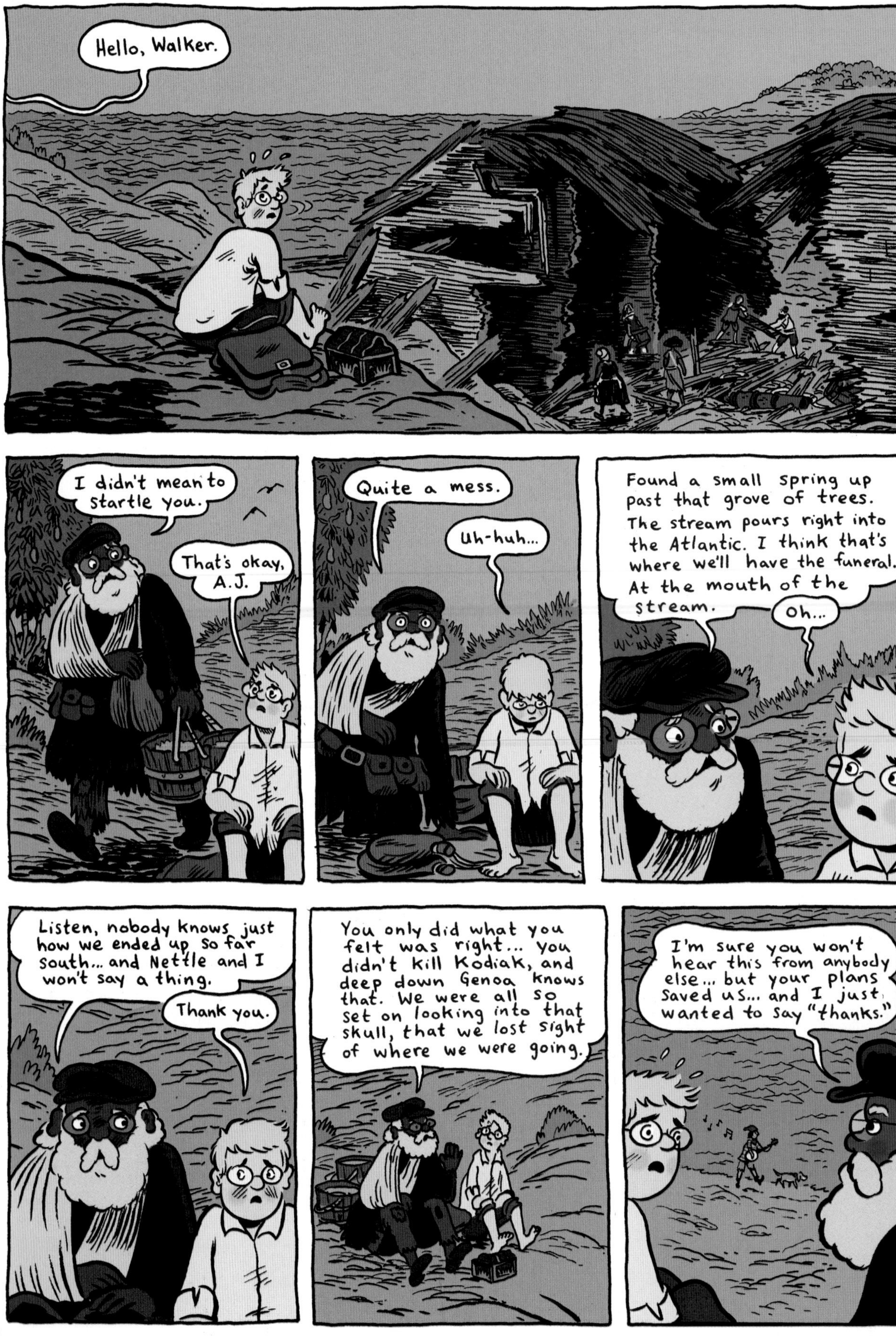
Hello, Walker.
I didn't mean to startle you.
That's okay, A.J.
Quite a mess.
Uh-huh...
Found a small spring up past that grove of trees. The stream pours right into the Atlantic. I think that's where we'll have the funeral. At the mouth of the stream.
Oh...
Listen, nobody knows just how we ended up so far south... and Nettle and I won't say a thing.
Thank you.
You only did what you felt was right... you didn't kill Kodiak, and deep down Genoa knows that. We were all so set on looking into that skull, that we lost sight of where we were going.
I'm sure you won't hear this from anybody else... but your plans saved us... and I just wanted to say "thanks."

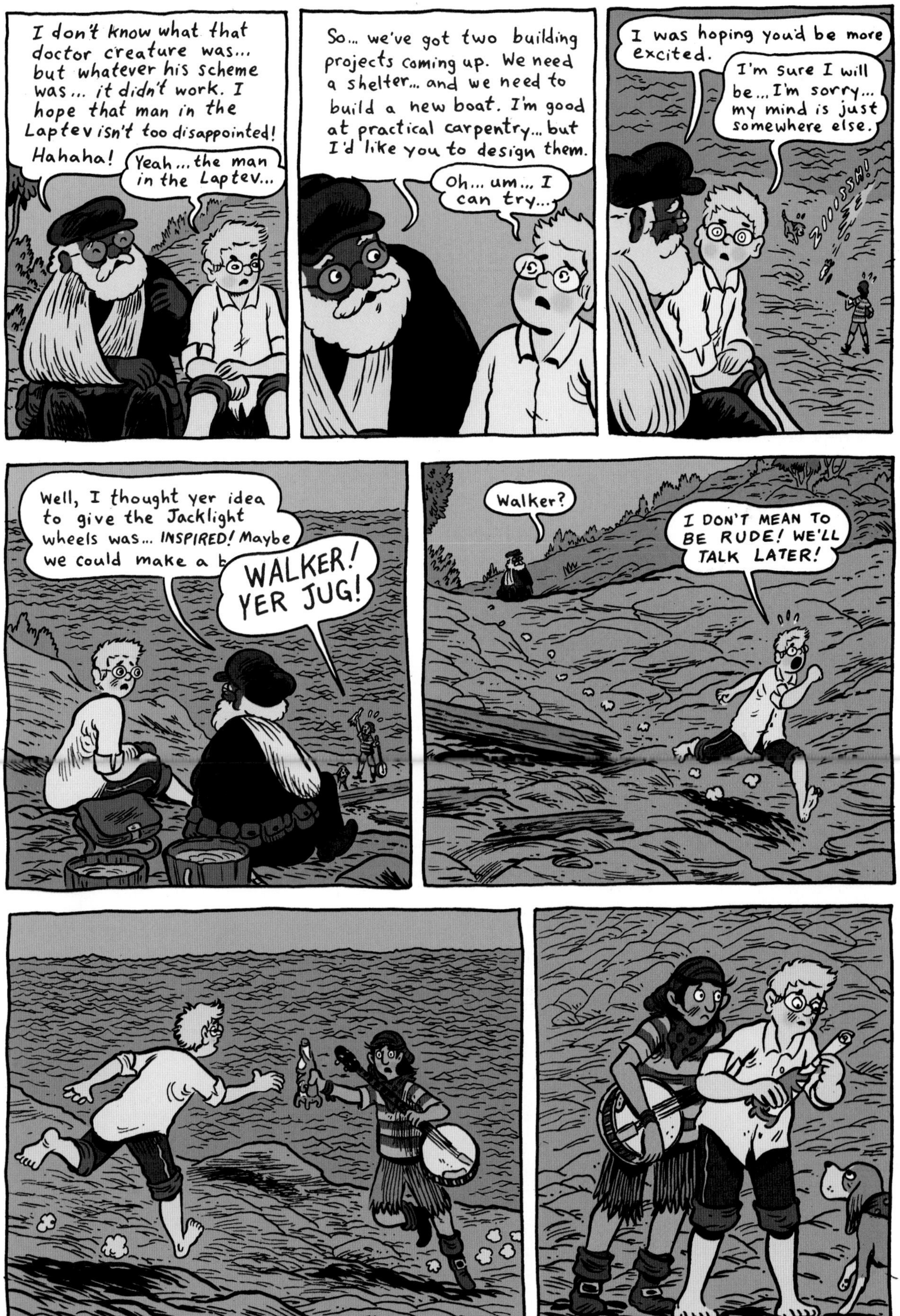
I don't know what that doctor creature was... but whatever his scheme was... it didn't work. I hope that man in the Laptev isn't too disappointed! Hahaha!
Yeah... the man in the Laptev...
So... we've got two building projects coming up. We need a shelter... and we need to build a new boat. I'm good at practical carpentry... but I'd like you to design them.
Oh... um... I can try...
I was hoping you'd be more excited.
I'm sure I will be... I'm sorry... my mind is just somewhere else.
ZIIOOSSH!
Well, I thought yer idea to give the Jacklight wheels was... INSPIRED! Maybe we could make a b
WALKER! YER JUG!
Walker?
I DON'T MEAN TO BE RUDE! WE'LL TALK LATER!

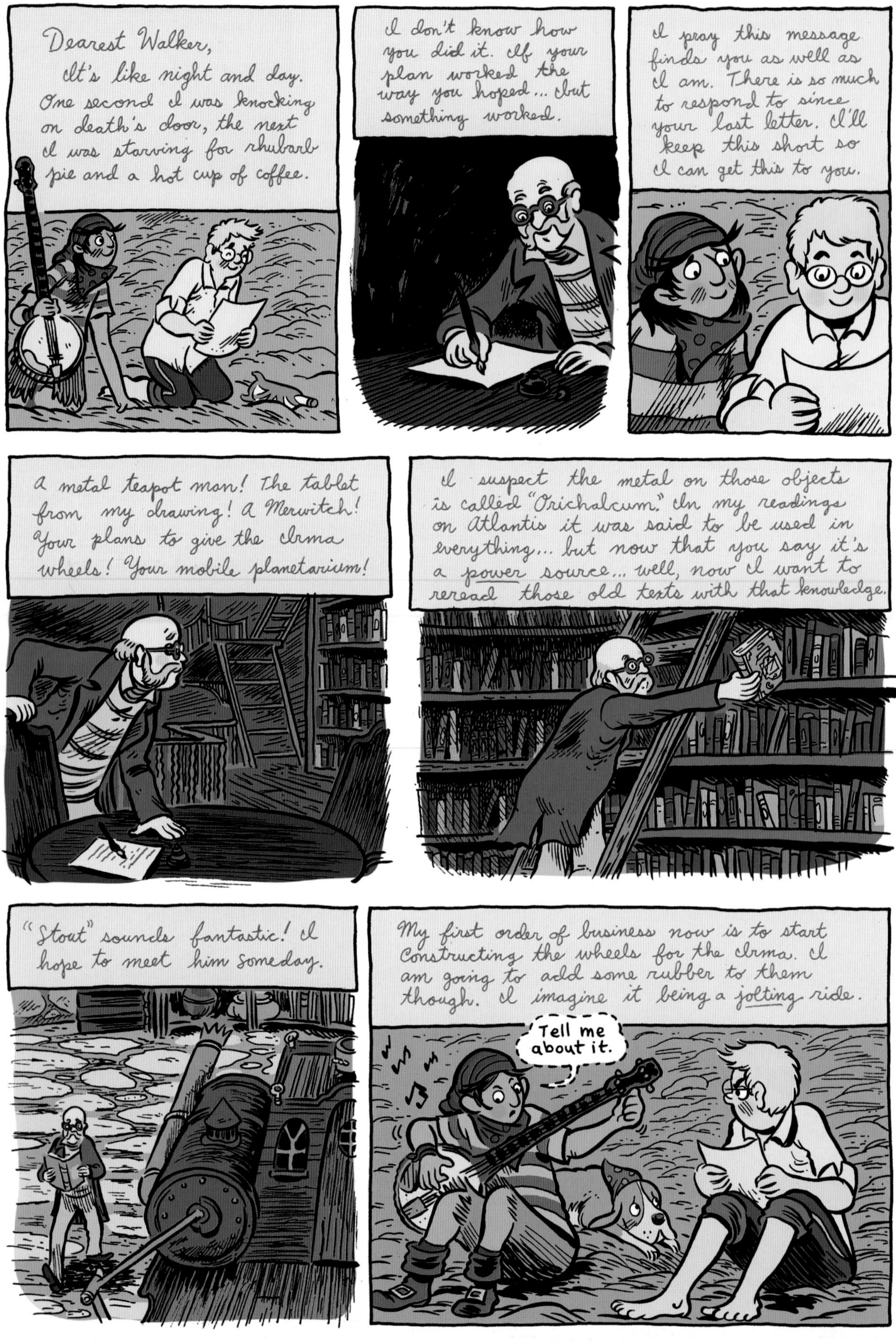

Dearest Walker,
It's like night and day. One second I was knocking on death's door, the next I was starving for rhubarb pie and a hot cup of coffee.
I don't know how you did it. If your plan worked the way you hoped... but something worked.
I pray this message finds you as well as I am. There is so much to respond to since your last letter. I'll keep this short so I can get this to you.
A metal teapot man! The tablet from my drawing! A Merwitch! Your plans to give the Irma wheels! Your mobile planetarium!
I suspect the metal on those objects is called "Orichalcum." In my readings on Atlantis it was said to be used in everything... but now that you say it's a power source... well, now I want to reread those old texts with that knowledge.
"Stout" sounds fantastic! I hope to meet him someday.
My first order of business now is to start constructing the wheels for the Irma. I am going to add some rubber to them though. I imagine it being a jolting ride.
Tell me about it.

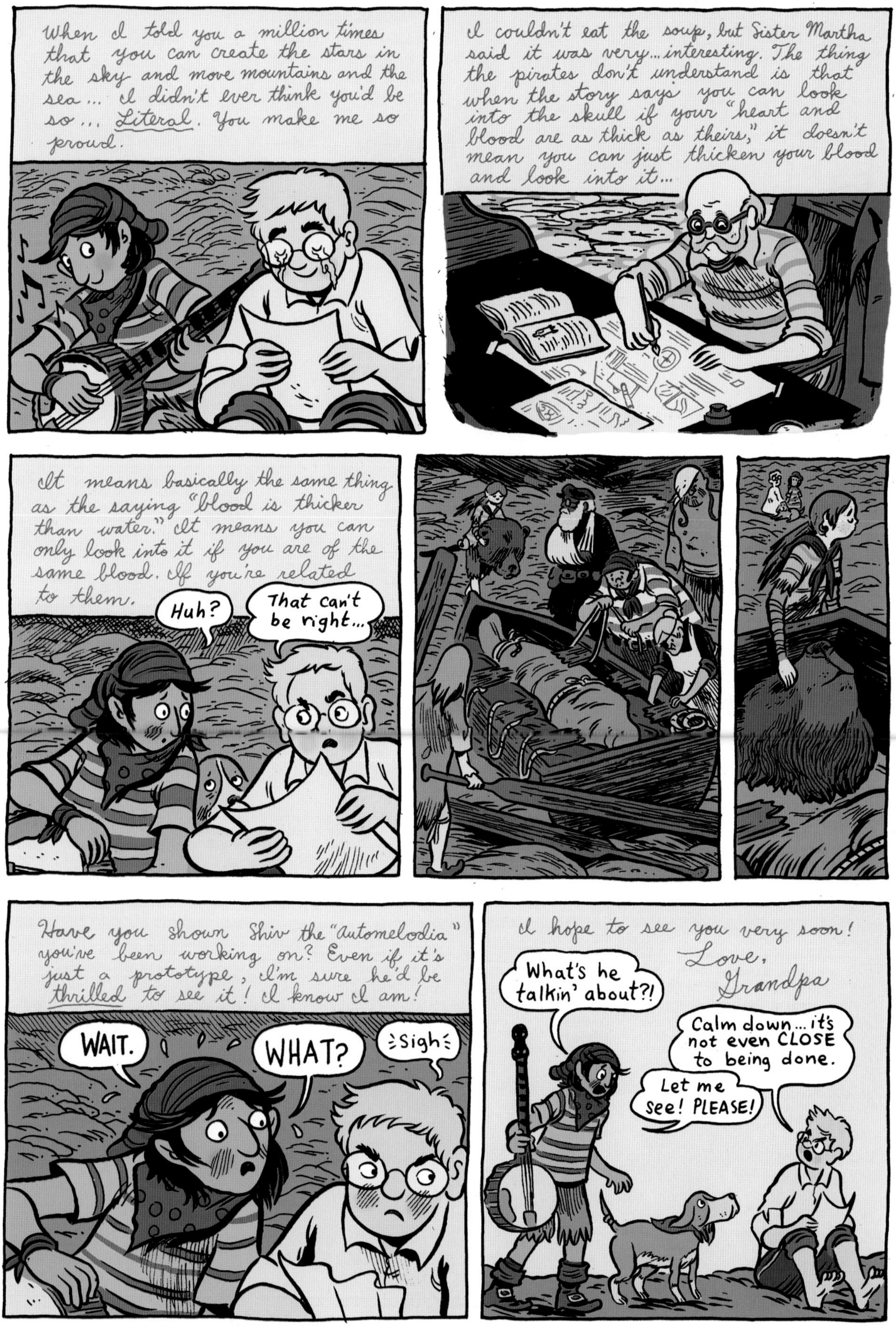

When I told you a million times that you can create the stars in the sky and move mountains and the sea... I didn't ever think you'd be so... Literal. You make me so proud.
I couldn't eat the soup, but Sister Martha said it was very... interesting. The thing the pirates don't understand is that when the story says you can look into the skull if your "heart and blood are as thick as theirs," it doesn't mean you can just thicken your blood and look into it...
It means basically the same thing as the saying "blood is thicker than water." It means you can only look into it if you are of the same blood. If you're related to them.
Huh?
That can't be right...
Have you shown Shiv the "automelodia" you've been working on? Even if it's just a prototype, I'm sure he'd be thrilled to see it! I know I am!
WAIT.
WHAT?
Sigh
I hope to see you very soon!
Love,
Grandpa
What's he talkin' about?!
Calm down... it's not even CLOSE to being done.
Let me see! PLEASE!

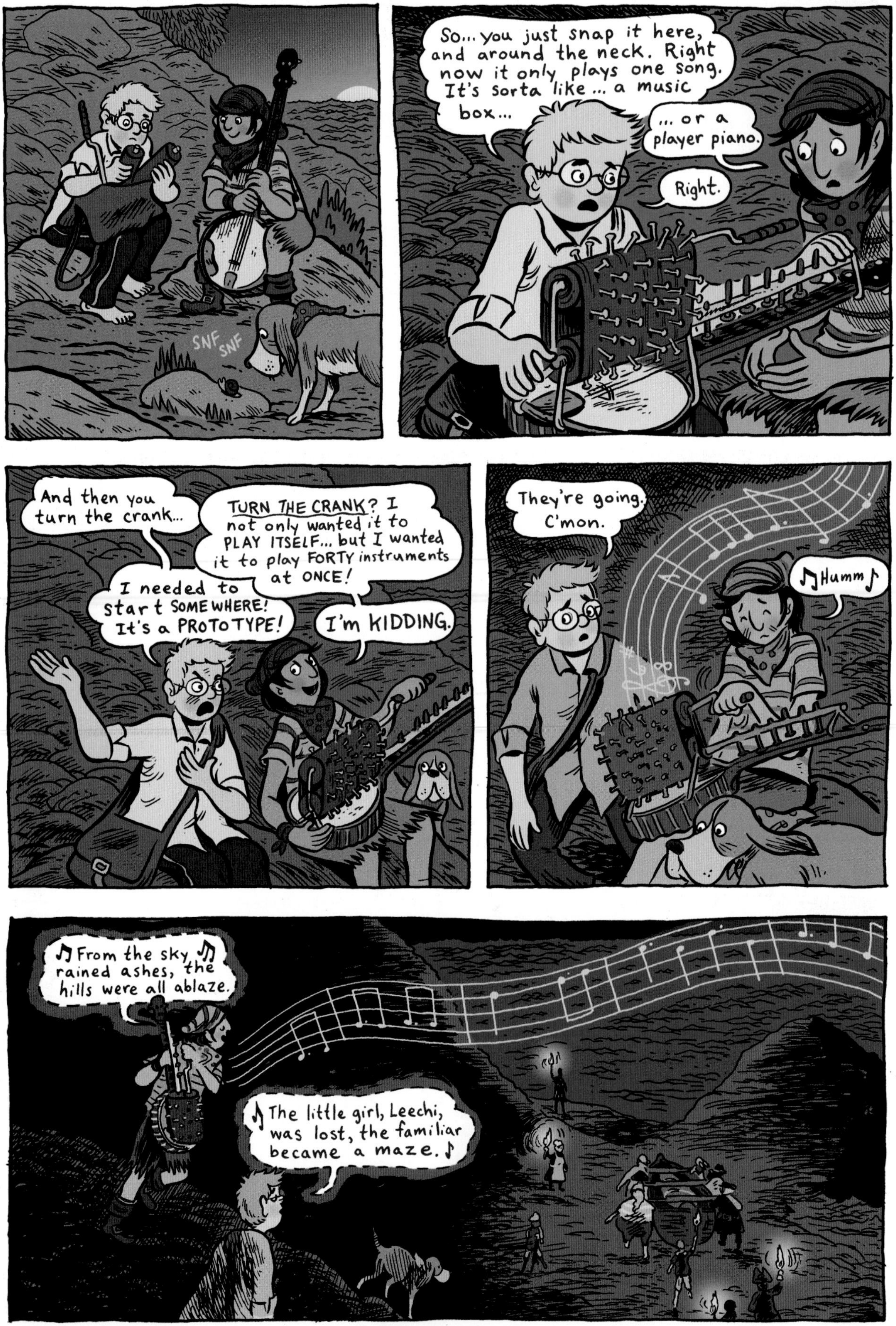
SNF SNF
So... you just snap it here, and around the neck. Right now it only plays one song. It's sorta like ... a music box...
... or a player piano.
Right.
And then you turn the crank...
TURN THE CRANK? I not only wanted it to PLAY ITSELF... but I wanted it to play FORTY instruments at ONCE!
I needed to start SOMEWHERE! It's a PROTOTYPE!
I'm KIDDING.
They're going. C'mon.
♫Humm♪
♫From the sky♫ rained ashes, the hills were all ablaze.
♪The little girl, Leechi, was lost, the familiar became a maze.♪

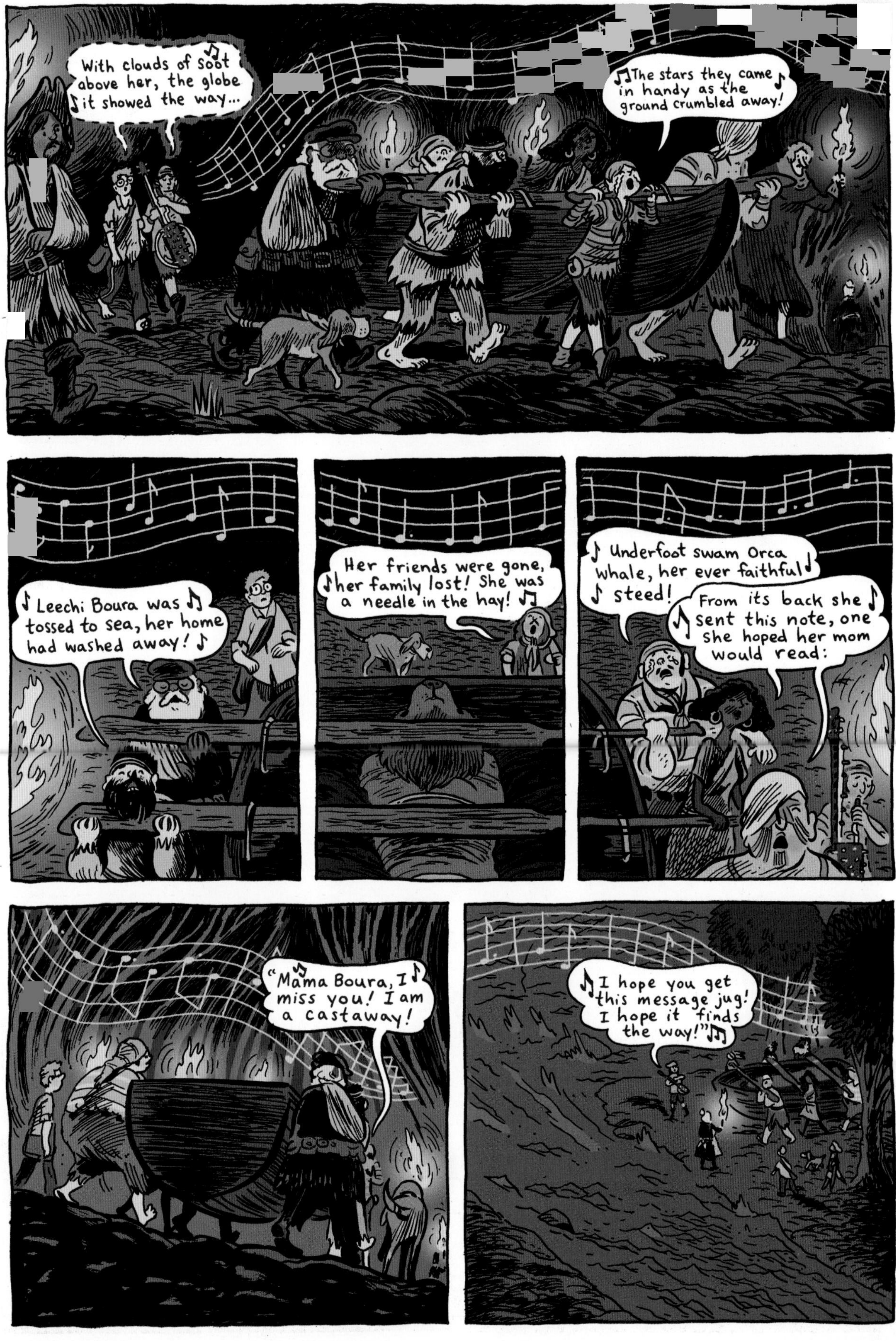
With clouds of soot above her, the globe it showed the way...
The stars they came in handy as the ground crumbled away!
Leechi Boura was tossed to sea, her home had washed away!
Her friends were gone, her family lost! She was a needle in the hay!
Underfoot swam Orca whale, her ever faithful steed!
From its back she sent this note, one she hoped her mom would read:
"Mama Boura, I miss you! I am a castaway!
I hope you get this message jug! I hope it finds the way!"

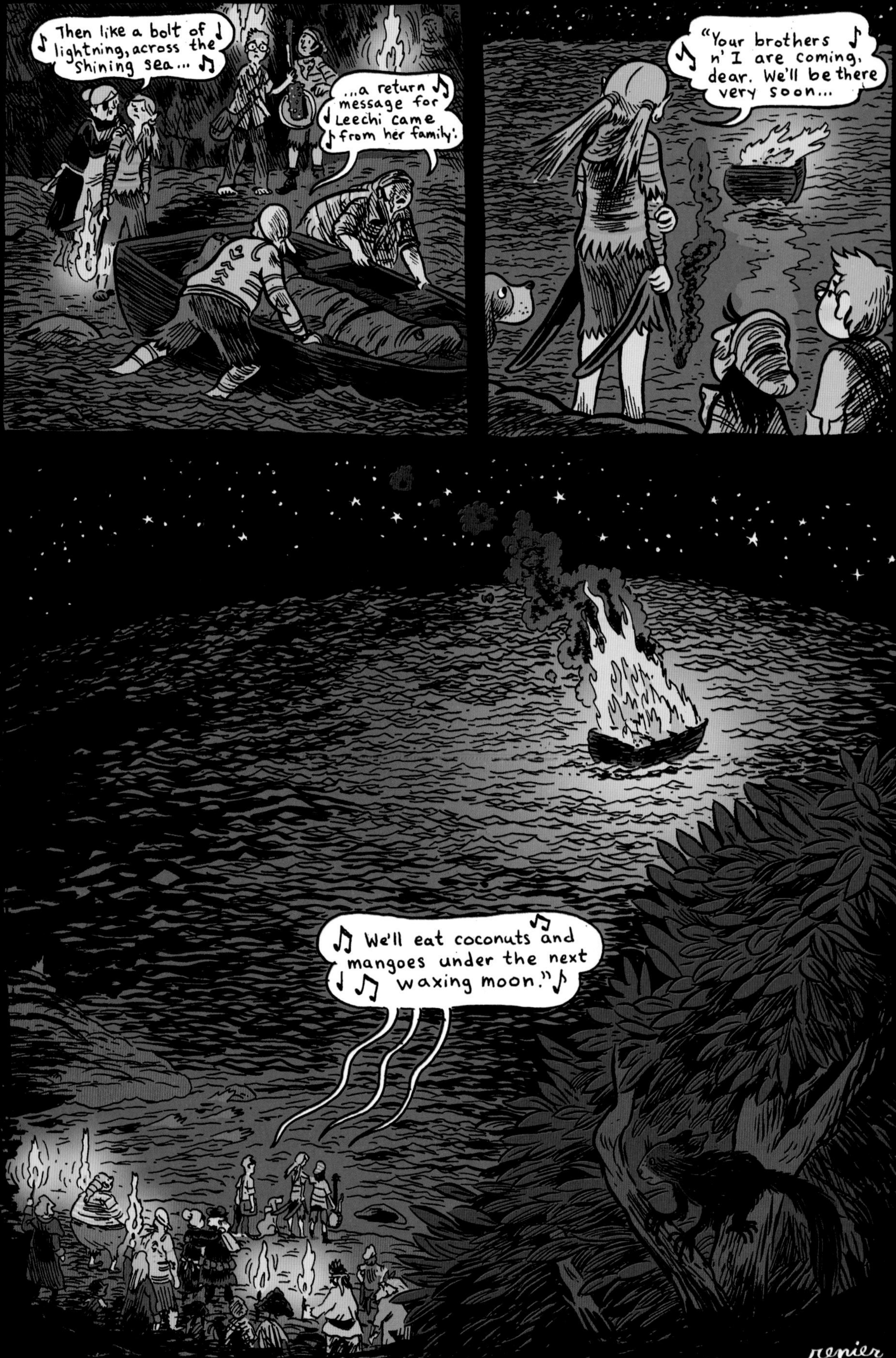
♪ Then like a bolt of lightning, across the shining sea... ♫
...a return message for Leechi came from her family:
"Your brothers n' I are coming, dear. We'll be there very soon...
♫ We'll eat coconuts and mangoes under the next waxing moon." ♪
renier

ACKNOWLEDGMENTS

For trust and guidance: Janna Morishima, Steven Malk, Mark Siegel, Calista Brill, Alec Longstreth, Craig Thompson, Brett Warnock, Colleen Venable, Chris Staros, Laura Park, Sam Carbaugh, Jeff Smith, Sheila & Dave, and last, but hardly least, David Coyle for the music composition.

For inspiration, life, and love: My family, Beluga, Daniel, Grandpa Koch, Gina, Lauren, Nate, Gabrielle, Matt & Truen (pssst... Hi, Axel!), Paul, Shiren, Liz, Kaz, Greig, Carson, Austin, Karen, Jon, Julia, Alex, Tom, Sarah, Daria, Evelyn, Jeff, Jen, Brian, Alison, Nate, Jeremy, Corinne, Ezra, Grant, Kazu, Claudia, Uncle Jerry, Kollodi, Philipos, all the people who enjoyed *Spiral-Bound*, and to all my great friends in New York, Portland, Milwaukee, and Chicago.

And an ecstatic welcome to the world to Soleia Ray!

The adventure continues in

THE UNSINKABLE
Walker Bean
Book 2

Early Sketches of book #2

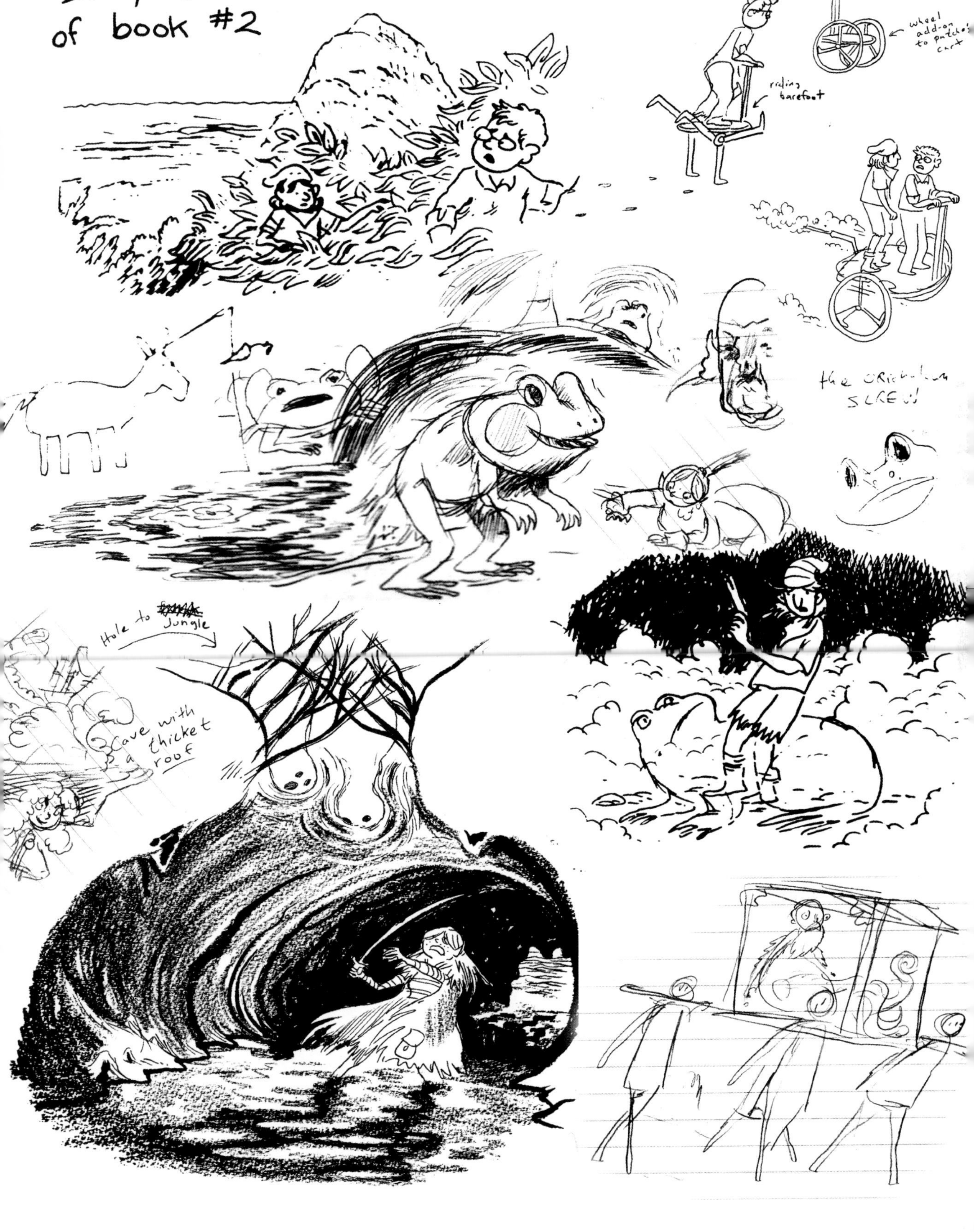

riding barefoot
wheel add-on to patchet's cart
SCREW!
Hole to Jungle
cave with a thicket roof

WALKER BEAN preliminary doodles & ideas

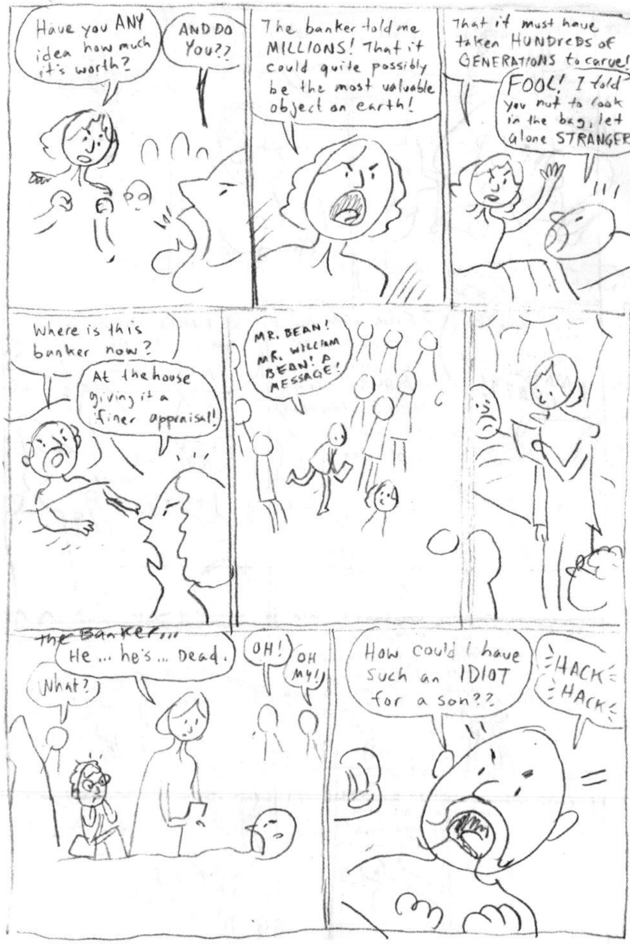

Have you ANY idea how much it's worth?
AND DO YOU??
The banker told me MILLIONS! That it could quite possibly be the most valuable object on earth!
That it must have taken HUNDREDS of GENERATIONS to carve!
FOOL! I told you not to look in the bag, let alone STRANGERS
Where is this banker now?
At the house giving it a finer appraisal!
MR. BEAN! MR. WILLIAM BEAN! A MESSAGE!
the Banker...
He... he's... Dead.
What?
OH!
OH MY!
How could I have such an IDIOT for a son??
HACK HACK

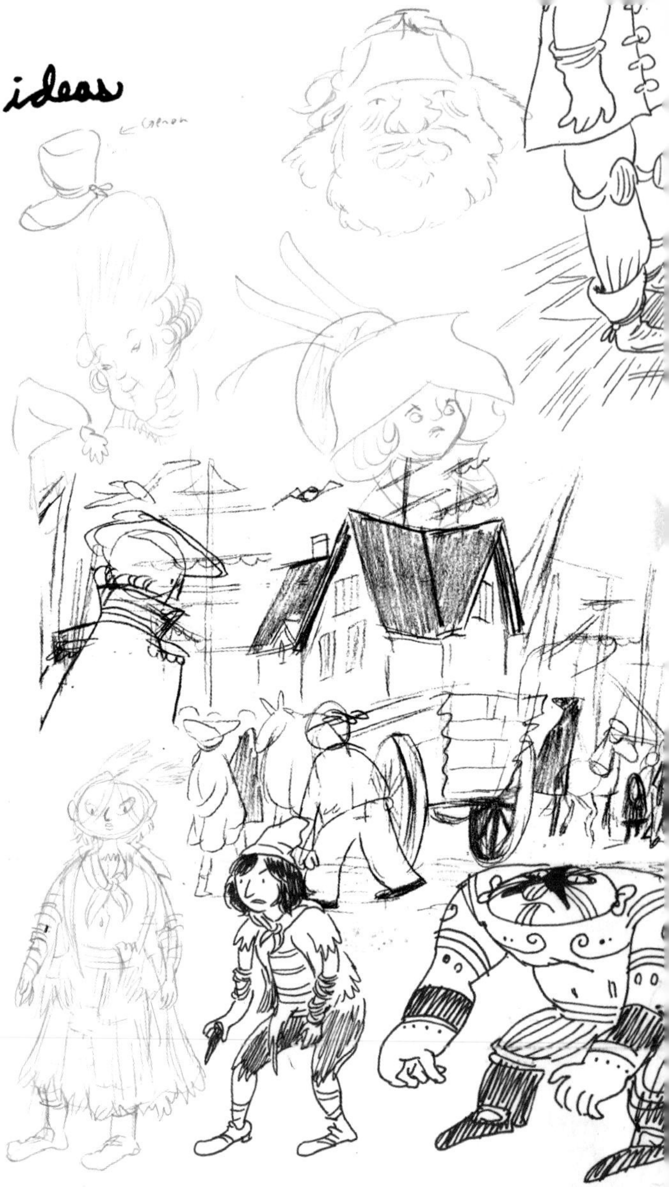

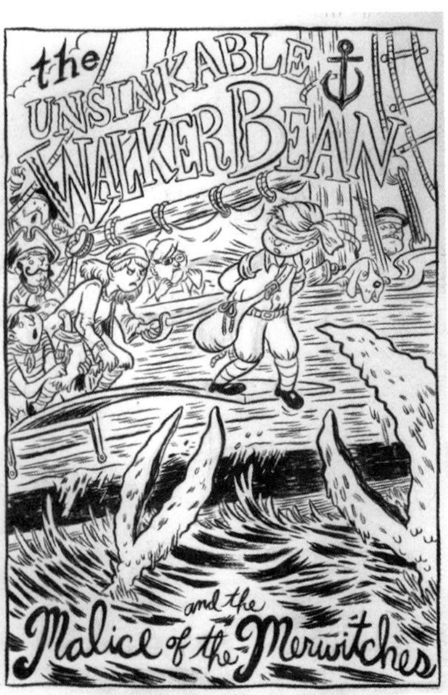

the UNSINKABLE WALKER BEAN
and the Malice of the Merwitches

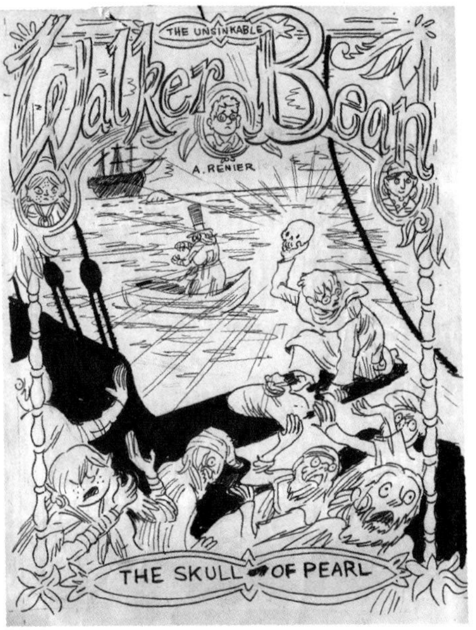

THE UNSINKABLE
Walker Bean
A. RENIER
THE SKULL OF PEARL

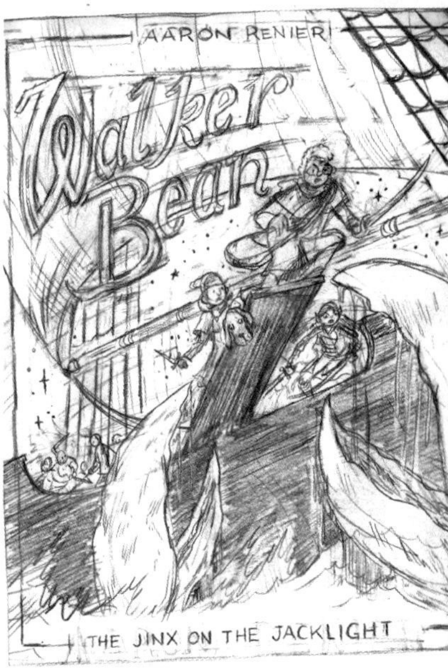

AARON RENIER
Walker Bean
THE JINX ON THE JACKLIGHT

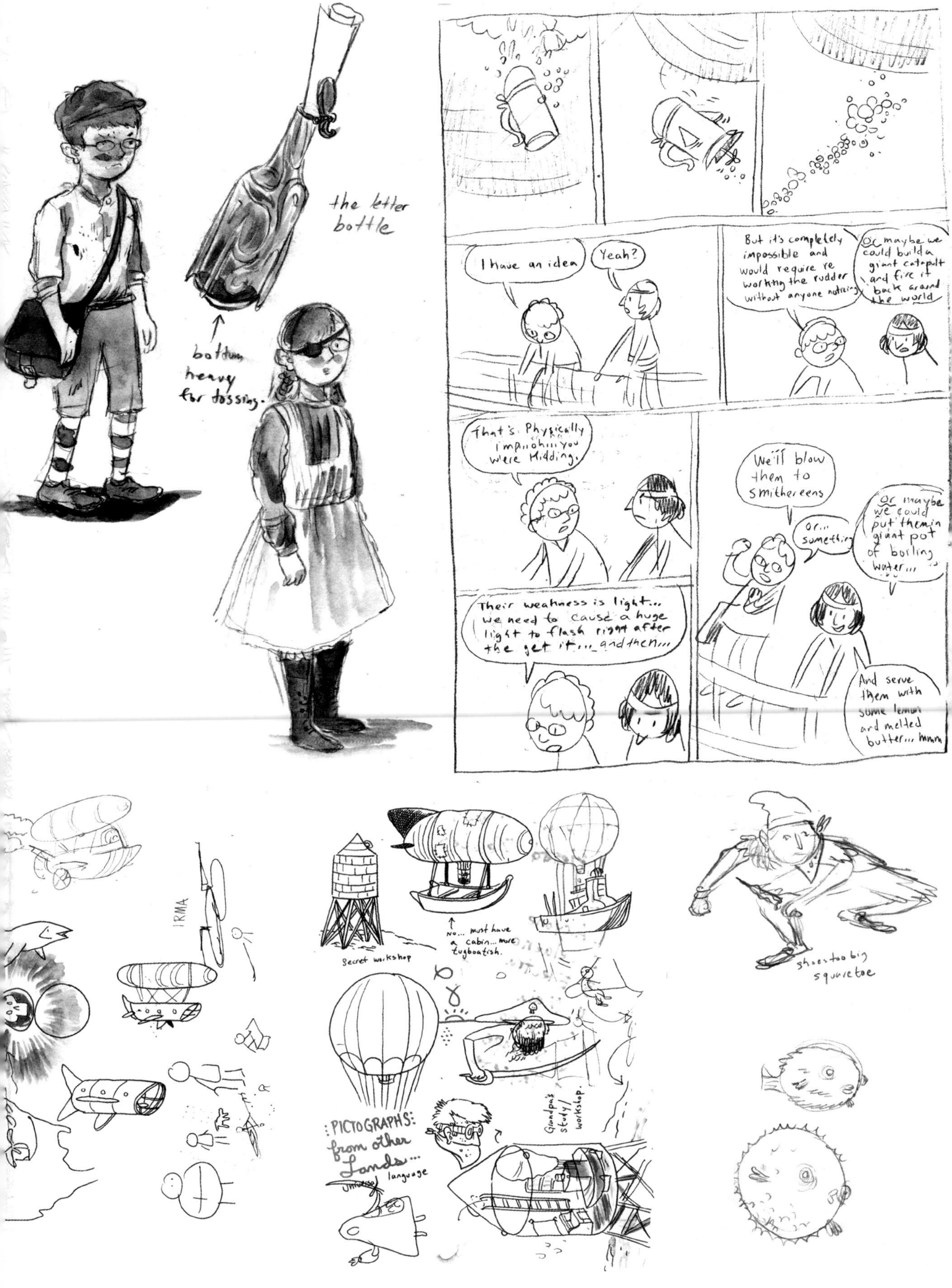

the letter bottle
bottom heavy for tossing.
I have an idea
Yeah?
But it's completely impossible and would require re working the rudder without anyone noticing
Or maybe we could build a giant catapult and fire it back around the world
That's Physically impo... oh... you were kidding.
We'll blow them to smithereens
Or... something
Or maybe we could put them in giant pot of boiling water...
Their weakness is light... we need to cause a huge light to flash right after the get it... and then...
And serve them with some lemon and melted butter... mmm
IRMA
secret workshop
No... must have a cabin... more tugboatish.
PICTOGRAPHS: from other Lands...
language
Grandpa's study/workshop.
shoes too big
square toe

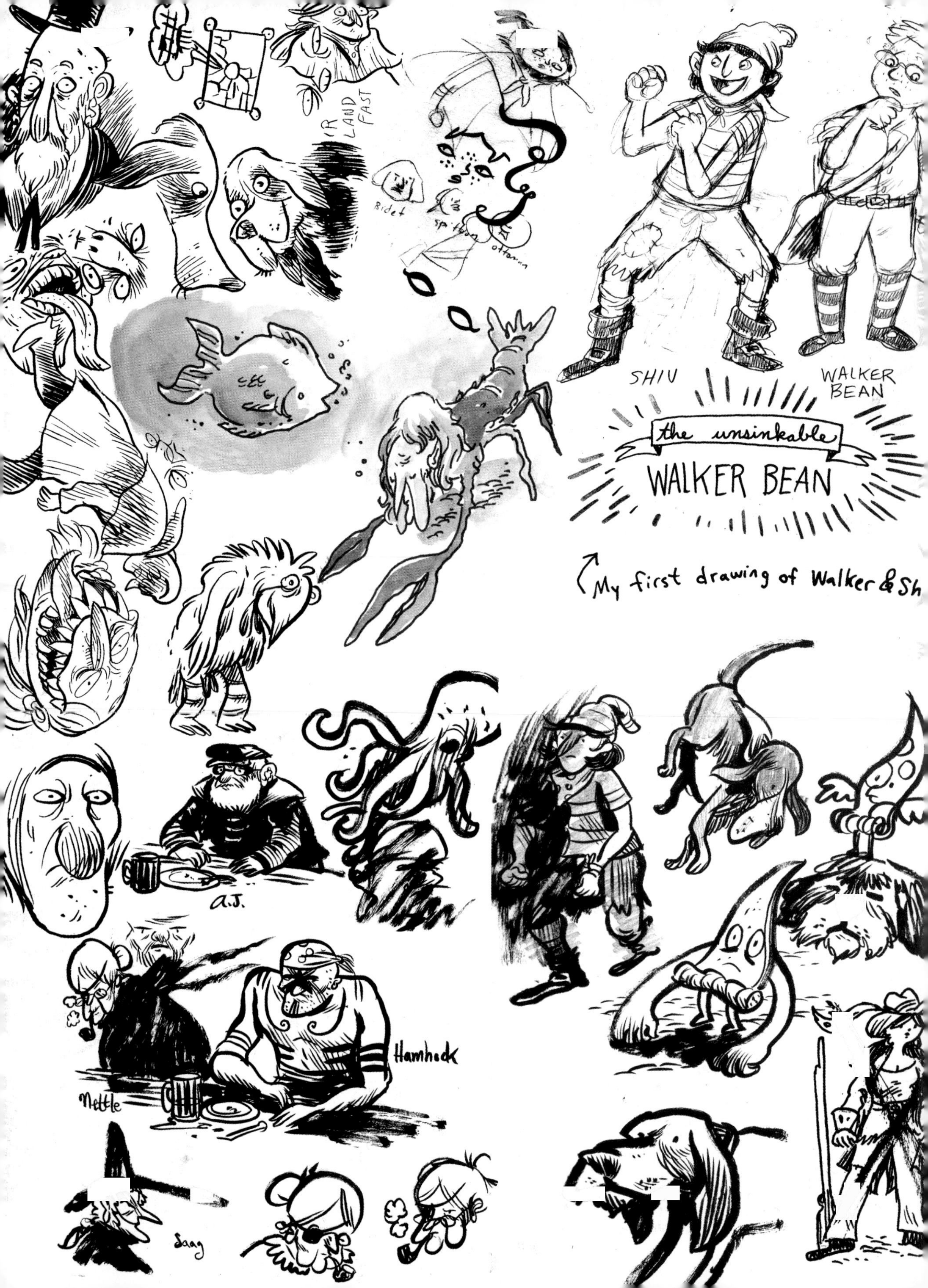
LAND FAST
Bidet
SHIV
WALKER BEAN
the unsinkable
WALKER BEAN
My first drawing of Walker & Sh
A.J.
Hamhock
Nettle
Saag

Huge old Map
the world

rons of
books
artifacts

walker and trotoires

grandpa's desk

IRMA

workbench

strange half
finished ship

Stove

Inside the Water Tower

ABOUT THE CARTOONIST

AARON RENIER was born and raised in Green Bay, Wisconsin. He has been drawing comics, in one way or another, for as long as he can remember. His illustrations have appeared in a wide variety of places, including the exterior of an entire city bus, making it look like an aquarium. He won the Eisner award for cartoonist deserving wider recognition for his first graphic novel, *Spiral-Bound*. He is the illustrator of a series of books about the Knights of the Roundtable by Gerald Morris, and a picture book by Alice Shertle titled *An Anaconda Ate My Homework*. This book was drawn in Brooklyn, New York and Chicago, Illinois, between trips to various parks and lagoons with his trusty hound, Beluga.

ABOUT THE COLORIST

ALEC LONGSTRETH was born and raised in Seattle, Washington. In 2002 he graduated from Oberlin College, where he majored in technical theater and in 2007 he graduated with highest honors from Pratt Institute, where he majored in illustration. After living in many different cities around the country, Alec now resides in White River Junction, Vermont, where he teaches at the Center for Cartoon Studies, self-publishes his comic book *Phase 7*, and works as a freelance illustrator and colorist.

ABOUT THE BOOK

The art was drawn on Strathmore vellum bristol board, with a standard yellow #2 pencil. It was then inked on with a Pentel Brush Pen, Rapidograph pen, and fountain pen. Words were lettered with a Micron 08 felt tip pen. After it was inked and pencil lines erased, some pages were scratched and ripped with razor blades to make rain and splashes. Wite-Out with a foam applicator was also used to make white shapes, and black colored pencils were used to draw Walker's illustrations. In Aaron's opinion, the tooth of the paper combined with the brush pen make really nice flowing organic lines, the variety of pens allows better control, and the colored pencil, razor, and Wite-Out add fun textures. The colors of this book were applied using Photoshop CS3, an iMac, and a Wacom drawing tablet. After drawing and inking, each page was scanned into the computer. The colors were added to the file on a series of layers underneath the drawing (sort of like an old animation cell). Using some old, faded children's books for inspiration, Aaron and Alec created a custom palette of 75 colors, which are the only colors used in this book. Coloring a big book is easier when one has only a limited number of colors to choose from, and it makes the colors feel very unified.

US $13.99 CAN $16.99

ADVENTURE ON THE HIGH SEAS!

A CURSED SKULL! FEARSOME PIRATES! WICKED SEA-WITCHES! And almost CERTAIN PERIL! Boy inventor Walker Bean and his scruffy new friends must summon their courage to face the direst scourges of the sea!

"*The Unsinkable Walker Bean* is gorgeous. Jump feet first into this rip-roaring, wild-eyed, high-sea adventure story. Join up with a young, pudgy, bespectacled hero, a brave powder monkey, a terrifying girl with the best red pigtails since Pippi Longstocking, and two seriously revolting sea-witches. Be prepared. You're going to love it."

-Brian Selznick, *Caldecott award winning creator of The Invention of Hugo Cabret*

"Aaron's work makes me feel ten years old again. He makes me want to whip up a root beer float, climb into a pirate-ship-playhouse, slap on a record of sea chanteys and read *Walker Bean* over and over. The guy's a bit of a mad genius."

-Lane Smith, *illustrator of The Stinky Cheese Man.*

"So beautiful are the drawings, that I can smell the sea salt and feel the spray as giant creatures of the deep draw near the ocean's surface. Outrageous, and wonderful!"

- Jeff Smith, *multiple Eisner award winning creator of Bone*

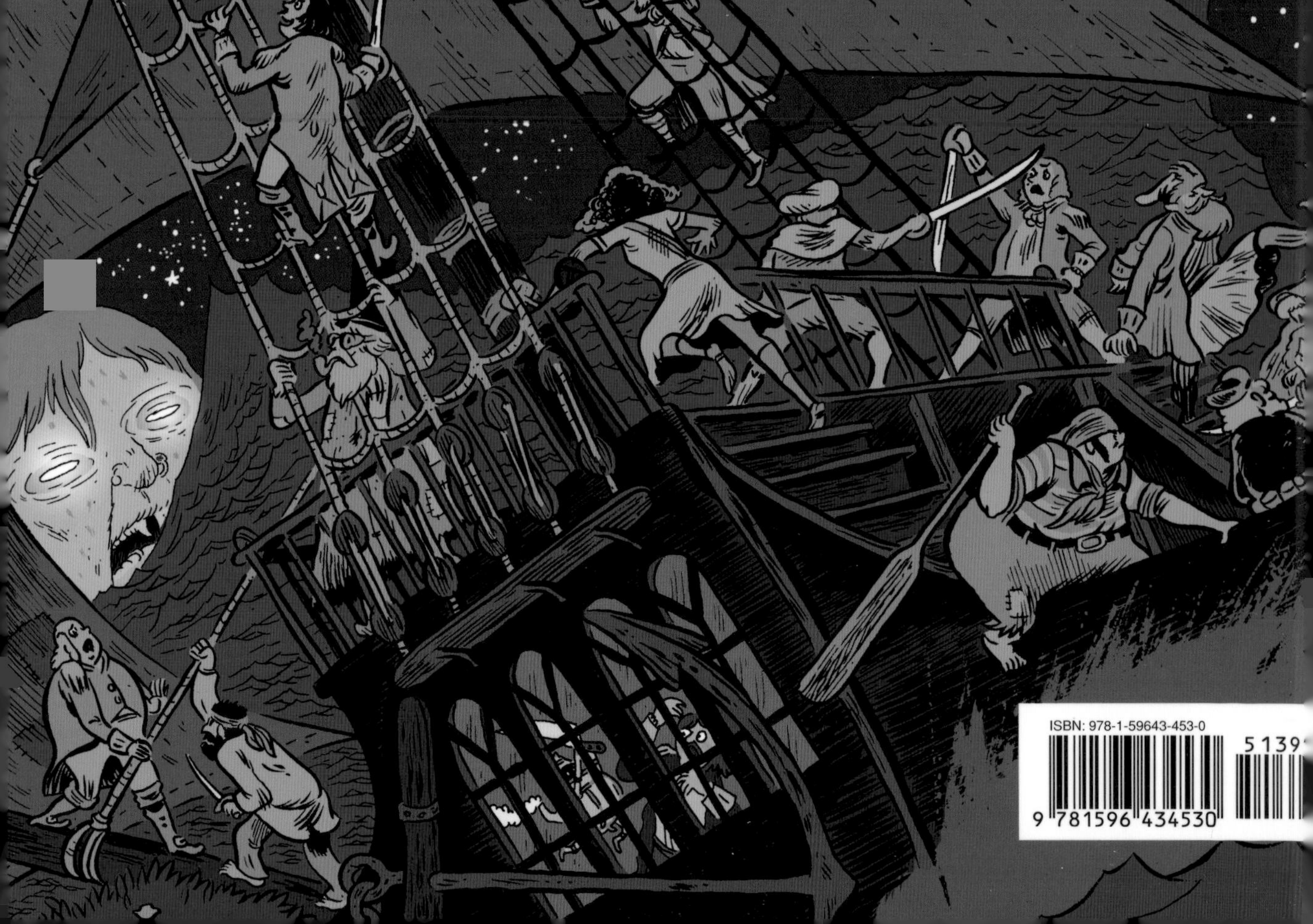

ISBN: 978-1-59643-453-0
51399
9 781596 434530